Shakespeare's Mistress

KAREN HARPER

D0996168

EBURY
PRESS

3 5 7 9 10 8 6 4 2

First published as *Mistress Shakespeare* in 2009 in the USA by New American
Library, a division of Penguin Group (USA)
Published in 2011 by Ebury Press, an imprint of Ebury Publishing
A Random House Group Company

The Random House Group Limited Reg. No. 954009

Addresses for companies within the Random House Group can be found at
www.randomhouse.co.uk

A CIP catalogue record for this book is available from the British Library

The Random House Group Limited supports The Forest Stewardship Council
(FSC®), the leading international forest certification organisation. Our books
carrying the FSC label are printed on FSC® certified paper. FSC is the only forest
certification scheme endorsed by the leading environmental organisations,
including Greenpeace. Our paper procurement policy can be found at
www.randomhouse.co.uk/environment

MIX
Paper from
responsible sources
FSC® C016897

Printed and bound by CPI Group (UK) Ltd, Croydon, CR0 4YY

ISBN 9780091940423

To buy books by your favourite authors and register for offers visit
www.randomhouse.co.uk

Did Will have two wives?

Several mysteries surround the life of William Shakespeare, and one of the most fascinating concerns whom he married. Will evidently promised to wed two women at nearly the same time. In records that survive today, he is listed as being engaged first to Anne Whateley of Temple Grafton, a village near Stratford, England. But on the next day in the same book of marriage bonds, he is recorded as being promised to Anne Hathaway of Stratford in the diocese of Worcester.

Two friends of Anne Hathaway's family laid down a goodly sum of money and vowed to produce Will Shakespeare for what we now call a shotgun wedding. Other events in his life and parts of his plays point to the possibility that Will was forced to wed a woman he had gotten pregnant but did not love. It's well known that he and Anne Hathaway lived quite separately, so could Anne Whateley have been the Dark Lady of his sonnets, the love of his life, and his London wife?

Scholars have both ignored and debated the "two Annes" theory" for centuries. Here, Anne Whateley tells her story.

Let me not to the marriage of true minds
Admit impediments; Love is not love
Which alters when it alteration finds,
Or bends with the remover to remove.
O, no, it is an ever-fixed mark
That looks on tempests and is never shaken;
It is the star to every wandering bark,
Whose worth's unknown, although his height be taken.
Love's not Time's fool, though rosy lips and cheeks
Within his bending sickle's compass come;
Love alters not with his brief hours and weeks,
But bears it out even to the edge of doom.
If this be error, and upon me proved,
I never writ, nor no man ever loved.

William Shakespeare
Sonnet 116

Prologue

༄

When I opened my door at midmorn and saw the strange boy, I should have known something was wrong. I'd been on edge for three days, not only because of the aborted rebellion against the queen, but because Will and I were at such odds over it—and over our own relationship.

"You be Mistress Anne Whateley?"

My stomach knotted. The boy was no street urchin but was well attired and sported a clean face and hands. "Who wants to know?" I asked as he extended something to me. He must have a missive saying someone was ill. Or dead. Or, God save us, arrested.

"'Tis a tie from a fine pair of sleeves meant for you with other garments too, once adorning Her Majesty's person," he recited in a high, singsong voice as he placed a willow green velvet ribbon laced with gold thread in my hand. In faith, it was beautiful workmanship.

"Didn't want me carrying all that through the streets," he added. "'Tis all waiting for you at the Great Wardrobe nearby."

"I know where that is, lad, but have you not mistook me for another? I have naught to do with the queen's wardrobe."

"Three figured brocade gowns, two fine sleeves with points and ribbon ties, a butterfly ruff and velvet cloak for the Lord Chamberlain's players to use at the Globe Theatre. Since they be busy today, I am to fetch you to receive the garb."

Of late certain nobles had given me donated garments to pass on to Will's fellows. I'd done many things for the players behind the scenes, as they put it. I'd once helped with costumes, and that at court too. In the disastrous performance but three days ago, I'd held the book and prompted the players. I'd copied rolls for Will and his fellows as well as taken his dictation. Many knew I had helped to provide the fine cushions that padded the hard wooden seats beneath the bums of earls and countesses who graced the expensive gallery seats at the Globe. So mayhap the word was out that I was the Jack—or Jill—of all trades at the Globe.

Yet things from the queen's wardrobe? It was said she had more than two thousand gowns, so I supposed she could spare a few. The Shakespeare and Burbage company had performed before the court both at Whitehall and Richmond, but after the catastrophe of the Essex Rebellion, three days ago, Her Grace was donating personal pieces to them? Surely, she had heard that they had staged Will's *Richard II*, a play some whispered had intentionally incited the rebellion against her throne.

I'd told Will—another of our arguments—that promoting that

tragedy at that time could be not only foolhardy but fatal, so thank the good Lord the Virgin Queen valued her favorite plays and players. The promised garments must be an olive branch extended to them. At least this would prove to Will once and for all something else I'd argued for years. Elizabeth Tudor was a magnanimous monarch, not one who should be dethroned or dispatched before God Himself took the sixty-seven-year-old ruler from this life.

"One moment," I told the boy. "I must fetch my cloak, for the wind blows chill."

And blows ill, I thought, as I put away the pages of *As You Like It,* so-called a comedy, for it was larded with serious stuff. Will and I had been feuding over what was love, and I was looking at a copy of his role as Jaques, the part he'd written for himself. Like this character, Will had been "Monsieur Melancholy" lately and, looking closer at Jaques' lines, I'd been appalled by what I'd found. And though Will and I were not speaking right now, I meant to take it up with him too. More than once he'd stripped our tortured love bare for all London to see, devil take the man, and he meant to do it again in this play!

"We're off straightaway then," the lad called over his shoulder as I followed him out the door into the courtyard. I lived in the large Blackfriars precinct, but it was still a goodly walk to the Wardrobe. Ever since I'd set foot in London eighteen years before, I'd loved this area and Will did too. When we were young and even more foolish than we were now at thirty-six years of age, Blackfriars was our fantastical place. We'd oft pretended we owned a fine brick mansion set like a jewel in green velvet gardens among homes of the queen's noblemen and gentry.

And to think that Gloriana herself had dined at Blackfriars earlier this year in the Earl of Worcester's house! She'd been met at the river and carried up the hill on a palanquin, I recalled with a sigh. At Blackfriars too the queen's noble cousin, the Lord Chamberlain, the players' patron, lived in elegant style in Hunsdon House. Maybe, I thought, his lordship had put in a good word for Will and his men in this Essex mess, so the queen had decided not only to forgive them but to reward them.

Still hieing myself along apace with the boy down the public street edging the area, I had to watch where I stepped to avoid the reeky central gutter and the occasional pan of slop thrown from upper windows. Others were abroad, but the streets still seemed greatly forsaken in the wake of the ruined rebellion. The half-timbered facades and their thatched brows frowned down on us, making the narrow streets even more oppressive.

We entered through the eastern gatehouse I so admired. As ever, I craned my neck to savor the venerable grandeur of its three stories. Its diamond-paned windows gazed like winking eyes over the city with fine views of mansions and their great privy gardens, old Bridewell Palace across the Fleet to the west, the city walls and even the bustling Thames.

Will and I had once found the gatehouse's lower door ajar. Holding hands, we'd tiptoed up the twisting stairs. Standing stripped of goods, the rooms were being whitewashed for new owners. Such narrow but elegant, sunny chambers!

"Next time 'tis offered, I'll buy it for you," Will had promised grandly, though he had but three pounds to his name after sending money back to Stratford.

"Says you, the dreamer, my marvelous maker of fine fictions,"

I'd retorted. But our lovemaking had been very real, and I yet treasured the memory. Nor, I told myself, would I forget this one, for I'd never been inside the vast structure that housed the queen's wardrobe, that which was not of immediate need and kept at Whitehall Palace.

I'd adored Elizabeth of England from the first moment I'd seen her, gorgeously gowned, on a white horse, when I was but eleven and she'd come to visit her favorite, the Earl of Leicester, near my home in Warwickshire.

The boy led me round the corner into an alcove hidden from the street. He knocked thrice upon it.

"Do you serve Her Majesty?" I asked while we waited.

"I serve those who serve her," he said only.

I meant to question him further, but the door creaked open and an old woman with face wrinkles like cobwebs stood there with her sleeves rolled up. She wore a broadcloth apron as if she were tending a kitchen. "Follow me," she said, not waiting for introduction or comment. The boy did not enter with us but closed the door behind me. It thudded nearly as loud as the beating of my heart, which I told myself was only from our quick pace and my excitement to see this place.

"Farthingales here. Watch your head," the old woman muttered.

I trailed her through a narrow alleyway of swinging metal hoops, like lonely bird cages, over which the queen's elaborate kirtles and petticoats would be draped. We plunged down an alley of sweet-smelling sleeves arranged by color, though the limited lantern light made the rich tawny, ruby and ivory hues all seem dusky. Boned bodices came next, then an aisle of fur-edged

capes and robes. Of a sudden, the sweet scent of lime and lavender from the garments changed to some sharp smell that made
me sneeze.

"Camphor to keep out moths," my guide said.

I jammed a finger under my nose to halt a torrent of sneezes.
The maze deepened: swags of green and white Tudor bunting
lined the way, then dusty, draped flags and battle banners. Suddenly, my stomach clenched with foreboding. Why would not
the garments to be given me simply be ready at the door? We
seemed to have passed from attire to military materials. As we
rounded the next corner, my worst fears leaped at me from the
shadows.

Within a dimly lit grotto of garments, behind a small portable
table sat a man simply but finely attired all in black; his amber eyes
shone flatly, like an adder's. It took me but a moment to realize I
knew him—that is, I knew who he was. I had glimpsed him at
court the time the players had taken me with them. His hunchback form was unmistakable. For months, the whole city had
talked of naught but the bloodless battles between this man and
the Earl of Essex. If he was here to see me—or I to see him—I
dreaded to know why.

Robert Cecil, the Earl of Salisbury, the queen's closest council-
lor and chief secretary, was the avowed enemy of Elizabeth's former
favored courtier, Robert Devereaux, Lord Essex, and his compa-
triot the Earl of Southampton, the men who had led the rebellion
against her. It was through Cecil that the two earls had been arrested and rightly so. It was through Cecil that Will's patron, the
Earl of Southampton, was being held prisoner in the Tower under
the same terrible charges as his friend Essex.

"That is all," Cecil spoke to the woman, who scurried away.

I remembered to curtsy. I was pleased it was quite a steady one because my legs were starting to shake. I saw we were not alone; two men—guards or secretaries?—sat at another table off to my left side. Had I been snared in a trap baited with the promise of royal garments only to be summoned to an inquisition?

"I do indeed have the pieces of cast-off wardrobe for the players you were promised, Mistress Whateley," Cecil said as if he'd read my mind. "I do not speak untruths or half-truths, and I pray you will not either. I must inform you that, since Her Majesty much enjoys the talents of the Globe's players, I can only hope they will be able to remain at large to put the royal items to good use as costumes in their dramas."

After that initial assault, I could scarce catch my air. The memory of my dear, doomed girlhood friend Kat leaped into my mind's eye, for I felt like that—trapped, floating faceup, exposed, bereft of help, hope or even breath.

"Fetch a seat for Mistress Whateley, Thompson," Cecil said, and a man jumped to obey. It was some sort of folding camp stool. I perched poised on the edge, telling myself to sit erect and to show calm and confidence no matter what befell. Oh, yes, I could be a player too. And I was not such a country maid that I did not know this was to be a war of wits, and that this one the rabble called *Robertus Diabolus*—Robert the Devil—had the upper hand.

I tried to buck myself up: however much at odds Will and I were now, had I not been so close to him and the players that I was well armed with clever turns of phrase? I knew how to listen well for cues before responding. Yet this was the man who had inherited Sir Francis Walsingham's dreaded web of intelligencers, who had brought down the lofty likes of Essex and Southampton and had made mincemeat of lesser men and women like Will's kin.

"Thank you for your consideration, my lord," I said before he could speak again. The words, too many, I warrant, tumbled from my mouth. "For the seat, I mean, but I am also grateful for the gift of Her Majesty's cast-off garments to the Lord Chamberlain's Men, not only for them but for myself—to be able to merely care for them. We all honor our queen."

"Do we all?" he parried. "Mistress, I need straight answers from you. I have not hauled in the players themselves—yet—because I cannot abide prevarications or histrionics offstage. I have it on good authority you are forthright and have spoken your mind to the Globe's actors. And I will have you speak plainly here."

"Of course, my lord, but I cannot see why we must meet in such a place, away from others—"

"I did not think," he interrupted, "knowing Will Shakespeare as intimately as you do, a covert meeting was something new to you."

My insides lurched. He knew about me and Will. How much did he know, from how far back? He must be punning upon the word *knowing* in the biblical sense and be aware that Will and I had met secretly off and on for years. And worse, that I had been questioned once before by someone from Her Majesty's government about where Will Shakespeare's loyalties lay.

I fought to compose my features. Our eyes met and held. His face was not uncomely, but he was so misshapen in bodily form it was said the queen called him her Pygmy. I knew of nicknames that could sting, for I was of half-Italian blood and had oft been called Gypsy or Egyptian.

Cecil's enemies called him simply the Hunchback, and during the rebellion, someone had scrawled on his front door, in a near quote from Will's description of the hunchback King Richard III, HERE LIES THE TOAD! I well knew that playwrights had been imprisoned, tortured and killed for slanders stuck on doors in London.

"Let me speak plain, mistress," he said when I did not flinch under his gaze and did not respond again. "It is well known that Shakespeare and his fellow players performed *The Tragedy of King Richard II,* at the behest of the Earl of Essex and his dear friend-in-arms Southampton, just before the recent rebellion. I am certain I need not tell such a *devoted* friend of the playwright that scenes are in that drama that advocate the overthrow of a sitting monarch by a favorite of the English crowds."

"It's just a play, my lord, employing the past and hardly predicting the future." I saw where he was going now but had no notion of how best to navigate the dangers. "Indeed, the Lord Chamberlain's Men were paid a goodly sum for performing it," I continued. "They had no political statement to make, but simply needed the money, forty pieces of silver, so—"

"It should have been thirty pieces of silver!" he exploded, smacking his palm on his table, making it jump and shudder. "They are Judases, as much favor as Her Grace has shown them! And, yes, mistress, I hear you repeat the name of the Lord Chamberlain, as they bear the queen's cousin's name as patron. But," he said, thrusting up both hands when he saw me ready to protest, "I know Will Shakespeare's bread is buttered on the other side too, for he's been cozy with Southampton for years, and the Shakespeare family has a convoluted, questionable past as Catholics and rebels!"

I was dumbfounded. He knew about Will's beginnings, family connections, his life from the earliest days. Then he could ruin Will with this—ruin me too.

"All I can tell you of my Warwickshire friend Will Shakespeare in all this," I said, fighting again to control my voice, "is that he prays that your lordship and Her Gracious Majesty will spare the life of his friend and sponsor the Earl of Southampton. He merely did a favor for him and for the needed money. He meant no political statement."

I was lying and I felt myself begin a fiery blush from the tips of my ears to my throat. I could only pray that the tawny hue of my skin hid that. And here I was fighting for Will when I could have strangled him with my bare hands but three days ago.

"Both earls' coming trials will decide all that," Cecil said, "but we can hardly claim that poets and playwrights are above such political frays, can we? Praying we forgive Southampton, that's what he's been up to, eh? More like, London's favorite playwright has been writing something else to stir up sedition. Ben Jonson went to the Marshalsea prison five years ago for a slanderous play," he went on, jabbing a finger at me like a scolding schoolmaster. "Thomas Kyd was questioned under extreme duress and, sadly, died soon after. Christopher Marlowe—"

"Was supposedly accidentally stabbed in a tavern brawl," I dared to interrupt. My Italian blood was up; I could not help myself. At least he seemed not to know of my past with Southampton or Marlowe either. "And," I plunged on, "it was said Marlowe was an informer for Sir Francis Walsingham, so I'm not sure what it behooves one to be an informer, as it's whispered his demise could have been an assassination and not an accident!"

"Ah," he said, and his mouth crimped in either annoyance or amusement. "The beauty does have hidden fangs as well as a clever brain."

We stared at each other in a stalemate but hardly, I thought, a truce. Air from an unseen source shifted a battle banner behind his head. One of Jaques' lines from *As You Like It* leaped through my mind to taunt me: "The worst fault you have is to be in love."

With a shudder up my spine, I realized then what I said in the next few moments could save Will or damn him to torture, imprisonment or even death.

"But tell me," Cecil said, leaning on his elbows and steepling his long-fingered hands before his mouth, "before we go on, exactly what is William Shakespeare to you? Here you are, an exotic woman, a tempting vixen, when he has a wife and family back in Stratford-Upon-the-Avon. Tell me true, Mistress Anne Whateley, what is the man to you?"

That, I thought, was the question. For nearly two decades, since even before the day he'd publicly, legally wed Anne Hathaway, I'd not only loved but loathed William Shakespeare to the very breadth and depth of my being. What was he to me and I to him? God's truth, in my pierced and patched heart, I, Anne Rosaline Whateley, was above all else, the first Mistress Shakespeare, Will's other wife.

THE HISTORY OF ANNE ROSALINE WHATELEY

I would not have anyone believe I am untutored nor ignorant of how one's life's story is commonly constructed. I admit the previous scene of dialogue with Robert Cecil in London is not truly a prologue, for much of what I will write next came before. After all, an old adage says, "What's past is prologue."

But you see, that confrontation with Cecil caused me to search my soul to record my life. What, indeed, am I to Will and to others? What and who am I to myself?

Having inspired characters in Will's plays and worked closely with him in many ways—ah, both of us love to rhyme—I have decided to arrange the events of my story as if it were a five-act play, that is, divided into the major parts of my life and story. As Will wrote for a play last year, "All the world's a stage and all the men and women merely players." And since I have the London playhouses and their people in my blood as fiercely as does he, I shall relate my narrative in such a pattern.

This tale will reveal not only my life but Will's, so entwined are our plots, so to speak. Sometimes I fear his rivals will consign his work to oblivion, or that theatrical tastes may shift yet again and judge him of no account, or that plague or the prating Puritans will shut down the playhouses permanently. If so, I pray this account will let others know him and his work even better—and justify my part in his life too.

The rendering of my thoughts, emotions and experiences is part comedy and part tragedy as well as history, for life is such a mingling. And so, I write this report of the woman born Anne Rosaline Whateley, she who both detested and adored a man named William Shakespeare.

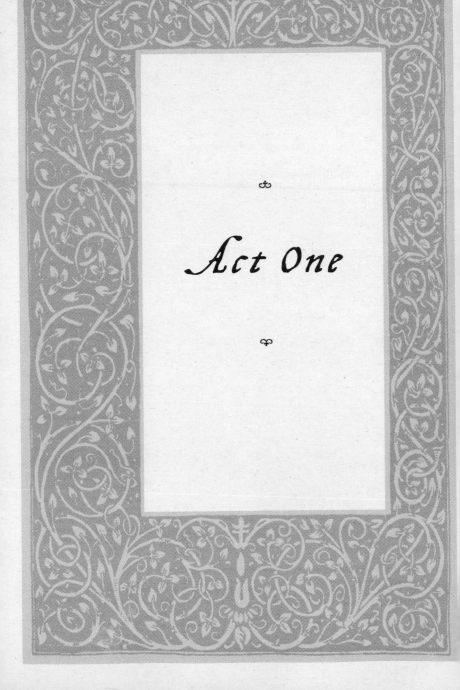

Act One

CHAPTER ONE

✢

My entrance to this world was in the same year as Will's, 1564, though he made an appearance in the spring and I in the autumn. Looking back, I can say that the most startling discovery of my early life was how gentle and lovely lay the land where I was reared but how fierce and brutal the blows of life that soon assailed me.

Among other local children, I always knew that I was different. In the heart of the sweet countryside of central England, where most folk were blue- or green-eyed, fair-skinned and light-haired, I had snapping dark eyes under brows of inky arches, a tawny complexion and a thick, unruly mane of raven black hair. Yet I believe I was comely in an exotic way, like some rare bird the winds have blown off course. How could I be else with an Italian mother? She was, of course, Catholic born and bred, which she kept quiet in Gloriana's Protestant England. I yet possess my mother's violet-tinted-glass rosary beads from Venice; I pretend they are a crystal necklace she bequeathed me, but these dangerous days, I wear it only with my night rail in my bedchamber.

Odd too in the very heart of rural England where few strangers, as foreigners are called, abided, was that my mother had not been a milkmaid or a tradesman's daughter but a ropedancer my father found in London.

In my mind's eye, I catch glimpses of Anna Rosalina de Verona only through a veil, for she died of the sweat when I was but four. Of all the people I have known, I have met only one other who had a country English father and an Italian mother, and that Will's friend, the playwright John Marston. But Marston's mother was the daughter of a learned Italian physician, not that of a traveling tumbler.

So I treasure only haunted memories of my mother. I can sum-mon up the sound of her silver laughter, her lithe body, how she held my hand as we danced through flowered fields when Da was away. She was, I pried out of him one time, "light on her feet and quick to caper." Though I heard him once whisper to her in the night that she was his "cloud dancer," he'd made her swear that she would never mount a taut rope again to dart along it as if she walked on wind.

She vowed she would never more dance even upon the ground for groats and ha'pennies under the avid stares of other men. So sad that someone who had seen sunny Italy and famous France and most of England, someone so graceful and ethereal, should die burning up with fever, twisting in sodden sheets in a tiny, earthbound bed.

The day she was buried in the graveyard at old St. Andrew's in our village of Temple Grafton, outside Stratford-Upon-the-Avon, was the only time I saw Da cry. I hear he bedded with another woman after, but I'm sure he never loved but once. For my down-to-earth da to call anyone a cloud dancer, he must have loved her desperately.

"Won't you tell me more of her, Da?" I'd ask off and on.

"Naught more to tell," he'd mutter, frowning as smoke from his tobacco pipe curled around his head.

He was about our timber and plaster cottage but a few days now and then and, when he was away, I was shifted off to distant cousins in Stratford. Da owned four packhorses and worked for the Greenaways who, with up to twenty sturdy carriers, took goods back and forth from Stratford to London every fort-night.

Pack trains were goodly sized, for robbers still lurked on the roads near Bloxham and High Wycombe. Cheese and lambskins, linseed oil, woolen shirts and hose and Will's da's fine gloves made the trip from Stratford to markets in Londontown. After more than a week away—the plodding trip took three days and two nights one way—the pack train returned with fineries like sugar, rice, dates, figs, raisins, almonds and special orders for Stratford folk.

The packers unloaded the horses near Market Cross, down the way from the Shakespeare house and not far from where I stayed. I recall the thrill of hearing the pack train was back in town, of running with the other children to see what would be unloaded and to hug my da. Having seen naught of the world, I thought the market town of Stratford was the big city, especially compared to the clumps of cottages huddled about the old church in Temple Grafton. Even when I squeezed descriptions of London out of Da, I could not fathom how fat and full a place it was.

"But tell me again about when you first saw my mother in London," I urged him many times. He stayed bent over his bread and cheese, which I delighted to serve him in her stead.

"'Twas in the churchyard of St. Paul's there," he would say, speaking slowly. "Packed with people, it was too."

Da was not quick with words or movement nor could he sign his name but always made his mark with a cross. Since he'd lost my mother, who had somewhere learned to read, write and do simple sums, he'd paid an old former priest to teach me those skills, else I'd have stayed illiterate. In the gentry class and the gentles above them, most women could read and write, but Da had barely dragged us off the bottom rung of England's ladder of ranks and rights. His dream was for us to keep our own accounts for our own pack train to London.

"Got to keep good records," he told me. "We'll not prosper on our own if you can't keep writ down the count of what goods we send and bring back. Else, no need for you to have no fancy learning."

"But you said, if I get even better at learning words you will bring me a book or two to read. Da, you promised!"

"Aye, I said so, and I'll bring it from the very stalls in Paul's Churchyard where I first saw your beautiful bird of a mother tiptoeing across the very air and knew she must be mine."

So he had not forgotten that I asked him about my mother. And when he talked like that, I knew my da had a poet's heart, and I wanted to have one too.

. . .

I'd like to create some wondrous, bejeweled day when I first exchanged words with William Shakespeare, but, since I'm telling true, I must admit it was this way: Will was walking past my cousin George Whateley's wool drapery shop one gray-sky day the April when I was still eight and he was newly nine. He was on his way to deliver a pair of fine calfskin, wool-lined gloves, and I brazenly fell into step beside him. He had auburn hair and bright hazel eyes so alert in his pale face. Even then he was taller than me by a head.

I'd seen Will about the Henley Street neighborhood before, usually running errands for his father or setting out for high adventures with his best friend, Dick Field, a cooper's son, but I'd never really been alone with Will. I spent most of my free time with Katherine Hamlett, called Kat, the haberdasher's eldest daughter, but she was working in her family's shop that day. I loved Kat and liked Will and Dick well enough because they'd never made sport of my dark skin nor called me anything but Anne.

When my da was away and I stayed in town, my cousin by marriage Mrs. Whateley ordered me about a good deal, but never watched me overmuch if I went outside. A bit bored and in full knowledge that Will was the eldest of the Shakespeare brood and that his father had been master chief alderman, bailiff and ale taster—quite a well-respected man—I asked Will, "May I go along then?"

"I don't mind," he said with wide eyes and an exaggerated shrug. "If you won't be missed."

"I won't be missed."

"My mother would smack me good for just walking off without a word."

"I don't have a mother, and Mrs. Whateley pays me little heed."

"She should," he said, picking up his pace.

I thought him a bit of a nitpick, but looking back, I wonder if he didn't mean I was worth something and should be better watched. Freedom was fine with me. I was on the brink of turning hoyden and liked nothing more, when not doing household chores, to dance about to made-up verses or venture on walks away from Henley Street and even out of town.

I entertained Will with songs and dances most of the way, despite the fact that the week before Da had caught me skipping and whirling along a grapevine I'd laid out like a rope on the grass. He'd boxed my ears 'til they rang. Smiling, then laughing, Will matched me back, rhyme for silly rhyme. He showed me the finely stitched pair of men's gloves but put them back straightaway in their packet of parchment paper.

I'd not fathomed he was going so far that day, nigh on a half hour's walk to a gate in the hedge hard by the southeast edge of the Forest of Arden. There, by a big oak, in a meadow of bobbing wildflowers, he met a finely garbed and mounted servant of one of his distant Arden kin. Will's mother was an Arden, an honorable name, stretching far back. The Ardens were possessed of many properties. Will told me that plain enough and more than once. I'd heard the whispers that Will's da had "married up" and come into goods and fine, fertile land through his wife's handsome dowry.

I reckoned our two sets of parents were about as far apart as the earth and the moon. My little village of Temple Grafton was nicknamed Hungry Grafton for the poverty of its soil, though the fields produced stone and lime. Sadly, its claim to once belonging to the heroic Knights Templar was a sham as the land had been held by the humble Knights Hospitallers before Great Harry, the queen's father, overthrew the Catholic Church in England. I told Will my tutor had said my cottage was on land once bestowed on Henry de Grafton by King Henry I, which I thought was so wonderful.

"Imagine," I said with a sigh, "the very land on which I live was once the gift of a king! And that same Henry de Grafton then gave some of it to Simon de Arden, one of your ancestors, that's what my tutor said."

He sobered even more when I told him I could read and write, even if I admitted I needed much practice yet. "But the Shakespeares are related to the Ardens, and you aren't kin to Henry de Grafton, are you?" he asked, kindly enough, though that burst my bubble. Still, he didn't call me Gypsy or Little Egypt as some of the other Henley Street children did.

"And what's this about a tutor?" he demanded. "My best friend, Dick, and I attend grammar school in Church Lane, but we have no tutor."

"It's old Father Berowne from up by Knowle, then he used to pastor St. Andrew's," I told him. "Besides paying him a shilling now and then, Da brings him things from London to pay the fee and lets him sit at supper with us too."

"School keeps me busy," he said, "and I'm always getting spastic hand from learning to stitch gloves and control a quill.

I keep snapping off the nibs of the pens and pluck our poor goose until it's nearly naked. I'm learning Latin and Greek, though it would truly suit me to stay with our own mother tongue. There are enough words in it and more to be made just like cobbling up a shoe, but Master Hunt caned me at grammar school when he heard I'd said that about both of those old, honored languages."

I knew not one whit about lofty Latin or Greek. I was envious, but didn't let on. "I have a bargain with my da," I said, still trying to top him. "If I keep our records and sums straight, he'll bring me a book from London once a year, one with pretty poems, maybe even sonnets. He's soon going to have a pack train of his own. Then maybe I'll get even more books to read."

"I truly covet books, and my father says he can borrow me some from Edward Arden, the head of my mother's family. But my father won't like your da's rival pack train," Will said as we tarried. We were skipping stones in the Avon, upstream from the bridge a bit where the fierce eddy always snagged things and swept them round and round. "Among other ventures, he's put money in the Greenaway business," he added, I suppose hinting that my da indirectly worked for his.

"Your da's a busy man," I said only.

"More like, he is hardworking and important to our town. It's his ambition to make us worthy of the Ardens. But his livelihood is not just inherited wealth from my mother's side with their fine coat-of-arms and vast Park Hall lands about eighteen miles from here. You know," he added as he sat down with a sigh on the riverbank and rested his elbows on his raised knees, "the best thing is my father's the one who signs the permits when the companies of traveling players come to perform in the Guild Hall. A troupe called the Queen's Men are coming back soon and Lord Leicester's Men too. You ought to see them prance about and dance jigs."

"Oh, they have dancing?"

His eyes took on a distant look as if he saw things I could not. He suddenly sounded awed, and his voice fell to a mere whisper. "Even if there are supposed to be corpses on the stage, everyone gets up and dances at the end, the merriest of jigs."

"I'd like that better than deaths and sorrow to be left with. Do they know Her Majesty and have they seen her close?" I asked, clasping my hands against my chest. To glimpse the queen of England in the flesh was then my life's desire.

"I warrant they do and have. 'Tis said she fancies all sorts of play and pastimes."

"But does it cost dear to see these players?"

"Oh, aye, there's money in it, for a certain. Standing between my father's legs on a bench at the Guild Hall, I saw my first play when I was five. The clown made me about split my sides. Wintertime, it was when it was so cold my little brother Gilbert's tongue stuck to a pewter cup when he licked it, and everyone was blowing on their fingers who didn't have warm gloves, and people spoke with white puffs of air as if those tiny clouds could carry their quick words to stinging ears."

"I shall see these players this time and hereafter, just like you," I vowed as I tried to skip my last stone, only to see it devoured by the mouth of the eddy.

Two more things I recall after that day, besides the fact that Will never just said something plain, like the weather was cold, but always made word pictures to prove it. I worked harder than ever at my reading and writing. And, after that first day I spent with Will, I always called my sire *Father* to others and never just *Da* again.

CHAPTER TWO

ꤷ

The most thrilling event of my younger years was when the queen came to visit our part of the country on what was called her summer progress. As mayor of our town and Arden kin, Will's father took him to see her grand entry into Kenilworth Castle, the country seat of Robert Dudley, the Earl of Leicester, Her Majesty's longtime favorite.

Kenilworth lay fifteen miles from Stratford, so I never would have been able to go on my own, though I vowed to my father I'd run away if he didn't take me. But, God be praised, all pack trains in the area were hired to bring in supplies for the queen's visit. After much cajoling and pleading, I was allowed to accompany my father and his men. Poor Kat, my best friend, sobbed and sobbed at not being able to go, but I vowed I'd describe every royal detail, down to the rings on her fingers and bells on her toes. Will's father also took Will's friend Dick Field, but my father said one wench was enough to watch with all the carters and carriers about.

Everyone knew that the earl—'twas said the queen always called him Robin—would like to seduce or coerce Her Majesty to wed him. But ever since his wife had died under mysterious circumstances, which threatened both Leicester's and Elizabeth's reputations, she had managed to keep him in his place while still enjoying his good company. The earl had planned a fine supper for her vast train of courtiers under a big tent at Long Itchington. After what Will called their "*al fresco* repast," Leicester would escort Her Majesty seven miles to his castle for a visit to last at least a fortnight.

When my father and his men—he had four laborers now and a dozen horses for his own pack train—finished delivering their last load of victuals to the castle, he left the animals guarded by two men and found us a place along the road where the queen would pass before entering the huge, redbrick edifice of the castle.

I noted well the whispers from the crowd as we waited, pressed in together like cod in brine: "Leicester wouldn't have this grand place to entertain her if she hadn't given it to him—and his title . . . His family's full of upstarts . . . Maybe murdered his wife so he could court the queen . . . Leicester's father a traitor . . . beheaded . . . rumors afoot that the Catholics in the area will turn their backs on the queen or try to do away with Leicester, her watchdog here'bouts . . ."

All I knew was I'd never seen the likes of Kenilworth Castle. Massive, with many fine towers guarding its stalwart flanks and rows of banners fluttering from its ramparts, it sprawled between a spring-fed lake and a vast hunt park full of deer. On the lake, I saw a man-made floating island, which, 'twas whispered, was to be part of the queen's welcome. If I squinted, I could see a woman on the wooden platform, gowned in white silk, her hair golden in the sinking sun. Oh, if that could only be my place in this vast, shoving array of folk, for I could barely see from here. Lord Leicester had ordered an arched bridge built over the water for a special entry, and I had to get close to that to be sure I could espy that lady all in white greet Her Majesty.

And then I spotted Will, or rather his father, who had already uncapped. The bald spot on the back of John Shakespeare's head shone in the sun. They stood not far from us, but closer to the road in the second row behind the many local men of import in their blue velvet Leicester tunics embossed with the chained-bear symbol of his coat-of-arms.

"Can I edge closer?" I asked my father. "I won't go far."

"All right, but don't lose sight of me," he ordered, craning to look down the road in the direction from which the procession would come.

I didn't tell him it was the Shakespeares I saw, for between the Greenaways and my father, Silas, there was bad blood. Despite being offered more money to stay with the Shakespeare-supported carriers, my father had formed his own company and, by under-pricing the Greenaways, was off to a sound start. Will and I never broached the subject, but so we wouldn't be seen together, we now met under Clopton Bridge to take our rare walks. When our companions, Dick and Kat, went out to the country with us for a stolen afternoon, they knew to meet there too.

At last the buzz of the crowd changed from murmurs and mutterings to shouts. "Hey, ho! Huzzah! She's coming! Uncap there, knaves! Stand back, get back! Make way! Make way for the queen's majesty!"

I wedged myself in the press of people one body away from Will, but he saw me leaning out to look. He reached over to squeeze the hand I held out to him. I was surprised he spoke to me with his sire so close, but the noise of the crowd covered his words.

"That's Edward Arden, the head of my mother's family, in the first row," he said, pointing at a thin, glowering man, garbed all in black. He stood out like a harbinger of doom amidst the bright colors, especially in the row of Leicester livery.

"Did he forget his tunic?" I asked, for a man as important as Edward Arden in this area owed direct allegiance to Leicester.

He shook his head and leaned closer. "More like, he's foregone it. Leicester's been as mean as that bear on the tunics. He pesters and prosecutes recusants, and Cousin Edward's spleen is up over it. But in this crowd, Her Majesty won't notice."

Recusants were those with Catholic loyalties or leanings. They were recorded and fined if they didn't attend the Protestant church. In the early days of her reign, the queen had commanded that everyone could keep his conscience private, but since several attempted Catholic plots and rebellions, she'd let her advisors convince her to change her policy.

But none of that mattered to me now, only glimpsing the great and glorious queen of England. Menfolk tossed their caps into the air. I had to remember to breathe as the parade came in sight. Guards on horseback, prancing steeds of the nobility raised a great cloud of dust, for it was said, a hundred courtiers and four hundred servants traveled with her. I grew dizzy in the press of people as the scarlet-and-gold-clad yeomen guards rotated past, each ahorse, each holding his ceremonial halberd upright from a stirrup. Then someone shouted, "The earl! Lord Leicester!" and I saw a handsome bearded man in peacock blue, mounted on a huge black horse, and the queen in white beside him on a pure white steed with gold saddle stitching that gleamed in the sun.

A pox on it, I was on the wrong side to see her well! Maneuvering for position, I jostled others back when they bumped me. My ears rang with the cheers, then I was screeching too, "God bless Your Majesty, God bless good Queen Bess!"

Suddenly, it happened.

The earl looked straight at Will's father and reined in. No, not at Will's father, but at Edward Arden, standing with his legs spread and arms clasped over his chest—with his cap on his head—three people from me.

"Sir?" the earl clipped out as if it were a question, then said in a darker tone, "Sirrah!"

The only thing that vexed me was that the earl was blocking my clear view of the queen. When she moved a bit, I saw she had a golden hat with sweeping plumes perched on her red curls. It seemed she had no eyebrows, they were so fair. Her face was narrow, her chin pointed and her skin pale as milk despite her rouged cheeks. She nodded, smiled and waved, first to one side then the other. I thought her a goddess, eternally young, though she was over forty years of age. I was hoping she would speak to the crowd, but she said only—and I had to read her cherry red lips—"Robin, not here."

But it was Edward Arden's voice that rang out from the buzz

of the crowd. "I'll not wear the livery of an upstart lackey!" he cried. "A chained bear indeed! Would that it were chained and not free to harry those who are not heretics but—"

Someone seized and stifled the shouting man. It might have been Will's father. At the same time, the earl's boot, still in a heavily encrusted metal stirrup, gave a kick or a shove and both Edward Arden and John Shakespeare toppled back into the crowd. Folk bounced into me, and we went down like bowling pins at least four rows deep. I righted myself and leaped up before the rest, even before Will.

In that brief moment, ere the earl and the queen rode on, I stood looking eye to eye with Elizabeth of England. However fair of face, her eyes were as dark as mine. That's why I loved her even more, from that moment on, no matter what befell.

When the queen paused on the bridge over the lake, my father and I scrambled to get a good vantage point. We heard the Lady of the Lake greet the queen from her floating island, declaring in fine words how tradition said Kenilworth was once upon a time one of King Arthur's castles of Camelot and how the lady had stayed in the lake awaiting the arrival of the next great monarch.

The couplets of the poem carried quite well over the water, once everyone hushed. I hoped Will could hear these glorious words for, as far as I was concerned, they surpassed any in the two plays we'd seen in the Guild Hall.

"And now," the lovely lady on the island said to the queen, still ahorse on the bridge,

> "Pass on, Madam, you need no longer stand;
> The Lake, the Lodge, the Lord are yours to command."

"Is the lord indeed mine to command?" the queen's bell-clear voice rang out. "I would prefer to win all of your hearts!"

Everyone gasped as she swept an arm toward us and then rode into the castle. I mouthed those few words over and over. Such a short speech but so full of wisdom and wit—and power over a man, over a land, over us all.

I felt giddy and hardly startled when a gunfire salute rent the air, nor later when the sky boomed to life with the shooting stars, pikes of pleasure and whirling squibs of fireworks that reflected in the water. The bridge on which the queen had entered stood empty, and when at last the sky slipped into silence, my father pulled me away to sleep on the ground with him and his carriers around a fire.

But I didn't sleep a wink and knew there was naught else I would ever want from life now that I'd seen the queen. That is until I overheard the next morn that one of Her Majesty's entertainments one week hence would be on the bridge, given by an Italian tumbler who was "skilled at somersaults, turnings, caperings, and, upon the thin railings above the waters, fanciful flights."

Of course I was wild to return to Kenilworth to see the Italian tumbler, but my father's pack train was bound for London the next week. He forbade me to go back, even if someone would take me. So, I vowed I would go with no one. But once I was deposited with the Whateleys on Henley Street and the pack train disappeared over Clopton Bridge, I set my plans in motion to go on my own.

"I'm bound and determined to see and speak with that tumbler," I confided to Will, Dick and Kat as we met under the bridge the next day. "I won't tell a lie to my father, even if he asks me later if I went—"

"Which," pretty, brown-haired Kat put in with a toss of her curls, "he probably won't ask, because he doesn't say much. And you said he doesn't like to bring up anything to remind him of your mother. I should like to have a love that dear someday," she added with a sigh and sideways glance at Dick.

"Hell's gates, leave off!" he declared, using one of the oaths he'd picked up when he delivered new-made tuns, kegs and firkins to the Burbages' inn on Bridge Street. "Let's just cut to the quick. How's Anne going to get to Kenilworth and back without being caught?"

"And without being harmed," Will added. He kept twisting his new seal ring his father had bought him. It bore some decorations and his initials W.S. in reverse so the blob of wax into which he pressed it would be readable. He prized it above all else, yet, it seemed to me, the ring made him feel as anxious as important.

"Anne," he said, "you saw the hangers-on round the castle precincts. You may be yet young, but you are a fetching maid, and someone could give you trouble."

Our gazes snagged. His face flushed, and something strange and unspoken leaped between us before he looked away. It was the first moment I felt more for Will than gratitude or envy, somehow all mixed up with other emotions I could not name.

"But the tumbler is to entertain at midday," I argued. "If I go at first light on one of my father's horses he's left behind to rest in our stable back of our cottage, I could see the show and return before dark."

"But you can't ride," Will protested. "And it's not as easy as it looks, especially sidesaddle, which ladies always ride."

"Do you think I'm a lady, Will Shakespeare?" I demanded, hands on my skinny hips. "Oh, I'd like to be, but never will. I'm going to tell Mrs. Whateley I need to walk to Temple Grafton to get something I forgot. I'll dress like a lad, take one of the mounts and ride to see the tumbler and that's that. Only, please, no matter what anyone asks of you, my friends, don't let them know what I've done."

I could tell Will was in a wretched mood. He'd hardly been able to enjoy anything since catastrophe had befallen the Ardens the day the queen arrived at Kenilworth. Edward Arden had been heavily fined by Lord Leicester and told privily to stay away from the earl's august presence or he'd find his "Arden arse in prison." But today, mayhap my crisis distracted Will.

We all swore secrecy and friendship forever. Dick pricked a fingertip of each of us so we could mingle blood to seal the vow. It hurt, and I know Kat and I flinched a bit, though both Will and Dick took the tiny cut with manly pride. Amazing how much that small wound bled so red as we touched fingers, holding our hands out and moving in a circle as if we were spokes in a turning wheel. More amazing, how many times I thought of that silly little rite over the years, and then how the pain was not on a crimson fingertip but deep in my heart.

Five days later, at dawn when I arrived at my father's stables, Will was waiting with two horses saddled and a spare set of his clothes laid out for me in the straw.

. . .

When we arrived at Kenilworth, I saw that people had set up temporary camps along the roads, forest edge and lake, hoping for another glimpse of the queen. 'Twas said she ventured out almost daily, sometimes to hunt in the forested chase, sometimes to walk the bridge and wave to the crowds. It was hard for me to believe that in one week I'd become so intent on seeing the Italian tumbler that Elizabeth Tudor had become of secondary import to me.

Perhaps because we both led big, sturdy horses or because we looked like lads waiting for their masters to arrive, people let us through to a good place to view the bridge.

"My mother used to dance upon a mere cord, thin as a cobweb," I told Will, craning my neck to look up and out at the narrow railing.

"Pretty words," he muttered, twisting his seal ring. "Yet tales become more fantastical with time and the telling, you know."

Ordinarily I would have been vexed at him for throwing cold water on my fancies, but I was so grateful he'd come along. Since I was garbed like a lad, he'd even given me hints about riding astride. My thighs were so sore I could barely walk steadily, but I tried not to let on. I knew Will could get in terrible trouble for this. He was always worried about letting his father down, and I shuddered to think what his mother would do if she'd known the Shakespeare heir had ridden off for the day with the Whateley wench. Will's sister Joan had called me that, and of a certain she didn't hear it from Will.

The queen and her courtiers evidently strode out upon the

bridge, for the crowd farther up the banks of the lake let loose a mighty cheer. Our angle of sight was bad to watch Her Majesty but good to see the tumbler when he began to tiptoe upon the narrow railing high above the lake as if he had not a care in the world.

He was handsome too and wore a fool's motley with the diamond-shaped harlequin designs in bright hues. Not only did he prance along the railing but bent over it forward or backward and put his hands upon the rail as if his backbone were as limber as a lute string. He'd somersault onto his hands and walk the board railing before cartwheeling back to his feet. Will and I were both in awe. From the bridge and banks came wild applause and cheers. As we stared up at the man, it seemed only the sky and battlement banners were above him and all the earth below.

He sang a song, evidently in Italian, full of words I didn't know but which Will guessed meant things like sweet and love—*dolce* and *amore*, I remember that well. I mouthed those sounds silently, thrilled I now knew words in my mother's language.

"Look! Look, he's coming off the bridge this way!" I cried to Will when the queen's retinue went back inside and the bankside audience drifted away to other pursuits. "Will, please, hold the horses for a moment. I must try to speak with him, to see if he knew my mother, if he could be kin to her and me."

"Bring him back over here," Will insisted as I thrust my reins at him and darted off through the thinning crowd.

"Master Tumbler, do you speak English?" I cried as I caught up with the Italian. I sounded breathless. He had seemed so tall and robust balancing above, but now I saw he was quite short and thin. Up close, his costume looked gaudy and worn.

"Aye, lad, what is it then, 'less you've come from your master to beg a show." Though he sounded weary and vexed, he spoke in a lovely, lilting way, pronouncing little words like *it* or *is* as if they were *eet* or *eez*.

Still perspiring from his exertions, he seemed to gleam. Such a handsome face with bronze skin, dark eyes and sleek eyebrows framed by hair so black it shone blue in the sun. My heart went out to him, for he had like coloring to me. He had evidently noted that well too, for he said, "Or do you ask, because you are *Italiano* too, my boy?"

"I'm part Italian because my mother was, but she died years ago. Her name was Anna Rosalina de Verona, and her family were tumblers. She could walk a taut rope, even at St. Paul's in London. That's where my father first saw her. He's there now on a trip, but he's missed her horribly too."

He smiled as his eyes flickered over me. He motioned me away from the little rabble of children who had followed. I was about to tell him my friend Will wanted to meet him too, but all that flew right out of my head when he said, "Ah, but you resemble her greatly, our Anna Rosalina. Had she not told you of me, her cousin Bruno de Verona? And, do I not detect a beautiful young woman in that lad's shirt and hose and breeches, *si?*" he asked with a light pat on my hip.

I nodded so hard my pinned-up hair bounced loose from my cap. He spoke good enough English and was kin to my mother. His very voice haunted me with long-buried memories of how she spoke. I began to cry.

"Ah, *bellissima,* a woman indeed, so slender, so light and lovely with her feelings brimming over, *si?* Come, come with me and let us talk of her, our poor, departed Anna Rosalina. Ah, her loss is such a shock to me also, but did you ever think to learn her craft then, *cara bella*?"

"Of tumbling or ropedancing?" I asked as I swiped at my wet cheeks with Will's shirtsleeve and followed him away from the lake. "I had thought of it, dreamed it," I admitted.

I felt I danced with Bruno de Verona even now upon the bridge railing in the sky with the queen's courtiers clapping in approval and awe. Once I glanced back, hoping to see Will, to gesture him to follow, but I saw him or the horses nowhere. I could not let Bruno go, not someone who had known the beautiful cloud dancer who had left such a hole in my heart. I had to know everything about her.

We walked into a field, set off by trees but not far from the castle where many small tents were staked and roped in the ground, perhaps the temporary abodes of the queen's carters and servants who could not fit within the bursting castle walls. At this close range, I saw the tents were muddied and tattered.

"You make a very pretty boy, but I could use an Italian-looking maid to train to my talents, to know and respond to my arts," Bruno said with a wink. "Come, sit within." He swept his arm gracefully toward one tent staked a bit off to the side. "We shall share some sweet ale and talk of the queen of England and your queen of a mother. Families should keep together, *si*?" He lifted the flap of the tent and smiled again at me, teeth and eyes gleaming.

Some deep-set instinct made me hesitate. I stooped to peer inside the dim, empty interior, then, still bending over, glanced about to see if anyone else might be near. The area was greatly deserted at this midafternoon hour; the few folk I saw seemed busy about their tasks.

"Come, come. Do you not expect a tumbler to give you a tumble?" he said with a laugh and gave my bum a shove that toppled me to elbows and knees inside.

That shattered the haze of my daydream. I had overstepped and now this man would too. Suddenly sprawled beside me in the dim tent, he turned me faceup and covered my mouth with a dirty hand. His other clutched hard at the crotch of my—of Will's— breeches.

I tried to kick and bite. He cursed in Italian and pulled his hand back. That gave me a moment to scream, and I did, screeching out I know not what as I now recall the dreadful scene I myself had caused. As we struggled, the man spoke to me in soothing English, then Italian, his tone harsher, his hands harder. I believe I screamed Will's name again, again, for all the good it would do me.

Then he was there, my friend, my hero, yanking the flap up so daylight streamed in to make my tears blur my vision. Somehow Will ripped the tent half down, or the horses did. I never asked him later. I tried to forget it all, especially how stupid I had been, how desperate.

But I never did forget how Will charged one of our horses at the man as he tried to scramble away from the tent on all fours, then got up to limp crookedly into the bushes as the much ado brought others to the scene. I shall always recall how Will helped me straighten my clothes and did not say that he had told me a maid could meet with dangers here.

Rather, claiming to be my brother in most convincing style,

Will drew me and our two mounts away from the whispers and prying eyes. He held me on his horse ahead of him until I stopped shaking. Then, with a quick kiss on my cheek, he boosted me up on my own mount and led me quickly on the road toward home.

CHAPTER THREE

℘

In the autumn of 1577 a great comet streaked across the English sky, provoking many predictions of woe from ministers and sooth-sayers alike—even from the queen's astrologer, the famous Dr. John Dee. 'Twas said that the heavenly torch portended famines, plagues and wars, so even the most stouthearted hunkered down, expecting the worst. Some were looking for the signs of heavenly retribution or the end of the world in daily events.

I hardly cared a fig for all that talk as I was finally looking less the lanky girl and more the blossoming woman. My father's en-deavors were prospering enough for me to afford a brass mirror and a pretty piece of fabric and, now twice a year, a book from the sellers' stalls at St. Paul's Cathedral. Another blessing was my three good friends.

But soon it didn't take a comet to convince me that things were taking a turn for the worse. The wool trade that propped up all of us midlanders collapsed; poverty, like a wolf in the fold, devoured rural profits and properties. People began to murmur against the queen's rule, especially in our part of the country where the pope was still revered by those who could not abide a monarch as head of the Church of England. Just as my family helped support old Father Berowne, other folks hid former priests as servants so they could celebrate the Mass in secret.

However, Will's next-door neighbor, the one east toward Bridge Street about six doors from where I stayed, may have caused his own dire misfortune during this comet-cursed time. Despite his tailoring trade and ownership of several local properties, the man had to leave town when it was discovered he had two wives, one here and one in Oxford. Will said the Stratford aldermen had charged this William Wedgewood with "marrying another wife while his first was still living." A stiff fine and shameful public penance awaited him, but where he had fled to, no one knew.

Will's great catastrophe was that his father had to withdraw him from school. No longer a city councilman, John Shakespeare could not keep his sons in the King Edward VI Grammar School for a free education. In past years, he could have afforded such for Will, Gilbert and, later, Edmund too, but not now, for besides making gloves, Will's father had invested much in wool trading. Besides, Will was needed part-time in the glovery since Gilbert was bound to Kat's father as an apprentice in the haberdashery.

Will had bravely joked that at least now his spastic hand would come only from too much stitching, but I knew he was deeply grieved to leave his formal learning. The Shakespeares owned a Bible and a prayer book but little else. I started sneaking Will the few books I owned for his sparse free time, but soon his father hired him out to work mornings as a lawyer's scrivener, despite his hand cramps.

The only times I saw him privily for long periods the next summer was Sabbath afternoons. I rode behind him on his horse as he went to his cousin Edward Arden's Park Hall to borrow books from the fine library there. I simply waited for Will an hour or so just outside the gates; he always came out with some sort of sweet for me. Twice I had lovely conversations with the Ardens' elderly gardener, a man amazingly learned for his calling. He always lifted his hands in the sign of the cross and gave us a blessing as we left.

As we jogged back to Stratford, sometimes I read one of the newly borrowed history or poetry books to Will. He would not let go of his ambition to be a poet, which, indeed, was about as likely as my dancing on a rope or the queen being elected pope.

But the increasingly complicated rhymes Will and I used to spout to try to top each other now went by the wayside as did other merry pursuits. It seemed to us and to Dick and Kat that our childhoods had streaked off into the black sky with the comet's tail.

"My father has to mortgage another piece of rural property," Will told the three of us at an increasingly rare meeting by the river. "After all, he has five children to feed, and, as eldest, I hope to help him." He sighed heavily and glared down at his seal ring, maybe thinking there was no way in all Christendom his father could afford such a gift for him now. "One of his hopes was to buy great Clopton House in town, but, by the rood, we'll be blessed to keep the Henley Street house and shop now. We've stopped making wool-lined gloves, and few can afford even the unlined ones anyway. Still, he sends the expensive rabbit-lined ones to Edward and Mary Arden when I borrow books there."

Dick put his big hand on Will's shoulder. "And I know your sire must be paying fines for not attending church," he said. "Hell's teeth, I wager those can add up too."

"Though my father and the Ardens privily favor the old faith, that doesn't mean he's not loyal to the queen!" Will cried. He yanked away from Dick, his voice strident. Kat and I took a step back. Not only was Will proud, but he had a temper. "At least the Earl of Leicester's not about as much," Will plunged on. "He's sticking close to court and queen like a burr on—or up—her skirts."

Kat gasped, and I frowned. I didn't like the way Will disparaged the queen, but I held my tongue. Since his rescue of me at Kenilworth, I was fiercely loyal to him. I fancied his affections too, but struggled to keep him from noticing in these tough times. Still, with Will Shakespeare, who delved into everything people said and did and could recall all that was spoken, I thought perhaps he knew. Sometimes we would finish each other's thoughts and sentences, and then we'd gaze at each other with a certain surprise and recognition of—of I know not what.

Kat was far gone in whirls over Dick too, but he cared for naught but his own advancement as an apprentice to a London printer. He had great plans for escaping the midlands, spreading learning abroad through his calling and making a pretty penny too. Already Kat was ruing the dwindling days before he'd leave Stratford. Her parents had their eye on the widowed eldest son of the miller for her, though he was cross-eyed, stuttered and was nigh on twenty years her senior. I urged her to speak to them about

Dick if he'd but vow to send for her when he was well established in London.

But we had some good times those years too. All England rejoiced at the news that Francis Drake, who hated the vile Spanish as much as they hated him, had circumnavigated the globe. Will loved the sound of that all-encompassing mouthful of a word—the *globe*.

To celebrate Drake's feat, huge bonfires were lit on hilltops, and some managed to dance and sing, including the four of us, down on the riverbank. At least, we told ourselves as we pressed our hands together, holding them high and walking in a ring-around as if we circled a maypole, we never went hungry, not for belly food or for the food of friendship either. Though we didn't mingle our blood from pricked fingers then, that moment the four of us again celebrated our friendship cut deep into my soul.

But grievous times cut short our joy. Brutal winter came with flooding and cold. Da said even the Thames overspilled its banks and flooded Westminster Hall. Worse was the death from weak lungs of Will's sister who bore the same name as I. It was the first time I'd seen Will cry and was touched that he trusted me enough to sob on my shoulder. He'd never faced a loss of life, though I'd carried such a burden on my back since I could remember. It was also the first time since that last awful day at Kenilworth that we'd clung to each other. They said still waters ran deep; I supposed that was the way of it with Will and with me too, so what would happen if those tides would ever meet?

Despite their tumbling fortunes, the Shakespeares paid well for the pealing of the mourner's steeple bells when they buried their Anne in the graveyard by the stony skirts of Holy Trinity. Though

I knew Will's mother didn't care a fig for me, I grieved for her. Surely the agony of a mother losing a daughter must be like unto that of a daughter missing her mother. Anne was the third daughter Mary Shakespeare had lost, the other two before Will was born. Dick did a rough count and reckoned that nigh on two-thirds of Stratford infants died before their first year, so at least, he said in an attempt to cheer Will up, little Anne had lived longer than that.

But naught lifted my spirits or Will's either that cruel winter. As he wrote years later in *The Tragedy of Hamlet*, "When sorrows come, they come not single spies / but in battalions" and "One woe doth tread upon another's heel." It was that way for us then, and, I warrant, all England too. But for Will and me, the worst was yet to come.

In the depths of that second dreadful winter, when Dick had been gone to London for two months with not a word sent back, Kat's parents betrothed her to Guiles Willoughby, the miller's heir. Kat told me that immediately increased the bounty of bread for their table, fine white flour manchet bread too, 'twas said to be the queen's favorite bread.

Bitter cold though it was, I met Kat under the bridge and we walked along the slippery banks of the half-frozen river. She was wrapped in a shawl and carried a milk pail.

"I'm on my way to the mill," she told me. She looked ashen-faced with gray half-moons under her eyes as if she'd been ill. But her bloodshot gaze showed that sleepless nights and crying were the culprits for that too.

I tried to lift her spirits at first, as Will and I had done after Dick first left. "Not giving out milk at the mill now, are they?" I asked.

"Don't jest. Mother thinks I've gone for flour."

"What is it then, my Kat?"

"What is it?" she cried, turning to face me and throwing the pail down. "I'm going mad as a Bedlamite not hearing from Dick after Will sent that letter to him for me. You told me he wrote in it that, if he cared for me, he should declare his plans before the first banns are read for Guiles and me, and that is this coming Sabbath!"

I took her hands in mine. We both wore gloves Will had made for us from scraps of calfskin—fine, supple gloves, though a bit like a motley coat of patched pieces where he'd practiced his small stitches. "Kat, even after the banns, you might hear from him and could change Guiles' mind, if he knows your affections lie elsewhere."

"Stuff and nonsense! What have affections to do with this bargain? Dick had to get that letter weeks ago. Your friend Stephen said he delivered it personally."

"So he did. He told me."

Stephen Dench was my father's most trusted worker. I had asked him for a privy favor for Kat's sake, though I had the same worry with him that Kat had with Guiles. True, I'd paid Stephen a kiss to take the letter from Will to Dick, but at least my father had no burning desire to match me to anyone this soon. I was worth too much to his business. I just hoped he didn't get the idea that a betrothal for me to Stephen would strengthen the Whateley pack train endeavor, as he had no male heir.

"Kat, keep your hopes and heart up then," I urged. "And even if Dick only looks on you as a friend—"

She pushed me away. "I suppose it wouldn't hurt you one whit if Will took off for London to make his fortune, or decided to go off with the queen's players he so adores without a backward glance!"

"Yes, of course it would, but I intend to have a life with or without Will Shakespeare."

"Oh, brave words!" she cried, kicking her pail so it rolled down the bank and skidded onto the ice. The center of Avon's current was open water, but the river was icing up from both sides.

"Kat, I am sorry."

"I'll run away, I vow I will!"

With that last declaration she sank onto the muddy, slippery bank, put her head on her hands and began to sob so hard I thought she might choke. I knelt beside her, one arm around her quaking shoulders, one covering her hands clenched on her knees.

I just held her, until I was crying too, but silently. Tears froze on our cheeks. Her heavings muted to mere hiccoughs, and she quieted at last. When I saw she meant to rise, I helped her up and fetched her pail for her, careful not to go out too far upon the ice. I wanted to tell her something like, *Surely you will grow to love Guiles* or *When you have children, you will live for them and life will be worthwhile.* Or the worst lie yet, *I am sure Dick will write or come in time.* But the words would not form, so I spoke the bald truth.

"Oft we cannot control or choose where we love," I told her. "I believe that is the fate of womankind, my Kat, from the queen with her Leicester on down—down to the likes of us. Desire wars with duty, but we must still march bravely on. And I will ever be your friend."

"You have been a dear friend, you and Will too," she whispered, not looking at me now. I was astounded to see her nod and press her lips into a taut smile as she dashed her tears from her face.

"I will see you later!" I cried as she started away.

"You will for a certain, ninnyhammer," she said, using one of our pet names we oft used to call each other. She did not look back as she headed down the riverbank toward the mill where the water turned the big wheel.

She sounded more steady now, pray God, accepting of her loss. Feeling relieved and hopeful I had helped my friend, I hurried up the slippery slope in the opposite direction.

Later that chilly day, I was sweeping out the stale and greasy rushes from Mr. Whateley's wool shop floor when I saw Will come tearing up Henley Street. I knew that his younger brother Gilbert had been ill, and I prayed he had not taken a turn for the worse. He ran up the walk where I was now gaping out the front door at him.

"What?" I barely got out before he grabbed my wrist and pulled me outside so hard I nearly left my feet. I dropped the broom and, holding up my skirts with my free hand, tried to match his strides.

He was out of breath. "Fulk Sandells from Shottery—sells us fleeces—just came into the glovery and says—a girl's caught in the ice near the brook."

My heart filled with foreboding.

"Says it's the one who's to wed the miller," he choked out.

I gasped as we ran pell-mell toward Clopton Bridge. Still holding hands, we did not cross it, but half ran, half slid down the bank to our old meeting spot under it, then followed the slippery path in the direction I'd seen Kat walk earlier. I nearly dry-heaved from fear. Neither of us was dressed for the cold, but we were both sweating.

"But—no one's wed to the miller," I protested, trying to hold back the horror of what this could mean. I remembered the way Kat had suddenly seemed resolved—but resolved to do what?

"He must have mixed that up," Will muttered. "But Master Sandells says the girl's drowned!"

I nearly collapsed, but he pulled me on, past the place where Kat and I had talked just hours earlier. No! Dear holy Jesus in heaven, please protect her—please, not Kat.

"It can't be Kat!" I insisted. "I talked with her a while ago, and she said—well, of course, she's overturned about Dick and Guiles—but she promised I'd see her soon."

He slowed but did not let go of my hand. "Watch your footing," he ordered. "We don't need to slip in too, if that's what happened. People will be here soon. Come on! Maybe she's only knocked her head, and we can save her. I saw a limp cat get pulled out of a well once, and it breathed again."

Too soon and yet too late, we reached the spot we both feared to look but knew to search. There a willow grew aslant a brook that fed into the river by an eddy that always pulled things down into it. In the sweet months, crowflowers and daisies grew there; now only frozen reeds adorned its hoary bank.

I saw Kat's discarded pail and, pointing at it, let out a scream.

The gloves she'd worn—Will's gift to her—were neatly folded on the upturned pail. All grew silent in my head and heart as we went closer and looked down to behold our friend staring up at us through the clear ice that edged the banks.

Her eyes and mouth were open, as if in surprise or expectation. Her thick, curly hair had straightened and darkened, yet it seemed to crown her head with a wreath as the current swept past where her body had wedged. Her open, empty hands floated at her sides, palms up as if she were beseeching us to give her something, and her sodden skirts shifted as if she danced. Was this an accident or her own design—suicide? Will held my hand so tight it went numb while we gaped down at her.

"God save us, she's killed herself over it all," he whispered.

"No—don't say that. Not that, or they'll bury her by the cross-roads as a heathen where everyone throws stones. I couldn't bear it."

"I know, I know. But unless we can convince the crowner and bailiff it was an accident, they'll not allow her in hallowed church ground."

We could hear other voices coming closer, random shouts and cries, no doubt her family as well as others. Fulk Sandells perhaps, leading people in. Yet we did not move but held tight to each other, gazing down in awe as if our friend had been preserved in a glass coffin.

"Damn Dick Field!" I said. "Her parents and Guiles too! They killed her. It's murder!"

"Leave off!" Will ordered, giving me a shake. "If you talk that way, you'll turn everyone against our common cause."

"What common cause?" I demanded as I pulled away from him

to kneel on the bank. I reached out to put my hand upon the cold, slick ice over Kat's face. Tears had frozen on that face earlier; now it seemed a torrent of tears encased all of her. If only she could get up and dance a jig with me as we were wont to do, as Will had said corpses did upon the stage at the end of the play to make everything right again.

"I've learned a lot at the law office where I've been copying documents," he said, speaking fast now, though his words hardly pierced my stunned brain at first. "If we both testify—you, especially, since you saw her but a while ago—that she was calm and of sound mind, happy enough about her coming nuptials, they will have to rule that she drowned by chance, not what they call *felo de se*—suicide. Anne, do you hear me? Would you stand up with me on that, both as her friends? We must let no one gainsay what we claim."

The ragged group of people turned the bend in the riverbank and burst upon us. Kat's mother was with them and began to moan and wail. Will's mother put her arms around the distraught soul. People pushed the women back and simply stared at first. Then men led by Will's father and Fulk Sandells began to hack at the ice to retrieve the body.

Will and I stood apart and moved away. If we testified thusly to allow poor Kat to be buried in consecrated ground, everyone would know of our secret meetings—that we were covert friends. And it might come out about Dick and Kat to further sully her name. Though we were yet young, folks might suspect the worst of Will and me too. Purity and honesty were valued in this town, and people oft sued each other over slurs or accusations of sexual affairs. The Shakespeares would be appalled and angry, and my father—I knew not what he would say. Mrs. Whateley would believe she should keep me on a shorter leash—that was certain. I'd be as bereft as Kat was to lose the one she loved if I lost Will.

"Yes," I whispered to him in the din of cries and shouts and sobbing. I nodded fiercely. "Lord help us, we must hazard all, for it is the least that we can do for one we love."

"Loved," Will said, as if he spoke the amen to Kat's lost life and mayhap to all our days together.

The next morn in a back room of the Stratford Guild Hall, I testified to Katherine Hamlett's state of *compos mentis*, as the crowner, who had examined the body, put it. That man and the bailiff presided.

I soon saw that this hearing was to be quite formal and official with Latin terms thrown about willy-nilly, ones I didn't understand. I hoped Will did, as he'd not only studied Latin but now worked for the lawyer who sat beside him and his father on the opposite side of the room from my father and me. As I write this from my memories of twenty-one years ago, I cannot recall the name of the lawyer Will worked for or if John Shakespeare had hired him or whether he attended from curiosity or as a favor. And, despite the fact Will had a mind like a trap, I won't ask him, because I don't want him to know I'm writing my love story and life story, not yet at least.

At any rate, I felt I was on trial myself. My father and I—he had just come back into town the day Kat died—sat on one side of the officials' table with Kat's parents seated two benches back.

Arrayed on Will's side of the room—I had thought we were to be on the same side, so to speak—were his parents; the lawyer; the Greenaways, my father's business rivals; and even the miller's family, including Kat's betrothed, Guiles, who looked not as much grieved as gruff. Perhaps some of these folk had chosen their seats at random, but it seemed something dire was to be done with me that day too.

Standing before the table where sat the crowner and bailiff, with tears in my eyes but in a clear voice, I answered the questions put to me. It reminds me now of a plot from *The Merchant of Venice* (though that was supposedly a comedy), which Will wrote a few years ago, where Shylock demands his pound of flesh. Would that I then had the heroine Portia's brightness and boldness, but I spoke out as best I could.

Perhaps the real horror of that day was that Will and I had resolved to lie, or at least slant our remarks in Kat's favor. I took strength in our now unspoken bond that Kat must not be buried in a desolate, shameful place where she would be deserted after death as she had been in life. Above all else, that would have galled me sore.

"So you were a friend of the deceased—*sub rosa*, secretly so," the bailiff began as I stood before their table.

"We both had household duties but enjoyed each other's company when we had the time."

"Not quite what I asked, but I see."

He didn't see, but I didn't say so. I reckoned he'd bring up Will and Dick being part of the whole thing next, but he didn't. I wondered if Will's father still held sway with his old fellows, since he'd served Stratford so well before his financial problems.

"And you had a conversation with the deceased on the riverbank but an hour or so before she must have drowned."

"Yes, before she must have slipped in. As you know, the riverbanks were frozen mud and ice. I found the footing very slippery so—"

"Simply answer the questions put to you, Mistress Whateley. I want you to have it clear that we are here trying to determine if this death was *per infortunium,* that is, by accident, or *felo de se,* committed wittingly—a suicide," he said as he rose to his full height behind the table and walked around it to look down on me.

I wanted to give ground but I did not. "I understand that, Master Bailiff."

"How would you adjudge Katherine Hamlett's state of mind at your last meeting then?"

"She was a bit agitated about her coming nuptials but was preparing for them. She gave me a little smile as she left and said I'd see her again," I expounded, grateful that those statements were true. "She was headed to see her betrothed and was going to bring back some flour to her mother in her pail."

"A pail which was found upside down on the bank with her gloves folded neatly atop it as though, with clear aforethought, she didn't want them to get wet," he said, glancing at my hands I had gripped before me. Slowly, I lowered them to my sides, telling myself to keep calm.

"I warrant she didn't want them wet or the pail either, if she was to fetch flour in it," I said. "She no doubt put the pail and the gloves down to look into the ice like a mirror to see that she looked well enough before she approached the mill. You probably would not know, Master Bailiff, but it's easier to arrange one's hair properly without gloves on."

I was rolling along now, seeing a scene I knew in my heart had never happened. But I didn't care what these people—all but Will and my father—thought of me. It was wrong that the church declared someone who took her own life should be banned from a proper burial. Yes, suicide was even more wrong, for God had given that life. But the judgment and punishment belonged to Him and not to such as this man. I wanted to declaim all that in the loudest voice, but somehow I managed to rein in my temper.

"Mistress Whateley, do you not think if Mistress Hamlett had leaned over the ice to peer at her image and had accidentally fallen in, the ice at that spot would have been broken through?" he said with a knuckle knock on the wooden table that startled me.

"I do not know how fast it might have healed itself on that cold day. I recall it took several men to break through"—I dared to rap on the table too—"to pull her body out. If she slipped on the ice, she could have skidded into the center current or that eddy and could have found herself wedged under the ice by accident, indeed *per infortunium.*"

The man looked like a beached fish gasping for air that I'd used the Latin back to him. In my line of vision behind his broad shoulders I saw Will, who had obviously been told not to so much as look at me, try to smother his broad smile with his hands.

The bailiff was not to be put off. "Mistress Whateley," he said, his voice taking on a sharper tone, "since it was so cold a day, was it not highly irregular that Mistress Hamlett was going such a distance—and tarrying to talk to you—in merely a shawl instead of a cape or something warmer?"

"I warrant, your honor, you've never been in love and heading to see your betrothed. 'Tis said it heats the blood. Though she did not mention it, perhaps Kat hoped that Guiles Willoughby would notice and give her a hug or even offer to take her back home on his horse. But, now, so sad to say, she'll never go home again . . ."

My voice caught and I nearly burst into tears, and it was not playacting either. My shoulders shaking, I cried silently for Kat's loss of Dick and of her young life. For my looming loss of Will I saw coming. My brave words to Kat about bearing up at the loss of Dick, my bold speech about the battle between desire and duty but that we must keep marching on all seemed now so like dancing on empty air.

"That will be all, Mistress Whateley," the bailiff said, strutting back to his place at the table. "And we would ask you to wait outside."

I was not to hear what Will would say, if he was to testify at all. Not trusting my voice, I nodded. My father, forever turning his cap in his hands, rose to go out with me. At the last moment, I saw Kat's mother, teary-eyed, nod either her thanks or encouragement to me.

Outside, when the door closed behind us, in the vast hammer-beamed Guild Hall, a man stood to face us. It was Fulk Sandells, the Shottery farmer who had first found Kat's body. Perhaps he had testified before I had arrived and was to wait out here for the verdict too.

"I've a message for you from John Shakespeare," he said, looking only at my father. "He wants your daughter to stay clear of his son Will, and the boy has vowed the same. Nothing good can come of it."

"I spoke to her," my father told the man as if I were not able to speak for myself after testifying a moment ago, "and she says they were but honest friends. The Shakespeares and their business fellows, the Greenaways, have no right—"

"This has naught to do with that. Will Shakespeare's not of age to be going off with womenfolk of no acquaintance with his family."

Of no account to his family, I thought I heard the silent accusation echo. I had known that it would come to this. My entire being wanted to rebel, to scream at this man and them all that Will and I were special, that we were of like mind in many things—and, though I would never say so and Will might not realize it—that we were in love.

At least I had one brave victory amidst my losses, for the bailiff and crowner ruled Kat could be interred in hallowed ground. They buried her in the far corner of the churchyard of Holy Trinity, barely inside the wall, but it was enough for me. I took flowers to her grave whenever I could and still do.

Mrs. Whateley told me that town gossip said the bailiff was vexed that I'd been "upstart and sassy" when I testified. Yet in gratitude for what I'd done, Kat's parents sent me two gifts I will ever cherish. One was a long-handled fan with ostrich feathers that they had bought for her wedding. The other was an emerald green velvet, white-plumed hat that, in all but color, reminded me of the one I'd seen the queen wear at Kenilworth.

Though I partly blamed the Hamletts for Kat's demise, I accepted both gifts graciously in memoriam of my friend. I dreamed almost nightly of her, about the four of us walking and dancing together, happy dreams, not nightmares, for those came with my waking when I realized Kat was gone forever.

As for Will, I locked away my memories of him tight in my head and heart. However much I missed William Shakespeare, for no man would I languish and die—at least, that's what I thought then.

But for distant, hurried glimpses, I was not near Will until a year later, the afternoon the Queen's Men performed in the Stratford Guild Hall, where our time together had ended. A pox on him, but Will waved and smiled at me, took his seat with his father and stared only at the stage. Afterward Will went off with the players to the Burbages' Red Hart Inn on Bridge Street. I know because I walked that way—the long route back home to Temple Grafton.

I'd come into Stratford on my own to see *The Fantastical Floating Island of Atlantis*, if I recall the name of the play aright. I heard it was by "Anonymous," whom Will had once jested was the most prolific English playwright of the day. He'd said if he ever wrote a poem or play, he'd be proud enough of it that he'd put his name upon it.

The title of the drama reminded me of that wonderful time Will and I had seen the Lady of the Lake greet Her Majesty at Kenilworth Castle. But this was a romance about strange seas with soft sand shores and an enchanted cavern where a party of four fine folk was shipwrecked. The only characters, but for a few flitting sea creatures and the gods Poseidon and Neptune, were two men and two women, though the females were, of course, played by painted, gowned and bewigged boys, just as they had been in the days of Greek dramas. Still, I liked the way the four main characters exchanged banter and danced and sang.

But if I'd written those parts, I would have the actors at least making speeches about foraging for food or getting rescued. That seemed to be of no concern to them at all. A silly play, I thought, especially because the players made broad, set gestures to demonstrate particular emotions. They declaimed even fear and awe in bellowing voices and fell too suddenly in love and planned a double wedding out of the blue. *Too* happy and *too* fantastical to suit me.

Still, I loved the jig at the end. I kept glancing over at Will, for I could see his profile. He was, I guess, much enamored of it all, the dog-hearted popinjay.

After the upheaval when Kat drowned, my father had declared I was old enough to stay in our cottage at Temple Grafton when he was away instead of being boarded with our Stratford kin. And so, in exile just as surely as if I were shipwrecked alone, I kept house and tended the two horses the Whateley carriers left behind on each run. I kept all the records and made out reckoning slips for how much people owed us. On occasion, I went afoot to Shottery or Stratford to collect our due.

And sometimes I lingered by the banks of the Avon where I had once met with Will or where Kat and I had spoken that last day, even the spot by the eddy where she'd drowned. I made coronets of posies and cast them in as a memorial to her or sailed leaf boats toward Stratford with the tiny initials A.W. to W.S. punched in them with a hairpin. I pretended Will would find them and know they were from me. More than once, I invented elaborate scenes in my head with witty dialogue and long, heart-wrenching soliloquies of how I had missed him. I knew such plots were as fantastical as the Queen's Men's play.

But I cursed Will too, for he had evidently been cowed by his parents' decree not to seek me out. That last moment, by Kat's corpse before the others came upon us, we should have vowed we'd meet in secret at least at certain times. What about that finger-pricking blood oath we'd taken years ago? He had evidently abandoned it and me as completely as Dick had left Kat.

The years slipped by and my warm memories of him grew colder, until they barely moved—like a torrent turned to ice in the frigid river.

CHAPTER FOUR

❧

As I had feared, Stephen Dench, the best of my father's carriers, bided his time, yet wanted to court me with a vengeance. He was broad-faced and brawny, kind enough but loud and untutored in social graces as well as learning. I knew he watched me with hungry eyes, which did not scare me half so much as it intrigued me. But I still said no and wrenched a promise from my father to give me more time. Because Stephen could not read or write and my father trusted no one else with his records, he spoiled me and gave me my way.

"For one more year," he said, shaking a finger at me when I turned seventeen. "Stephen would be a good match for both of us—for the business. He's as hardworking as we are, and you could grow to love him if you'd but give him his chance. You've still got your head in the clouds, missy."

"Maybe after I've seen London. You said I could go with you to see London."

"Someday, I said. But I repack and turn right round, you know that. You'd have no time—"

"Just once, you could give me time. You could stay a few days. Da," I wheedled, using my old pet name for him that sometimes softened him up, "I know there's so much to see and do there. I could go to a real play at that place—the playhouse—"

"Heard tell there's three of them now," he said, when I fumbled for its name. He drew in a breath from his pipe, then blew a wreath of smoke into the air. "No, girl, London's not a place for you. But if you was to wed with Stephen, I could see it clear to give the both of you a week or so there between runs. Aye, I could do a run or two without him, and someone would be there to be certain you are safe. You could see the Maiden Head Inn where we unload. You could let a chamber from John and Jennet Davenant, who have a shop there. They live upstairs on Lilypot Lane, a fine couple, though sadly they've lost more than one—"

"That's a bribe," I interrupted. "Truly, I need more time to decide about Stephen or anyone else."

"Talk to Father Berowne about it when he comes by. He says he loves to hear you read. You just cease that chattering about poems and plays long enough to ask him what he thinks of real life—of you and a man."

"Father Berowne is dear but in his dotage, and the world's changed," I protested. "Besides, he never wed."

"He's known enough who did, conducted many a ceremony, including your mother's and mine," he muttered, pointing at me with his long pipe stem. And that was that, though I never said one thing about Stephen to the former priest.

I did ask Father Berowne, though, if he'd heard how the Shakespeares were getting on since it was whispered they were Catholic recusants, just like their Arden kin. He said only he'd heard that they were trying to keep their heads down, but it wasn't easy since Edward Arden was so blatantly disloyal to Lord Leicester and the queen and, though in an increasingly dire financial bind, John Shakespeare bravely paid his fines rather than attend the queen's church. I thought it strange that the English Church did not try to keep people like that out of the graveyard rather than poor distraught souls like Kat.

And so the weeks, months, nearly two years, slipped by like water in the Avon until the month I would turn eighteen. For on the sunny, windy day of September the ninth, 1582, just after noontide, Will Shakespeare passed my cottage heading west through Temple Grafton. He stopped apurpose and leaned on the stone fence as if twenty-one months had not passed since Kat's death.

I'd been pulling onions out of my garden to ward off coughs and cold this winter and had just straightened to arch my aching back when I saw him. Like a statue, I stopped and stared, frozen in time, however fast my heart began to beat. When he spoke, somehow all the long days we'd been apart fell away—as did my better judgment, the loss of which got me all too soon in water way over my head.

"Anne, it's been a long time," Will called to me over the stone fence as he doffed his cap, then held it in his free hand. "How beautiful you are."

I managed to loose my tongue from the roof of my mouth. I

had expected I would cry if we ever acted out a reunion scene I'd rehearsed forever in my heart. But I was shocked at what I said.

"It's the beautiful day that's thrown you, Master Shakespeare—or something has addled your brain in these few months or so since I've seen you. My, but time has flown like a bird." I was pleased with that rejoinder. Polite but tart and clever, but how my voice shook.

"I realize," he said, frowning in the sun, "I do not deserve to stand in your good graces, but you do look lovely. Indeed, you have blossomed into—"

"Into a sharp-tasting onion like these I've been yanking up by their roots," I said and tossed one in his direction. It sprayed soil and just missed him, but he didn't budge. "You're no doubt merely passing by," I went on. "Forgive me, but I must return to my petty tasks, and I don't want to keep you."

But I did want to keep him. He looked fine with his auburn hair gleaming in the light and his hazel eyes clear and piercing. His face and form had filled out in manly fashion; muscles molded his loosely laced shirt and swelled his breeches. And tall—so much taller. He was quite well dressed for a rural walk, surely, not for me.

"Anne, you did a remarkable thing the day you testified on Kat's behalf. I swear, it was your brains and bravado that kept them from daring to rule her a suicide. I thought of you as Lady Tongue that day, sharp with your thoughts and words—even as today."

"It was the least I could do for a dear lost friend, in truth, the dearest I've ever had and lost." I could tell he took that barb four-square. He didn't even try to smoothly change the subject, but jumped topics like a frog, holding up a packet in his hand. "I am to deliver gloves to a Percy Berowne here in Temple Grafton, a former priest. I believe you know him." His own bravado seemed to be slipping; he looked both uneasy and annoyed.

"Ah, you simply stopped at random for directions. Then, here they are. Keep going."

"I—I had to promise my sire I'd stay away from you. He said if I didn't, he'd make it hard on you and your father. I regret our long separation too."

"Too? *Too* is a synonym for *also*, Master Shakespeare, and there is no one else here who rues our brief separation. How long was it now—ah, a week or two at least, I wager."

"Anne, please—"

"I am pleased with my life, thank you. But am I to believe that poor old Father Berowne walked clear into Stratford to order gloves? The dear soul's gone senile, you see."

"My father is sending them to him *gratis*."

"If that is true, your father has gone senile too, forgetting that those wretched Whateleys live but a half mile from the old man. That way!" I declared again, pointing toward Oversley Wood to the west.

"Is Father Berowne yet your tutor?" he inquired, as his eyes examined me, bare toes to the windblown crown of my head and lingered at all the stops between.

"Unlike your eyes, his are so bad that I read to him now," I said. "Not long and he'll be resting them forever in St. Andrew's churchyard."

As I crossed my arms to keep from hugging him over the thick stone fence and frowned to keep from exploding into tears, Will added, "I'd forgotten the name of the little church where the old man used to pastor. So you live in the shadow of Saint Andrew's.

I've read he was the patron saint for unwed women. 'Tis said if one such prays to him and sleeps naked on St. Andrew's Eve, she'll see her future husband in a dream. So if you have not had a good dream lately, I pray you will have one tonight. I hear it really works."

That was the old Will, stubborn and shrewd. And newly naughty. Again, especially when he prated of sleeping naked, his eyes bored into the very depth of me, and I felt that down to the pit of my belly. But I wasn't going to give in yet.

"On the other hand, Master Shakespeare, I've heard 'tis said if a man tries to amble and jig his way back into a woman's life after he's let her down, she's a ninnyhammer and he's the greatest fool in all Christendom!"

He made no retort but walked along the fence to the gate and pushed it open, then came slowly through it as if he feared another blast of onions and rebukes.

"Is your father home?" he asked. "I would pay him my respects. Anne, my father's feelings are not mine, though I owed him respect too and help at home."

"Yes, my father's here but he's sleeping," I lied. He kept coming closer. He obviously didn't credit that and was intent on his purpose no matter how I protested.

"I can't fathom," he said, "there has not been a parade of suitors through this gate, but is there someone special, some swooning swain?"

"Indeed there is, one of my father's fellows in the trade, quite acquainted with London, he is too, which we shall visit when we're wed. And you, of a certain, have a list of maidens in line to woo."

"Quite a few, but never one like you," he rhymed, just the way we used to toss couplets back and forth. But this time, I held my tongue. To my surprise, he swept me a courtly bow. I blinked back tears that prickled behind my eyes.

"Anne Whateley, queen of my thoughts and, even after all this time, my heart," he said, straightening to his full height but a body length from me. "I have failed to be a good friend to you, but circumstances were my foes, the arrows of sad misfortune. No!" he cried, holding up his hands when he saw I would answer, "Don't browbeat me further, but let me have my say. Then if you ask me to go and waste another twenty-one months shy ten days away from you, I shall at least consider it."

I stared agape, with nothing else to say. He spoke so well, in such finely measured, moving tones and sweetly selected words. His presence emanated confidence and manliness. I studied his strong mouth, the slight stubble of the buckskin-hued beard that shadowed his chin. At the side of his strong brown throat a rapid pulse was beating—beating for me.

"Your friendship and encouragement in my younger days were shining stars to me," he went on, his gaze holding mine. "Our times together were precious, even to a foolish, addlepated boy. But that boy has become a man."

"I can see that, and—"

"Shh. I must tell you that I have written sonnets, several to you without ever the hope I could share them, but I could stay away from you no more. You are soon to be eighteen, a full-fledged woman. I had to see you—and to speak. Listen to this poem, I pray you, the start of it, at least, and then you may judge my sincerity and my art:

"Those lips that Love's own hand did make
Breathed forth the sound that said, 'I hate,'
To me that languished for her sake.
But when she saw my woeful state,
Straight in her heart did mercy come . . ."

"There's more," he said, "but I'll write it out for you, if you'll but let me return to your friendship and your arms so that I might court you and—"

I nearly knocked him down when I ran to hug him.

Father Berowne did get his gloves when he arrived that evening to sup with me and listen to me read. I fed and read to both him and Will from my new book from London, *The Writing of Artful Poesie.* Will was totally entranced, and not only with the book. However much Father Berowne's old mind wandered, I thought he was surely a good enough chaperon when my father was away.

All that first afternoon we were reunited, Will and I had rambled about the meadows and through a woods called Alcock's Arbour, holding hands we swung between us. I did not ask him when he was going home; I never wanted him to leave. We picked up the threads where we had cut off our relationship, talking of everything and nothing.

With a fine, sweeping view toward the Cotswolds, we sat on a lofty slope of land where wild thyme and oxlips grew and the scent of woodbine and musk roses seeped into our souls. We lay on our backs in tall meadow grass and stared up at the sky 'til Will changed everything when his enraptured face blocked my view and we drank deeply of each other's kisses. Then the whole world spun faster, and I believed in enchanted isles and castles and rushing streams that did not drown a maid but only swept her away to find herself again.

That first month we were reunited swept past too, and we lived only to see each other. When Will was sent on errands, he came posthaste to Temple Grafton; if he had less time, I took one of the pack train horses and rode anywhere to meet him. We had a special trysting spot along the Avon, though not where the eddy still swirled. When we could, we met under the oak tree at the edge of the Forest of Arden where we'd walked the first day we were together nearly ten years ago. Time was more precious than gold; we snatched at its nuggets of minutes and moments.

We talked of marriage, though we knew it must be a ways off. As the trees turned scarlet and gold and leaves pelted all around us, our caresses and kisses flamed to passion. More than once we threw our garments aside and caution to the winds. When it came to coupling, I didn't quite know what I was doing, but Will seemed to. I knew it was a risk, but he was worth it all. It was common for those promised to each other to share a bed, and what was better than one filled with drifting golden leaves? Because I lived close to others in the village, we dared not stay long within my cottage unless the former priest was with us.

"We'll be found out again," I warned Will as we lay in each other's arms in the aftermath of loving on a strangely warm day in mid-November. My skirts hiked up and his breeches unlaced, we yet lay spoon fashion on our sides as if I sat in his lap. "We must tell our parents," I rushed on, "petition their support, but if they will not give it, stand up to them."

When he did not answer, I sat up and straightened my bodice and petticoats as my skin quickly cooled. I still tingled everywhere his hands and mouth had touched me. His beard stubble had rubbed my breasts and belly to a delicious ache.

"Not until I settle something," he said, lacing his codpiece back to his breeches. He'd seemed rushed, almost harsh in his loving that day. If not for his pretty words of adoration, I would have thought he was actually distracted.

"What is it you must settle?"

"A debt I owe—not money. Just a proper explanation and change of plans."

"Are you going to leave your trade as scrivener?"

"I long to leave both that and glove-making. I've had an offer to go on the road with the Queen's Men the next time they come through these parts."

Ah, I thought, so that was the big change he was considering. He looked as if he'd lost sleep over it too. Will was, above all—even above his passionate self—very ambitious. Or, as I would come to learn later of him, his chief passion was his ambition.

"Tell me all about it," I prompted.

"They're led by a James Burbage. His son Richard's with them. They are distant cousins to the family that owns the Red Hart on Bridge Street. I long to go with them, but the truth is, I still want to try my poor, cramped hand at poetry and playmaking as well as acting. Only, here's the rub. I fear the Queen's Men are not out and about the countryside only for their art or even profit."

"What do you mean? They are recruiting new players?"

He took my hands hard in his. "They were founded by and are subsidized by the queen's spymaster, Sir Francis Walsingham."

I gasped and floundered for words. "But, you mean, that's kept quiet because he fears no one would want to see the plays if it was known he is their patron? I warrant that could be true in these parts."

"No—I wish it were so simple. They spread Protestant propaganda and feed intelligence to him and the queen, probably to the Earl of Leicester around here too."

"About rebels, about covert Catholics and recusants," I reasoned aloud, my mind racing. "But then why would they take you on, a kin to Edward Arden and one who has a recusant as a father?"

"I hope it would not be to get inside information on my family, but I will be wary. I'd like to think they want me because they see such promise in me—that's what they say. At the Red Hart, I've read through scenes with them. They were astounded at my memory and facility with words, and of a certain I can learn their emotive gestures and tricks."

"You would be a fine actor, Will! I'll never forget that time you convinced all those people staring at us near Kenilworth that you were my brother. Even with the chaos of the ruined tent—and ruined leg of that horrible Italian man—you talked our way out of there."

"I'd have liked to convince them that the rutting jackanapes should have been hanged on the spot for trying to ravish you. But to get a foot in the door with the players—any players, and ones who also act in London when the theatres aren't closed by plague or Puritan decrees—'tis my fondest—no, my second fondest—desire."

I smiled as we clasped hands even tighter.

"But the play we saw them put on," I said, still thinking, "about the island of Atlantis had no Protestant propaganda in it."

"Richard Burbage told me the play had been much amended for the performance that night. They removed apurpose the shipwrecked character who was a minister and wed the two couples. They cut the role of a sea captain who rescued the shipwrecked souls and took them back to London to tell their story to their great and glorious queen." He shrugged. "It seems they often change their lines to suit their own—no doubt, Walsingham's—objectives."

"I see."

"And, I surmise," he added, his eyes glistening, "they did not want to alarm my father. They want me in their troupe that much."

"And rightly so. But do they think you will go along with their true intent? Or would you? Would you go with them, even if you disdain their methods or their motives?"

He looked away, out into the distance. "I need to hazard all. I must have my chance. Once I have a foot in the playhouse door, I can change companies, maybe start my own."

"If you joined the players, would your father let you go?"

"He won't like it, and I don't truly come into my majority until I'm twenty-one. But I cannot always live to please him. As you can tell, I feel desperate sometimes, as if I will burst if I must stay in Stratford. I used to look for diversions—I grapple with despair in the night and can't sleep . . .

"Besides," he went on, "there could be more money with the players, and the Shakespeares need such, make no mistake about that." He reached up to stroke my wind-tossed hair, then wrapped the length of it in his fist. "I won't give up this chance!" he cried, tugging my face close to his. "I will choose where I go and what I do and that includes having you!"

"You do have me, my man, and I refuse to lose you again."

"Never! I swear, as soon as I can make some sort of living, I will send for you, but can we not be married first?"

"I could hardly go on the road with players," I protested as he loosed my hair. Actually, I'd have liked nothing more, to be with Will and to see more of England, especially London.

"I could not take you on the road, but you could join me in London for most of the year," he went on as he laced his shirt. "Could you not keep your father's records for him there? We must be wed here when we can manage, then go to London."

"Yes. Yes, of course. I'm sure I could convince my father to let me go to London if we were wed. But if we had the banns read here, they would try to stop us. Will, they wouldn't even let us be friends before, and now this . . ."

"I would not leave you to pursue my dream without your promise to be mine, not with that Dench fellow sniffing about."

I hooted a laugh. "I never mentioned him at all."

"You did not have to. I've seen him look at you—that day last week you came into town while your father's carriers were unpacking."

"And is there no fond maiden who gazes on my Will that way?"

"Oh, no doubt. Legions. Entire battalions of them I must beat off. But whatever they may think or do, I am now yours alone. What would you say to our speaking to Father Berowne about a troth plight in private first, so they cannot pry us apart?"

My head jerked up. I'd never fathomed that. "A handfast marriage?"

He nodded wildly and seized my hands again. "I've studied it all at the lawyer's. Such an alliance could turn our family's rancor to acceptance. I know your cleverness and beauty would win them over, Joan and Gilbert, my parents too."

"Your father—possibly . . . but your mother?"

"All! Now listen to what I've gleaned. The Church of England no longer considers marriage a sacrament. It's the spousal contract and the recording of that—a license—that counts, not the formal solemnization of marriage in a church. Let us speak plain. The queen is the child of an illegitimate second marriage, so the secularization of the act is fine with her."

I nodded. That made sense, at least.

"A couple only has to make a vow and marry before a witness, then consummate the union," he went on, speaking faster. "There should be hand-clasping and ring-giving. Anne, my seal ring," he said, turning his hand so I could see it. "When we wed, I shall give it to you until I can buy you one of your own someday. An unsolemnized and even an unwitnessed union, though irregular, can be fully binding. We must only take each other's hands as man and wife, using these Latin words: *per verba de praesenti*. Or canon law recognizes spousals in words of the future tense, *per verba de futuro*, a contract to marry, rather than a contract of marriage."

My head spun faster, faster. I tried to hold to each thing he said, to cling to reason as well as the rapture that swept me. "I would want to vow it in the present and for all time," I told him.

"You are stronger than anyone I've ever known." He stood, pulled me to my feet and grappled me full length to him. I laughed, insanely happy, linking my hands behind his neck and leaning back from him, which only melded our hips closer. We spun around a bit as if we would dance. Will Shakespeare might be a man of thoughts and words, but he was ever ready for action too. I could feel his urgent need for me again.

"Stop that," he teased as I moved my hips against his. "Stop that by the time we have been wed forever and a day. Man and wife, two bodies and hearts and souls as one—that is our future. Let's hie ourselves to Father Berowne to have him see our license is registered in Worcester."

"And then in this land and in God's eyes, William Shakespeare and Anne Whateley will be linked officially and eternally."

"Amen, my love," he whispered with tears in his eyes. "Amen."

Just over two weeks later, on November 27, Will arranged for the bond for the grant of a marriage license for us to be recorded in the Worcester archives by the scrivener there, a friend of Father Berowne. He told me our names would read in Latin, *Wm Shaxpere et Anna Whateley.* On that same day, in the old church of St. Andrew's in Temple Grafton, Father Berowne let us in through the side door at midafternoon.

Sunlight spilled in through the plain glass windows and the remaining stained glass one with Adam and Eve and the serpent. It was the only one in St. Andrew's that King Henry VIII's men had not destroyed, and it cast colors on the stone floor and even on Father Berowne's old prayer book.

I had worn my hair loose and stuck in late-November blooms of goldenrod and marigold I had foraged for. We joined hands and plighted our troth, speaking the legal Latin words Will had said we must and listening to a meandering blessing from Father

Berowne, who was so shaky that day that I believe he thought at one point he was marrying my father to my mother.

No matter. We were ecstatic, giddy with it all. Will put his ring on my finger; it was huge and I would have to wrap it. For the first time I noted that between his initials was a decorative knot—a lovers' knot, I silently decided. I gave him *The Writing of Artful Poesie* I'd read him the first day of our reunion. We kissed before the bare altar and smiled into each other's eyes. And we had plans— oh, we had plans.

But we had to move quickly, stay apart for a few days, until my father, who was due back with the pack train tomorrow, would set out again. We planned to tell him just before he left next time. If he would agree to find the Queen's Men in London to give them Will's agreement to work with them, we would go there the next time with the carriers. Will's family we would tell either before if Will thought the wind blew favorably; if not, he might write them a full explanation from London and we would win them over later.

"Parting is sweet sorrow," he told me, as he made ready to leave me at the church to hie himself back to Stratford for his daily duties. "We must both be the best of players until we can proclaim our love and union publicly."

I smiled through my tears as he left me. At least I'd had a premonition when we were separated the day after Kat died, for I had not the slightest hint that the devilish destruction of all my dreams would soon befall.

CHAPTER FIVE

❧

That afternoon I wrapped my wedding ring in yarn so it would fit my finger and hummed about the house for an hour, lost in reveries and hopes for a wedding night and lovely life yet to come. I hugged myself and spun about, dancing with my dreams. Will was going to tell his folks he'd promised Father Berowne he'd come to read to him and spend some time so that we could have an entire night together. That would surely work since John Shakespeare was tenderhearted toward the old clergy who had lost their place. Then Will and I would have a night together here on my narrow bed and plan how best to break the news to both our fathers.

I gasped when a loud knock rattled the front door. The cottage was small with only a front room and two tiny back ones, the latter which we used as bedchambers. I rushed to answer, praying it was Will at the door. He must have gotten nearly home, then come right back. He could not stay away. He wanted another kiss and caress or all of me. He would insist I go home with him to tell his family our news now.

I flung open the door with his name on my lips. At first, I could not place the two men standing there; then I remembered the taller one. Fulk Sandells, the Shottery farmer who had found Kat's body and told my father to keep me away from Will. The other man I did not know.

A chill wind blew in past them. My insides cartwheeled, for I sensed they were harbingers of doom. I was so terrified that I blurted out what I should have kept silent—

"Will—is he all right?"

"He will be soon," Sandells said, "once his father and us is done with him."

They knew? We'd been found out!

"This here's John Richardson of Shottery, 'nother friend of the Hathaways and the Shakespeares."

I feared a trick or a trap. "The Hathaways?" I asked.

They exchanged quick looks with each other. "The Hathaways be farmers from Shottery, a good family and friends of our'n," Sandells said. He seemed to be the spokesman. Richardson just frowned; he was built like a barrel, stocky with no neck.

"But what are you saying about Will?" I demanded.

"Same as afore, mistress," Sandells said. "We heard last week from Stephen Dench that Will been sneaking off with you, so we're warning you to stay clear—forever."

Stephen! That traitor! But they were too late to keep Will and me apart now.

"And Will Shakespeare," Sandells went on, crossing his arms

over his chest, "must needs wed with Anne Hathaway next week, and we've put up forty pounds—"

"Forty pounds!" Richardson repeated.

"—as assurance bond to be sure we get him to the church to be wed or else!"

Though shocked and trembling, I had the strangest urge to break into hysterical laughter. Will and I had outfoxed them all! Forty pounds assurance bond or not, these two enforcers or not, Will was already wed. Our license was registered, no doubt, in the same record book where they would not dare link his name to any other. Anne Hathaway? I could not place her, but I'd only been quickly in and out of little Shottery, which lay a mile north of Stratford.

Though I had to sidestep to avoid the men, I went outside. "Where you think you're going?" Richardson said with a grunt.

"I'm showing you off my property," I told them, pushing wider the gate they'd left ajar. "Will cannot marry Anne Hathaway, for he's—"

"He's a two-faced, bootless, codpiece blackguard, that's what he is!" Sandells shouted. "Tupping two maids at once, I wager, the young varlet. He'll wed Mistress Anne Hathaway in a proper church with a proper minister, or he'll rue the day he was born—his family too. Her father was a good friend of our'n, and we'll see the Shakespeares sued for every cent they're worth if the lad don't make right what he's done."

With utter horror, I saw the ramifications of it all. No one would credit a senile, rambling former Catholic priest who had married us by sneaking in the side door of a backwater church. Worse, Will was not of age to fight his father on this, and family reputations mattered in Stratford. John Shakespeare no longer mingled with men in high places. He was struggling to stay solvent and respectable. How blind we had both been to think we could win our parents over.

At least Will did not wed me just to possess me. Oh, no, I'd given myself to him gladly, fool that I was. Another woman! That must have been what he was stammering about the day he proposed: he'd said he had something "to settle . . . a proper explanation and a change of plans." He'd been missing sleep and agonizing not just over me, but over how to end his courting of Anne Hathaway. But then—then—my frenzied thoughts stopped to snag on what else Sandells was saying.

"They been courting, and she's carrying his child. He'll be a father come spring, and he's got to make it right. The law says so and the queen's church does too!"

I grabbed the gate for support, but it swung out, taking me with it. I sat down hard on the ground, hitting the back of my head on the corner of the stone fence. Lights pulsated before my eyes. I was certain I would be ill.

Sandells' voice droned on while the other man helped me up. "We're friends a Mistress Hathaway's deceased father and, with John Shakespeare, we'll see justice done. Will's parents are giving him what for right now. Anne Hathaway and her brother's there too. Got a pass on the reading of the banns, we did, happens oft enough," he added, taking my other arm as they propelled me back toward my cottage.

The wind blew cold. Richardson lost his hat, and my skirts—my best petticoats that had been my wedding gown—were now sullied from the soil. My head pounded with pain.

And I could have killed—killed with my bare hands—my once beloved husband, William Shakespeare.

I shook the men off and staggered toward the door, trying to seize hold of my thoughts, to rein in my agony and temper. I had Will's precious seal ring, and he never would have given it to me had he not intended to wed me. All our plans of London and a life together. Had he been so clever an actor with me? And this other Anne—he had lain with her—too.

"Had—did Will know he was to be—a father?" I managed to ask, leaning in the open doorway.

"Only now," Sandells said. "And if'n he knows what's good for him, he'll do his Christian duty."

Mrs. Birkstead, a widow from down the way, hurried along the road and called to me, "Anne, not bad news? Your father or Stephen not been hurt?"

"All's well, goodwife," Fulk Sandells answered for me and waved her off. It was a good thing, for I'm sure, as they took their leave, I'd lost my voice and my senses.

The crushing weight of the old longing nearly suffocated me. Those years Will and I had been friends, then forced apart . . . it had happened all over again. I was deluded to think I could ever have him. I'd been deceived by the only man I'd ever loved. Whether he'd known his other Anne was with child or not, he'd managed to have us both. He'd never told me about her, and of a certain, she'd known naught of me—or had she? No matter, I told myself, for I detested Will Shakespeare whether she had known of me or not. Perhaps the poor woman was just another distraction for him while he awaited his great glory as an actor far away from here, the lying, rutting cur.

Despite my dizziness from hitting my head, I wanted to break every piece of pottery I owned over his head, to stab him with my cutting knife and drown him in the rushing waters that had taken Kat from me, because her love had let her down, selfish sot that he was—that all men must be.

My head pounding, I lay flat on the floor and kicked and beat the ground with my fists as if I were a child in a tantrum, cursing Will, and, though I damned him to the lowest depths of hell, still loving him.

After I regained control of myself, I was terrified of what my father would do when I had to tell him what had befallen me. I reckoned he would storm into Stratford to take on Will and his father this time, maybe with Stephen to back him up. I vowed to myself I would go with them and curse Will before them all.

But I never had to tell my father, for he returned from that trip with a raging fever and stomach pains that doubled him over on his horse. The sight of him made the headache that still raged behind my eyes suddenly seem nothing.

Stephen had brought him straight home and helped me get him off the horse while the other carriers took the pack train into Stratford to be unloaded.

"It came on fast, like a hectic in the blood," Stephen told me as we got my father into his bed. "Maybe something he ate—or caught in London—don't know. I'll go into town to fetch the physician."

I mouthed a "thank you" to him, but the words would not come out. I'd planned to scream at the man, tell him he was a spy and a traitor and I'd hate him 'til the day I died for what he did. But what was the use of that now? Will had ruined us on his own.

Before they'd left, the two messengers of doom that were Anne Hathaway's friends had told me that she was twenty-six years of age—twenty-six! Eight years older than Will! Those words came back to me now that my spleen had abated a bit. So had she set her cap for him, seduced him? No good to face spinsterhood when there was a handsome, clever lad about ripe for the plucking. With the innocent babe involved, I would never try to stop their union, however I longed to. Children needed their parents, mother and father too, I knew that only too well.

But now all that was momentarily thrust aside as I desperately tended my father. He lay in the same bed in which my mother had died of fever. Since he'd been in London where the summer visitations of the plague sometimes closed the playhouses and sent the actors' companies to the shires, I prayed it was not that, but Dr. Wentworth said not.

"Hardly ever plague or pox in the winter," he told me after he'd smelled his breath and bled him. "He's a strong man. My herbs and curatives will restore him. This is a fine elixir for fever with a touch of gold in it, and the chamomile will soothe his stomach and his nerves and, God willing, put his bodily humors back in balance."

It was true that my father's nerves needed soothing, for he raved on and on in his delirium after the doctor rode back to Stratford. Stephen knocked on the door after dark to see if he could help.

"No, you've done enough," I told him, frowning. "Now leave us—especially me—alone."

"I heard in town your swain's to wed the Hathaway girl and that she's carrying his child. Anne, I only wanted you to be free of him, the double-dealer."

"Thank you for taking care of my father. Now leave before I say things to you I do not want a suffering man to overhear."

"You'll see things different when he's better. My offers to you still stand, Anne. I—"

I was so exhausted and bereft—and furious with Stephen, with Will, with the world—that I slammed the door in his face and rushed back to the sickbed.

"Ah, there you are," Da said, his eyes glassy, his gaze darting and distracted. Yet I felt some relief as he seemed to be in his own mind. He wasn't ranting and raving about prices and lame horses, at least. Dipping a cloth in rosemary water, I wiped his ashen face again, realizing I should have asked the doctor for something for my persistent headache. Da's bedclothes were drenched with sweat; I longed to change them, but was loath to move him.

"Yes, I'm here," I whispered. "Just rest."

"Will you not come to bed, my Anna?"

My hand froze. He thought I was my mother.

"Are you still longing for London?" he asked. "Or even for your people yet? I told you I'd make it up to you, be everything to you. It's just—I had to leave to make ends meet. In the summers, the sun here's like in Italy's winters, aye? I told you it would be so. Can you not feel it, so warm even now? You forgive me and still love me, say you do . . ."

I had not cried after I'd learned of Will and the other Anne, but it seemed now my father in his delirium spoke words Will would want to say to me. "Are you still longing for London. . . .

You forgive me and still love me, say you do . . ." Only this time, I could not want him back, could not forgive. Nor could I bear to live in a place where I could come upon him—or her and their child.

I jolted when my father, who had been weak and limp as a babe, grasped my wrist so hard he hurt me.

"Say you forgive me, Anna, that you love me!"

"Da, I'm Anne," I choked out.

"I can't die in peace if I don't know you forgive me!" he shrieked so shrilly that it turned my blood cold.

"Yes—yes, I love you and forgive you," I said. "Now, rest, please rest. You need your strength."

But he evidently only needed to know those things from my long-dead mother, for he loosed his grip on me and died.

At my father's funeral in the bitterly cold shadows of St. Andrew's, I thought I would go mad. Father Berowne managed to jumble a marriage ceremony with a funeral's final words. If I had not been so utterly bereft of emotion and dead inside, I would have laughed and cried at once, especially when I saw that I still wore Will's ring. I had been in such a dazed state that I had not yet taken it off. I'm sure he wished he had it now for his other Anne, but I had no intention of taking it off or sending it back. I'd hide or bury it somewhere—another sort of funeral.

Stephen, who stood behind me with the five other carriers, tried to take my arm, but I shook him off and walked back to the cottage alone. Widow Birkstead and three other neighbor women had laid out a cold repast for us. I thanked them repeatedly, for I could no more have fed even myself than I could have flown. This was Will's wedding day, and his father was at a wedding feast. How I would have loved to ruin it all, running through their house, shrieking like a banshee, cursing them all and throwing their fine feast in their faces.

Though I was doing little thinking then, as I write this years later, I am reminded of Prince Hamlet's rant that the wedding feast for his mother, Queen Gertrude, could have been furnished from the leftover funeral meal of her dead husband, King Claudius. No matter: all that was in my brain the day I buried Da was the sonnet Will had written me. Years later, though it was one of the first poems he ever wrote, it was published with his other sonnets as Number 145.

There was a line in it about "gentle day / Doth follow night, who, like a fiend, from heaven to hell is flown away . . ."

I guess that's the closest thing I had to a thought after we buried Da. Everlasting night had come for me like a fiend. Once in heaven, now flown to hell . . . If I felt anything at all, that was it.

It was dark when the couriers and neighbors left me with kindly words. Stephen lingered. "I know you are distraught and grieving, Anne," he began.

I forced my eyes to focus on him but did not speak.

"When you're done mourning that—your da and . . . the other—I pray you will recall now how much your father wanted us to be together—to keep the business going—so I could take care of you. I hope you will come to your senses later."

"I'm not good at coming to my senses," I whispered.

"Then let's us be business partners for now. That's all I ask. The

Whateley carrier business is building up—you know that. I'll keep things going, and you keep up the records."

"Yes."

"Good—that's settled then. No need for a contract between the two of us, not for that. Then is it all right if I hire on another man? No one can replace Silas Whateley, but we need another."

"Yes."

"We've got goods ready to be loaded in town. I'd like to be able to take a period of proper mourning but—"

"But the play must go on."

"What's that?"

"Yes," I said, standing at the table from which I hadn't budged for hours. "Yes, get everything ready. If we lose this week's business, it will set us back. There will be one change, though. I'm going with you."

"To see London, you mean? But—that's good. Change of scenery and all. It was what your father said to me more'n once and—"

"But not the way he wanted. I will see to things in London, stay on that end of it to keep the books, either for a while or—forever."

"Stay there? But—what about here?"

"I'll move Father Berowne into this cottage, and we'll have to hire someone to keep the books here. I am going to London."

The moment I said that, the pain I'd had for three days since hitting my head on the stone fence departed.

"Will you come into town to leave with us?" he asked.

"No. I'll take one of the extra horses and meet you beyond Clopton Bridge."

"All right. Will you want a second horse—a packhorse for your clothes or goods?"

"The saddlebags on my mount will be enough. I have little I want to take with me. Leave me now."

Looking amazed, he hesitated as if he would say more. Then he nodded and went out.

No, there was little I wanted to take with me from my past. I vowed to start anew and somehow to bury my wretched love for William Shakespeare at least as deep as I'd buried Da.

A note from Will, obviously dashed off by the looks of the careless script, came to me at dawn the next day, brought by Kat's father, Master Hamlett, who came ahorse. I recall it was the morning of our first snow that winter. The ground was white, but the skies had cleared.

"You two done us a great favor, standing up for our Kat to get her buried proper in the churchyard," he said as he thrust the note at me. I had packed both saddlebags and was preparing to mount my horse. "Sorry for your loss—your father's death, I mean. This be from Will, and he prays you read it, then burn it."

"Tell him I might burn it before I read it," I blurted. Then, in a kinder tone—the quiet, listless drone that seemed to be my voice now—I added, "Thank you. I think oft of my dear friend Kat."

"You put flowers on her grave sometimes, I think."

"I do."

"If you will do that, e'en after my wife and I are gone—" His voice cracked, and he sniffed hard.

"If and when I am in Stratford, I will, as long as I live," I promised.

He smiled enough so I could see his crooked teeth. "I'm off then," he said, doffing his cap to me and giving a bow as if I were a great lady before he mounted and turned his horse away.

"I'm off too," I whispered to myself, "and in more ways than one."

Still hurt, furious and exhausted from all that had happened, I leaned my shoulder against the horse's flank. I was tempted to simply burn the note—or to bury it where I'd interred Will's ring under the bare, thorny blackberry bushes behind the cottage. That way, I would cut all the ties for good—or ill.

But I looked closer at the note. It bore a blob of red wax, but no seal since I had his ring. Perhaps he would dare to ask for it back. Whatever this missive said, I must read it fast, and hie myself to meet the pack train on the far side of Clopton Bridge.

My dearest Anne, it began.

"Bastard!" I clipped out but read on.

I had no idea Mistress Hathaway—

"Yes, your mistress indeed, even as I was!"

—was carrying my child. We had a dalliance, but I saw that we were not suited and told her I wished to end our alliance and then I came to you, my love.

"My love—my foot! But you didn't see fit to tell me, did you?" I shook so hard, holding the paper, that it rattled. Pent-up fury poured through me like the river torrents in rain-soaked spring.

I swear to you, I never intended to deceive you. I am most bereft and wretched. I send my most heartfelt condolences for the loss of your father, especially at this difficult time. I sincerely wished to spend my life with

you and now face not only your loss but a life with one I have not cho-
sen. But for the unborn child, my parents' good name and my own
honor . . .

"Honor! I spit upon your honor!"

I have faced up to my responsibilities. Whatever happened, it is not
the child's fault. I have kept our vows secret and assume you did too,
since no one seems to know of it. I have admitted only that I had begun
to court you.

"Coward! Lily-livered, clay-brained, flap-mouthed coward!"

I hope you will at some future time—

"Never!"

—allow me to explain my soul-sick regrets and to give you all hom-
age due your beauty, dreams and God-given talents.

"Fie and curses on your devil-given talents!" I cried. "My talents
lying with you when you had no right to my maidenhood? My
dreams? I hate you and ever will—Will!" I screamed at the letter.

It was only when the horse sidestepped in alarm that I realized
I stood in the front yard of our cottage hard by the main road of
Temple Grafton.

The note was unsigned and might as well have been unwritten,
as far as I was concerned. I was free of Will Shakespeare, free of
country ways. I was going to live in London, to buy my own books
at St. Paul's, to see plays Will would never see and never write, to
glimpse the queen outside her own palace.

I rushed around to the back of the cottage and grabbed my
hand spade to disinter the small metal box holding Will's ring. I'd
just add this pompous, monstrous, wretched letter to it. Maybe
someday, I'd flaunt it, blackmail him with it, I knew not. I only
knew I suddenly could catch a glimpse of how poor Kat had killed

herself over a wretched, bootless, selfish man and the families and rules that ruined lives!

But when I dug up and opened the box in which Da used to keep tobacco and saw the W.S. ring lying there with its lover's knot, all wrapped in wool to fit my finger, I put the letter in the box and took it with me.

Act Two

CHAPTER SIX

❦

Even in my dazed state, London stunned me. From our view on the Hampstead hills above the city, everything seemed crammed between the wall and the huge silver snake that was the River Thames. So many houses and people, nearly two hundred thousand, so Stephen said, though how anyone could count them all, I know not. As daylight waned, our pack train passed St. Giles' Church and a public water conduit just before we approached the city on Wood Street.

Oh, the smells and noises! I could barely imagine what it would be like in warm weather, for a ditch with partly frozen offal and refuse ran right down the center of the street. The sounds of horses, of course, I'd expected, but the clatter and calls of the vendors hawking everything from hot sheep's feet to pigeon pies assailed me. "What do ye lack!" they shouted over and over as well as calling out their particular wares. Carters and carriage drivers screeched at those on foot to get out of the way, and our own carriers shouted at people to stand clear. Once in a while, a rough voice called out rude greetings I tried to ignore.

"Ho, then, that dark beauty for sale with yer goods, man?"

"If we be invaded by the Spanish, hope they look like that wench, eh?"

"Over here, Cleopatra! Look my way, and I—"

That voice too blessedly faded in the tumult and turnings. I had hoped that in London I would not stand out as being so different, but the old taunt of "Egyptian!" haunted me again. At least, I tried to buck myself up, Cleopatra was Egypt's queen. Despite my fears and grief, I lifted my chin higher.

"What do you think of it all?" Stephen called to me as we passed through a redbrick, turreted city portal called Cripplegate.

All I could manage was, "I think I'm not in Stratford anymore." But Will was. However hard I struggled to banish him from my mind, he would not budge. Would he ever come to London to follow his dreams? If so, I would somehow get even with him then.

The Whateley carriers headed our pack train down the street past inns, livery halls and ordinaries—alehouses that served food, Stephen explained. Tenements three stories high seemed to teeter over the busy thoroughfare. The huddled buildings blocked out the biting winds but dimmed the late-winter daylight. This area was stuffed with packers from the northern shires of the kingdom, Durham, Yorkshire and Worcester; their journeys ended at the sprawling carrier inns like the White Hinde, the Swan with Two Necks and the Castle. I glimpsed quieter side streets lined by craftsmen's shops with wooden signs trumpeting their wares.

"That's Silver Street," Stephen called, pointing down one to our right. "Metalsmiths, goldsmiths even, ones to make pretty gifts for ladyloves."

I just nodded and ignored his implication. Each night when we'd stayed at some rustic inn, he'd managed careful hints of his devotion. But Will's ring bounced in its box within the heavy sack I wore over my shoulder, because I did not trust it to my saddle packs. Also there was my record book, Will's sonnet to me—only saved, I told myself, as a piece of paper to muffle the sound of the coins I'd brought—and the fan that Kat's parents had given me when she died. The plumed hat her father had made for me took up too much room in the saddle packs, but I couldn't bear to leave it behind. Besides, should I ever go to Whitehall Palace to see the queen pass by, I shall wear it, I told myself.

I felt exhausted as we turned into the sprawling Maiden Head Inn, the one we midlanders used. Will was married to two maidens now, my thoughts tumbled on, wed to both of his Annes. A pox on the man, for our union had been binding! Instead of vacating the field of battle, I should have marched to the center of Rother Market to declaim to all Stratford that Will had two wives. Then, like that Henley Street neighbor years ago, Will would have had to leave, and if he'd come here, I'd tell him exactly what I thought of him!

What if I too were with child? Would Fulk Sandells and his ilk hunt me even here to tell me to keep clear of Will, the Hathaways and the Shakespeares? Would I then be forced to marry Stephen Dench to keep my child from being a base-born bastard?

Before I could dismount in the central courtyard of the inn, Stephen jumped off his horse and helped me down. This area was cobbled and swept quite clean. Boys ran everywhere to help the men unsaddle and unpack. My knees almost buckled; my side and back hurt from riding without a proper sidesaddle. I walked my aches off, staring up at the three tiers of railed balconies above, realizing as I saw the square of sky that I'd fulfilled one of my great desires: though God's great heavens seemed so small here, I'd set foot in London. Yet I could summon up little joy at that, and it was all Will Shakespeare's fault.

I saw I was drawing stares again. Because a woman rode in with a pack train of men? Because I looked exotic and different? Or because word had spread that Silas Whateley was newly dead and his daughter didn't look one whit as if she were in proper mourning, but had come to town to take the reins of his business?

When I heard Stephen send a boy for a Mistress Davenant, I recalled that Da had mentioned that name when he'd tried to get me to wed Stephen with the promise of a visit to London. What else had he said about her? It was so hard to believe I'd never hear Da's voice or see him again; he'd been away enough that it seemed he'd soon be coming back, that he—unlike my past with Will— was not dead.

Stephen had another boy fetch me a pewter mug of something. "Good small beer," the boy said. "Not that dragon's milk or mad dog ale."

Ordinarily, I would have laughed at those names. Was I entering a world where they spoke with a foreign tongue, even if it was the queen's English?

The man who kept our accounts here, Thomas Kingery, introduced himself, and I found I could at least make sense to him. I explained that Stephen would hire a bookkeeper for Stratford, but that I would see to the records here now. He was not pleased, though I know he served other carrier companies.

Then a vision appeared, one of the most beautiful women I have ever seen, like an angel, I thought. She was fair with hair like sunlight and had clear blue-green eyes framed by golden lashes. Her skin was flawless, her slanted cheeks burnished by the winter air above her dark blue cape. Her nose was reddish, though she must not have come too far to fetch me. I decided she looked like a Venus rising from the sea, one worthy of greeting the queen on that floating platform years ago at Kenilworth. The men around, who'd been eyeing me, swiveled their heads toward her and parted to make a path as if she were Moses at the Red Sea.

"Mistress Anne Whateley?" Her smile showed perfect teeth, a rarity among those with missing or yellowed ones. "I'm Joan Davenant, a friend of your father, and you must call me Jennet, as everyone does. My husband John and I live nearby, and Silas spoke oft of you. I am so sorry to hear he has left us."

She took my cold hand. Mine were bare, for, despite the weather, I'd refused to wear gloves Will had made. Her warmth almost made me burst into tears.

"I am shocked to hear of Silas' departure," Jennet said as if she too thought he'd be back soon.

"It was so sudden. I had to get away, and I needed to see to things—see things here," I stammered as if I were a child. My lower lip quivered.

"Come with me, for we oft spoke of your staying with us should you visit. And as for wanting to escape when there's a dreadful loss—I do know whereof you speak. Master Dench," she said, turning toward the hovering Stephen, "will you then be so kind as to see Mistress Anne's things delivered to our door on Lilypot?"

"I will and be there myself afore we turn about and head back on the morrow."

Jennet took me through the moving maze of horses being led away to stables; we went out a side door of the courtyard. "About your loss—knowing whereof I speak," I said as we traversed an alley into the very teeth of the wind, "did your father depart this life recently also?"

"My little babes," she said as we turned down another street. Her voice quavered. "Three of them, one each in the past years."

I did cry then, as if a stuck millwheel had now loosed a torrent of tears. Surely, so much worse to lose babes in arms! And three in three years? Jennet tugged me in the front door of a tall house and let me cry, leaning close, holding me by my shoulders, or so I thought, until I realized I was propping her up too.

I knew then we'd be fast friends, this stranger and I. I'd had no one since Kat and never would have Will again. Finally, we both blotted our faces and blew our noses. I looked about to see we were in a room where small kegs and bottles, all lying on their sides, lined the four walls. The glow from a glass-paned lantern on the counter in the middle of the room was reflected in the bottoms of the bottles like an audience of eyes upon us.

"My husband imports wines," Jennet said, walking behind the counter and hauling up a half-empty bottle. "And we're both going to have some before we go upstairs to greet him."

. . .

I soon saw the contrast between Jennet and John Davenant was day and night. He was of a grave countenance and demeanor, which, I learned, had naught to do with the loss of their three infants. Though he was devoted to his lively wife, his was an inherent melancholy. He was quiet and, though industrious, seemed to me just bland—brown eyes, brown hair, brown clothes, brown, or mayhap gray, personality. Jennet, despite her tragedies, could be all sparkle and smiles. She did everything at a hectic pace—movement, words, tasks. I was so grateful when she vowed she would take a day away from their shop to show me some of London.

The Davenants rented me a cozy, sparsely furnished chamber at the back of the third floor of their large, three-storied house. I insisted on paying them, despite their kind offer I could stay as a guest. My room had a charming, crooked floor under the slanted eaves that reminded me of my Temple Grafton cottage, which, I told myself, I did not miss. Even mice scratchings I could hear in the thatch over my head at night did not disturb me, but were a familiar sound among all the strange ones of the city.

The views out my two mullioned windows, when they were not thwarted by frost, were, to the west, more roofs, busy Noble Street and the city wall, and to the north, more roofs, some tiled, to the steeple of a church called St. Mary Staining, which had a mournful bell that tolled for funerals. It was where my hosts, and so I too, attended. Though the Davenants had no servants, there was an outside, covered servants' staircase I could take up or down to my chamber to keep from walking through their wine shop, dining parlor and kitchen, but I took most of my meals with them in those early days.

It seemed to me that John and Jennet's wine shop was doing

well, for it was a busy place during daylight hours. Yet the third full day I was in London and somewhat rested, Jennet and I bundled up and set off to visit places I told her I would like to see and those she insisted that I must.

Though I learned she could only write her name and do numbers, she let me wander the bookstalls at St. Paul's where Da had bought me gifts. I had often wondered why my mother had been rope-dancing on holy ground, but I soon saw the so-called sentinel of the city was hardly hallowed as a patron-saint church. It looked as forlorn as I felt, for its steeple had perished in a fire more than twenty years before and had not been replaced. A lottery was held at the west church door to raise funds for repair of the kingdom's harbors, but I thought the money should go to renovate the church.

I was also astounded to see traders had set up stalls to hawk their varied goods among the tombs and baptismal font. Had not the Lord thrown the money changers out of the temple? I kept my eyes peeled for Richard Field. He was apprenticed to a printer in the area, and I was sure I could find him if I but inquired. Yet I could not bear to face him—not after what he'd done—and then I'd have to tell him what Will had done too.

Besides booksellers stuffed in cheek-by-jowl, lawyers received their clients at St. Paul's, for the Deanery could no longer afford to maintain the building just for worship. A veritable parade of fancily garbed youths called gallants with long, crisped and curled hair walked up and down the nave, chatting and laughing—preening like peacocks, truth be told. Jennet said they whiled away the time 'til eleven of the clock, went to tobacco shops and spent two or three hours over dinner and then returned to St. Paul's for the rest of the afternoon.

Most amazing of all was that noisy, smelly horse fairs were held in the very nave of the church. Called Paul's Walk, the nave was an expansion of the Cheapside Market, where we walked with our hoods pulled tight about our heads, not only to avoid the wind but people's stares and the unwelcome remarks.

"They see you are a beauty," I whispered to Jennet as we walked on. From time to time she sipped from a small brass flask of cough elixir, for she said she'd had the winter blains.

"Open your country eyes, my friend, for they are speaking to you also," she insisted. "Dare I say you draw even more attention than I, for you are much more intriguing than a winter-pale face that hides a broken heart."

"But you bear up so well."

"What choice have I? To cast myself off the parapet of St. Paul's or throw myself in the Thames?"

I started visibly when she said that. My dear Kat's face staring up at me through the river ice jumped into my mind as if she were newly drowned. Jennet pulled me into the recessed doorway of an apothecary shop with its sign of an extended tongue with a lozenge on it.

"Anne," she said, gripping both my arms, "I mean not to affront you, but I am terrified to conceive another child. Yet we desperately desire one, and I will risk all for that—and for John."

Tears sprang to my eyes, and I nodded. Only today the onset of my monthly flux had proved I was not carrying Will's child. I praised the Lord for that, and yet, I mourned too. His other Anne had tied him to her that way, and I—I had nothing but memories, no doubt as flimsy and fleeting to Will as the breeze. And, of course, thanks to the knave, my battered heart.

"There's more, isn't there?" Jennet asked, most unexpectedly. "More than the sudden death of your father? You've lost someone else, and I just wondered if you too—not a child, of course, but ... Oh, please do not take my prating, prying tongue amiss!"

"It's all right. Yes—I lost someone I loved to another, so to speak."

"So to speak? Then I shall speak of it no more unless you choose to share it someday. Come on, then, my sister of sorrows. We've much to see and do, and, if we do it fast and furious enough, perhaps we shall brace ourselves to face another day. Getting through each hour, each day—that's the victory."

The Thames was choppy with a big breeze blowing, but we walked down to see it. We stood staring at varied watercraft struggling against the current and the white-capped waves. Its vast width made the Avon seem so small and distant. Why could Will not seem that way to me? After what he'd done, why did he not shrink in my memory?

"I've never seen boats with both canopies and seat cushions," I told her to break our solemn silence.

"Wait 'til you see the queen's royal barges all tricked out with green and white Tudor flags and cloth-of-gold bunting. But those are wherries for hire. Quite comfortable. In warm weather you'll oft hear the oarsmen singing too. It carries over the water just like their calls of Eastward or Westward Ho."

"More are going across the river than up and down it."

"Nothing keeps Londoners from their pleasures and vices. That rural south bank is called Southwark or just plain Bankside. Can you make out the bear- and bull-baiting gardens?" she asked,

pointing at large, oval buildings. "But it's unruly and even dangerous over there."

"Pickpockets?"

"The least of one's worries. Besides men and whores flocking
there for animal baiting, there are stews and prisons—King's
Bench, the Marshalsea and the Clink. It's a vile sanctuary for
rogues and lawbreakers too. Since Bankside is out of the city lim-
its, it's also out of the reach of the men who control England's
pastimes, with their license fees, inspectors and censors."

"But the theatres—where are they?"

"Of the freestanding ones, two are about a mile north of the
city at Shoreditch and one a mile south of London Bridge at New-
ington Butts in Lambeth. But instead of that, I shall take you
someday to the plays given in the large carriage inns at St. Helen's
Bishopsgate where even the Queen's Players perform."

"The Queen's Players," I echoed. "I would like to see them,
indeed."

"Then we shall go next time John can spare me."

But a ship that had braved the winter seas from France brought
new wine to the shop: sweet Osney, Rochelles, Gascoignes and
rich clarets that needed unpacking and recording. And, I saw,
though Jennet kept the bottle hidden from her husband, for sam-
pling. So I went one sunny, cold afternoon to see the Queen's Men
on my own.

At four of the clock nearly a week after I came to London, I saw
my first play. I had walked eastward to the neighborhood of St.
Helen's Bishopsgate and followed John Davenant's directions to

the Black Bull Inn where the Queen's Men were playing. It was not the only galleried, tiered inn where companies performed, but it was the only one then with a permanent stage.

The place was packed with more men, but women were there too; I was soon wedged in like a fish in a brine barrel. The mingled smells of garlic, onions, stale beer and even sweat, despite the chill and the extra layers of clothing, assailed me. No wonder several herb girls stood outside selling sweet bags, pomanders and tussie-mussies. I saw a few of the better-dressed women on the balconies above held such to their noses. But it was the heady scent of anticipation and excitement that made my head spin.

For today's play was to be a stirring drama of the English victory at Agincourt more than two centuries ago. Drummers in the streets had announced the play. Drumming up business, I heard it called; they evidently heralded each performance that way. Those drummers as well as trumpeters and pikemen now lined the bare wooden platform soon to be transformed into a battlefield.

Though I had come early to get a good view, I made the mistake of getting jostled clear to the front where I had to crane my neck to look up. Yet I didn't care. Was this not revenge against Will, for I was where he longed to be and he—he was at home with his pregnant wife, or punching a needle through calfskin, or copying someone else's writing.

"Jus' come to see the clown Tarlton," a big lout behind me told his companion. "He'll have us rollin'."

"Oh, aye. Hear tell the queen loves 'im too. Told 'im to get off the stage and outa her sight once so her sides wouldn't split from laughin'."

"Heard the Earl of Leicester found him just tending swine, and he's been tending to London's swine e'er since," someone else put in as they dissolved in mirth.

I'd seen Richard Tarlton in Stratford once, so I knew whereof they spoke. What I remembered best was the rogue's skill at jigs and how he capered about to put all the Guild Hall in a roar. I needed that, I thought. I needed to learn to let go and laugh again.

Soon words and sounds transformed the small stage to the vast battlefield of Agincourt where the outnumbered forces of the English king Henry V and the huge force of the pompous French monarch Charles VI met with their armies. I knew the basic story; I warrant all Englishmen did. I had heard Will recount it more than once from some book he'd borrowed at Edward Arden's house. Encased in armor, the frog-eaters used old feudal tactics of lance and sword, but our cloth-clad yeomen relied on their quick-shooting longbows and won the day.

I thought the players did a splendid job with battle cries, trumpet blasts, distant drumming and the clash of swords on shields. Battle banners were carried back and forth through the melee. Somehow fewer than twenty players reenacted two armies. The actors were adept at swordplay, even in armor, though they merely mimed shooting their bows. Men cried out and fell with blooming bursts of blood they cleverly exploded—so Will had said once—from pigs' bladders. Horses snorted in the distance; I think it was men whinnying behind the stage. But through it all, despite grand speeches from the deep-voiced James Burbage as England's king, it truly was the clown Tarlton who won everyone's hearts, however much it seemed he intended to make tatters of the play.

He entered as a common English soldier but soon tripped over his sheathed sword, then could not wrench it from its scabbard. And when he got it out, despite the fray all around him, he pretended to pare his fingernails with it. I was astounded to see the tricks he pulled and expressions he made even in the most serious of scenes. It seemed he worked against the impact of the play, and yet the audience adored it, cheering him on just as they did the actors playing the heroic roles.

Squint-eyed and flat-nosed with an unkempt mustache, Tarlton played the country innocent, even trying to stuff a French battle banner in the back of his breeches where it stuck out like a tail. Wherever he went onstage, his russet costume and buttoned cap amid helmets and hats cried, *Look at me!*—and we all did.

During the final scene, a wedding feast for the French king's daughter and the English king, Tarlton sat on the edge of the stage, pretending to eat a drummer's drumstick rather than the meat ones the actors devoured. All the while, the clown swung his feet and bantered with the groundlings. It felt so good to laugh, to be unable to catch my breath from guffawing with the others instead of from sobbing into my pillow alone. But then, to my amazement and dismay, Tarlton's eyes fastened on me. Too late, I realized my hood had slid back and I was bareheaded.

"Ah," the clown declared as he pointed the drumstick at me, "now there's the one I'd fight for—not some princess of France, treaty or not, especially since our fair princess is actually a boy player, eh?"

Amidst the roar of the crowd, I saw heads turn my way, felt their eyes. I was tempted to pull up my hood, but I could make no retreat, hemmed in as I was. To my utter amazement as well as the approval of the crowd, I answered, "But I'd only consider it for one of your jigs!"

The crowd bellowed their approval, and I blushed to the roots of my hair when the clown dared to make an obscene gesture and retort, "I'd jig with you, my pretty, day or night!"

As he leaped up and began to dance, people turned away from me and a good thing too, for my cheeks were as hot as Jennet's looked when she downed too much of their fine wine. I was embarrassed but not ashamed. And how I longed to tell Will what had happened, that, somehow, I'd been a part of the play. Why, if I'd but had time to consider a thing or two, I could have come up with a clever comeback that could have set Tarlton's teeth on edge.

As I was swept out at the end of the play in the press of the crowd, a few glanced my way. Even, for a moment, a sweet-smelling, fancily garbed and very handsome man blocked my path and stared into my face with a ravenous look before he thrust a note into my hand. I saw it was directions to his house in a place called Blackfriars and wadded it up to sail it into the sewer trench in the middle of the street. And then, despite London's noise and smells, I happened to look up into the eyes of one of the herb girls with her big basket of sweetly scented goods.

The other girls around her were screeching out their wares, including claims their nosegays were sure protection "'gainst the return of the plague." I knew London had been repeatedly visited by this catastrophe and that the disease was borne by foul smells, so no doubt a strong-scented bag held to one's mouth and nose could help. But why scare buyers about the Black Death on a blue-sky, sunny winter day?

Amidst the din, the thin waif stayed silent, yet, for the first time, I wanted to buy something in London. I'd bought food, of course, but had not wanted anything else, not even a book from St. Paul's. I'd not so much as looked at any of the secondhand garments that had been displayed today when I came past Petty France where the Huguenots lived and the nearby area where the Jews had their stalls.

The young female vendor whose eyes met mine was rail thin; she wore clothes too big for her. Her hair hung stringy and greasy beneath a mobcap. Her nose was long, her face pinched, but her eyes were lavender, the hue of that sweet-scented dried herb I could smell.

A huge, crashing wave of homesickness spread over me. For my own herb and flower gardens, for my cottage, for the meadows, even for the Avon. And for myself as a young girl, somehow standing unsure at the edge of life.

"What have you here?" I asked her in a tremulous voice before I could clear my throat. I wondered for a moment if she might be deaf or dumb.

"Mistress, I've sweet herbs that can make the body glad but heal the mind and heart too."

"Magic elixirs, then? Tell me all."

I listened patiently to her recital about "virtues enveloped within the green mantles and flowers wherewith special plants are adorned." I was amazed at how well she spoke. Besides, I was so desperate for comfort that I half believed her recital of cures for a heavy heart, indeed a malady of its own.

"This sweetbag has dried marjoram for those given to oversighing," she went on, displaying a small sack made from scraps of satin stitched raggedly together. "Basil can take away sorrowful-ness and rosemary cures nightmares . . ."

I overpaid her for two sweetbags, which both, truth be told, smelled only of meadowsweet and lavender. But, ah, if they could only heal my heart. Before I left, I asked the girl's name.

"Maud, mistress. 'Tis Maud Wilton."

"Maud, you look cold but ever so bold," I rhymed, which made me miss Will even more. "I shall trust what you say and come back when I can, and then talk to you more of my plan."

She looked puzzled but she gifted me with a sweet smile that tilted her lavender eyes. I laid yet another coin on her rickety little stand and hurried off.

CHAPTER SEVEN

☙

Like the great Thames rushing under London Bridge—like the Avon at home—time slipped past. In the eleven months leading up to mid-October 1583, I kept the pack train company going, even prospering. I helped John in the shop when Jennet's next pregnancy weighed her down. I attended plays and helped Maud Wilton buy a proper stall so she didn't have to cart her heavy herbal baskets every day. I even got her the opportunity to make sweetbags for wherry passengers if they'd pay an extra ha'penny for their fares. I'd come up with that idea since the Thames stank like a sewer in the hottest weather.

And one crisp autumn day, I decided to go find Dick Field—though I'd not forgiven him for deserting Kat—at the print shop near St. Paul's Churchyard where he was an apprentice. I realize that perhaps, looking back, I was just desperate for news of home, even of Will, and I never got a bit of that from Stephen. He'd become sulky and sullen when I'd turned his offer of marriage down again last month. He'd muttered curses against both me and Will.

The only thing, it seemed to me, he'd delighted in telling about Will and the Shakespeares was that Will now had a daughter named Susannah, born in May, and that the family seemed to be in increasingly dire financial straits. That, he had gleaned from the fact Will's father had appeared in debtors' court and gossip that Will's wife had borrowed money. I didn't ask Stephen, but could the glovery still be doing so poorly and Will's work as a lawyer's scrivener be so unprofitable? Of course, there were now eight mouths to feed in the family packed into the Henley Street house.

Dick Field was easy enough to find, for I recalled that the letter Will had sent him about coming back for Kat was addressed to the sign of the White Greyhound in Paul's Walk. I only inquired once and was sent straight to it. As I went in the shop door, though I saw no one at first, I heard the rattle of type being returned to its trays along the back wall. Drying printed pages were draped over dowels clear to the ceiling; the smell of paper and ink was sharp and good. From books, both shelved and stacked, emanated the rich smell of vellum or leather, which added to the compelling aroma. How Will would have loved this shop—and I did too.

I closed the door noisily and a man emerged from behind the press. It was Dick; he stopped dead in his tracks. Like other London apprentices of any trade, he wore a flat, round cap over close-cropped hair. His traditional blue gown was calf length and contrasted with his white cloth stockings, however smudged those were. He looked as if he'd seen a ghost—perhaps he was seeing Kat instead of me.

"As I live and breathe," he said.

"You do, some don't," I cracked out when I'd meant to just extend a greeting.

Dick frowned and wiped his hands on his big canvas apron. He had much filled out with muscle. His hands and face were more smeared with ink than I'd ever seen Will's. Turning away, he poked his head into a back room.

"Master Vautrollier, the title page is done and ready for proofing. I mean to step outside a moment."

I heard no reply, but Dick walked past me, opened the front door and gestured me outside ahead of him. We leaned our hips against an empty hitching rail in the slant of autumn sun. The large copper beech down the way wafted its leaves at our feet as we spoke.

"Will said I should look you up," Dick said, crossing his arms over his chest. "Hell's gates, I wrote him to leave well enough alone."

"I wager that is your life's creed," I told him. "It's a good one, if you think what happened to Kat was 'well enough,' what happened to Will and me was 'well enough.'"

He hung his head. "I've suffered over it all too, Anne, truly I have. I can't help what Kat did. I rue the day I heard of it. And I rue that my friend Will is wed to a woman he did not choose and cannot love."

My head jerked around, and my insides leaped. "He writes his thoughts to you. But he—they—have a daughter now. I have heard the glovery and his scrivener work doesn't bring in enough to—"

"Hang it, do you think he should be doing scrivener work?"

Dick interrupted, thrusting himself away from the rail to round on me. "He's dying there, just as surely as Kat died there, only it's taking him longer! I suppose that makes you feel better!" he accused, glaring at me. "If you want revenge, you have it."

"You dare not attack me just to make yourself feel less guilty!" I shouted at him, turning to face him down.

"Did you come here to berate me, Anne? Leave me alone, then. I'm just trying to get on, day by day, learn my trade, make a living and a life."

"Yes, I know. I have a friend here in London who is doing the same with her regrets . . ." I squared my shoulders. Kat would not have wanted me to detest Dick so. "Then, good fortune and health to you, Dick Field," I said as I turned away. Why had I come? To glean news of Will? Nothing now could help Kat.

"He should have wed you, Anne!" he burst out. I turned back. Perhaps that was what I had wanted to hear, not that Will regretted his marriage or that Dick thought Will and I were suited, but that Will still kept our secret, as I had. Evidently, Will had not even told Dick that we'd handfasted, a legal marriage. I'd told both Jennet and Maud some of my story, but not that I had wed Will or that I believed I was really Will's wife and not that other Anne who had his name and his child.

"Yes, he should have," I said, my voice much stronger than I felt. "I would have been everything to him."

"As he is yet to you," he whispered so quietly it might have been the dry leaves of the tree sifting down.

I did not admit to that but glared at him and walked back to Davenants'. To my amazement and chagrin, at the wine shop a black-clad stranger awaited my return with questions that terrified me.

. . .

"Ah, there you are, Anne," John greeted me as I passed the door of his wine shop where he was conversing with a buyer. "A Master Mercer is waiting to speak with you by the hearth."

That did not bother me unduly, for London merchants who wished to send goods to Warwickshire had called upon me before. Rather than take the stairs to my chamber, I went in through the shop to the back room that served the Davenants as dining parlor, kitchen and pantry. I had thought to find Jennet waiting with the man, but she must have gone back to bed, for she was having a difficult pregnancy. "Hard times now when I've sailed through before," she'd remarked with forced cheeriness the other day. "It might mean, God willing, a different result after birth too, and I'll have a baby live, one who will live to bury me someday."

I hung my hooded cape by the door and approached the man who was staring into the low-burning fire on the hearth. He had a calm, kindly profile now outlined by the silver-orange coals. Before he saw me and rose, he gave a turn to the spit with a loin of mutton Jennet must be preparing for supper. He smiled broadly and gave me a half bow. I must confess I liked him instantly, more fool me.

"You wish to inquire about the Whateley pack trains to the midlands?" I asked. I could tell he was somewhat startled by, perhaps even entranced by my appearance, but I was becoming used to that. Unless I was in the Jewish area over by Bishopsgate, women the French called *brunettes* were few and far between, and then not ones with such tawny skin as I.

"In a way, mistress, for I am a tariff taker of sorts."

"I pray I don't owe taxes I knew nothing of," I told him as we sat across the hearth from each other, he on his bench and I in Jennet's favorite chair.

"No, nothing like that. Rather, I need a bit of information. I must tell you I have already spoken to your overseer Stephen Dench, but thought I would inquire of you also."

"About what, pray?"

"I'm afraid I have reason to believe that certain parties in Warwickshire might be sending contraband to London and receiving such in return."

"We ship nothing covertly, Master Mercer, and I keep good records you are welcome to examine."

"I would never cast a shadow of blame on you, of course, but I cannot help but wonder if certain parties might be bribing some of your carriers to transport such things."

"If so, I shall ferret this out immediately," I said, gripping the chair arms and leaning toward him. "But what certain parties? And what things?"

"You grew up outside of Stratford, I believe Dench said. So perhaps you know of the Arden family who reside in nearby country at Park Hall, for the Ardens and their kin are well known in that area."

I hesitated, hoping he thought I was only trying to place the name, but my heartbeat kicked up. Did he imply that the Ardens and perhaps their Shakespeare relations were smuggling contraband goods?

"I cannot credit that," I said. "Aren't the Ardens wealthy—I've heard tell? Why would they do such a thing?"

"Mistress, let me say this flat out. The things I fear that may be going back and forth covertly are Catholic prayer books, papist roods, crucifixes, rosary beads—and, more fearfully, perhaps plotting."

Jagged images tumbled through my mind. My mother's glass rosary beads upstairs in my room . . . Edward Arden loaning Will all those books . . . Arden shouting out in public at the Earl of Leicester and the queen that she was the heretic . . . Will's family's pride in their blood ties to the Ardens . . .

Blood ties! Men had been tortured and executed for papist plots against this queen, and her own Catholic cousin Queen Mary of Scots was imprisoned in the north even now with political intrigue swirling around her.

"I can tell you honestly, Master Mercer, that I have no knowledge of any such contraband goods or such doings."

"As I know you attend the church nearby and are loyal to the queen, I do believe you," he assured me with a smile as he rose. "Well, these things need looking into, and they will be, especially now that the Arden son-in-law John Somerville has been arrested and taken to the Tower."

I gasped. "For sending contraband or for secret plotting?"

"For slandering both the queen and the Earl of Leicester. But worse, for waving a pistol about and quite blatantly boasting he was on his way to London to kill Her Majesty," he said, for once not smiling. And all the while, my inner voice was screaming, *The Tower! Only traitors are taken to the Tower!*

"He was just brought in today," the man went on, "and we will be questioning him and his family quite closely, gathering evidence on all the Arden relations here and there. It is good that you reside in London now for, I fear, the Stratford area is crawling with way-ward, doomed souls."

We made more conversation after that. I told him how I'd once seen the queen at Kenilworth and how I hoped to see her here. I spoke of how much I admired the brilliant, bold woman as ruler of our great land. Of course, I was trying to feather my own nest. But of all he had said, certain words kept catching in my mind: not only *the Tower*, but *here and there*. The government—run by the queen's spymaster Sir Francis Walsingham, for I knew now Mercer was no mere tariff official—was going to gather evidence here and there. Stratford, where lived *doomed souls*.

The Shakespeares had never made a secret of their prideful ties to the Ardens, and Will's visits to borrow books could implicate him. What if someone said he brought books—with plans and plots hidden in them—back into the bosom of his family?

But, my shrill inner voice cried, if Will and his wife—his parents too, who aided and abetted his marriage to Anne Hathaway—were fined or taken prisoner, what righteous revenge!

Once the man was out the door, I stood trembling with the power of the possibility of all that. John Shakespeare ruined. Will's mother, who surely thought I was not good enough for her son, left destitute or even widowed. Will linked to Edward Arden, his high and mighty wife left with their child if he too were sent to prison, though surely not to the Tower.

I went out in the alley so that John or his guests did not come upon me, for, if they had, surely they would have seen some demon-possessed soul at that moment. I bent over double as if I would be ill; I tore at my hair, then hit the wall with both fists.

I could either warn the Shakespeares or hold my tongue and let whatever befell them happen. And it would be naught that I did to actually hurt them; I would not really be to blame, but their own stubbornness and snide superiority would ruin them.

Weak-kneed, I leaned against the back of the house. I gripped my hands between my breasts and frowned so hard my eyelids pinched tight shut.

But then I saw Will's face and heard his voice, heard in my head his letter to me claiming, *I swear to you, I never intended to deceive you. I am most bereft and wretched. . . . I sincerely wished to spend my life with you and now face not only your loss but a life with one I have not chosen. . . . I hope you will at some future time allow me to explain my soul-sick regrets and to give you all homage due your beauty, dreams . . ."*

But now all his dreams, his talents, his very life could be destroyed by my silence. And I would be forever soul-sick too, if I let that happen. I would not, could not, revel in his destruction or that of those he loved. Did he yet love me? I longed to know. But above all, I had to bridle all my hurt and hatred to try to save him.

I did not even take time to check on Jennet or go back inside to fetch my cloak but rushed out through the back alley that led to the Maiden Head Inn. I looked behind me more than once, for what if I were followed? I sent a boy to find Stephen and bring him to me.

"Now, isn't this a rare honor?" he said as he swaggered toward me where I waited out of the wind in a corner of the, for once, quiet courtyard. Ever since I'd firmly denied his suit last time, the man had turned snide and mulish. If he didn't stop all that soon, I'd decided, I would have to replace him and wouldn't that be a pretty pickle? But worse—what if he'd implied something untrue to Master Mercer about the Ardens or the Shakespeares just to get revenge on Will?

"I hear you were questioned by a tariff taker," I said.

"Started out 'round Robin's barn, but was looking for Stratford ties to the Ardens, far's I could tell."

What I could tell was that Stephen had been drinking, but what he did on the day before he turned the pack train around was his concern. His speech was slurred and he looked bleary-eyed, but his reading of Mercer had been a sober one.

"Worried for your old swain, wedded Will?" he asked with a snort. "Heaven knows, his folk've boasted 'bout their ties to the high and mighty Ardens."

"Will has not a thing to do with this—with me or with whatever the Arden son-in-law has done," I insisted, but I knew that could be a lie. I'd heard Will speak against the queen, and that's evidently just what the son-in-law had done. *The Tower . . . gathering evidence here and there . . . doomed souls in Stratford.*

"I pray it's not a possibility that any of the carriers *are* hiding contraband," I told him.

"Not a chance, or I'd know it. But you know what I think?" he said, leaning his big shoulder against the wooden wall. "I think, 'less you're still mooning for the man—and I don't mean Mercer," he added with a lopsided grin and a hiccough—"here's your big chance to bring the smug Shakespeares down for what they done to you. 'Sides, if there's no Will, distant, sure, but still desired, you'd wed with me, wouldn't you, Anne Whateley?"

"No, I would not, and I'm through with William Shakespeare," I spit out.

At least, the fact he was suggesting I take revenge made me

believe he had not done so. And I cursed myself for having thought exactly the mean-minded things he had just suggested. As for Mercer, if he were a spy and knew my past, perhaps that's even why he thought I might try to implicate the Shakespeares.

I have no idea what else I said to Stephen that day, but to wish him well when he set out with the pack train on the morrow. I was grateful he was going, though that would make my quest even more difficult and rushed.

I might be mad in risking much, but, whatever it cost me, I was going to warn the Shakespeares that they were in deadly danger.

I told the Davenants that I was going to visit friends at home; I know they assumed I was going with my own pack train. But before they were out of bed the next morn, with my hair pinned up and wearing secondhand breeches, shirt and jerkin, I hurried up Wood Street to the White Hinde Inn and hired two boys and three horses. Since I knew my own pack train would leave at dawn, we rode fast to be sure we were ahead of them and then pounded toward Stratford. We slept a few hours in the common rooms of inns along the way, then were off again. At least the roads were frozen mud and not mire. In just two days, exhausted, we rode across the Clopton Bridge and into Stratford.

My first impulse was to take my gown from my saddle packs, but I was in too much of a hurry for that. Though the pack train had to be nearly two days behind us, I had no notion of when more "tariff takers," as Mr. Mercer had dubbed himself, could be arriving here.

I sent my hired companions to the Thorn Bush Inn, for I was

even fearful to trust the Burbages at their more familiar establish-ment. Will might hang about there and, as James and Richard Burbage of the Queen's Men served as spies for Walsingham, it was best to completely avoid the Burbages' inn now.

This time of day, I expected to find Will either at the lawyer's or in the glovery. Pulling my cap over my forehead and screwing my courage to the sticking point, I tied my horse in front of my cousin's house a few doors down and strode straight for the Shake-speare house. The last time I'd worn boy's garb, Will had saved me. I prayed that now I might save him.

I glanced in the glovery window. Will's father had his back to me. I cast a shadow and Will, bent over stretched cloth with a knife tracing around a wooden pattern, looked up. His hand with the knife jerked; he stood, wide-eyed, before he lifted his other hand. I saw he'd cut himself, though he paid it no heed and kept staring at me as though he'd seen a ghost. I rushed inside.

Strangely, there were no greetings; we began to converse as if we'd never been apart.

"Despite all that," Will said, gesturing at my cap and garb, "I knew it was you from the tilt of your head and slant of your cheek. But why are you clad like a boy? What's amiss? Are you back from London?"

"We've no time for all that. I've come to warn you and your family."

At first John Shakespeare just gaped at us, turning his head back and forth. Then, just before I blurted out about the Ardens, he interrupted, "Will, is this who I think it is?"

I pulled off my cap and let the bounty of the hair I'd pinned up in the crown of it sweep free. Whether or not Will had confided in his father all the truth about us, I did not know. I opened my mouth to explain everything when someone filled the doorway that linked the shop to the house.

"Will," a brown-haired woman said, "Susannah just sat up all on her own. You must come and see."

She too stared at me, then at Will. "Father," she said, as if she could no longer speak directly to her husband—for I knew this was not Will's sister Joan—"why is *she* here—like this?"

And so, though I never wanted to so much as be in the same city as the other Mistress Anne Shakespeare and was shocked to know she knew me, I ignored her and said to Will, "I've just come from London where I have learned that Edward Arden's son-in-law has been arrested and taken to the Tower of London for proclaiming his plans to kill the queen."

Will gasped. His father muttered, "By all the saints! John Somerville? He's unhinged half the time, and now he'll take us all down with him!"

"Somerville is his name," I said. "And anyone who is kin to the Ardens are suspect and may have their houses searched and perhaps be questioned too."

"But why would *you* know all this?" Will's wife asked. Her voice was not only petulant but shrill, much more so than the lads who played women's parts on the stage.

I faced her at last. "In London, my head carrier and I were both questioned about whether our pack train carried covert Catholic books or letters of plotting from the Ardens or their kin."

John Shakespeare took charge then, locking the shop door and hustling all of us into the back of the house where he barred that door too. Despite my fears for them all—even for myself—I took a good look around. Imagine, I was Will's first love and first wife, yet I'd never stepped inside his house.

It seemed spacious in comparison to the Davenants' narrow town house, and a palace next to my old cottage at Temple Grafton. The floors were stone-flagged and covered with rushes; the walls clean-looking with their contrast of dark timbers and whitewashed plaster. A worn Turkey carpet covered the long table, and faded hangings of biblical scenes covered two walls. The furniture was oak and heavily carved, though it seemed this sturdy house was now shaken by a fearful wind.

Anne scooped up their daughter from a rug near the hearth as if I'd harm her, though she was probably just panicked to keep the child safe. Little Susannah began to fuss, then cry. I tried not to look at Will, who had wrapped a cloth around his cut finger. It was the same one, I noted erratically, that Dick Field had pricked on all four of us the day we vowed a blood oath.

John Shakespeare gave me a warm mug of cider and sat me down on a stool before the hearth; he and Will took the bench facing me. "Mary," John said over his shoulder to his hovering wife, who kept wringing her hands, "send Joan for Gilbert and tell her to be quick about it. Anne, go tend the child upstairs if she's going to cry, and take Richard and Edmund with you," he added, referring to Will's two younger brothers, aged nine and three, who hung about staring at me.

"I want to stay here," Anne protested. "This concerns me too, really concerns me."

I gave her a slant-eyed look. Anne Hathaway Shakespeare was well favored enough with milky skin and a spray of freckles across her nose. Her eyes were blue-gray and her hair pale brown. Her eyebrows were over-thick for a woman and straight across, which made her look perpetually indignant. She was hardly thick-headed for she'd made a clever pun on the meaning of the word *concern*. But did Will trade couplets with her? Did she read to him and listen to his dreams in the depths of their bed?

Despite her protest, when Will glared at her, she flounced off with the baby and the two youngsters while the three of us sat before the hearth.

"We are grateful for the warning," John said. "You know of our close ties to the Ardens, I warrant, having been Will's friend, and still his friend now."

My gaze collided with Will's. As if no one else were in the room, as if no one's safety or life was at stake, we just stared. I know not what I thought or felt then. Love, anger, jealousy, fear, even fury. I suppose only a moment passed, but it might as well have been eternity.

"Yes," I said, tearing my gaze away, back to his father. "And, like many, I observed a public clash between Edward Arden and the Earl of Leicester, even before the queen herself. I fear this might give the earl an excuse to settle with the Ardens too, and since Will's been there to borrow books . . ."

"I trust Anne implicitly, Father," Will said. "If you are thinking she's here to try to glean information for our enemies, you think wrong."

In my haste and panic, I had not even considered that. Will always did see all sides of an issue, all sides of a character, and I rejoiced silently that he had stood up for mine.

When the entire family was gathered but before plans were

made, Will led me out the back door so that I could get to my horse in a roundabout fashion. I saw his wife standing at a back window, holding her baby, watching as he walked me through the kitchen herb garden and along the edge of their duck pond and paused a moment.

"This has been looming for years," he said. "We've been holding our breath. I can't thank you enough, Anne—especially, considering our . . . our mutual hardships."

I had no reply to that. I wanted to say so much, but this was hardly the time or place.

"How is it, then, life in London?" he asked, his voice wistful as I frowned out over the pond, for I could not bear—and did not dare—to look into his eyes again.

"Busy and exciting. The theatres call for you, Will. They call for Will and ever will," I rhymed and walked away from him as fast as I could.

I dared not even visit old Father Berowne at my cottage, for, though I stood on the fringes of Will's life, I did not know how thorough a search would be made or when it would begin, or what the old former priest would recall or babble about our secret wedding. Midland families had been heavily fined in the past for housing former priests, but the penalty could be worse now, for all I knew.

I fed my two London lads well at the Thorn Bush, where the innkeeper let us sleep by the hearth all night. Thus we rested our horses and headed back toward London the next morn, passing my pack train heading the opposite direction that afternoon near

Oxford. Stephen and the men looked half asleep in their saddles and, as I had gambled, hardly looked at three fast-riding lads.

I was in a sweat until my carriers came back to London almost a week later, for I'd only heard rumors of what could be happening in Stratford. It had been noised about London that John Somerville of Edstone, near Stratford, who had "extreme views," had claimed the queen was morally corrupt and that the Earl of Leicester was an adulterer and an upstart. Somerville had vowed that our queen's Catholic cousin, Mary of Scots, would make a far better ruler and he would like to see it so.

"Ha!" John Davenant spit out when he heard that much from a customer. "Mary of Scots goes from husband to husband, helped kill one of them and was ravished by her lover before she wedded him as her third!" It was the most animated I'd ever seen him. If a placid man like John could erupt like that, I knew the city itself must be like a tinderbox.

I also gathered that this Somerville was going to be questioned under duress—torture—to see who else he would implicate. But when my carriers came back, I heard the rest.

On October 31, the very day Mr. Mercer had spoken with both Stephen and me, a warrant had been issued for the apprehension of—Stephen had asked our bookkeeper in Stratford to write it down for me—"such as shall be in any way kin to all touched, and to search their houses." On the second of November, a clerk of the queen's Privy Council, a Thomas Wilkes, had arrived at the house of a local and very well-to-do justice of the peace, Thomas Lucy, just outside Stratford to make that his base of operation. The Ardens' home had been raided and Edward's wife, Mary, their daughter-in-law and a former priest whom Edward Arden had passed off as his gardener—whom I knew, but had not realized was a father—were arrested and sent for questioning and trial in London. Other homes in the area were to be searched also. Edward Arden himself had been arrested at the home of the Earl of Southampton here in London.

"Keep safe, Will," I whispered as I went to bed that night. "Keep safe." It worried me too that I'd chatted with that priest the Ardens had kept on in disguise there and that he knew of Will's many trips to Park Hall.

The news for the Ardens grew worse from that day on. Edward Arden was put to the rack, and a trial date was set for him, his wife and their son-in-law. With their gardener-priest, Hugh Hall, they were to be tried at the London Guild Hall on November the sixteenth.

All London was abuzz with both reports and rumors, and which was which I was not sure. I knew I did not dare to go near the accused and yet I was eager to know the outcome. And so was Will, for he showed up on the Davenants' doorstep the day before the trial.

CHAPTER EIGHT

❧

"I—can't believe he's here!" I said breathlessly, gripping my hands together when John told me I had a gentleman caller from the midlands and I peeked through the doorway to see it was Will. John had also said my visitor looked like a ruffian, and indeed he did. But he spoke like a gentleman, John had added—one with a midlands accent as broad as the one I had intentionally lost since I'd been here.

Praying Will did not look so unkempt and was here in London because he was hiding out, I hurried to him.

"What now? Will, I—"

He gripped my hands in his and spoke in a rush, his voice a mere whisper. His face was dirty; he'd pulled his hair forward and wore workers' clothes as if he were a ruffian indeed.

"I rode in but an hour ago and found the Maiden Head," he told me. "Though your carriers are en route home, I used a false

name when I asked for you. I'm here as Andrew Whateley, one of
your distant cousins from Henley Street. Father and I must let
Edward Arden know we have not abandoned him. I'm going to
try to catch his eye when they bring him in for trial. A dreadful
way to see London my first time."

I was amazed at the reply that fell from my lips, when I had
spent so many months cursing this man. "Come meet my friends
and sit down at our hearth. I can get you some food, and you could
stay—"

Looking surprised he still touched me, he dropped my hands.
He folded his under his armpits. "I can't, though I'd like to talk to
you to get caught up. We are so grateful to you," he plunged on,
"all of us, despite how Anne acted. Can you step outside with me
for a quick walk?"

I hesitated. But this was not for us to resume our relationship;
it was rather life and death for others.

"Yes, of course."

We strolled Wood Street for a quarter hour, ignoring everyone,
hearing none of the noise. I tried to convince him not to go near
the Guild Hall or Newgate Prison, where I'd heard the crown
prisoners were being held after being tortured in the Tower.

"I can't believe Walsingham and the Privy Council would stoop
so low as to charge Mary Arden too," he said more than once. "You'd
think the queen would have pity on the womenfolk, at least."

"She wasn't tortured, at least. But Her Majesty must think like
a man in all this. Besides, she's no doubt seen the duplicity of her
own cousin, the Queen of Scots. That woman is the passionate,
impulsive woman our queen can never be."

He frowned that I would dare to gainsay him or stick up for

the queen. "But Walsingham and the Privy Council must know John Somerville's deranged," he argued. "I can see why they think he must be silenced, but to pull everyone down . . . Anne, they stormed in and searched our house. Thanks to you, my father had hidden his prayer book and other things, but they found where I stowed the books I had from Edward Arden—just to keep them safe because I could not afford such, I told them."

My insides cartwheeled with fear and the shock that I cared so deeply about that. "Did they believe you?" I asked.

"I'm not sure because the one in charge—Thomas Wilkes— looked page by page through each one. Two of them had Edward Arden's name in them—"

"Oh, Will . . ."

"But even when Wilkes read the tiny notes Cousin Edward had made in the margins, he found nothing to incriminate me. Anne blurted out to them that my ambition was to be a poet and playwright—as if she was proud of that, when she berates me for such airy dreams all the time."

"If you go to see the Arden trials in the Guild Hall, I will go with you," I vowed. "And I am certain you could get a room for the time you're here from the Davenants—"

"No, Anne! I hope to stay with Dick Field. Besides, if I stayed near you, my wife would get it out of me and scold for days and—I agree with her—I can't be near you. I mean, here we are, but I can't be with you at night, or in private, I swore it. She does not know we took vows, but she knows . . . I cared for you. Anne, I'm so sorry for all that's happened between us. Those two friends of the Hathaways vowed to ruin my family if I did not comply—and it was my fault—the babe she carried."

"And hers."

"Be that as it may, all this too may mean the ruination of all the Shakespeares."

He seemed so distraught that it terrified me even more. This turn of events kept all I had ever meant to say to him—scoldings, accusations, curses—at bay, at least for now. I did convince him to take a meal with us, and I believe he calmed a bit in the Davenants' company, even when John told him he should wear a sword in the city streets not for style but for safety's sake.

After farewells, John and Jennet went into the shop, I believe to let me walk him to the back door alone. As Will went out into the twilight city with an old sword and scabbard borrowed from John, he turned to face me again.

"Anne, I had to see you, to tell you all. But I will stay away now, so that no one can link us."

"No one but ourselves, Andrew Whateley!" I called after him as he hurried down the darkening alley and disappeared as if I'd dreamed him. I might not, I thought, be able to go by the name of Shakespeare, but, even if in pretense, he had taken mine.

Despite the fact he'd told me to stay away, I could not bear to let Will go alone to the Guild Hall for the trial. He had gone with me when I had risked much to see that Italian tumbler so long ago. Yet I knew I often drew stares and realized Will was right that we should not be seen together and not only so his wife would not interrogate and scold him later. Just like the deranged John Somerville on trial today, who knew what senile Father Berowne would say about me if someone questioned him? And then what might Stephen do if we were seen together here?

So once again I bound my breasts and dressed in the second-hand clothes I had bought in the Jewish market. I smudged my face and knotted and pinned up my long hair and played my part in the crowd of restless groundlings outside Newgate Prison, which was actually a three-story gatehouse with rooms and cells inside. The male prisoners were brought out, loaded in drays and driven through the raucous, insulting crowd down Newgate Street and then up Milk Street to the Guild Hall.

I kept scanning the mass of Londoners for Will, though my eyes were drawn back to the three pitiful prisoners, who seemed so alone. I had not seen Edward Arden since he'd insulted Leicester before the queen at Kenilworth when I was a girl. He looked old and enfeebled, but defiant. Somerville, the man who had triggered this upheaval, did indeed look as if he belonged in Bedlam. He was twitching and crying but smiling too; he kept squinting up at the sky as if some heavenly visitation would swoop in to rescue him. The priest Hugh Hall, the kindly man I had known briefly as the Park Hall gardener, looked crooked and all bent over, yet seemed deep in prayer. He spoke now and again to the other two, though how they heard over the tumult, I know not.

But no Will.

I followed along to the Guild Hall and then I saw him. Still in his rude garb, he had positioned himself near the top of the stairs leading up from the street so that the prisoners would be marched right past him. Someone whispered that the female prisoners had already been taken inside; I wondered if Will had seen them. I held my breath and braced myself against the wall of the Haberdasher's Hall, just across the way, as the prisoners were unloaded from the dray.

The little scene played out just as, I'm sure, Will would have wished to write it. Edward Arden's head jerked noticeably when Will took his cap off as the older man was herded up the stairs. Will bowed his head but kept his eyes up. Edward lifted his folded, manacled hands together briefly above his shoulder as if to signify they had clasped hands. Then the carved double doors closed to devour him.

We waited for several hours. I edged closer to Will but did not try to catch his eye. At four of the clock, the very time, I thought, the Queen's Players were performing at the Bull, the doors opened for the next act of this dreadful drama.

Guards spilled out with pikes and shoved the street crowd well back. The prisoners were brought out, the two women first, who were taken off, and then the three men, pushed quickly toward their dray. I could tell—and I prayed no one else did—that Edward Arden was looking for Will again. Caught by the wall on the top of the steps, Will waved to him and Arden, tears slicking his cheeks, nodded.

Word of the prisoners' fates spread through the crowd like wildfire, even before a black-garbed man came out to read the verdicts for all those associated with the Arden plot. Somerville's wife was to be released; Mary Arden's punishment of being burned at the stake was to be commuted. But all three men were to be hanged, drawn and quartered at Smithfield three days hence.

It was easy enough to get to Will when the crowd dispersed. He still leaned against the wall as if he were frozen there. When he saw me, his eyes widened but he didn't move.

"Come on then," I said, not climbing the last few steps to him. "Let's away. There's naught else you can do. He saw you—he knows you care and send him your strength and prayers."

"As you have always sent yours to me, my Anne."

I felt my blood heat, and my legs went weak. "Don't talk so. Come on."

I started to walk away, and he came after me, walking jerkily as if he were a jumping jack with wooden limbs strung together. "I heard," he said, still whispering, "they will put their heads on the bridge. I saw some there yesterday. Such deceit—and power—and pride crushing mere men . . ."

I waited for him to say more; he looked horror-stricken. I decided to change the subject. "Are you staying with Dick?" I asked, but his gaze stayed somewhere far away.

"What? Oh, with Dick on a pallet in his little room behind the print shop. It's a wonderful shop. And I've been to see the Queen's Men."

"Are you demented?" I cried, propping my hands on my hips in a most unmasculine fashion. "You told me once they are spies for Walsingham and you went to see them at this time?"

"I was told to."

"What?" I cried and yanked him off the street into a narrow close that led mazelike to who-knew-where. "You're overthrown, distraught. You're not making sense," I accused.

"I—I forgot to tell you before. I was told to see them by the man who was looking through the books Edward Arden had loaned me. He made me sit by him while he read each scribble in them—Arden's, not mine. In faith, I've never owned a book I dared to write in but the one you gave me when—"

"When we wed, Will. But tell me what the man said."

"It was after Anne piped up with the comment about how I wanted to be a poet and playwright. I glared at her and motioned with my head for her to leave us, and she did. Then he—Thomas Wilkes, a clerk for the Privy Council—said to me, 'I'm sure some of the Queen's Players could use a clever man like you. Best you go and inquire about that employment.'"

"Did he mean for you to come clear to London? Did he say it as a threat?"

"By all that's holy, Anne, everything was like a threat that day! And when he left he whispered to me, 'See you on the stage in London and the shires soon.'"

"Walsingham's spies and intelligencers have spun a huge spiderweb. I fear for you if you get involved."

"I fear for myself if I don't. What if I defy these hints—these invitations I keep getting? Oh, I know you think I'm just looking for excuses to come here to try my hand at it all, but the terrible thing is—despite the horror of this Arden mess—I truly love London. I want to come, and in better times . . . Hell's gates, listen to what I'm saying. Would I be getting in bed with those who will kill my own kin?" he cried, raking his fingers through his hair so hard that his cap flew off behind him.

Before he could retrieve it, I seized his wrists in a hard grip. I was thinking, *And would you ever again try to get in bed with me,* but I said only, "There's one thing I am certain of, Will Shakespeare, alias Andrew Whateley and alias my brother that day you saved me at Kenilworth. You can play parts, and I know you can rhyme and write. Whatever you decide to do, you have the God-given gifts for it and have worked hard to increase those. As Father

Berowne used to say before he lost his senses, 'To whom much is given, much is expected.' Will, if you are taken on by any players, it will be because you are good—and can be great."

His mouth open, he stared at me. I was as shocked at what I'd said as he. All those lonely, wretched, angry hours I'd rehearsed telling him I hated him and I said that. His distracted gaze finally focused on mine. He lifted his chin and straightened his spine so that he looked strong and settled as he had not in days.

"Two things," he said, his voice calm and clear, "no three. Above all else, I regret that I have lost you, but I will always love and cherish you in my heart and mind and soul. Anne, swear to me you will not come near Smithfield the day they execute those men."

"If you will stay away."

"I swear it, for I could not bear that. But I will see you before I leave the city, I swear that too."

"Is that the third thing?"

"The third—no, the third is that, if and when I come to make my name and fortune here, it will be alone—alone but for knowing you are here. I will not rear a child in London, and Anne, the murderess of dreams, would never come with me."

I gasped at how brutally he'd put that, but he dashed a quick kiss on my cheek and was off at a run toward I knew not where.

I did see him again, the morning after the executions; he was leaving the city later that day. He sent a note saying he'd call for me at my back door, and we'd just be two country lads together. So I wore my boy's garb again and off we went.

Almost like old times, we headed for a river, but the Avon was but a ripple compared to the torrent of the Thames at high tide. I felt that way about Will too. Whatever love I'd borne him earlier and whatever passions I had felt in Stratford were like a drop compared to this sudden surge within me. And yet, I held my tongue and played the part of his friend.

He hired a boat, a cheap one without a canopy, cushions, or Maud Wilton's sweetbags. I could have afforded a better one, but said naught about that either.

"Where are we going?" I asked as we headed "Eastward ho" on the river.

"Though I spent the time Edward Arden was publicly butchered on my knees in St. Giles' Church, in prayer and remembrance of his kindnesses to me, I have to see what they've done with his head. No one else would understand but you. Someday I'll write about such passions and power that can turn one's world upside down and destroy destinies. And I swear I will put the name of Arden in my plays and the name of poor, mad Somerville too."

Will did just that. He oft used the Forest of Arden, and he put the name John Somerville in one of his earliest plays, *Henry VI, Part 3*. Will gave Somerville but three lines, in which he told an earl, a man far above his rank, he'd misjudged something and was mistaken.

Now I nodded as he took my hand. John Somerville had managed to hang himself in prison before he had to face his torment and execution, but his parboiled, tarred head was still to be placed with other traitors' on the bridge's south end.

The current took us faster as it flowed toward London Bridge, for the water was forced between the arches there. Only skilled, licensed men called bridge shooters could take a craft as small as ours through the churning water of high tide. But our oarsman pulled hard to keep us far enough away from the cauldron of the current. Holding hands, we looked up to see the three new heads on pikes, gory and gruesome, their features drooped in agony and yet recognizable—Arden, Somerville and the priest Hall. They weren't alone, for at least a dozen other heads in various stages of decay seemed to stare down at us.

I thought I would be ill, but forced the bile back in my throat to help Will bear up.

"I feel my past is dead," he said, "and yet I shall build on all I know and all I am to make it live again." His deep voice resounded over the current and the noise from the street and shops up on the bridge. "I have seen the worst this city has to give but I want to see the best, and I vow I will be back for it—and to see you."

A sad and strange place for a vow, I thought as the boat bucked and we gazed up at the remains of mortal men so crudely displayed. Worse, I actually believed Will once again, and yet it took him more than four years thereafter to make his words and his future begin to come true. And in that time, I became almost another person.

Act Three

CHAPTER NINE

❦

I counted the days waiting for Will to come to London to make his fortune and his future. I was certain he could outact and outwrite even the best of London's new breed of young, brash dramatists. Thomas Kyd, Ben Jonson, John Lyly, George Peele and, especially, Christopher Marlowe had the love—and entry fees—of the masses. They were the men who wrote for the Queen's Players and other theatre companies, when it should have been Will.

And what would I be to Will when he came? An encourager, a friend, a lover? I still felt betrayed in my deepest woman's heart. I still held his other marriage against him. Perhaps I would be his enemy.

I put off a wealthy, handsome suitor, Nicholas Clere, one of John's wine buyers, who lived both in England and France. He promised to take me to Paris and give me the world. But like a Bedlamite, I waited for word of Will. Besides, I believed I would be committing bigamy if I wed someone else. And was that the real reason Will had kept our union a secret? Not for my sake, but for his? In my darkest moments when I still missed him, I cursed myself for loving him yet.

When Will did not arrive, I considered visiting Stratford, now that the purge of midland plotters seemed to have passed. I was wild to know if he was ill or had changed his mind about his destiny. But then, an entire year after the execution of Edward Arden—just before Christmas, it was—I saw Richard Field among the bookstalls at St. Paul's, and what he told me turned my world topsy-turvy again.

"What news from home?" I asked after we chatted of the cold weather, the threat of Spanish invasion and the latest plays.

"You have carriers in and out of Stratford each week and you ask me that?" He went back to rearranging a pile of finely bound books; I assumed he had printed them.

"Yes, I ask you that. I don't want gossip, and I know Will writes to you. I am just praying that the ruination of the Ardens has not made it worse for his people and kept him from his destiny here."

He looked up at me. "A heartfelt hope, so I will tell you. I told him I would not play go-between for the two of you, but since our lives seem intertwined—the three of us—here it is."

He cleared his throat. "Will was ready to leave Stratford twice, but once his parents prevailed upon him to stay a bit longer, for they are deep in debt—and his wife is big with child again."

I put my hand on the edge of the wooden stall to steady myself. I felt sick to the very reaches of my soul. If he still bedded with her, did he love her? Another child! Would he stay home for them?

I'd missed my father sorely when he was away. I did not wish Will's loss on them—and yet, I still wanted him here—so that I could kill him not for one betrayal but now for two!

My blood beat hot through my veins. I sucked in sharp breaths.

"So big with child," he went on, when I said naught, "'tis thought she's carrying twins. I'm sorry, Anne—for you, for me even—and certainly for Will. He's promised his wife he'll help her through the next few years."

Few years . . . few years, those words echoed in my head. Looking back at his precious books again, Dick chatted on. Were all men so blind, so stupid? Did he not see I was dying?

"He's beside himself," he said, now edging slowly away from me. "When he was here, he said he was desperate to leave—to live here. Desperate and determined. It's tearing him apart. He's a very moral man, you know."

I gave an inelegant snort. It was all I could manage, or I was going to scream aloud in pain. Or perhaps beat Dick into the dust to murder the messenger.

"Moral at least," he went on "compared to the iconoclasts and free thinkers today, many of whom are writers. I swear, Anne, some Londoners have their minds in the sewers—even at court. 'Tis enough to turn one to a Puritan."

Ignoring his desperate attempt to switch subjects, I found my voice at last, though it didn't sound like mine. It was hard, cold, bitter. "Perhaps the Puritans have a point to hate the plays and players and condemn them. And, no doubt, books like these you have helped to publish."

He looked up again, surprise on his face. At that moment, I

hated and wanted to hurt Dick, Will and every man jack of their species that went by in the street or had ever trod the earth. Thank God, Will was not coming to London, for he would have been a marked man with me.

Dick took a step back, a kind of awe or fear upon his face. Perhaps he finally realized how I had taken his matter-of-factly delivered news, for he tried to fill the space between us with words.

"Yes, I guess that's—that's t-true," he said, stammering now. "I feel torn too, Anne, perhaps a human condition, eh? They say even the q-queen is wrenched apart about whether to sign the death warrant for her conniving cousin, the Scots queen, but I say Queen Mary should pay the price for her treachery."

An even better try at a new topic, for I loved news of the queen, but I said only, "Someone always pays the price for treachery."

"Anne, I know I have no right to invoke Kat's name, but you would not do something desperate, would you? Over Will? I mean like—"

"Like throw myself into the Thames? No, not that." Then, not wanting him to think I meant to ride hell-bent to Stratford to murder Will—for he knew I'd gone last year to save him—I added, "I shall throw myself into life. There are things I want to do here which I haven't. It's as if—as if I've been waiting for the main character to make another entrance to the stage in the play of my life. I've lived like a nun in a cloister and for what? Should our once mutual friend in the midlands ever inquire about me, say I am writing poetry and perhaps I shall try my hand at a play. Now, did you print those books you have there?" I added, desperate to think of something besides Will and fearful I never would again.

"I did," he said with a nod and sigh of relief as he showed me the embossed spine of one. Poor man, he had no idea I was still so angry with mankind in general that I could have burned all his damned books and him and Will with them. "I'm in the last year of my apprenticeship. Look you, Sir Philip Sidney's verses, *Arcadia*, though the bookbinder has put the price too dear."

My hands still shaking, I opened the book he handed me to a random page and read, "My true-love hath my heart, and I have his, / But just exchange one for the other given . . ."

"I'll take a copy, dear or not," I declared, silently vowing that nothing the world had to offer—especially love—would be denied me now—if and when I wanted it. Although I could not kill Will Shakespeare as I longed to do upon this moment, he was henceforth dead to me, and that was that.

Still that was not that. I ranted and raved, pacing the floor at night. I broke things. I was ill-tempered to men, even to poor, placid John Davenant. I became the highest order of malcontent. Although I longed to escape Will's hold over me, I could not bring myself to accept a betrothal from Nicholas Clere. His pride punctured, he went back to France in a huff, and I could only hope he would not halt his imports for John's business because of me.

I tried to force myself back to the loving person I had once been. I strove to cherish my two best friends, Jennet and Maud, for at first I vowed to need no man. Jennet had cruelly lost yet a fourth infant, this one because its birthing cord was wrapped around his neck and had strangled the little mite. Through it all, I held her hands and wiped her brow, then went with John to bury the tiny coffin on top of three others, because Jennet could not bear to.

In the aftermath of grief, as I had learned the day I lost Kat, wise words could not help, but my simply being with Jennet was some solace—to her and to me. Though I wished to cheer her, I found myself telling her my entire sad tale of Will, the first time I'd admitted our handfast marriage to anyone. Somehow our mutual losses and longing bonded Jennet and me closer. When Stephen Dench—who, thank the Lord, had wed a London tavern maid—told me that the Shakespeares had twins, a boy and girl named Hamnet and Judith, Jennet and I both cried for our own reasons, but we cried together.

Though I wrote my own poems and began a play or two—surely not good enough to ever see the light of day—I also became more bored, bitter and reckless. Fed up with men trifling with me on the street or even accosting me, I began to go to plays garbed as a boy. It worked well enough; only Maud and Jennet knew, though Jennet did not know I ventured to the two theatres in the tawdry section called Shoreditch a mile north of the city and a far hue and cry from the more reputable Bishopsgate neighborhood.

Sometimes Maud went with me, also garbed as a youth. She was much filled out and better dressed now, since my acting as agent for her sweet herbs had prospered her. Tired of sitting on hard gallery seats at the Theatre and the Curtain in Shoreditch, I hatched a plan for Maud and me to sell scented cushions to those playhouse managers. Enough herb girls clustered about the doors selling sachets and themselves, but we would top them all.

"I hope you're not going to see that horrid new drama by Christopher Marlowe," Jennet muttered as I headed out the back door where Maud was waiting in breeches, shirt and doublet. It was an unusually warm early February day, I recall, in 1587.

"I am. It's being performed by the Queen's Men, and they are great actors. Since it's a company that performs under Her Majesty's aegis, I'm certain the play is quite respectable."

Jennet snorted and shook her head as if I was a lost soul heading for Hades. "'Tis said Marlowe's an atheist, you know, mad and bad."

I went back to hug her. "I promise I shall not let his words convert me to the Moslem religion his hero espouses," I told her, with a little pinch to let her know I was jesting. "But his play is all the fashion. I must hear how his heroic verse sounds, when mere ruffians in the street are not butchering their favorite lines from his plays."

"They say he's a sodomite and drunkard too!" she protested as I made for the door again. I turned back to face her. Even as she said that, she held gripped to her bosom the tiny flask she had used to tell me was cough elixir.

She fidgeted as our gazes snagged and held. I walked slowly to her and took the flask, though she tugged it back for a moment. I knew she could easily get more of the garnet-hued claret she kept close. Indeed, hidden bottles of it were about the shop and house.

"Jennet, I know that calms you, but if you and John yet hope for a child—"

"A living child, you mean."

"Yes. Then perhaps drinking less of this might make a difference."

"The Lord knows something must change!" she declared, smacking her hands on her skirts. "But I never drank a drop of anything but ale and small beer before I lost the second babe. I swear—as with the Black Death"—like many Londoners she lowered her voice when she spoke those two dreaded words—"it must be the unhealthsome night air of the city that makes me a bad breeder. After all, your Will's country wife has just had two more and— Oh, Anne, I'm sorry. I didn't mean . . ."

"It's all right. It doesn't matter," I lied, for however much I ran about and tried to keep occupied, it truly did. "I'm off now, and we'll talk later. I mean to find the manager of the playhouse afterward and propose Maud sew him scented seat cushions for his gallery guests. Then, when I make my fortune, I shall help you and John buy a country inn you've been dreaming of, and I shall visit you each summer." I waved jauntily and went out, depositing her flask in a pile of refuse down the alley.

But later that afternoon, as I stood openmouthed among the groundlings in the Theatre, I realized Jennet had been right about something. Christopher Marlowe must be one of those free thinkers Dick Field had disparaged. His hero was pompous, brutal, cruel and unrepentant. The Tartar conqueror Tamburlaine slaughtered virgins by the score, but did love his wife Zenocrate, the daughter of an Egyptian sultan, no less. Still, he murdered his own son Calyphas, because he was a coward.

Everything in the play seemed outrageous, big and brazen. The lead role was played by a tall, commanding actor named Edward Alleyn, whose voice boomed out the mesmerizing lines with broad gestures and whose mere presence ruled the stage. Despite the shocking content of the words, the language itself, called unrhymed iambic pentameter, was so bold, so heroic of its own accord, that it was surely the center of the performance:

By sacred Mahomet, the friend of God,
Whose holy Alcoran remains with us,
Whose glorious body, when he left the world,
Clos'd in a coffin mounted up the air
And hung on stately Mecca's temple roof . . .

An infidel indeed! Why did this playwright Marlowe earn a pass in London, spouting such lines when Christians, be they Catholic instead of Protestant, were prosecuted? Why had not Edmund Tilney, the queen's Master of Revels, censored this content and levied fines, or demanded revisions, as he did of other playwrights? No wonder the Puritans and some of the city fathers not only reviled the raucous playhouse crowds but questioned the purpose of some plays.

But as the powerful language swept me up in its embrace, I became seduced by it too. No couplets here, few rhymes, no hints of sonnet structure. It boasted a beat but was more like natural speech. Even the groundlings stood raptly at attention.

I began to cry, not for the deeply moving impact of the actors or the genius of the daring mind that had written this drama, but because that damned Will Shakespeare was not here to hear it and to top it.

After the play, as I had planned, I hustled Maud to the back door and waited for someone important-looking to step out. I knew James and Richard Burbage would be possibilities; I planned to tell them I'd seen their plays in Stratford. A few others hung about too, herb girls, the slovenly wenches who sold oranges and hazelnuts and a few blatant whores. A small rabble of men also watched the back door like hawks. I hoped the theatre manager would not be detained by any of them.

As we waited, I studied the Theatre and its environs. The half-timbered, three-story building was built of lath and plaster walls; it boasted two outside staircases by which guests could climb to their gallery seats. The small lot was crammed between a garden and Great Horse Pond, where those who rode left their horses to be watched by boys. On another side of the structure, pens of complaining cattle waited to be dispatched in a nearby slaughter-house. In addition to the stench of the animals, a sewer ran past, heading toward Finbury Fields. If patrons came from the west, they entered the area through a hole in a brick fence and skirted the sewer. Yet, once inside, the skill of the actors made everyone trade raucous reality for fine, faraway fictional scenes.

Finally, a chestnut-bearded man came out the back door with his arm around a younger sloe-eyed one whose unruly dark hair looked as if he'd combed it with a spoon. The young man was flashily garbed in a padded black doublet with bloodred slashings, and gartered purple tights outlined his shapely legs.

To my dismay, several of the people waiting leaped at the older man for whatever purposes, chattering away at him. He wasn't one of the Burbages, but he would have to do. I stepped closer, doffing my cap before I realized I should keep it on. Though I quickly replaced it, the younger man's eyes fastened on me, raking me up and down. He shrugged himself away from the cluster of men and came straight for us—or me, rather, for Maud was timid and hung back.

"Did you see *Tamburlaine the Great*?" he asked with a smile.

"Yes, and it was great indeed," I told him, trying to pitch my voice low.

He smiled even broader, displaying large, strong teeth. A slight mustache above and a thin goatee below edged his full-lipped mouth. His eyes were strangely shiny, like silver shillings.

"What part did you favor most?" he prompted.

"I found it all amazing and daring, as does everyone."

"Ah, but I have not chosen to speak to everyone."

I tried to place this young man as an actor, but realized I must be speaking to the playwright Marlowe himself. "You wrote those bold words?" I asked, wishing I sounded more learned, more clever.

"And have more where those came from—such as, will you come have a drink and talk with me, my lad?"

Of course, he thought I was a lad—didn't he? "But why me? I'm sure you have friends, and your friend there—"

"Has seen the play two score times not counting endless rehearsals, so I can hardly ask his opinion, can I? Is that other lad with you?"

"Yes, and truth be told, we intended to talk to someone about buying scented cushions for the gallery seats. My friend makes herbal pomanders, tussie-mussies, and we've sold such to some wherry owners so I—"

"Ah, I have it!" he declared and took Maud by the elbow to march her up to the cluster of men. "Roger," he said to his friend, interrupting several conversations, "this lad needs to talk to you about making us seat cushions—for a fair fee, mind you, whether they are provided by the Theatre or rented by the audience for each performance—scented ones too. I insist you take him up on it, and I'm going to discuss such with his partner over there. I'm sure you can talk the Burbages into it. See you later at the tavern on Holywell."

Whether he thought I was fish or fowl, I was grateful to Christopher Marlowe. But I was not such a country maid that I did not realize he must have seen I was a woman in disguise and that had intrigued him. I was pleased he had mentioned the Burbages, but it went right out of my head to discuss their Stratford ties with him or tell him I had seen them perform there.

"I need to wait for my friend," I insisted, but my feet kept easily up with his as he steered me along. To have the ear of the nation's premier playwright, to be able to probe his brain . . . I only hoped that his ear and his brain were all I would have to contend with if he'd noted I was a woman. "I don't mean to mislead you," I told him, "and I wasn't born yesterday so—"

"But you are country born and bred," he said, stretching his strides and keeping a hand on my arm so that I hurried apace with him. "I can hear it in your flat vowels, though you've done quite a good job of covering it. Coventry? Oxford? 'S bones, somewhere in the midlands, I warrant. But I assure you, I favor rural ways, and you have such a striking face."

"Then you know."

"Know what?" he demanded as I pulled back when he would have dragged me in the door of a very noisy alehouse.

"That I'm in disguise."

"My sweet boy, we're all in disguise one way or the other. Are you a runaway apprentice? I promise to give you a place to hide."

"I'm a woman, Master Marlowe, one who didn't want to flaunt herself as others do to come to Shoreditch without a man."

"'S bones!" he clipped out and pushed me against the outside tavern wall.

"You knew that, didn't you?" I challenged. "Because else, why would you pick a mere lad to be with y—"

He pressed his palms against my bound breasts through my doublet and shirt and swore a string of oaths. Like other Londoners who considered themselves stylish, each curser used God's name in vain, coupling that holy word with something common, such as God's nightgown, God's teeth, God's bones. The curser left off all but the final *s* of God's name, so it came out *'s teeth* and such. Perhaps I was yet a country maid for "Faith!" and "Devil take it!" were the main meat of my swearing so far.

"'S teeth, I knew it was too good to be true!" he ranted, stomping both feet like a boy denied sweets. He yanked me to the door of the tavern and held me there a minute. My eyes adjusted to the dim light; I took in the men and lads within—and then I realized that the boys were *with* the men. Devil take it, Jennet had said Marlowe was a sodomite! I blushed to the roots of my hair.

"So you didn't know my sex?" I stammered as he tugged me outside again.

"You're exotic enough I could almost say it didn't matter."

"Tamburlaine's Egyptian wife come to life?"

"'S bones," he said, snapping his fingers, "perhaps that's it. Let's just say I had hopes, damn you, the prettiest boy I've seen in ages—but then, what a woman, eh? Will you tell me your name? Are you one of the Virgin Queen's naughty unvirginal ladies in bold search of forbidden fancies?"

"You had my speech aright—I'm from Stratford and run a business in London now, but I'm no lady."

"I like the sound of that. And your business is to make sweet cushions for sweet bums?"

"A side interest. But I am an admirer of plays."

"And playwrights, I pray."

"*Do* you pray, Christopher Marlowe?"

"Ah, a clever and tart tongue is tastier than a sweet one," he said, wetting his lips, deliberately, slowly, as if he planned to devour me.

I tried to ignore his blatant provocation and said nothing. Will had called me Lady Tongue once, and Marlowe's parry that he hoped I admired playwrights had hit home. I felt a rush of longing for Will, but fought it back.

Marlowe ogled me again and reached around to pat my bottom. "I must tell you, lady or lad, you sport a lovely cushion of your own. Will you not tell a poor poet and playwright your name? And you may call me Kit, as do my closest friends."

"Your male friends?"

"*Touché*," he retorted, though I knew not what he meant by that word and had no intention of asking or standing here longer. Several men going in had made rude comments. I was just starting to walk away when the man Marlowe had called Roger strolled up with two other men in tow.

"I hope you've struck a good bargain with the lad," Roger said as he tipped his hat to us and headed in. "I've promised the quiet one of the two a pretty penny for a passel of pillows. Mark that alliterative line for your new *Doctor Faustus* play, you Cambridge-educated sot," he called back to Kit.

"Speak for yourself and find another friend for yourself, you goatish wag-tail!" Kit shouted. He winked at me, pinched my bum again, but followed the men inside.

As I ran home, bells began to peal and distant shouts echoed in the streets. I found an excited Maud with a written promise for cushions in her hand waiting for me with Jennet in the kitchen. Rushing in from the shop, John hurried to join us, clapping his hands over his head as if he would dance.

"A citywide celebration!" he cried. Maud and I glanced at each other as if it could be for us. Or, I thought in the instant before John said more, it might as well be a revel that I am finally over my past with Will. I've met and befriended and escaped unscathed from the most popular playwright in the city—in the entire land!

"Word's come that Mary, Queen of Scots, has been beheaded for her plotting 'gainst our queen!" John announced. "One Catholic threat to Her Majesty's throne down and one to go, when we singe the beard of the king of Spain! We'll sink whatever Spanish galleons he dares send into our sovereign waters!"

I had seldom seen him more excited. Jennet ran to his arms, and he swung her around. I glared at them until I caught myself. Of a certain, they would lie together tonight, and I feared the results. Jennet would never bear up under the loss of another child. And, sad to say, I resented that I had no one to hug and love and bed with myself.

About seventeen months later, in late July of 1588, as John Davenant had predicted, the Spanish Armada approached England's shores. The queen herself played a role in rallying her troops on the beach at Tilbury for, costumed in chest armor, she rode among them to demand victory. She delivered a fine soliloquy about being a "weak and feeble woman but with the heart and stomach of a king and a king of England too!" Whatever some thought of her, I loved her all the more for her boldness. She was hardly weak and feeble, but brave, and I longed to be like her.

Praise be to God, in mid-August, the large, lumbering Spanish Armada proved to be no match for the quick, smaller English fleet, cobbled together by the queen, her nobles and certain sea captains. It was Agincourt all over again, with swiftness and agility conquering bulky weight and old ways.

In the midst of the city celebrations, three theatre passes arrived for John, Jennet and me to attend the premiere of Kit Marlowe's latest play, *Doctor Faustus*, the title I had heard mentioned that day I'd met him. The dimwit boy who brought the tickets said the donor was "Nonny-muss."

I had not seen nor heard from Marlowe. Had it taken him this long to track me down? Maud must have given something away when the last of two hundred cushions was delivered to the Theatre and James Burbage paid our fee.

But John refused to attend a work by "that pagan Marlowe" and Jennet was heavily pregnant again, so I took Maud and another herb girl. We went garbed as lads to celebrate our good luck and thank Kit for the tickets, though I had no intention of going off with him alone again.

I had seen one other play by Kit Marlowe since our meeting, a revenge drama called *Hamlet*, full of blood and guts and no subtleties of character at all. I hated myself for it, but I spent most of the days after that wondering what Will would have done with that story. It would be nearly thirteen years before I found out.

But today at the debut of Kit's third play, the expectation was palpable.

"Everyone's still excited about the Armada's defeat," Maud said, settling herself on her own cushion, for the passes were for the first row center of the gallery. We faced the musicians just above the stage in their own elevated box; I noted well the music they played was stirring, not soothing, yet I'd heard this story was a domestic drama, not one set on the battlefield.

"I can tell these seats are from the playwright," Maud's wide-eyed friend Dorothy whispered. She was rightly awed, but it annoyed me that she said everything in such a breathy way. "The finer folk here are staring at us, I can tell."

"There are no finer folk than us today and don't forget it," I told her as I nonchalantly peeled an orange. It smelled a good bit better up here than in the pit, that was for certain. Our cushions were a great success.

I was determined to soak in this show. Perhaps I'd even send a missive home to Will through Dick Field, whom I hadn't seen in ages, all about what popular playwrights were doing with the London stage. Yes, I felt far enough removed from my passion for Will now to encourage him again in his own writing. Whatever he did, I told myself, it was no skin off my nose. Besides, the truth was, I knew such a letter of my worldly, literary pursuits would rot his very bones, still stuck in Stratford as he was.

As soon as the play began, I saw why scandalous comments had leaked out about *Doctor Faustus*. Why was Kit's work not censored like everyone else's? Not only did the main character, a

German scholar, practice black magic, but he summoned up Mephastophilus, a devil whose master was Lucifer! Faustus promised his soul in trade for twenty-four years of wishes from the devil and began to enjoy a life of sin. A clown named Robin, Faustus' servant, also summoned up a minor devil in his bumbling way, but somehow the comic relief of that did not belong in this tragedy. If Kit asked me what I thought, I'd tell him that, I vowed.

Yet it was as compelling as *Tamburlaine* had been, and, I assumed, would have a good moral at the end to boot when Faustus had to go to hell for his life of licentiousness. Kit Marlowe should heed his own writing, I thought. I wagered he did not have to do one bit of research for the characters of Faustus or the devil.

Near the end of the drama, Faustus had Mephastophilus summon up the beautiful Helen of Troy to impress a group of scholars. Each scholar spoke, warning Faustus he was in danger of eternal damnation for his terrible bargain.

When the third scholar spoke, I jerked on my cushion. That voice, ringing out deep and clear ... Despite his cap, wig and ruddy coloring from face paint—devil take us all, it was Will!

I gasped so loudly, people looked my way. He had several more lines. How long had he been in London and not let me know? And these theatre passes—from Kit or Will?

I gripped the railing of the gallery so hard my hands went numb. In the last scene, the devil carried Faustus' soul to hell, and the scholars found his bloody limbs scattered on the stage and decided to hold a funeral for him. Will spoke the play's final words, the moral, though not one so pious as another playwright might have used.

"Anne! Anne, are you all right?" Maud kept asking as the players danced their closing jig and took their bows. Will's footwork was superb. It took me back to our cavorting days, to how we danced in the meadows those weeks we courted before disaster struck— before my soul was taken from me as surely as Faustus' had been.

My feelings were a jumble. I was proud of Will and happy for him. He was here. He was on the stage. But I feared and hated him too, especially when he looked straight up at me and, despite my own costume, smiled and nodded. Yes, he'd known exactly where I'd be sitting.

I was still too stunned to speak. When my friends pulled me to my feet during the thunderous applause, I stood frozen. Then I saw Dick Field farther down the first row and knew Will had sent the tickets, however much these four gallery seats must have cost him.

Furious, fearful I would throw myself at him, I mumbled something to my friends and pushed ahead of them through the exiting crowds. I knew Will would be waiting below, the conquering hero, but I'd have none of that. I'd not bounce back into his arms only to be deceived and deserted again.

I was right. He had managed to dash outside; his eyes were skimming the people pouring out. He saw me, smiled and dared to motion me to him. Rather than tear right by, I saw my salvation as surely as Faustus had chosen his own devil.

"Kit!" I cried when I saw Marlowe being congratulated by friends. "Kit, it was wonderful!"

I could hear Will's words from here—my name, once, twice. I did not look askance. Marlowe saw me coming and, whether he recognized me or not, opened his arms as I hurled myself into them. I could barely glimpse Will out of the corner of my eye and did not turn to look. Maybe now he could grasp the terrible pain of what he had done to me.

"My favorite lady-lad!" Kit cried.

In my rising hysteria, I gave no thought to my own predicament if I went off with Marlowe and his fellows. All I wanted was to get away from the power of Will's eternal allure for me, to bury the agony I had fought so hard to hold at bay or turn to loathing. Not once looking back, I let the laughing Kit lead me off into the crowds.

Uncertain where I was, I awoke with the most crushing head pain I had ever felt. It was agony to even open my eyes. I knew I was not home in my bed for this one felt like a featherbed, not a chaff-filled one. Dark—dark in here—but where was here? In faith, I felt as if I were with Faustus in the dimmest reaches of hell.

I racked my pounding brain to recall where I could be. Had Maud taken me to her room? And then it hit me like the weight of the world. I had gone drinking in a tavern with Kit Marlowe. He and his raucous fellows had talked of plays, people and politics, and I had drunk it all in—and drunk so much—and . . . and that was all I could recall.

I tried to move my legs but was like one sodden with sleep, lead-footed, trying to run from a nightmare's fiend. Was Kit in bed with me? At least I yet seemed to be fully garbed. What was that stuff Kit's friends had been drinking, that elixir they called dragon's milk? They had vowed it would turn any day-hired, walk-on actor into a well-paid performer at the royal court.

Then I realized someone was whispering. Someone distant, thank God, more than one person—men. Yet Kit's voice stood out.

"But with the Scot's queen separated from her head and King Philip separated from his fleet, why must I still keep it up? I've no time or patience for such anymore!"

"Do you not think others will still plot to overthrow her?"

I fought harder to clear my head, to concentrate on what they said.

"But I've got London at my feet now, man."

"Let's just say you've made a Faustian bargain and must play by the original rules. If you have London at your feet, 'tis partly because your work is treated by Tilney with a gentler hand than most. You'll have to go to France, he says."

"Tell Wally the Spider to bugger off! I've served him well and—"

"Keep your voice down. You've been given free artistic rein when that could all change with the stroke of a pen. It just so happens sodomy is a capital offense. You'll do what's best or there may be an arrest."

"Rhyming couplets, are you now, Mercer?"

Mercer! The man who had questioned me once before. And here Kit Marlowe—like the company of the Queen's Men—was a spy for the queen, or at least for her spymaster Walsingham, if that's who Wally was. I knew I now had two reasons to flee before Kit came to bed, if he had not been here already. But I didn't feel sore in places I would if he'd assaulted me, only, for the first time in my life, so sodden drunk I was not certain if I could move.

I slid carefully to the far side of the bed. It looked like a curtain separated me from the men. My shoes were missing. My head throbbed when I lifted it so I could slide off the bed. Nausea racked me. I tried to hold back the taste of bitter bile. I could only pray there was another door out of here, but only shifting shadows stretched out from each wall and corner.

I saw a window and made for it, sliding across the floor in my stockinged feet. Pitch black outside; no noise in the streets. A curtain covered the window too; I pulled it aside. A full moon; the light of it hurt my eyes and made my head pound even harder. I turned aside for a moment and gasped. Kit stood right behind me!

No, not Kit but his portrait hung there, and a strong shaft of moonlight struck it on the opposite wall. He looked bored and daring in it with his arms crossed and one corner of his mouth quirked in dislike or disdain. He wore the same black and red-slashed padded doublet from the first time I'd seen him. I dragged my eyes away from those of the portrait, which seemed to pin me right where I was.

Dangerous, I knew, to be about the streets at night, especially in Shoreditch, if that's where I was. But more dangerous to stay in that bed. If I escaped his clutches again, had I given away anything to Kit so he could find me?

The window was ajar this warm September night; I shoved it farther open and froze when it gave a little squeak. The men's whispers hissed on. If they discovered my flight and Mercer real-ized what I had heard, would he insist they silence me? And then Will would never know what became of me. Maybe he'd question Kit Marlowe someday, maybe . . .

I was not on a high floor as I had reckoned when I'd seen the moon so clearly without eaves or thatch. This chamber was on the second floor, so if I could get a good hold on the lower window ledge, then drop carefully below . . .

Not taking time to find my shoes, I stood on a wooden coffer and shifted shoulder-first through the narrow window. I shoved one knee and hip out, then the other. Concentrating on each move, I tried to ignore my pounding head pain, the dizziness and nausea that assailed me.

The window ledge hurt the inside of my fingers when I hung from it. I could not tell what was under me, but now—now! I dropped hard to the packed-dirt alley, fell on a stinking pile of refuse and vomited into it.

I lay there but a minute, sweating, slippery, hating myself. I had to hurry home, and I'd have to avoid the night watch to keep from being fined for a curfew violation. My friends would be beside themselves with fear for me, whether they thought I'd gone off with Kit Marlowe or was missing somehow else in deep, dark London.

Feeling not only physically ill but sick to the depths of my soul, I lurched to my stinging feet and stumbled toward home. No bones were broken, but my heart was, and I blamed Will.

CHAPTER TEN

❦

I never told Maud or Jennet, both of whom were waiting for me when I dragged myself home, that I had actually been in Kit Marlowe's bed or knew about his spying. Noising the latter around could get me arrested or worse. I only told them I'd gone to a tavern with Marlowe to celebrate the triumph of his play, had gotten drunk and stumbled into an alley on the way home where I'd slept for a while. They helped me clean up and vowed not to tell John, who had gone to bed and didn't know I was missing.

The next morning—midmorn, it was, I knew that much—I lay abed feeling at least half as sick as I had the night before. I rehearsed everything in my throbbing head again: the shock of seeing Will, my desire to hurt him, the mess with Kit. The summer sun pouring in my window made my head ache much more than the moonlight had last night.

Jennet came in carrying a tray with a few items—bread, cheese and a tankard of ale, it looked to be. She was big with child; I pictured Anne Hathaway carrying twins. Will had a son and two daughters—all men longed for a son.

"Jennet, you should not be toting trays up those stairs," I chided gently. My voice sounded rough. I'd seldom spoken last night in the tavern, but when I had, I'd been forced to pitch my tone low and yet raise my voice to be heard over the babble there.

"Nonsense. I'm fine this time, and after how you helped me last time, it's the least that I can do. Now, I know you're still feeling a bit rocky, but Maud told me that this warm posset with chamomile and borage would help you."

I knew enough about Maud's herbal remedies by then to realize that, though chamomile was standard brew for stomach complaints, the borage was to help lift one's spirits. Maud had said that it purged melancholy, but she'd also mentioned it could comfort the lunatic person. At that thought, I did not know whether to laugh or cry. I had no doubt acted as if I'd lost my mind when I saw Will on the stage. I'd been insane to throw myself at Kit, however much I wanted to hurt Will. And if lunatics were even more maddened by moonlight, the shaft of it that had burst into Kit's bedroom had perhaps made me more demented—such were my rambling thoughts the morning after.

I sat up against the headboard and let Jennet put the tray upon my lap. "And something else for you there—under the posset," she whispered, twisting her apron over her distended belly with both hands as if she were wringing out laundry.

It was a note, not sealed but with a blue ribbon around it. I could almost wish it were from that demon Kit, but I instantly recognized the handwriting.

"He's waiting in the alley," Jennet blurted as I simply stared at the note as if it would bite me. "He won't step in unless you give permission and says he must be off to play practice, but he longs to see you. At least to have you read that note."

"No."

"Anne, I can't read it to you. The man's been out there nearly since dawn, and he won't take food or drink."

"Tell him not to be late for play practice, though I have seen he is a fine actor without a bit of rehearsal."

"Won't you read the note? He says he would have sealed it but someone dear has his seal ring. Now, I know you told me—"

"Perhaps he wants the ring back, and I should toss it out the window."

"Oh, Anne, for heaven's sakes! You told me how dear he'd been to you—how much—how . . . I'm sorry. I know both of you yet long for each other and—"

"That doesn't matter. Tell him to go back to his life and do his best and that will be enough for me. Tell him not to come back here or try to contact me again."

As she flounced from the room muttering, I was tempted to make her return the note to him, but my wretched curiosity got the best of me. I had never been able to turn down knowing what that man was thinking or writing. I pulled off the ribbon and picked up the piece of parchment, folded in quarters. My hand shook as if I had the palsy, just as Will's right hand sometimes did when he used to sew gloves, do his scrivener's work and write for hours on his own. The paper was warm from the mug or perhaps from his hand. It crinkled loudly in mine as I opened it.

Dearest Anne,

In addition to the acting, I have been madly writing both poems and plays and owe much of my courage to your continued good will. Let us now at least be friends. I will wait each day just after dawn at Puddle Dock at the foot of St. Andrew's St. to speak to you. I recall another St. Andrew's on the best day of my life. No more now, but I long to tell you my heart. One of my sonnets I have written with you in mind begins thusly:

Let me not to the marriage of true minds
Admit impediments; love is not love
Which alters when it alteration finds,
Or bends with the remover to remove.
O, no, it is an ever-fixed mark
That looks on tempests and is never shaken . . .

Devil take the man! He'd tricked me into forgiving him once before with one of his love sonnets. But how did I know they were not written for his other Anne? The note was signed, "I beseech, your Will."

It was a clever signature and an outrageous message after all he'd done. A poet must be a skilled seducer of emotion; a playwright must be a master manipulator of character and plot. William Shakespeare was both and more. At least he had not berated me for going off with Kit. He certainly knew the man and his reputation, for he was acting in his play. So then, perhaps he didn't care—and yet . . .

I was lost in mental mazes with only dead ends. I had to fight him. I could not rush back to his arms as I had done once before with disastrous results. And yet, a little voice inside me insisted that I was his wife and his helpmeet. I had wed him before his other Anne, and if it had not been for one child—and now three . . .

With a sob, I sailed the note across the room. I lifted the tray off my lap, spilling the posset onto the bread. Rushing weak-legged to my window that overlooked the alley, I stuck my head out and looked down from the overhang of my top story.

I saw him, head down, shoulders slumped, turn the corner out of the alley into the street. He looked totally dejected and defeated.

I thought to scream his name. I could run downstairs after him, even in my night rail, no matter what the customers in John's wine shop thought when I tore through. But I just held hard to the window ledge, sucking in deep breaths of warm summer air and telling myself I was much better off without my Will.

That next week Stephen Dench brought me word that Father Berowne had died. Though he had already been buried in St. Andrew's churchyard not far from my parents' graves, I went home to mourn them all—and mourn for myself. I spent a week wandering the fields and forests near Temple Grafton, many of which Will and I had walked and used for a bed in our happy days. I saw him wherever I looked, beckoning from darkening woodland shadows, on the broad brow of a hill, sprawled amidst wild thyme, musk roses and woodbine.

I leased the cottage to a young couple who I thought would keep it up, for I could not bear to sell it. I did not go into Stratford but once at sunrise to put flowers on Kat's grave just before meeting my men to return to London.

The graveyard did not haunt me, but the Avon and that bridge did. Waiting for my pack train, I glanced toward Henley Street, wondering how things were there. Had Will's wife come to believe in him and set him free to try to make his name? Did she value his genius and try to tend it rather than rend it?

The day after I returned to London, everyone was abuzz with news that the queen and her retinue would go by river from Greenwich Palace, where she had spent part of the summer, to her city palace of Whitehall. Although upon occasion I had seen her pass in a coach or royal barge, I longed to see the water pageant, as Jennet called it. Since my friend was due to deliver her fifth child in a few weeks, I went alone, walking through the beautiful Blackfriars area to stake out a space along Puddle Dock. It was the site Will had vowed he'd wait for me after dawn each day, but this was nearly noon.

I walked along the wharf, trying to find a good spot, avoiding the loud wherrymen, several, I saw, who sported Maud's cushions even on their craft's finely padded seats. They were calling for people to go out on their boats to catch a closer glimpse of queen and court, but I hadn't thought to bring coins.

Music from one of Her Majesty's gaily bedecked barges heralded the approach of the water parade. I saw yeomen guards filled the first barge. In the second, musicians wailed away on their sackbuts, crumhorns, fydels and the softer lutes. Barges farther back were packed with courtiers. Bright colors, the glint of sun on halberds, blowing bunting and flapping banners blurred past.

The queen's barge of state came third, all awash in green and white Tudor silks and draped cloth of gold. And Gloriana herself in a gown of cloth of silver that shimmered in the sun. She was smiling and waving—yes, waving my way!

I waved back wildly. Tears blurred my vision as always when I beheld her, a woman in a man's world, a bold woman. I felt she could have risen from her carved chair and walked upon the water.

"It reminds me of that time we saw her and the Lady of the Lake at Kenilworth," a voice behind me said.

The entire scene on the river shrank to nothing. I thought I might topple into the water. I fought to keep my voice calm. "It's not 'just after dawn,' you know," I said, not looking at him.

"Ah, then you did read my heartfelt letter to you. Perhaps I have been here ever since, just pining for you."

For the first time in ages, I cared how I looked, for I wanted Will to see me as prosperous and proper. Thank heavens I'd attired myself a bit better than usual, almost as if the queen could see me as I did her. I wore a starched ruff today and the bodice of my willow green gown was finely embroidered. My scalloped petticoat hems showed fashionably beneath my newly shortened skirt, which came just to the top of my red leather, cork-soled shoes.

Gritting my teeth so I would not erupt in tears, I swung about to face him. His eyes raked me head to hem. A pox on him, but he looked handsome. He was not finely garbed, but wore the new style of full, loose breeches called venetians with black stockings and a sleeveless leather jerkin, which contrasted with his white shirt, open at the neck. The brimmed hat he held in his hands was not a stylish beaver one, and it boasted a single white goose feather instead of the burst of plumes the gallants wore—and then I saw he'd stuck a quill pen there.

But beyond how he was dressed, Will emanated a strength more than his physical impact on me. True, he was a bit pale—but tall and as regal in bearing as if he'd been on the queen's barge with her courtiers. Despite what a fine presence he'd made on the stage, until I was this close to him again, I'd forgotten how broad his shoulders were and how rich the hazel hue of his eyes, which now seemed to swim with gold flecks in the sun. His mustached mouth looked both sweet and sensual. All this I took in as a moment fled before I forced myself to speak.

"Have you been in more of Kit's plays?" I asked, fishing by misdirection for how much he might know about Marlowe and me.

"But for his brilliant work, I don't give a fig for the man as long as you truly don't. Besides, however comely a lad you make, once Kit got down to it, he must have discovered a woman and lost his—his interest. Anne," he rushed on as his eyes searched my face, then thoroughly examined me—again—throat to shoe tips, "I keep looking for you in the audience, as male or female. But has not your bosom friend Kit told you I had an argument with him?"

"Over . . ."

He dared to laugh. "Perhaps over how I shall surpass him as London's premier playwright someday. Surely the new actor and scribbler from the country would not have dared to challenge him over you."

"How nice you are in such a fine mood."

"If I am, it's only the heady joy of seeing you, breathing your air and—"

"Reeky Thames air, more like. Are you still in love with London?"

"Are you giving me an opening to talk of what and who I am in love with?"

I shrugged elaborately. "I must be going." I had to flee him, flee that old feeling that always came upon me when I was near him—and when I was not. "By the by, how is your Stratford Anne?" I added over my shoulder as I pushed past him in the crowd still craning to see the queen. Surely a mention of that would make him back off. Faith, I was not going to throw myself into his arms again. When he had needed me during the Arden disaster, that was different, but now . . . and since he had bedded her after that . . .

"She is furious with me," he said, keeping up.

"Ah, that makes two of us."

"But you have always urged me to come here to make my way, to write."

Men, I thought. *They are so thickheaded, for that was not what I meant at all.*

"I've been working day and night," he went on, "acting, yes, but making contacts to sell my work. Philip Henslowe, who buys and then agents many plays, is interested. I've begun several, a history, a revenge tragedy set in Rome, and one a comedy that you have insp—"

"If they are performed, do not bother to send me tickets you cannot afford," I said and kept going down the wharf. He walked with me easily, his long legs matching my flight. I slowed so he would not think I was as panicked as I felt. "I've been writing only tragedy," I told him. "And some love poems, though not as clever ones as yours."

"You have?" he asked, either not catching or, more like, ignoring my subtle cuts. "But I don't want to be clever," he added, pulling me around to face him. "I want to be good. I want to be versatile. I want to be rich. I want to be—if not loved—appreciated and admired."

"Not by me, I hope."

He gave me a little shake. His grip hurt me, but I was entranced by his passion. My own long-smothered feelings for him burst within me but I beat them down. "Anne, when I went back to Stratford from London, my father was in debtors' prison—prison! With the Arden terrors, I wasn't sure if Leicester's long arm had snared him too, but his earlier contacts and service to Stratford freed him. Then I learned my wife had borrowed forty shillings from a shepherd while I was gone! A shepherd was more solvent than the Shakespeares!"

"So you quickly got her with child and had more mouths to feed!"

"It isn't like that. It's never been like that—not with Anne Hathaway. It has always been a duty with her, not, as with you—"

"Lust?"

"Curse it, love!"

"Yes, I'd like to curse love."

"Listen, will you? Anne thinks I'm mad and selfish in general to want to write. Why she ever wanted me, I know not, but that I was available and gullible, ripe for the picking."

Such honesty from him today. It was a heady aphrodisiac. I wanted to hold him, to have him, but my own pain came pouring out. "An old story from a man, I fear," I accused. "Poor me, my wife doesn't understand me, but you do. Well, I don't!" I pulled away and went back to walking faster up St. Andrew's Street away from the river.

But he was not done. "I wanted to have some success—some money—before I let you know I was here this time because—"

"How long have you been here this time?"

"Two months, but I toured with the Queen's Men in the shires before that. I would have gone with them sooner, but I caught a swollen neck disease that laid me low for nigh on a month— mumps, the doctor called it. Anne, whatever I've done, whatever has befallen, I've been bereft without you."

"Let's see now, maybe you could write a sonnet rhyming the word *bereft* somehow. Maybe something like 'In Stratford, my heart was cleft / But I'm still glad my first wife left' or . . ."

He swung me around to face him again. We must have made quite a scene, for several people stopped to stare and one or two called out encouragement to Will, which both of us ignored.

"Mock and berate—and hate—me all you will," he cried, "but whatever success I have, the laurels will always be partly yours. But my love—far beyond the duty I owe the woman I had to marry, the mother of my children, whom I vow to support in a style befitting the Shakespeares—will be yours. Again, I say and swear it so, my love will be yours! Good day and good life, then, my Anne."

He loosed his hold on me so quickly I almost toppled over. One man staring at us dared to clap at that speech. Evidently oblivious to everyone but me, Will started away, then turned back yet again and spoke as if there were no one else in the world but the two of us.

"And even if you do avoid my plays, promise to see or at least read *Love's Labour's Lost*, for without you, I'd have none of it."

He swept me a courtly bow, more graceful, I wager, than any the Earl of Leicester ever gave his royal love. Before I could say aught else, he had disappeared into the crowd, leaving me standing under the big Blackfriars Gatehouse with a stranger applauding his exit.

'Tis widely known that deaths come in threes, so a week or so later, when I heard that both the Earl of Leicester and the London theatre's veteran clown, Richard Tarlton, had died, I dared hope that, counting Father Berowne's death, that meant Jennet would not lose the child she carried.

Amazingly, Tarlton, the darling of the London masses, was mourned much more than was Leicester. And, I'm sure, in the midlands, those who still clung to the old faith were dancing one of Tarlton's jigs over Leicester's demise. On the other hand, John heard from someone who delivered wine to the palace that the queen had shut herself up for days to grieve the loss of her "Robin."

Still, I knew too that Will and the Queen's Men must be overturned for losing their patron, the Earl of Leicester. Attaining noble patronage was not just a question of financial support. In 1572 Parliament had passed an act that set down conditions for punishment of vagabonds, a term that included common players and minstrels not supported by any person of great degree in the realm. In other words, if they did not have the blessing of a great lord, they could legally be whipped and burned through the ear for loitering, so low was the esteem of playwrights and actors at that time. And, with the queen's Warwickshire watchdog Leicester dead, would whatever funds or protection came their way for spying for Walsingham be cut off too? Will would be relieved to be out of that, at any rate.

I was glad Will had not told me where he was living, for I might have been foolish enough to seek him out. He had vowed he loved me—yet our mutual fulfillment of that love was impossible. He claimed that I was his muse—yet I stopped attending plays, afraid I would become one of those women who haunted the playhouse back doors.

Maud and I ventured to Tarlton's memorial service, which was held several days after he was buried. Not only did I wish to pay my respects to the man who had noticed me at the first London play I ever saw, but we figured Philip Henslowe might be there. Will had mentioned him as the purchaser of plays, but we had learned he was also a buyer of anything to do with London entertainments. We were hoping that for a small fee, he might promote our scented cushions to persons we did not know and buy some for his own playhouse, the Rose, in Southwark.

Since we expected a large, important crowd at the memorial for Tarlton, gowned in our feminine best, we went early. The big old church was in the area of the great carrier inns that also housed numerous theatres, quite close to the one where the famed clown had singled me out. Looking around, I reckoned the crowd of mixed theatre folk, a few gentles and plain Londoners was larger than any Tarlton must have performed for when he was alive.

I wore a hood and black velvet half mask and made Maud wear

one too. Not only did I not wish to run into Kit Marlowe, but, should Will be there, I did not intend to have another verbal fencing match with him. I'd been playing that one from last week over and over in my mind and did not need more reasons to lose sleep by night and patience by day.

I could tell by the way people reacted to Maud and me that they thought I was a lady *incognito* with her maid. Fine, I thought, let that be my disguise today. I stood by a very comely, finely garbed youth with long, golden locks, so luxurious he almost looked feminine. He was, I guessed, not yet twenty years. He looked to be with a guardian, for the other man—perhaps ten or so years older—seemed to be pointing out particular people to the youth.

"I adored Tarlton," the young man said to me. He gave me a shy smile while his companion was talking to someone on his other side.

"I too," I told him, using the fan Kat's family had given me to partially hide the lower part of my face. "He addressed me once from the stage, and I shall never forget it."

"I told my mother that when I come into my majority, I shall sit on the stage so I can feel more a part of the action!" His voice was petulant but polite. I fancied he spoke as a noble youth would. Amethysts in his doublet buttons winked at me despite the poor light in the vast, crowded nave.

I had seen gentles sit upon the stage, mostly to be seen rather than to see, but I nodded and smiled, flipping my fan. When his friend turned to look at me too, I asked, "I wonder if I could prevail upon you two gentlemen to point out Philip Henslowe, the theatrical agent, if you know him, for I would speak with him."

"Ah," the youth's companion said, leaning around him to eye me closer, "I'd steer clear of that one, unless of dire necessity."

"Why so, sir?"

"Do I know you, madam?"

"I cannot say, but I believe you know about Master Henslowe, and I would value that information before this service starts."

"Indeed, I'd not deem this a service," the youth put in. "More like a play where some who knew the clown will recount his virtues and, hopefully, not his vices. All theatre folk have vices, and that's the fun of them, the theatre offstage, if you will."

"Henry," the older man said, "that's the clown's wife there, coming in, Em Ball her name is." He gestured toward a red-faced, plump woman who was wheezing like a horse that had been run too far.

The youth raised his voice as the buzz of the crowd swelled. "Then, I believe, Lord Strange, this shall be better than a play by even Marlowe."

Lord Strange, be it a title or nickname, seemed to set the mood for the strange event. Not a prayer service indeed, but an impromptu drama as the youth had said: part history as Tarlton's early life was recounted; part tragedy as those who knew him spoke about his loss; and part comedy as some recalled his antics onstage and off and as his widow sobbed aloud as if she were a professional mourner, making those who spoke raise their voices.

Kit, looking wobbly-legged and a bit unkempt, spoke briefly about one time the clown came drunk to perform but didn't miss a cue. To my amazement, Will spoke, telling how kindly the clown had treated him as a new-fledged actor and playwright in London. Another man, whose name I did not catch, wept copiously into his handkerchief as he blubbered on about someone named Will Kemp who must now carry the fallen mantle of the immortal Richard Tarlton.

I had shifted to stand behind Lord Strange and the youth, though we were far enough back I didn't think Will would note me.

"Madam," Lord Strange said, turning around to face me when it was over and the buzzing crowd began to shift toward the door, "if you insist on speaking with Henslowe, I shall point him out—for one glimpse of your fair face."

"I am not fair in face, but in character, sir," I told him. I whisked my fan and mask aside and back in one quick motion. Startled at how fast I'd moved—or at my dusky or exotic appearance—he broke into a grin while the youth hung on our every word.

"There is Henslowe—in the high-crowned, popinjay blue hat," he told me, pointing at the man who had spoken last. "But I must warn you, he is a speculator, out to make money any way he can. Starch-making, usury, bull- or bear-baiting, and, yes, the theatre. 'Tis all the same to him. Just a word to the wise."

"I thank you, sir."

"To the wise and to the fair," he added and doffed his hat to give me a quick bow. "Let's get you back to Southampton House, Henry, before your mother sends the servants after us." Taking the youth by the elbow, he tugged him away through the crowd.

So both Lord Strange, whom I'd never heard of, and the youth—for Southampton was a well-known noble family—had been my betters and I'd won over both, I thought smugly. 'Twas well known that the Earl of Southampton, whose name was Henry Wriothesley, was as wealthy as King Croesus. His father had died when the boy was but eight, leaving the lad not only his title but much wealth and property. I'd heard he'd been given into the care of the queen's chief minister, Lord Burghley, until the age of twelve, but now lived with his doting mother. Gossip said he'd resented Burghley's wardship of him and now chafed under his mother's care, but at least he'd been out and about with a friend today. I couldn't wait to tell Jennet.

With Maud in my wake, feeling a bit more confident, I made for Henslowe, who was still wiping his eyes. Surely, Lord Strange had exaggerated this man's rapacity, for he looked most moved by Tarlton's loss.

Still wearing my mask, I introduced myself and made my speech about scented cushions. Suddenly dry-eyed, he looked me over thoroughly. "You're asking much too much per item," he told me, "but the idea has merit. I cannot believe I didn't think of that."

"That's the price the Burbages paid, Master Henslowe, and—"

"I might see myself clear to try a few and rent them out per performance. For the Rose, of course, my new theatre over on Bankside."

I'd never been to the Rose, for Bankside was full of stews, animal-baiting pits and prisons. It was across the river in an area where the city fathers had little control, the place Jennet had warned me against on my first tour of London.

"All right, then, for the Rose," I said. "And I was hoping you would agree to be our middleman for sales to the other theatres."

"My lovely young woman, I am middleman to no one, but front man to all. Alas, if you only had someone's plays to sell, for we need a steady diet of them for these ravenous crowds . . ."

Before I even thought, my long-honed business instincts took over. "I write, sir, but would you take a drama from a woman?"

"Highly unlikely," he said, stroking his shovel-shaped beard, "but if you wrote under a man's name—"

"Then if a woman with pen in hand is anathema, just as is a woman on the stage, you'd best buy Will Shakespeare's plays."

"The country upstart? He's finished them? I know he claims to—"

"I'm quite familiar with his work from the shires—both his acting and his playwriting. He is an original, brilliant talent. You, sir, will greatly regret it later if you do not get in line to buy them now."

"In line? But who else is—? I mean," he said, hieing himself after me as Maud and I moved away, "he didn't mention anyone else . . ."

"We will come to the Rose when we can with sample cushions, Master Henslowe. Until then, I'd suggest—"

Someone stepped aside to allow my exit, and I banged right into Will, who must have been intent on finding Henslowe too.

"Is this your wife or patron?" Henslowe blurted to Will.

Will and I both gasped at how Henslowe had worded that. Will set me back and removed his hands from my shoulders as if I'd burned him.

"Why do you ask, Master Henslowe?" Will said.

"Her ladyship is promoting her pillows and your plays, man. If you have aught prepared for me to see, bring them to the Rose first thing on the morrow, even if they're not quite polished up yet, you hear me?"

"I hear you. I will, and each play shall be signed 'I, Will.'"

Henslowe snorted a laugh. "Mayhap you should take Tarlton's place instead of Kemp," he muttered and pushed away from us through the remnants of the crowd. Maud gaped at us. I kept my hand on the lower part of my mask as if its removal would slay me. "Should I stay or go home, Anne?" she asked. "It's not far from here and—"

"Yes, *Her Ladyship* gives you permission to leave us," Will said. His hail-fellow-well-met expression had now flown.

"Yes, Maud," I said, when she tarried yet, "it's all right." Neither Will nor I looked away from each other as she left us.

"I don't know whether to thank you or spank you," he said under his breath and steered me out the door and up Winding Lane toward Bishopsgate Street. "My ladyship, indeed. It's one thing for me to bargain with Henslowe, but he's one to talk your petticoats right off you before you know what's happened."

"It takes such a man to know one."

"Stop it, Lady Disdain. You hardly hate me if you were promoting my plays to him."

"It was like giving alms to the poor to help you out."

"Curse you, Anne Whateley!" he cried and hustled me into the entrance to Swan Alley. "You're getting in the way of my writing—my obsession with you, wanting you—I need to write, I grip my pen until it bends and my spastic hand racks me but not so sore as do my memories of you. I have only pieces of plays to show Henslowe tomorrow unless I stay up all night and write with my pen in my teeth!"

"If I am in your way, will you hire someone to rid you of me? Will you—" was all I got out before he pressed me against the alley wall and kissed me hard, crushing my half mask askew.

I wanted to push him off, to tell him off, but I didn't. Somehow my arms got wrapped around his neck to grapple him to me. I pushed back against him as he flattened my petticoats and my breasts under my taut bodice by grinding me against a wall. The kiss went on and on, deeper, spinning the entire city around us. His hands raced over my waist, my hips and breasts. We slanted our heads to drink deeper of each other, open mouths, breathing hard in unison. He rained mad kisses down my throat to where my breasts swelled and I thought he might yank my bodice down. We both gasped for air as if we were being smothered.

When we broke the kiss and caress at last, he lifted a hand to pull my mask up and shove back my hood.

"Tell me Kit Marlowe is naught to you!" he gasped raggedly. "Tell me you haven't been in his bed."

"You know he favors lads."

"Tell me, vow it to me!"

"I was in his bed, but only because I was drunk. I swear nothing like you're thinking happened, and if he says it's so, he lies. I went out a window when he wasn't looking."

He stared at me, his eyes narrowed. "If I believe you, it's only because you just had the perfect chance to drive me completely mad by saying he's had you. If you'd let him—let him use you—"

"Does he say so, the wretch?"

"Ah, music to my ears that you don't care for him. But then, you have berated me and you once cared for me. Anne—my Anne, we can hardly go to your rooms with Jennet and John there, and I have had to hire a scrivener to copy my work back in my room. Besides, it's dank there, and if I fail as an actor or writer, I shall just hawk the mushrooms that grow in the corners of my room. 'Mushrooms, fresh mushrooms!' Ah, you're smiling."

"One crazed kiss does not mean I shall bed with you any more than with Kit Marlowe."

"Maybe I only desire that you read my work," he said with a wink.

"Will, my hand is strong and sure, and my penmanship good. I used to read to you, but cannot I help you write—that is, take your dictation so we can get something finished for Henslowe on the morrow? You must get a good start with him or the Burbages or whoever is to discover your work beyond your acting. And if your room is dank and dark, we shall just take part of the table from your scrivener and work all night by candlelight."

"It's a small, wretched room, that's the rub, and I left him with my last candle stubs. Damn, but those are dear in this town. Sometimes I sit up all night in a tavern writing because candles are free there, but the noise and stench . . . But you—our love—deserves much more."

"And we must be somewhere at least tonight where we would not be distracted from the writing."

"Anne," he cried, crushing me to him again and covering my throat with hot kisses, "I have missed you so, needed you so."

"I have it," I told him, though my voice was shaky and I could barely catch my breath. "We'll work the night in the Davenants' kitchen. Jennet has plenty of candles there, even a horn lantern we can light. How long before you can look in on your scrivener, then come to the back door with your work?"

"I'll run. An hour at most, as I'm up by Shoreditch near the theatres, on Holywell Lane. I'll keep him working at *Titus* and bring the comedy with me. But will you be all right, getting home? You look so—so stunning today that—"

"It's still light out. Her ladyship will be fine. Fine now that we are partners at least with the plays, if not with playing." I gave his firm midriff a light punch. "Hurry," I told him. "This is your place, Will, and this is your time."

CHAPTER ELEVEN

☙

Considering that I had been denied my wedding night, this was the most thrilling night of my life. Will and I took a quick supper with John and Jennet, and John helped her up to bed. The child was not due for several weeks yet, we reckoned. I had vowed to be with her each moment when her time came, and I was dreading that, however much I tried to bolster her spirits and mine too. When John and Jennet were gone, Will and I turned to our work.

"I may still not be able to show Henslowe the tragedy the scrivener's finishing in my room," Will admitted. "I won't have time to go over what he's copying, but perhaps we can have this play done by dawn."

He spread the pages out on the table in acts. Three of the piles looked completed but messily—that is, shakily—written. The final two seemed a bit sparse.

"The way we work at rehearsals," he went on, sounding as excited as the boy in him I recalled so well, "I can make changes up until the last moment anyway. Once the play's accepted—purchased, that is—it needs to be copied over in long rolls, the roll of the king, the roll of the princess, et cetera, for each player. Lines are sometimes amended by the company anyway."

"Let me look it over to see what you have before we go on. Then you can dictate and I can write, or we can act out scenes between us if that helps."

"Hold a moment," he said, backing me up to sit in John's big chair at the head of the table. "Let me give you the backbone of it all. And this time," he added, starting to pace around the table, "I believe you will well note that you—we—are the inspiration for *Love's Labour's Lost.*"

"Even in the title perhaps? But our labor of love for this play shall not be lost."

"I pray not."

"'Let us not to the marriage of true minds admit impediments,'" I recited from his sonnet to halt the pall of melancholy that suddenly seemed to cloak him. "We must labor to get this in shape and, unlike other nights, this one will end too soon."

"I know," he said, putting his hands on the arms of my chair and bending toward me. "And yet I'd almost give it all the heave-ho for another kind of night's work between us."

"*Almost*, you said," I countered as he bent to kiss me, a heavy, hot kiss. Then he straightened and instead heaved a huge sigh. "Will, let me hear the story of this comedy and quickly, for we have work to do and are in danger of doing nothing at all—of this sort."

He paced again, explaining how the plot satirized scholars and certain pompous playwrights who boasted of their Oxford or Cambridge credentials. But it was also a comedy of the sexes. Three men, including the King of Navarre, vowed to live a strict life of learning for three years. This meant swearing off all sorts of distractions, including wooing women.

"But of course, those are famous last words," I put in.

"Exactly. Three women, including the Princess of France, arrive on a diplomatic mission, so King Ferdinand and his friends must deal with them. He becomes much enamored of the princess, and his friend Berowne—"

"Berowne? You used Father Berowne's name?"

"In honor of the old man, I did."

"I am not in it, am I?"

"Not as Anne, but I have borrowed your middle name for one of the women."

"Rosaline? Tell me of her."

"All right then," he said, linking his hands like a cap over his head, elbows straight out, as he paced again. "She is described as a bright woman with velvet brows and two dark eyes. She is clever and independent and takes no rubbish from any man, even when she falls in love with Berowne."

"Let me see the cast of characters there on top," I cried, bouncing up and seizing the paper.

"No," he said, pulling it back from me, "rather look at Act V, scene 2, though that is a part which needs much work." He shuffled through the sheaf of pages and thrust one at me. "There," he added, pointing to a line of tightly scribbled words with asides thrust in here and there with arrows.

"I see why you need me," I said, tipping it toward the waning window light, for we had not yet lit the candles or lantern. "This is most difficult to read. But here it is the Princess Katherine who says that her friend Rosaline has a 'merry, nimble, stirring spirit.' What does the man who loves her say—what do you say, if I am the inspiration for Rosaline?"

"It's not like that. People always think it is, but it's not. The author's feelings and ideas are usually more patched together, conveyed more indirectly. Then too, Berowne and Rosaline are sparring, are at odds, when he says she is 'a whitely wanton with a velvet brow / With two pitch-balls stuck in her face for eyes.'"

"What? A wanton? With pitch-ball eyes?"

"See what I mean? It isn't exactly you, just inspired by you. He's teasing her when he says that."

"You're mad as a Bedlamite, but brilliantly so. Say on."

"You must add all the parts together to get the whole of how you are my muse for this play. For instance, there is another character who is so enamored of a country wench that he falls into melancholy and is driven to versifying. That man is but a piece of me—his love a snippet of you also. Toward the end of the play, the men admit that women are 'the books, the arts, the academes / That show, contain, and nourish all the world.' Indeed, whether with me or afar, you are my muse. This play may not tell the world that, but I pray it tells you so."

Blinking back tears, kissing far too often to make much headway—until John came down to fetch some pickled cod for Jennet and, thankfully, did not find us sprawled upon the table for a bed—we finally got to revising and copying the play.

"'By heaven, I do love, and it hath taught me to rhyme and to be melancholy,'" I read a line aloud from Act IV. "When you wrote this—ever since we were parted after being wed, we were suffering much the same, but in silence, Will."

"I did think to call the play *Cupid's Revenge*," he admitted, stopping his well-worn circuit of the table long enough to peer over my shoulder where I'd been taking his dictation.

"I saw your lines about 'love is a devil,'" I told him. "'There is no evil angel but Love.'"

"Tell me you didn't curse me many a night."

"And day."

"Ah, my Anne, 'The tongues of mocking wenches are as keen / As is the razor's edge invisible'—have you come to that line yet? Still, love is hardly a laughing matter."

"Yet there is fine humor here amidst all the lovely poetry, songs and sonnets of these lovesick swains. When you wrote the part for the clown Costard, did you mean it for Tarlton? You heard Henslowe. He's all for this new clown named Will Kemp taking Tarlton's place. You might mention tomorrow that these lines will turn to much money in Kemp's mouth."

"You've read Henslowe aright. Sadly, like Tarlton, Kemp, as bright and clever as he is, tends to take over a play and rip it to shreds to get his own laugh lines in—that's why I hope I can convince him to stick with these—if Henslowe will buy it."

Hours later when we both came up for air, Will massaged my aching back and shoulders and then my right hand. He kissed each fingertip almost reverently, then licked between each finger until I tingled all over and felt his merest look down to the very pit of my belly. When we saw light was breaking through the eastern windows, we sighed wordlessly.

I turned into his embrace; we collapsed into each other's arms as if holding each other up. "Are you sure you want to go with me over to Bankside?" Will asked. "That part of Southwark is randy and rough."

I pulled back a bit and looked up into his face, scratchy with a new day's beard.

"Of course, for I go on an earth-changing mission. After all, I intend to sell Philip Henslowe scented seat cushions."

He smacked my bum as I darted away, laughing. "Tease," he said, his eyes darkening with desire. "Teases always get what they deserve, whether they be called Anne Whateley, the Lady Rosaline, Julia or—"

"Who, pray tell, is Julia?"

"A character for another comedy I have not yet begun to write, a play about two gentlemen from Venice, or whatever I decide to call it. Perhaps we can manage that one in the daylight—if you can find time to help me. Anne," he said, coming back to seize my hands in his again, "if I sell a play or two, I can pay you to help me, and—"

"You'll not pay me. Never suggest that again, that is, not pay me with coins, Will Shakespeare."

"Let me offer a down payment then."

"I have not the time," I said, with a coy laugh, "for John will be down soon, and I must eat and change and meet you somewhere to go across the Thames. You'll head home to see if the other play's in fighting trim, your bloodthirsty *Titus Andronicus* then?"

He nodded. "Meet me at Puddle Dock two hours hence so we can cross the Thames to beard Henslowe in his den."

"I'll be there," I vowed.

"I'll leave this play in your care. It and my heart."

He kissed me hard, strapped on his sword, grabbed a day-old piece of bread from the table and tore out the back door on this happy day of his—of our—long-awaited destiny.

But that day of our dreams was not to be, for a nightmare, not of our making, soon crashed upon us.

"Anne," John cried as he ran into the kitchen shoeless with his shirt unlaced, "the babe's coming and so sudden. It's too early, and the new midwife I've hired told me she'd be at her daughter's house 'til next week. It's too fast and too early! Jennet's terrified."

Both of them were, I thought. His hair stood on end, and his eyes were unfocused. My stomach clenched and, despite how I had tried to uplift Jennet's spirits, foreboding leaned hard on my heart. I stood from a breakfast of half-finished frumenty and placed Will's play I'd been rereading upon a shelf of the sideboard. After being up all night, I felt exhausted, but now panic poured through my veins to give me strength.

"What about the midwife you used last time?" I asked as I dashed over to be sure the wash water was boiling on the hearth. It was not hot enough. I swung the chain suspending the pot over the banked fire and began to build the fire up.

"Jennet won't use her," he said, coming to help me. "Not after the last babe was lost. Even our maids and my prentice are down to the dock waiting for the Portuguese ship to be unloaded."

"Then you must go out to inquire if you can find another midwife while I stay with her. Is the child truly coming yet?"

As if to answer for him, Jennet's scream rent the air. "I'll go to her," I said, grabbing his old pair of shoes he always kept beside the back door and thrusting them at him. "See if you can find someone, even a neighbor who knows a bit about this—a doctor or apothecary, if you must. Hurry!"

I scribbled a note for Will, telling him where I was and that *"LLL"* was on the sideboard. I pinned the note on the back door. He would understand. I hoped he would not think I'd changed my mind when I did not meet him at Puddle Dock. But my frenzied prayer was that Jennet's child would be all right and that John would bring help soon.

John and Jennet's second-story bedchamber seemed as hot as an oven, despite the fact the sun was barely up, but it beat against the windows here. I longed to open the dreary, nut-brown drapes Jennet thought were so fine to catch a morning breeze, but she believed the city air was noisome, so I dared not. I should have told her about all those Stratford babes who had died breathing country air—two in Will's family—but, of course, I had never broached such a subject to her.

"Jennet, I'm here, and John's gone for help."

"Not Mistress Pierce—not the last midwife!"

"No, not her. Can you tell how far the child is along?"

"Anne, something's wrong!" she cried, stretching her sweat-soaked night rail taut across her big belly. "Wrong before it even comes. See, the head's not down."

I knew nothing of human birthing. And our horses had simply dropped their offspring and then licked them dry. One time I had observed my father put his arm beyond the elbow into a mare that was having trouble and pull the wet foal out, but surely that could not be of help here.

I sponged Jennet's face and throat while she tossed and raved. She was indeed in labor, for every little while she would bear down and scream. Once she seized my wrists so hard that both my hands went white and numb before she released them. In her frenzy, she pulled her night rail up to show the bulging, naked flesh of her distended belly.

"Anne, look! See the head here when it should be down. Dear God in heaven, what if this one strangles on its birthing cord too, or won't leave the womb? It has to turn head down—ah, it's kicking me here—see?"

I did see. There was a definite bulge to the side of her navel that must be the head, and the feet were kicking under the navel, almost atop the hip bone. Where was John? He'd been gone for an eternity!

"Help is coming," I told her. "A midwife or doctor will know how to turn it."

"We have to do it now! You have to help me," she gritted out, then screamed again. Her face contorted, she clenched her teeth and arched her back like a bowstring, but I saw nothing appear between her spread white thighs.

Praying incessantly for John to hurry, I put my trembling hands on her perspiring, vibrating belly. Yes, a head there, up, not down. I gave it a little push.

"Harder!" Jennet cried. "Please, Anne, don't fear you can hurt me—help me-eee! Ahhh—I want to die if this one dies!"

"Don't say such things. This one will live and you too!"

I tried desperately to push the head downward, first in little stops and starts and then by applying steady pressure. It seemed to move, then to return.

"Oh, no, oh, no, oh, no!" Jennet chanted between gasping breaths. "It's coming, coming like this! I can't bear it—I mean I can't stand to—I have to push, I can't hold back . . ."

Between her screams, while she lay panting for breath, I heard a man's tread on the stairs. Oh, thank the Lord, John was here with help. I spun to the door—it was Will.

"Did you see my note and the play downstairs?" I asked him.

"I came when you weren't at the wharf, but none of that matters compared to this. I heard her scream. Where's John?"

"Went to get help. Have you ever seen a child birthed?"

He came to the doorway. "The twins, from across the room. The girl first, then the boy—I saw my son come into the world."

All that would have pitched me into melancholy or a rant, but Will was right—nothing mattered but Jennet right now. "Should I go look for John?" he asked, not budging from the doorway. "Fetch a neighbor?"

"Fetch some hot water, so we can wash her and the babe."

"All right," he said, turning away. "It was boiling."

Jennet screamed again and threw herself so hard to the side I thought she might fly off the bed. With a wooden bowl of steaming water, Will was quickly back. He came into the room this time.

"What about my looking for John?" he repeated.

"You might miss him. Can you help me here? I was trying to turn the babe into the right position, but I don't know what to do."

To my amazement, he did more than help. He almost took over. He tied ropes of sheets for Jennet to hold and knotted those to the bedposts at the head of the bed. He propped stools sideways against the foot of the bed so that she had something to brace her feet on when she bore down.

"Let's try to turn the babe, head down," he said, when I explained the problem to him.

But too late for that. I was appalled to see the infant's head drop, but not to lead the way through the birth canal. "Don't push, don't push!" I ordered Jennet. "Maybe we can still turn—"

But my words died in my throat as a tiny foot thrust itself into view. Help us, Lord, help us, Lord, I prayed silently. Send John back and help us, Lord.

Jennet began to howl like an animal in pain.

"Breech," Will whispered. "I think it's called a breech."

"I don't give a fig what it's called. We have to save this child!"

Though I was terrified, I leaped to action. I had to get that babe out and fast, for what if it too strangled on the cord—or what if it got stuck and killed Jennet?

"Push when I tell you, Jennet," I said, taking hold of that tiny, warm and slippery leg with a shudder. "Will, give me a piece of linen to hold it firm."

He picked up a bolster Jennet had kicked onto the floor, stripped it of its linen cover and turned that inside out. I waited a moment, praying another foot would appear and I could gently pull the babe out that way. But no other foot.

"I don't mean to hurt you now, Jennet, but I'm going to feel for the other foot."

Her eyes glazed, she was panting in great, heaving breaths. "Do it—anything . . ." she cried.

I pushed my fingers up inside, then felt the other foot. Tiny toes, little toenails. Slippery, getting bloody too. Will sponged the mess off with a wet towel. Holding both legs with the piece of wet linen, I tugged.

Jennet went rigid but did not cry out. I thought she might have fainted but I plunged on.

"Yes, pull," Will whispered. "That's all you can do."

I pulled again, more steadily now. Jennet shifted her legs; she was still with us.

"Push, Jennet!" I ordered. "I have your child's legs and I want the rest of—of her!" I shrilled in excitement as the babe was born to her waist in a gush of wetness and blood. "Oh, it's a girl—a daughter, Jennet!"

John should be here. Where was John?

"Bear down, bear down," I told her.

"I am!"

Suddenly, I recalled something else my father had done. He'd had one of the carriers push on the mare's belly while he'd pulled the foal out of her.

"Will, gently press down where you feel the head. We have to do this fast."

"The cord!" Jennet gasped out. "The cord. The shoulders are stuck! It will cut off the cord!"

"I see the cord!" I told her. "It's pulsing with life!"

But even as I looked at it, wrapped around the baby's waist, I could see that the life beat within it was slowing. I touched the cord in awe and anguish. Will did too; our hands slid together and a jolt of energy from him leaped up my arm.

Will put both his hands on Jennet's belly. "Hurry," he mouthed. "Now!"

I wrapped the baby's lower torso in the linen to keep her warm and to get a better grip. What if I killed Jennet doing this? If John had to choose, he'd want his wife's life, and yet I knew Jennet would choose the child.

I curled my hands over the babe's slippery pelvis and thighs and gently pulled, then harder while Jennet braced herself against the stools and Will tried to push the head. I tried to rotate the body, hoping something would pop free. I blinked back tears; sweat dripped in my eyes and off my nose. My damp hair hung in hanks. The green gown I'd put on to visit Philip Henslowe clung to me like a soaked second skin.

I wondered if John had gone mad with fear and run away. No, not stalwart John. And here was Will with me, helping. Whatever fate had done to the two of us, I loved this man. Being with him made me go shaky and weak but ever strengthened me too. Ambitious and proud and maddening at times, he was proving here how brave and strong and loving he could be. This was our child now too, the child we could never have together.

The first shoulder popped out. We gave a little cheer. "Just one more big push, Jennet! Jennet?"

"I think she's fainted."

"Maybe she's losing too much blood. Can you push harder then?"

He did. The other shoulder birthed as easily, though both arms were still inside. As if I knew what I was doing, I reached up past the neck to bring them both down and out. What I thought was victory now panicked me again. The last babe had gone blue before he died. This birth cord was turning blue and the babe's legs too. The horrid memory of Kat, not breathing under the river ice, jolted me.

"Throw water on her face, Will. She has to push. You push too, and I'll pull."

He did as I said, and poor Jennet sputtered awake. "Push, Jennet!" I shouted. "Push now!"

"Cut me open if you must. Anything . . ."

But the head seemed snagged. We tried again. I flexed the head, for I now had a chin resting on the child's chest. The remainder of the face must be in the hollow of Jennet's tailbone but still inside her.

The tiny body got bluer. Maybe the stuck upper forehead was pressing on the cord. I had to clear a way for the little girl to breathe. The wet, warm body shuddered weakly in my hands.

"Will, turn Jennet on her side—toward you."

He did; she screamed and fainted again. My muscles were burning. I twisted the tiny body, lifted, pulled.

The sucking sound of the child trying to breathe inside Jennet sounded like a scream in my soul. The cord had collapsed. The little body was going cold in my hands.

"Now, once more!" I cried with a sharp sob.

Will accidentally bumped my arm. The tiny neck pivoted, the head freed itself, and our babe was born into the world.

We tended to Jennet and cleaned and cuddled the child. When Jennet regained consciousness yet again, I placed the swaddled bundle in her arms, though she was too weak to hold her daughter without my bracing her arms. Still, the look on her face was pure rapture.

Will went out looking for John and brought him back, sobbing with joy and relief when he heard all that had happened. His head was bandaged with someone's handkerchief, and he was as white as that. In his headlong rush to find help, he had darted out in front of a cart; he'd been knocked unconscious and was tended by strangers. When he regained his senses, they had walked him home.

We gave the new parents time alone with their daughter, but John soon summoned us back and motioned us to come to the bed where, looking almost as spent as Jennet, he perched next to her, propped up with the babe lying between her breasts.

"Perhaps the secret of success," John said, "is for both of us to be knocked out and for Anne and Will to handle it all. We can never repay both of you and shall cherish your friendship for life. And we would be honored if you would stand as the child's god-parents," he added, as he stared at Jennet and the child through his tears.

"By what name shall she be called?" Will asked.

"We were afraid to think of that before," John admitted.

"We've decided," Jennet whispered, "that you both brought her into this world as much as we and you shall name her."

"Anne, what say you?" Will asked, turning to me and taking my hand.

"Yes, to the godparenting and—if you all agree—I would choose to name her Katherine and call her not Kat but Kate. Will and I had a dear friend Kat, but this little one wants to live and—"

I burst into tears before I could say *and Kat did not*. Will held me while I cried on his chest, completing the ruination of the new doublet he'd donned to face Philip Henslowe.

"Oh, no," I said, wiping at my tears and pulling back. "Is it still morning? Will, we must hie ourselves to Bankside."

"It's past midday, and we'll find Henslowe on the morrow," he told me. "I hear he moves about to his various businesses this time of day, and I have a play rehearsal in less than an hour."

"All right then, let's seal it all," John said, getting unsteadily to his feet. "The apprentice and the maids are back downstairs with the new shipment of wine. I say we have them prepare a celebration meal, and we all drink cheers to Katherine Davenant's perilous entry to this busy, crazy world."

Jennet had drifted off in exhaustion, and John handed little Kate to me. I held her against my breasts, rocking her slightly as Will and John went out to see to the meal. I'd have to wake Jennet soon for her to try to nurse Kate, but my love for this little one was as fierce as if I'd borne her. I vowed to always cherish her as she grew and as she found her own life and loves. I was so happy for John and Jennet, so grateful to Will. But right now, in this fleeting moment, this newborn miracle was mine alone.

CHAPTER TWELVE

❦

Will and Jennet had been right about the Bankside area of Southwark. It reeked of forbidden pleasures and danger, even at this early morning hour, so I could imagine what it might be like in the afternoon when it was swelled with folk at the theatres and animal-baiting gardens, the inns and stews. But no one had told me Bankside bore the heady scent of excitement too.

I decided to forgo a comment to Will on the actual smells here. Not only the stench of horse droppings or the drainage ditch, but that from the animal gardens and, worse, the fact that Southwark was the site of the so-called "stink trades" meant no one wanted across the river. Brewing and leather tanning went on nearby, though, as I was forced to breathe the air, those smells seemed to lessen, so, no doubt, one became used to them. At least I could see that there were open areas with vegetables and flowers growing here. Better yet, it wouldn't take much of a walk to be out in the fields and woods beyond.

On our wherry ride across the river, Will had explained that the area was outside the control of the Puritan-leaning city fathers, for it was in the shire of Surrey in an area called a liberty or a bastard sanctuary. Such areas existed in other spots surrounding the city, such as Shoreditch. Yet I knew Bankside had a worse reputation.

He said that the liberties had been controlled by the Catholic Church in earlier times and were, therefore, outside the reach of royal justice. Such areas originally sheltered criminals and debtors; now they were home to prisons like the Clink here in Bankside. In the Protestant England of the Tudors, the liberties remained privileged places where vagrants, beggars, cutpurses, prostitutes—and yes—play actors congregated. Foreigners, watermen and soldiers lived here in great numbers because of the cheap rents. Of course, thousands of English citizens were drawn here daily by their desire to take advantage of all the entertainments.

"The Bishop of Winchester used to control the area," Will added. "He licensed the whores in the stews. There are aplenty still, though I warrant they are all abed this time of the morning. Some folk still call them Winchester geese for their flocking about the area. But then," he added as we walked away from the Paris Garden Wharf, "I've heard them called Roses lately too, since they've been hanging about Henslowe's theatre."

"I hope your knowledge of them is from observation only."

"Writers must study all at close range," he said only and went back to his lessons about the area.

As we walked along High Street by the river, he pointed out the Rose Theatre. People speaking foreign languages—Will said Dutch and Flemish—and hawkers hurried past us, but I did not feel threatened with him at my side, guarding me and the plays.

I held both *Love's Labour's Lost* and *Titus Andronicus* to my chest, as carefully as I had cradled little Kate. I carried them to keep Will's arms free, for he wore a dagger stuck in his belt as well as his sword. He'd given me a bodkin, a long, thick pin, to keep up my sleeve, and it poked me when I turned a certain way. It was like a little pinch to remind me all this was real: the only man I'd ever loved was on the cusp of fame and fortune—I was convinced of that. I had helped him and was here to share it all.

As we approached Henslowe's Rose Theatre, I saw it was smaller than the two at Shoreditch. The playhouse looked to be round but was actually sixteen-sided. The walls were lath and plaster; thatch so new it was still butter-hued covered the upper galleries but had a hole in the center to let in light.

Next to the Rose, almost dwarfing it, were two animal pits, looking much like theatres, where bulls and bears were baited. Although it was too early for that also, we could hear the roars of the caged bears and the deep-throated barks of mastiffs Will said would be sicced on the bears later, though it was often the bears that won the bloody brawl.

"How can a theatre audience hear the players' lines with all that going on?" I asked.

"It's just another reason the playwright has to be very good, the actors too, always ready to adapt. Henslowe didn't even put in a stage at first, hoping to use the Rose for other entertainments—jugglers, acrobats and the like—but he's got one now. And no, we are not going to look for any of that ilk to see if they could be Italian ropedancers."

He'd never mentioned, never even hinted at that dreadful day in our past before. I prayed he hadn't hexed this precious day by so much as alluding to it.

"I've a good nerve to stop by the Elephant Inn and buy us some ale to stoke our courage," Will muttered as we walked around to the back door. Our feet crunched hazelnut shells that patrons dropped everywhere about the theatres.

"I'm not afraid," I said. "I'm going in, and I think you'd best come along."

He kissed me, a quick peck, and opened the door for me. The backstage lay before us, half practice hall, half tiring room with costumes on racks, and shoes, hats and armor on shelves. We wended our way past painted wooden flats that conveyed palaces or forests. It was quite dim here behind the curtain, though we peeked through to the audience area.

"Henslowe had the floor banked, so the groundlings can see better," he whispered, pointing. "If I had this theatre, I'd have those wooden pillars painted to look like marble. His small privy chamber is back here." He let the curtain fall closed, returning us to the dimmer light.

Will's expression and whispers had become almost reverent, though I felt his sudden shyness and solemnity would not serve us well with the likes of Philip Henslowe. I could hear his distinctive, high-pitched voice even from here as he spoke with a man who used lower, resonant tones. We halted just outside his withdrawing chamber; the door was ajar. We sat on what must pass for the side of a sailing bark onstage and, shoulders pressed together, waited.

"Honored, honored, my lord, to serve you," Henslowe was saying in an unctuous, boot-licking voice. Gone was the stern, tutorial tone with which he'd lectured me. "I'll find you the very play, yes, indeed. Sir Walter Raleigh too, you say, and to be done after dark at his Durham house on the Strand a fortnight hence."

"Something for the ladies too," the other man put in. I thought I recognized the voice but could not place it. "We don't oft invite them to our School of Night, where the talk is all of manly pursuits such as science, reason and exploration, but they need a sop now and then."

"'Tis said the queen's astrologer, Dr. John Dee, participates in Sir Walter Raleigh's privy company of friends too," Henslowe put in.

"*Who* says?" the man inquired sharply, and then I thought I knew who he was. "Some clay brains say he practices black magic too, but they are much mistaken!"

"A man I know from Mortlake mentioned it, that is all," Henslowe stammered. "My source was merely an actor, so no one of consequence. But yes, I shall have the very play and the players for you too on that day, indeed I will, my lord."

I was sure now that Henslowe's guest was Lord Strange, the companion of the young Earl of Southampton, both of whom I'd conversed with briefly at Tarlton's funeral. I'd learned more about Ferdinando Stanley, Lord Strange, since then. His title was actually the Earl of Derby, and he had much in common with his young friend Southampton. Like the earl, he came from a powerful Catholic family. He also loved plays and players; he delighted to be their patron. But I'd heard too he was associated with the so-called School of Night, a group of brilliant men who met to speak of learned and even arcane subjects, so apparently that was the group of men he'd been alluding to.

As Henslowe said, "I bid you good day, my lord," and we heard a chair scrape back, I bent close to Will's ear and whispered to him.

"We'll sell the comedy as the perfect play for those lords and their ladies—without letting on we've overheard them. Come on." I pulled him farther away from Henslowe's door.

We hid behind the curtain as the two men came out. Yes, Lord Strange, indeed. Will put his mouth to my ear this time. "That's Ferdinando Stanley, Lord Strange, Earl of Derby, a rich theatre patron, very learned and artistic. He's one the Burbages mentioned might become our next sponsor."

We gave Henslowe but a moment back in his chamber after he showed Lord Strange out, then headed that way. But evidently, Lord Strange had come back in, somehow without throwing light into the dim area, for he spoke behind us and we both startled.

"My lady of the mask and fan?" We both turned to face him. "Or not?" he added with an arch look at Will.

"How lovely to see you again, Lord Strange," I managed to get out. I wasn't certain whether I should curtsy or not, but I did and Will bowed.

"I see you did not take my advice about Master Henslowe, though."

"But you too are here, my lord, and if you have some business with him, I can think of no greater recommendation. My lord, may I present to you a playwright and friend, William Shakespeare."

"But—an unfamiliar name."

Before Will could answer, I put in, "But your name is not unfamiliar to Will, my lord. His admiration of you from afar has been so great that he named the hero of his play—King Ferdinand of Navarre, with but a slight change in the spelling of it—in your honor, a worthy man, indirectly inspired by you and your learning—isn't that so, Will?"

"It is indeed," he declared, managing to cover up his surprise at my ploy. "You see, my lord, I'm an actor with the Burbages, formerly the Queen's Men, but I've written new plays for Master Henslowe." Will took the manuscript of *Love's Labour's Lost* from me. "This one's a comedy, one with much variety in it—poetry, sonnets and songs. The main characters are a group of men who would form an academy of learning but realize they cannot do so without the support of their ladyloves."

"Henslowe!" Lord Strange shouted, though I noted Henslowe already stood in the doorway. "Take a look at this play and see if it's of any account—if it would suit. I'd favor having one not performed elsewhere first. I just came back in because I failed to tell you that there is to be no blood spilt in whatever you come up with for my use on that night."

I was about to blurt there was not one drop in Will's comedy, but Henslowe already looked angry. Still he held his tongue until he had escorted Lord Strange out for a second time and, frowning, returned to face us.

"This had better be good," Henslowe said, propping both hands on his padded trunk hose. "But then, if it's only half as clever as the way you've set me up here, I'll not only forgive you for coming a day late, but buy it for the playhouses too. Give it here then, give it here."

"And a second one," Will said, "but it's bold and bloody."

"Come back on the morrow, and by then, I'll have had a look. 'S teeth, man, after the playacting you both put on for Lord Strange just now, I hope to hell you can write too."

CHAPTER THIRTEEN

☙

I saw our love as dangerous, though not forbidden. I came to think of the Stratford Anne as Will's other wife, for I had married him first. Will and I were legally registered to wed in our shire. We had been united in a church by a holy man we both trusted and honored, one Will's father honored too. Granted, Will and I both should have had parental consent, but we were convinced that without his seduction by Anne Hathaway and the connivance and coercion of her neighbors, we would have won over both his father and mine. As for Will's children, somehow that seemed a separate thing: he loved them, and I envied him that love.

Teeming, busy London seemed so far from little Stratford that it was easy to live in a world of our own. Discovery or shame seemed as distant as the Avon. Our love was heedless and headstrong, heightened by the aphrodisiac of the sales of Will's first two plays. We were together! Success was on the horizon!

Our problem was, however, that we could not be seen together by the world—even our London world—as lovers or certainly not as spouses, or it would mean my humiliation and his ruination. Our time alone as well as places for trysts were scarce. Will refused to let me come to his tiny room on Holywell in Shoreditch. The name Holywell invoked a pretty, peaceful location, but it was a raucous place packed with people, many in the theatre trade, including most of his fellow actors. However wicked people might be themselves, reputations mattered, especially if Will was to prosper and find a patron from the nobility.

Honoring our friends the Davenants as we did, neither could we bring ourselves to steal away to my chamber. I had a privy staircase, but my room was accessible from their lower floors and their bedchamber lay directly under mine. Rather, when Will was not acting or writing and the weather was warm enough, we took walks into the countryside, though the autumn days were turning crisp and cold. We lay together as we had once under Stratford's open sky, only now to the north of the great city beyond Moor Fields where laundresses dried their linens and men practiced shooting at the butts.

I would say more, but I believe such ecstatic memories are privy and sacred. I hope you have your own youthful obsessions and passions and that you think of them, and then you will know how we loved. Why I did not catch a child from him, I know not, but I always thought that for the best. Why, I might have had to marry the wine merchant Nicholas Clere, who still called on me when he visited the Davenants. But I must share one time, a special memory.

Will and I were walking through Blackfriars after seeing our old friend Dick Field in the midautumn of the year Will sold his first plays to Henslowe, the very month, I believe that *Love's La-bour's Lost* was performed for the gentlemen and their ladies of Lord Strange's so-called School of Night.

Fortune had favored Dick, for his master had died and he had inherited his widow and the print shop near St. Paul's. He informed us he was nevermore to be called just plain Dick, but Richard. The newlywed Fields lived on the fringes of Blackfriars, the fine liberty not far from Lilypot Lane where I resided.

We had called on Richard at his house, and Will had a book under his arm his friend had given him, Holinshed's *Chronicles,* I think, for he was working hard on his history plays then. He had left Richard money to take home to the Shakespeares. Will usually sent it with the Greenaway carriers—never with my men—but the Fields were going for a visit and would deliver it, with, of course, news only of Will and not of the both of us.

As we left the print shop and strolled away from the river, we saw that the door and windows to the beautiful Blackfriars eastern gatehouse stood ajar. Though its stalwart sides were attached to tall brick walls that surrounded mansions and gardens within, the structure nevertheless seemed to stand proudly on its own. The slate-roofed building was three stories tall, of muted red brick with black diamond designs that echoed the diamond panes of the leaded windows. It must have fine views of London in each direction, we thought, including the privy gardens of some of the noble mansions nearby. I sighed each time I beheld the place.

"Hello!" Will called in the open door as we stood at the bottom of the stairs. "Just passing by! May we come up and see the view?"

Only the sharp scent of fresh whitewash drifted to us. Because the gatehouse was an edifice with a passageway through the center of the ground floor, the two stories of narrow chambers were upstairs. Holding hands, we tiptoed up a few steps.

"Perhaps they've left it to air out," I whispered. Whether Will was shouting or I was whispering, our voices echoed in the stairwell, which looked newly whitewashed but, with the breeze sucked in and up, seemed dry.

We peeked in the two rooms on the first landing: not one stick of furniture on the polished oak floors and the sunlight streaming in danced along the snow-white walls, dazzling our eyes.

"Does no one live here?" I wondered aloud. "Or perhaps the tenants are about to change."

"Next time 'tis offered, I'll buy it for you," Will promised, though he had but three pounds to his name after sending money back to Stratford.

"Says you, the dreamer, my marvelous maker of fine fictions."

Still holding hands, we tiptoed from room to room as if we were thieves entering while the residents were abed. We ventured up to the next floor, which boasted an even finer view of rooftops, river and sky. This high above the streets, the air blowing in smelled heavenly as it ruffled our hair and buffeted my skirts.

"Of course, when we live here," I said, picking up on his promise, "this shall be our bedchamber, and we shall use the next room for your writing. We shall awake each day in a huge bed here, pull the bed curtains back and—"

"Shh!" he said and turned me to him, putting a finger over my lips.

"You hear someone coming?"

"I don't—that's the point. When someone does return, we'll hear their footfalls or voices before they get to us—to give us time."

Humming, we danced about the room in a fast lavolta, then a slow pavane. Smothering our laughter and love words with kisses, we joined our bodies and hearts standing against the wall between the windows with the panorama of London below and beyond. If the queen herself had come in with a parade of courtiers to see my bodice down and my skirts up to my waist and Will all unlaced, we would not have known nor cared. Not the view, not the city, not the vast world, nothing else existed but we two.

And the highest compliment to me: when we were finished with our loving, Will was so sublimely moved that he forgot his new book and had to run back a block to retrieve it. It was then I knew the power I had over not only the body of the man but his brain too.

I continued to live in the bosom of the Davenant family, but they presented problems for me. The more I cuddled my little godchild Kate, the more I felt guilty about Will's children back in Stratford without their father. The conception of his firstborn, Susannah, had nigh on ruined my life, but I could not blame her and wished her well. And his twins—I know he missed them. It was then I hit upon the idea of commissioning a portrait of Will for him to send home to them, like the one Kit Marlowe had hanging in his bedchamber—well, perhaps one with not so cocky a gaze and imperious a posture.

My second problem was that John Davenant was still fast

friends with my erstwhile suitor Nicholas Clere, who was back from France again and avid to court me. He believed that I was playing coy to become all the dearer. I feared I might even have to leave the Davenants' house to avoid him.

Finally, another problem was Jennet. I had foolishly assumed that when she successfully brought a living child into the world, she would stop drinking to excess. But she didn't; I could smell sweet wine on her breath right now as she helped dress my hair for my visit to Sir Walter Raleigh's house for the premier performance of *Love's Labour's Lost*.

(I had been invited to attend by both Henslowe and Will. Henslowe had turned down my offer to sell him Maud's cushions for the Rose and had—the bootless blackguard—given the order for them to his wife instead. People oft took other's ideas for their own, since there was no protecting such, whether it was seat cushions or plots, characters or lines from plays. As for Penelope Henslowe, I had heard she made "royal" theatre clothes from secondhand ones, so she was in Henslowe's money books already. Still, I held my tongue because he was wild for Will's work. He tried to pretend they were run-of-the-mill to keep his cost down, but Will knew better and bargained accordingly.)

As Jennet fussed overlong with the way my heavy tresses pressed on my standing ruff, the most expensive one I'd ever owned, I dared to ask, "Do you not think that all that wine you drink could get into your mother's milk and that's why Kate sleeps so much?"

"Nonsense, or the milk would surely turn as dark as the claret."

"Urine doesn't."

"Anne—really! But that reminds me, I was wondering if you'd

let me keep a few bottles of it up here—wine, not urine," she said with a jerky laugh. "John's become such a nitpick about counting bottles. He says, if we lose one here and there, it will set back our savings for a country inn. Oh, I long to rear little Kate and whatever brothers or sisters may come, Lord willing, in a smaller town."

"I would let you my cottage near Stratford, but you'd need much more room, and there are already four inns in the town."

"Oxford, John says, a university town with many passing through and droves of ever-thirsty students." She dusted my ivory-hued taffeta leg-o'-mutton sleeves with rose powder. "He has a lead for a place. So what about just a bottle or two stored up here?"

I stood and turned to face her with my polished bronze-faced mirror still in my hand. "Jennet, I want only the best for you and John and, of course, Kate. So you must try to stop drinking as much as you do—"

"You're in league with him, aren't you?" she cried, her voice suddenly dripping venom. Anger contorted her lovely face, and tears glazed her eyes. "Here I share my home, my heart, my child with you, and you can't do that much for me!"

"I fear it has become a crutch. I know it helps smooth over bad or sad feelings like—"

"Like that time you tumbled in here all sotted up after a tumble with Kit Marlowe!"

"You'll not say that. I did not have a tumble with Kit Marlowe! I told you I escaped before—"

"That's not what he says!"

"What? Kit Marlowe's been here? And he dared to say—"

"He's very charming, isn't he? Yes, a month or so ago, just about the time Will sold Henslowe those first plays. I don't know how Kit found us, but maybe he just came to buy wine. John was busy, and I talked to him, amused by how he flattered me. He's been very helpful to me and—"

"Helpful? What do you mean?" I cried, seizing her shoulders with both hands. I knew now Kit had slandered me, as well as trying to harm Will. What if Jennet, in her cups, had hinted to Kit the truth about Will and me? Will had said that Kit had thrown a raving fit over the fact that Henslowe had tried to talk him into taking a lesser fee because he had "stiff competition now, and someone from the shires and not the universities too."

"Let me go!" Jennet cried and twisted from my grasp. "You're not the only one with a good head for money, you know."

"Money? You've taken money from Kit Marlowe? For what?"

"Never mind! Just never mind!"

"Jennet, I'm sorry we have quarreled. I only want you to consider trying to drink less and—"

"You just fix your own hair and collar next time you go prancing out with your Will to a fine lord's home!"

"I'm not going with Will. I'm sitting with Philip Henslowe's wife as Will is acting too. Jennet, please—"

She backed against the wall and pressed her hands over her ears and shook her head like a child in a temper. "Jennet—Jennet—Jennet," she mocked my voice. "Just go with Henslowe's wife then, and she can be your new friend!" To my dismay, she flounced from the room and slammed the door.

The sound reverberated in my heart that evening, throwing a pall over the excitement of visiting the mansion of one of the queen's closest courtiers along the Strand. Here the great lawns rolled out like sheared emerald velvet from the front doors to the ornate water docks on the Thames not far from the palace. In the gardens of Sir Walter Raleigh's grand Durham House, fountains played and peacocks, as good as watchdogs against intruders, screeched and strutted.

As I was offered my choice of wines in Venetian goblets from a silver tray, I caught my breath: this was another world, one right in the heart of London, and Will and I were experiencing it at the same time—if not quite together.

It turned out that Penelope Henslowe and I sat near the back of the large performance chamber—a formal dining hall, it really was—far behind the chattering special guests in their carved chairs. Only household servants allowed to peek in stood behind us. But I didn't mind, as I could soak it all in—the performance, the performers and the spectators—without craning my neck and making a country fool of myself.

I thought Sir Walter Raleigh one of the most well-favored men I had ever seen. Ah, the queen did know how to pick her favorites. Still unwed, he was the only member of Lord Strange's coterie without a lady. Tall, dark-haired and sporting a pointed beard, Raleigh commanded everyone's attention. His gestures were bold, his speech cultured and learned.

"Hard to believe, isn't it," Penelope whispered to me, "that our host is a second son and a self-made man? The queen adores that ilk, I warrant, every whit as much as the titled ones."

"Is it true that he laid his cloak over a mud puddle to keep her dry-shod?"

"So I hear, and he brings her exotic gifts from the New World land he's named Virginia in honor of his Virgin Queen, so who could not be swept off her dry-shod feet by that?"

"And that older man with the long, unkempt beard?" I asked, nodding from behind my ostrich feather fan.

"Dr. John Dee, Her Majesty's brilliant strategist and astrologer—and, some say, spy on his foreign travels. I overheard that he's just come back from the Continent, though public word is out that he's still away. 'Tis also said," she went on, obviously relishing her role as town crier, "that he believes in visions—contact with angels—who speak with him, something or other about looking in a strange mirror."

"Hmm, it seems to me Lord Strange would be the one for that."

She giggled as if I'd made the wildest jest. "Oh, for a certain, Lord Strange is entranced by odd and secret things too. Who knows what they really discuss at their meetings of all men?" She lowered her voice but lifted her eyebrows. "Even witchcraft and the use of elixirs and poisonings, some claim. The School of Night indeed!"

I would have tried to draw more information from her, but I held my tongue. Richard Burbage, who was to play the lead role of King Ferdinand, walked out on the elevated dais to begin. Tears stung my eyes to realize this was the start of Will's London career as a playwright. Soon the masses at the public theatres would see this play and his Roman drama *Titus*, and he was working on a sweeping historical saga peopled with England's ancient royalty and nobility.

I jumped when someone bent to kiss the side of my neck, smashing the edge of my ruff.

I spun in my seat, expecting Will, wondering why he wasn't ready to walk on in the role of Berowne. Kit Marlowe grinned at me like a grotesque gargoyle and made a mocking bow. He darted several rows up to take a seat, though not with the guests.

Penelope sputtered, "A prodigy but a popinjay, that one!"

"What's he doing here?"

"'Tis said he's on the fringe of the School of Night too—the fringe of everything, if you ask me."

I tried to enjoy the first act. How I longed to tell Kit off, to warn him to stay away from Jennet and not to slander me further. Soon the characters and words I knew so well swept me into Will's play. After the first act, Philip Henslowe darted out from behind the makeshift curtain—two tapestries suspended on poles— rubbing his hands together with a proud smile until he saw Kit had come in late. Henslowe frowned and hissed something his way. Kit only gave him an obscene gesture as Henslowe came to sit on his wife's other side, laughing too loudly and tapping his toes at any snatch of song.

Thank heavens, the front-row audience laughed when they should. Blessedly, the ladies loved it. Even, it seemed to me from here, Kit nodded now and then as if the play were his.

I noted things for the first time when I saw it acted rather than read. The theme of being truly able to see things clearly stood out. The poetry was powerful, the sonnets witty, the songs sweet and bouncy, especially the two with country lyrics in honor of spring and winter that ended the comedy. I tried to ignore Kit Marlowe's clenched fist hitting his knee in beat with the familiar, final dance, even as the ladies and their husbands applauded.

My Will was on his way! Surely now, nothing could befall to halt his climb to wealth and fame.

I was thrilled for Will. *Love's Labour's Lost* and *Titus Andronicus* were popular enough, but the first two plays of his historical trilogy *King Henry VI* took London by storm. It was the patriotic passion in them, I reckoned, the battles with the French and final victory over them, but it was the wonderfully human characters rising to meet their destinies too. The groundlings and the galleries alike stood and cheered, but for me it was two nonhistorical rants in the plays that stood out. In the first drama, Will wrote these lines:

> *For what is wedlock forced but a hell,*
> *An age of discord and continual strife?*
> *Whereas the contrary bringeth bliss*
> *And is a pattern of celestial peace.*

In part three, even more to the point, he wrote, "Hasty marriage seldom proveth well," and on it went in all his later plays, should anyone care to consult them—if I pray, Will's work is still performed when you do read this work of mine.

But as for what Will called "the contrary," meaning willing wedlock, I cannot say our times together were "a pattern of celestial peace." We argued heartily and far too often.

"Now that Leicester's moldering in his grave and Lord Strange has become our company's patron," Will said as we took a wherry across the Thames on a Sabbath afternoon, "that doesn't mean I still don't need a noble patron to support just my plays and poetry. I do, desperately so, to give myself more time to write."

Patronage was also of key import for an ambitious poet—which Will was also—as it provided income and social recognition. And for the patrons of poetry especially, the flowery dedications praising them elevated their position even more among courtiers and scholars, even university students.

I sighed and leaned back on the cushioned seat as the banks of Southwark skimmed past. "So many of my hopes for you have come true," I told him, "so why not dream big dreams? Should Her Majesty command a performance at court, dare you ask her to be a patron?"

"I might dare, but I don't want her."

"Will Shakespeare, whatever is wrong with you? You sound as if—" I cried, until he held a finger to his lips and darted a glance toward our boatman. After all, if actors and astrologers can be spies, why not a man bent over his oars?

But as soon as we alighted at Paris Gardens, I was not to be put off. "You didn't mean it—that you would turn down patronage by Her Majesty. Surely not!"

"After what has happened to my family, to my shire, to my country, why not?"

"But—in a way, you speak treason."

"I speak nothing of the kind."

"She's only listening to her counselors, Walsingham, Cecil and the like when she strikes out against her enemies."

"She's the queen, Anne, so ultimately, she is responsible. I may bow and smile before her in a play at court—even my own play— but you may bet that the bow and smile are my best acting."

"Have you been invited to play at court? Oh, Will, if so, I want to go!"

"Ever rhyming couplets, my Anne, even when things get out of hand."

"What gets out of hand? I adore our queen and have since the day we first saw her at Kenilw—"

"A dreadful day burned in my brain. I was grateful when the players' having to spy for her went by the wayside with Leicester's death, so let's leave it at that."

There were other worse rows between us, especially when he played *Love's Labour's Lost* at court with Lord Strange's Men and didn't tell me until after. "Did you think I would beg you to go?" I questioned him when he told me. I was furious and vowed I'd ask his fellows the Burbages and the clown Kemp what it was like there, since Will said nary a word of it.

"Beg me? Rather," he said, frowning, "I thought you'd dress like a boy and slip right in with us, much as you did into Kit Marlowe's arms—I pray not his bed too—the day I sent you the tickets to his play, more fool I."

"He's not been spreading lies about me again, has he?" I questioned, jumping in front of him as he walked me home, so he had to stop and face me. "I know he'd love to disparage you and your talents. He's jealous of you, Will, and it pleases him to taunt and hurt you, that's all."

"A clever shift of subjects, Mistress Whateley. But if so, you have given him the gunpowder to do such, haven't you? All we need is for him to discover the truth of us and spread it around. It would do me in—especially damn any hope I have of attracting a powerful personal patron for my plays or poetry."

"A pox on the man! He's tampered with Jennet's opinion of me and now yours. I fear I'll have to face him down."

"Alone? In his hovel of a place with that leering portrait of him on the wall perhaps?"

"You've been in Kit's place?"

"Sat on the very bed you've been in."

"Will, that was a mistake, I grant you that—"

"That he's had you?"

"It's not true!" I cried, stamping my feet and clenching my fists. I could have pounded his chest in my frustration and fury. "I mean, yes, I was there, but only since he got me drunk on that poison they call dragon's milk, because I was angry with you."

"Ah, I see. It was my fault you ended up in his bed."

"After all we've been to each other, I—I can't fathom you believe that blackguard."

"All right then, let me mention someone I do believe. I believe," he went on, maddening me more each moment, "I recall a letter from Dick Field when I was still stuck in Stratford that you told him you were 'tired of living like a nun in a cloister and for what' here in London. Yes, according to him, I believe those were your exact words."

"How dare you shift this off on me! You are the one who wed elsewhere—after," I lowered my voice now, "you wed with me. I believe your work is addling your brain, making you jealous and for naught. What is that line in *Two Gentlemen of Verona*? 'For love, thou knowest, is full of jealousy.'"

"I swear, woman, but you can quote anything to suit your cause. I am not each character I create and—"

But I was past being seduced by his pretty words and ready

lines. "If you cannot trust me after all these years, I want no part of you," I insisted. "A pox on you as well as Marlowe! Devil take you! Your hand is better now that I've been doing all your writing and copying, so just write out all the plays yourself!" I screeched and left him standing there.

It was only one of our battles royal, and our making up was always sweet. But I should have realized not to curse people by saying "Devil take you!" or "A pox on you!" for all too soon, I was facing both.

CHAPTER FOURTEEN

❦

I did come to see Kit Marlowe as the very devil. He dared to send me a note via Jennet, telling me that his lips would be forever sealed about my tumble in his bed would I but meet him elsewhere—dressed again as a lad. Now, wouldn't that be a pretty lime trap for a little bird, I thought. I tore up the note and stamped on it.

I was tempted to send Kit a note back, hinting that I'd overheard him and Mr. Mercer talking about spying, but I feared he'd have Mercer get rid of me or do it himself. Finally, one day when I was tending little Kate for Jennet so she could take a nap—she was newly pregnant again—I found a way to at least put one over on Kit.

From my room one floor up where I was tending Kate, who had finally outgrown her leading strings, I heard Jennet scream.

"Mama crying?" the child asked as I scooped her up and took the stairs down as carefully but as quickly as I could. Jennet's crying out like that dragged me back to the dreadful day of Kate's birth, but this new pregnancy was barely showing yet. She'd never lost a babe this early.

"Jennet, what?" I cried as I rushed into her room. I could hear men's voices below in the shop. John must not have heard.

She was sitting bolt upright on her bed with the counterpane clutched around her. "Jennet, where does it hurt?" I asked. "I can take Kate down to the maids and be right back so—"

"I—it was a nightmare—that I lost this one," she said, looking more shaken than I'd seen her in months. She laid her hands over her still-flat stomach. "It was so real."

"I'm not lost, Mama," Kate declared.

"Here then," I said and boosted the child up onto the bed and perched on the edge myself.

"It reminded me though," Jennet said, hugging Kate to her with one arm, but reaching out to take my hand with the other, "how good you've been to me, even when you have had your own pains. And I've been a dreadful shrew about—about the claret."

"Auntie Anne have hurts?" Kate asked, looking at me.

"No, I'm fine," I assured my godchild. She was fair and blond like her mother, so different from me and yet I loved and tended her as my own.

"Anne," Jennet went on, "I know Kit Marlowe's been your cross to bear—well, one of them anyway—so I've decided to tell you—to ask for your help and give mine to you if we can manage. He's doing the same thing to me, threatening to tell John lies. He's given me an ultimatum. Ah, Marta," she said as her housemaid knocked and stuck her head in the door, "take Kate downstairs for a treat, will you now?"

At the magic word *treat*, Kate slid off the bed onto the mounting stool without a fuss and when we two were alone again, Jennet said, "I should have listened to you. I swear that man is Satan's henchman."

"He is the very devil, and I'd like to be rid of him, whatever loss it would be to London's stages. Will knows not to trust him, but he always takes Kit's bait—again and again. And that strange streak of jealousy that rises in him when I've given him no reason to—well, a pox on Kit Marlowe."

"Will's so good at probing everyone else's motives in his plays or in life, but Kit's got his goat, all right. It's because he loves you so, yet cannot really claim or protect you without risking everything you both hold dear."

"But what ultimatum from Kit to you?"

"Not a fate worse than death, at least. He says I have a face like an angel and he wants me to help him fool some old man who believes angels appear to him when he gazes in some sort of celestial mirror."

I snapped my fingers. "Dr. John Dee."

"Who?"

"Her Majesty's advisor in many things, not a medical doctor, but a learned man. Penelope Henslowe says that under Queen Mary Tudor he was accused of witchcraft because he rigged stage machinery so it seemed that the classical gods could fly in from the heavens to end the plays—a *deus ex machina*."

"I know you and Will understand all that stagecraft, but was this Dr. Dee persecuted for dealing with demons or the devil?" she asked, her eyes as wide as dinner plates.

"All false accusations. He ended up befriending his jailer and proving how silly the charges were."

"Well, I say, with your help, maybe Will's too, we can warn this Dr. Dee and ruin Kit's plans—put him in his place. He'd dare not tell John this babe I carry is his, which is what he's hinted he would do. I'd hire someone to kill him first!"

"Jennet!" I said, appalled at her vehemence, but had I not just said much the same thing? "Yet," I had to add, "I know how you feel about the man. I have another idea, one that will shame Kit so that—perhaps—he will learn not to toy with you, me and Will, if Will will help us. And mayhap John too. Are you game?"

"Oh, yes! Say on."

Despite the fact the Bible teaches, "Vengeance is mine, sayeth the Lord," the night the four of us—John and Will too—set Kit Marlowe back on his heels was one I shall not forget. Our intent was deadly serious, yet it brought all of us closer. We enjoyed it immensely, despite the dangers. Best of all, Will learned that Kit Marlowe was taunting Jennet as well as me, and he knew full well, however much Kit plied her with drink, she would not betray John.

So, I think, though he came by that knowledge the hard way, he finally learned that I had not lain with Kit Marlowe. What I had learned by now was that, despite Will's intellect and oft calm and analytic persona, he could be a raving fool when eaten by jealousy. I suppose it served him well years later when he created Othello, his love Desdemona and the lying villain Iago. As he wrote in *The*

Comedy of Errors, "How many fond fools serve mad jealousy!" That night, though we were perhaps foolish, we served not jealousy, but revenge on Kit Marlowe and had such fun doing so.

It turned out that Kit had arranged a private demonstration for Dr. Dee in the very second-floor chamber wherein Kit's portrait hung. According to Jennet, Kit had also hung a curtain there—of course, I knew right where the painting and curtain were. She said Kit had duped Dr. Dee out of twenty pounds for the purchase of a new "cosmic and celestial" mirror, which was in truth the bottom of a polished copper kettle. Therein, an angel was to appear when Marlowe tried to summon it, in a practice Dr. Dee called scrying.

Having crawled under the curtain from her hiding place beneath Kit's bed, then rising from behind the mirror, the ethereal Jennet was to stun the brilliant man until Kit revealed all and made a mockery of the old man's fervent if foolish beliefs. And then, I supposed, Kit could blackmail or taunt Dee as he loved to do others.

But our plan went like this:

"John," Will said, "be sure to pull the ladder away once we've climbed inside, but be prepared to get it back to us when you see Anne at the window."

"Both of you keep a good eye on Jennet," John insisted. "That blackguard tries to get the coins back he gave her, and I'll ram each one down his throat."

"I like your spirit," Will told him. "But if we get caught, there may be hell to pay."

"But this way," I put in, "Kit will have hell to pay. Let's go!"

While Kit entertained Dee and his wife, Jane, in the other half of the room before the demonstration began, Jennet had made certain the window was open for Will and me to crawl in, just as I had crawled out that other night. Will had groused that this was a daft scheme, but now a big grin of anticipation split his face. I reckoned he might use it in a play someday.

But he'd preached caution too. Though not in earshot of John, Will had wagered me that we would only end up rescuing Jennet before Kit could ravish her, however much he preferred boys. Yet the idea of the three of us besting his nemesis appealed mightily to him.

Fortunately, the buzz of voices covered any sound we made. Stealthily, Will lifted the portrait of Kit off the wall and I doctored it up with a mix of sticky salve and seacoal dust that Maud had concocted for us. Whatever we thought of Kit, we knew better than to permanently deface his fine portrait, and this stuff would wipe off well enough.

I thought again of the painting of Will I'd sent home to his children in his name and with his blessing. He'd looked so earnest in it, so clear-eyed and determined. Surely, whatever their mother told them of their sire, they would see those qualities in him someday and understand why he had to be away. At least his parents and his brothers Edmund and Richard still lived in the household with Anne Hathaway and the three children. Will had been especially close to little Edmund. I prayed his parents and siblings would say good things of Will, the family's breadwinner.

I tilted Kit's portrait toward Will so he could survey my handiwork. He smothered a snort at the sight. Kit Marlowe now sported horns, a heavier mustache and a pointed beard. I added a crude pitchfork in his hand, then stuck the gooey pot and brush down between Kit's sheets where I also wiped my hand. Kit's so-called polished mirror lay at the foot of the bed as if awaiting its cue.

"We are ready to begin, Dr. Dee," we heard Kit intone from the other side of the curtain. That was followed by a scraping of chairs, so Will and I dove behind the bed. "Yes, face the curtain, and I shall fetch the celestial speculum, given me by a man who adored my Doctor Faustus play, a man who believes in life after death according to our just deserts."

In the dim light from the fading day outside, I saw Will do quite a good rendition of Marlowe with his eyes crossed and his tongue hanging out as if choked by a noose around his neck. Now I had to stifle a giggle. Jennet, looking like an angel indeed, peeked out from under the bed. Her cue was to be, "See, it arises!" I wasn't sure why Kit didn't just bribe one of the boy actors to take this part, but then none of them could possibly approach Jennet in angelic beauty.

Kit went on, blathering to Dr. Dee about the magical powers of the mirror. I was grateful Will could be in on all this, not only so I wasn't blamed for coming back here on my own, but so that he could hear again what a liar Kit was.

Will got in position to have the portrait replace Jennet's appearance, which would be a mighty shock to clever Kit. I gave the high sign out the window to John to bring the ladder back. I reckoned we'd been here about a quarter of an hour and, despite our behind-the-curtain merrymaking, my stomach was knotted like a rope. The moment Will placed the portrait before the mirror, he would follow me down the ladder, while, in the confusion, Jennet would dart out the doorway to the hall. We feared not only that she wouldn't make it down the ladder in time, but that she could fall and hurt the child she was carrying. If Kit tried to stop her escape, we—her husband included—would come charging to his door to get her out.

The scene worked as smoothly as if Will had written it instead of me. Poor Dr. Dee gasped as Jennet appeared as an angel, but he broke into huge guffaws when the devilish portrait of Kit suddenly seemed to levitate in her place as Jennet lifted it into their view. Though Kit swore a string of oaths, Jennet reported, as she ran breathless out into the street to meet us, he had no choice but to pretend he'd staged the joke.

"Let's go," Jennet cried, hugging John while he and Will shouldered the ladder. We were all holding our sides, sore with laughter. "However jovial it all seems," she gasped out, "if he sees us . . ."

"If he fusses about it at all," Will declared, "I shall write it into *The Comedy of Errors* with a topical allusion to be sure he's the butt of the joke, and then what can he do?"

I wanted to say that he could do plenty, but it was a wonderful night—the last for years—as the four of us hurried away with our ladder, buoyed up by laughter and love.

CHAPTER FIFTEEN

꠵

As far as I was concerned, another cursed comet might as well have come slashing through the sky to signal dread and destruction. For one thing, poor Jennet miscarried yet another child, which made Kate all the more precious. The new decade of the 1590s, which should have showered Will and me with joy and bounty, brought nothing but ill fortune—except for the fact that Sir Francis Walsingham died that year. But just as Robert Cecil was taking over at court as the queen's chief minister for his increasingly ill father, Lord Burghley, the young Cecil also took over Walsingham's covert yet blatant watch on us all.

Will had described these days best in a play he was writing about a pair of passionate but star-crossed young lovers beset by feuding families. *Romeo and Juliet* was taken from earlier stories but was also based on our early days in Stratford, though Will had transplanted the play to the popular site of Italy. (All things Italian, including my dark looks, were in fashion these days, but more on that later.) Will's line was "These violent delights have violent ends." And so it seemed for us and all of London.

Will was working both as an actor and playwright with Lord Strange's Men at the Curtain while the Lord Admiral's Men played at the Theatre next door, but the Burbages oversaw both places and sometimes mingled casts. By then, Will's plays were performed in those theatres, in Henslowe's Rose, in the great carrier inns and, even, more than once at court—the latter a subject we avoided so we wouldn't argue about the queen.

Our terrible times that year began with a bit of violence that was somehow both domestic and yet public too. One in which we were innocent bystanders and yet suffered for.

As Will and I were leaving the Curtain one chill November eve in 1590, we heard screeching. At first, I thought it was a wounded bear in a nearby cage, but we saw it was a woman with a small band of rough-looking men in a shouting match with Will's friend and mentor, James Burbage. Burbage faced the small mob just outside the Curtain.

We finally made out something besides curses. "You been cheating me and mine, Burbage, pocketing gate receipts, now hain't you? You still owe my husband more than a pittance."

We went a bit closer. The brawny woman was shaking her fist in the silver-haired Burbage's face.

"You must have mistaken me for the quick-fingered Philip Henslowe, Mistress Brayne," Burbage shouted back, "so take your rabble and be off with you!"

Will told me over the noise, "That must be the actor John Brayne's widow. At least Tom Kyd or Ben Jonson aren't here to pitch into this fray. They'd love nothing more, and Jonson's drinking and brawling will get him in real trouble some day."

Will was right. Later, Jonson killed an actor named Gabriel Spencer in a duel in Shoreditch Fields. He was tried for it and narrowly escaped the hangman's noose by being able to read the so-called neck verse in Latin, Psalm 51, admitting sin and begging for redemption. Still, he'd been branded with the Tyburn T on his thumb so that if he ever assaulted another person, he'd be hanged outright.

As for playwright Brayne and his vociferous widow, as with Marlowe or Jonson, this just went to show that many of the artists of the day—actors and playwrights alike—were not coddled, heads-in-the clouds persons but brazen brawlers. Even the Widow Brayne carried on that legacy, and I recalled how loudly Richard Tarlton's widow had bellowed at his memorial service, interrupting the speakers. It made me grateful that Will spent his free time either writing or with me—usually both and the same. He had a reputation for diligence among his fellows, unlike those who loved to drink, brawl and whore.

Meanwhile, the Widow Brayne was not to be put off. She was obviously after funds she felt were owed Brayne or her, and was not a bit shy about publicly berating Burbage.

"My friends come here to see you pay up! Not quick-fingered, but sticky-fingered, that's you and your ilk!" she screamed and launched into a string of oaths that would have made a sailor proud.

Suddenly, James' son Richard, the great actor Will was hot to write for, appeared with a broom and began to swing it at Mistress Brayne's men. His deep voice rang out over the crowd, "You'll not gainsay my father! I'll send you scum packing! Go bray, bray, bray your lies somewhere else, Widow Bra-bra-brayne, you bawdy, beslubbering, beef-witted harpy!"

Fists flew with insults and curses. I feared more than a broomstick would become a weapon and sensed Will was tempted to wade in with the Burbages. I tried to tug him away, but someone heaved a brick. It grazed Will's temple, making a small stream of blood that I tried to stanch with my skirt.

"Hell's gates," he muttered as he sat against a building around the corner while I tended him, "I'm seeing shooting stars!"

That was the harbinger of our newest onslaught of tough times, for soon the battle was of another sort. Lord Strange's Men had a falling-out with the Lord Admiral's Men and split into two groups. Will stayed with the Burbages at the Theatre, while the rest of Lord Strange's company left with famed actor Edward Alleyn for the Rose across the river. That was pretty much the end of Lord Strange's patronage of their company. Burbage's actors later picked up the artistic benefactor William Herbert, the Earl of Pembroke, but for a while they were adrift, and Will was panicked to find a patron for his own plays and poetry.

Ironically, he wanted to ask someone I had met years before at the clown Tarlton's memorial service, the handsome young Earl of Southampton. For one thing, it turned out the earl was distantly related to Will through the Ardens. He was still shy of twenty years now, but he adored poets and playwrights; it was all the rage for them to dedicate sugary sonnets to him. Will said the next time Henry Wriothesley, Lord Southampton, sat upon the stage to see a play all the better, he'd slip him a flattering poem and dare to introduce himself.

The only good thing to come of the rift between the actors was that, though Will had at first alienated Henslowe by not going to the Rose with the others, he was now the Burbages' chief playwright. And it turned out that Henslowe still could not resist Will's work—if there was to be a venue for such work at all.

For next in our onslaught of misfortune, a riot of apprentices erupted on Bankside, led by ruffians who spread the fray across the river. The queen's Privy Council promptly closed all the playhouses for three months, forcing the players to take a tour of the country-side to stay solvent.

"I must tell you," Will said as we walked back into the city from a rural tryst, a farewell for we knew not how long, "that our travels will include three nights in Stratford on the first three days of October."

"Ah, so you'll be home. You'll see everyone."

"I will be glad to see my children and my parents, make no mistake about that. As for the other . . ."

"The other Mistress Shakespeare."

"It brings it all home again—you know what I mean," he told me as he tightened his arm around my shoulders to grapple us closer as we walked reluctantly back toward the city. "How I long to make things right between us. To rewrite our history, so I don't have a country wife and a—"

"A city wife."

"Yes, well, there's nothing good about the situation, except for the exquisite depths of anger and agony to which the situation has plunged me."

"You mean it's all fodder for the passions in your plays."

"You realize how we almost finish each other's thoughts?" he asked as the walls of the city came in view. "I pray that on the road without you, I shall be able to complete my long *Venus and Adonis* poem and have time for the plays too, though without my muse . . ."

"And her pen writing down the words that spill from you . . ."

"Anne," he cried and turned me to him, "I shall miss you so. But we'll be back in three months, opening again for London crowds, together forever, I pray."

I bit my lip to keep from crying. Forever was such a very long time when one did not even have tomorrow.

We walked a bit apart as we entered the city. It was a good thing, for someone soon spotted Will and ran up to him, waving a piece of paper.

"A reprieve?" I heard him ask the man, someone I did not recognize. "Did the Council agree to hear our petition to reopen the theatres?"

I could not catch the man's reply, but he shook his head as Will took the paper and bent over it. What? I wondered. Something about the queen? At least it did not look as if it could be a letter with dire news from home.

"Have the Burbages seen this?" Will asked the man. "No? Then best show it to them—no, let me keep this. There are many ways to stage a fight, and this reeks of a sneaky one."

When the man left him, Will came to me at once. "I've been attacked and by my so-called fellows," he said, thrusting the printed page at me. "Here!" he said, pointing, and his fine voice broke. A frown furrowed his brow; he looked as if he would cry. I tore my eyes away from his distress to read aloud:

"There is an upstart crow, beautified with our feathers, that with 'his Tiger's heart wrapped in a player's hide,'

"He's quoted a line from your *Henry VI*," I said, then went on:

"supposes he is as well able to bombast out a blank verse as the best of you, and being an absolute Johannes Factotum, is in his own conceit the only Shake-scene in a country."

"Who wrote this drivel?" I demanded. "And what, pray tell, is a 'Johannes Factotum'?"

"Who wrote it? Playwright Robert Greene, the drunken lout. And the pompous Latin phrase means I am a jack-of-all-trades, a do-it-all—at least in my own eyes. More like a pompous jackass," he muttered.

"You are talented in many ways, and Greene is jealous."

"You said the same about Kit. I can understand competition, but must they roast me publicly on a barbed grill? Even Ben Jonson, a bricklayer by trade, no less, though he was educated at Westminster, has assailed my lack of education, telling people I have 'Little Latin and less Greek.' I'll just show them with *Venus and Adonis*! It's rife with classical characters and allusions."

"Curse them all, you are not writing in Latin and Greek. You have a way with depicting real people who, like your audience, don't speak to each other in Latin and Greek."

"I pray you, don't say the other writers are just jealous again."

"All right then, they are bitter. You've proved that playwrights need not stick to their precious classical unities of time and place and can use all classes of people who try to solve their own problems without the silly pagan gods riding in on clouds with wheels to help them out! I don't care what you say, they are jealous of your God-given talents!"

He almost smiled. "I detest jealousy. It's a weakness and yet it shows a sort of perverted strength. It eats at me. I can't help it, and I have no right, but I am ever jealous of others' attentions to you. Yet you have every right to go off with someone else, since I can't give you what you deserve."

I stood amazed he had admitted such and apologized for it too. It continually angered me that, after all we'd been through, he thought I would betray him with another man—however much I had once wanted to do such, *anything* to get back at him for putting me on the rack of tormented love.

"Will, the others have you doubting yourself, so stop it. Just promise me on your days on the rural roads—and at home—that you won't forget me."

"Impossible! I will love you—I, Will, love you."

Though he was still seething, we continued on our way, parting near St. Paul's with forlorn, mutual waves. Before turning my face toward home, I watched the milling crowds swallow him up. Despite our looming separation, I hoped for better times soon.

But a few days after he'd left town, more than the theatres closed from a cause worse than rioters or slurs. Like a monstrous demon, ravenous for human lives, the Black Death came to devour us.

People who had the means to do so left London like rats off a sinking ship. In his dray that usually brought wine bottles from the wharf, John and Jennet took little Kate and went to Oxford to stay in the inn they were considering buying. Before they fled, John buried some of his bottles of choicest wine in their tiny herb garden and took others, swathed in sheets, with them.

They offered to take me too, but I said I'd leave with my carriers who were due in two days. Where I'd stay at home, I wasn't sure, for my little cottage was still leased to others, but I could rent a room from someone in Temple Grafton. If it were not for the Shakespeares right down Henley Street, I would ask my Whateley kin to take me in again and pay them this time too.

Both Davenant housemaids and John's shop man had not come in, but I was grateful for that and even more relieved that the actors were already out of town, so I knew Will was safe from the plague. Rationing my food and drinking only wine, I'd not gone out for two days and kept the house quite closed. With an onion stuffed with figs, rue and treacle about my neck to ward off deadly air, I dared to venture outside. Maud had brought me this smelly protection; she was making a lot of coin selling such. Though it was a nice enough day, I was careful not to take deep breaths.

As I walked toward the Maiden Head Inn to meet my carriers and tell them we must turn about and head home at once, I was surprised to see how deserted the streets were. I stopped to read the *Bill of the Dead* posted on the apothecary shop, though I stood a ways back from it and squinted to make out the words. I couldn't read the names from here, but I could make out the numbers. Five hundred and seven Londoners dead already—forty-nine in this ward, but nearly two hundred up in Shoreditch! Damnation, but the theatres there would be blamed again.

On one door just before I reached the inn were displayed the telltale signs of an infected house. Cursing myself for not taking the alley shortcut, which I'd feared might trap more dangerous air, I beheld the dreaded bundle of straw, the red cross painted on the door and, in whitewash, the scrawled plea, "Lord have mercy upon us."

I stood still and stared. It was the first time terror had truly immobilized me. Then, from within the house, someone began screaming, maybe in pain, maybe grieving.

I went on but pressed myself to a wall once again as two men walking beside a cart pulled by a lumbering ox approached me. Someone selling food at steep prices, I thought, for I'd heard them go by in the streets the first day or so. But the stench struck me before the sight of the bodies did, piled in the cart like cordwood.

"Bring out yer dead!" the driver shouted as he reined in at the plague house I'd just passed. "Bring out yer dead!"

Holding my reeking onion clear up to my nose, I ran toward the huge, bustling inn where I'd first alighted when I came to London ten years ago. But the doors where carrier trains entered and set out for the shires were closed and bolted. Silence ruled here too but for the barking of a distant dog. I ran around to the side door that faced the alley. It was unlocked, so I darted in.

I saw only an old man burning something in the middle of the courtyard. That stench, too, hit me in the pit of my stomach, and I almost dry-heaved. Old shoes? Yes, it looked to be just that, with a saddle and leather reins and traces in the flames.

"You there!" he shouted when he saw me. "Stand clear."

"I'm Anne Whateley. I have a Stratford pack train coming in today," I shouted, not going closer.

He snorted and shook his grizzled head. "City gates closed,

though there's a way out of the city. It'll spread, mark my words. It'll spread if folks don't prevent the distemper by burning leather like this to cloak the pest'lent air."

I leaned back against the wall to steady my shaking legs. Without people coming in, that meant no food—and no pack trains with which to escape the city. Trapped. I was trapped like poor Kat under the river ice where she couldn't breathe as I was afraid to take a breath of this contaminated air.

"The contagion got ye?" the old man demanded.

"No, but I just didn't realize . . ." My voice trailed off. "Are there any horses here? I can pay."

"One old nag, may have to eat her if this goes on."

"Can she hold me? I need to leave the city by the way you mentioned—what is it?"

"Money means naught to me, mistress. Old as I am, I want to live—not sure why. Someone would take the horse right out from under you, but you can try walking out."

"But if the city gates are closed—"

"Just after dawn, watchmen open the gates on the bridge for coaches, though hear tell most of the nobles already gone. You can run out beside a coach if they don't stop you—food for sale right outside the gates, 'tis said too."

Stunned, I went out and closed the door behind me. A rat scurried across my path, not an unusual sight. I took the alley home this time, opened the door with my key and shut myself in. I slumped at the table, feeling alone and scared. I was flushed—that was a first sign, was it not? Yet I had just run a ways. My stomach hurt, another dreadful harbinger, but it could be just fear and despair. Tormented perhaps by ordinary aches and pains, I was afraid to examine my armpits, neck and groin for the sore places that bloomed to the telltale black, putrid swellings called buboes.

How had it come to this, so alone without my friends, without Will, without anyone? Unless Maud came to stay with me as I had asked, I had no one, no one . . . Then too, not only Will's livelihood but mine was now ruined by this visitation of the Black Death, and I could only pray my life would not be forfeit too.

The death carts rumbled by daily. Drinking too much wine, just like Jennet, I planned my escape. I had a fat purse of coins I could not leave behind, for I'd heard thieves ransacked empty houses. I hid some up in the thatch over my room and sewed the rest into the hems of Jennet's black mourning gown and into pockets I made inside my best boots until they became too heavy to lift and I took those back out. The coffer of stylish clothes I'd been so pleased with meant nothing to me now as I donned the black mourning gown with the heavy hem full of my fortune.

Whatever befell, I vowed, even though I would have to make the journey partly in the dark to be at the bridge at dawn, I was going to walk out of plague London. The child's chant I hadn't heard for years danced through my head: "London bridge is falling down, falling down, falling down, my fair lady . . ."

For yet another day, I lived and slept in the kitchen and pantry, closing off the rest of the house, including stuffing rags up the chimney. Outside air was the enemy, that and my dwindling hoard of food. I reckoned I had two more days of it left, and some of what I had was rotting. I saved dried apples and last year's walnuts to take with me when I fled on the morrow.

The day I planned to leave, I slept fitfully on a pallet before the hearth where dreadful nightmares assailed me. I lost little Kate when she slipped out of my hands into the Thames . . . Kit Marlowe and Mr. Mercer with a rabble behind them pounded on my door to get in . . . I was pressed down, down by reeking corpses in a death dray . . . I was carted off to be tortured and hanged for being Will's other wife.

I jolted awake so fast that I wasn't sure where I was. There *was* knocking on my door, the alley door. And Maud—Maud's voice, calling my name.

I scrambled up and tripped over my blanket to sprawl on all fours on the hard, cold hearthstones. "Maud? Just a moment!"

"I've more preventions and cures!" she shouted through the door. "I've sold much but saved some for us."

For us, I thought. That sounded so good. I was glad she had returned. I would have company, a travel companion for my escape. And she had safeguards against the pestilence!

As I pulled the bolt on the alley door, I began to cry with relief. Was it noon yet? If so, we had hours to kill before we could head toward the bridge and Southwark beyond. Perhaps we could go to the sea, where the air must surely be fresh and free. Perhaps we could—

The moment I opened the door, Maud fell at my feet in some sort of swoon. Her basket of powders and perfumed waters spilled out and something sweet broke; a pile of groats with some shillings tumbled out to ring and spin merrily on the floor. She was sweating so hard that her bodice stuck to her as if she'd been swimming. I gasped and pressed both hands over my mouth as, appalled, I stared at her.

It must be the plague, and if it was, odds were we would both be dead by the morrow.

But I nursed her for hours, into the next day. I could have fled, but I washed her in white wine and covered her up on my hearth pallet. With some diseases, it was essential to sweat the poisons out. I wasn't sure about the plague, but I was certain Maud had it. A big, black bubo had bloomed under her left arm. It horrified me and agonized her. Though she knew who I was, she babbled incessantly; some of it made sense, but some was feverish gibberish. I was so exhausted that I jerked asleep and dreamed I was tending my raving da before he died.

"A man told me drinking mummy in wine would help," she said, waking me. "But we can't get a dead body off the street. They've had the plague. We can't use something so defiled." She seized my wrist as I tried to bathe her throat and arms again. I'd stripped to my shift because it was so hot in here, even with no fire.

"Unicorn horn mixed with angelica root," Maud rambled on. "I have the roots but not the horn, or I'd have made a pretty penny. But maybe both of us have been too greedy—theatre cushions and all. The Almighty has punished me with the Lord's token," she cried, referring to her bubo. "If He spares me, I'll be a safe nurse and you too, hired by the nobles to nurse their sick . . ."

"Don't talk, Maud. Just rest."

"Remember that first day you saw me selling sweet herbs to make the body glad but heal the mind and heart? Remember that basil can take away sorrowfulness and rosemary cure nightmares?"

"Yes, I remember. Would to God it were all true."

"It doesn't work, does it? I must have lied. The Lord is punishing me with the Black Death."

"Then why do some good folk die and the evil live?"

"You love him, don't you?"

"Yes, I love the Lord."

"No—your actor, Will, your genius."

"Yes, that's the way of it," I said, because it felt so good to say it. Then I realized I was only admitting it to Maud because I believed she would not live, when I should not give up. And if she died, would I not be close behind without anyone to care or love or nurse me?

She began to recite recipes for tussie-mussies or herbal cures—I didn't know or care. Her voice became weaker until she seemed to sleep. I nodded off . . . off the bridge into the rushing river.

To my horror, I jerked awake to see she was up, wandering the room. She tried to lift the door latch with all her wasted might. I'd heard those afflicted sometimes ran like demented souls through the streets.

"Maud! Maud, come over here and rest."

"No rest for the wicked," she told me with a strange laugh, but she came back into the center of the room. In a singsong voice, she said "Angelica, ivory, mithridate and black pitch to smear on that man's face you hate. That wicked man, who has sold his soul somewhere, somewhere . . ."

When I tried to lead her back to her pallet, she pushed me away. "No!" she shrieked. "I want to die outside where I can see the sky. I want to be buried with sweet herbs, not in a mass grave with sick people—no!"

She swung a fist at me but missed and, like a rag doll, crumpled into the rushes on the floor. Rather than trying to drag her to the pallet, I brought the pillow over for her head, but I need not have. My friend lay dead at my feet.

I felt like a traitor, dragging Maud's body out when the death cart came. I stared horrified when the two men took her slender form, swung her once and heaved her atop the pile of corpses. But I had stuffed every sweet herb I could find inside the winding sheet I'd made from a curtain: dried roses, lavender, rue and basil and sweet summer meadow woodruff.

The man who approached the front door with both red and white paint stunned me. "Inside, then," he ordered, pointing with his bloody-tipped brush. "Lord have mercy, because that and the cross is what I must put here now. Your back and front doors will be sealed, but someone will be by to see if you need victuals or water once a week, come Wednesday next, and you can haul things up to a second-story window."

Wednesday, I thought. Three days away and I too could be dead by starvation or plague by then, and how would I ever get out of the city if they sealed me in?

I knew protest would avail me naught. Without a word, I went back in and closed the wine shop door. I hugged myself hard as the banging of nails in boards sounded from the front door and then the back as if I were being sealed in a coffin. I sat on the floor behind the counter in John's shop and stared into the darkness. At least I did not feel feverish but cold, so cold, like being encased in ice. For the first time—no, perhaps the second, counting that day I'd heard Will must wed another—I understood why Kat had killed herself. She felt abandoned, all alone. She did not want to face life; she did not want to live.

But I did. I did! I had things to do, places to go, poems to read and Will's plays to see. Huddled in the dark, I made a vow to myself: if I was not feverish or laid low with inward burning or agonized by a blasted bubo by two hours before dawn on the morrow, I was escaping this house somehow and getting out of town.

I had never prayed so hard in all my life, but I prepared in other ways to flee too. Still shaking from losing Maud so terribly and so quickly, just like my da's death, I dressed in my boy's attire and bound my breasts and my hair. Gathering my last apple and a pocket of walnuts, I cut the hem with its sewn coins off the black skirt and wrapped and tied it around my waist. I rigged a rope as if ready to haul up food and water Wednesday next, but, Lord willing, I hoped to be far away from London by then. And the Lord must be willing because I had no signs of the Black Death on me, at least not yet, and I knew it always struck suddenly and finished its work as quickly as it had with Maud.

I mourned her, but I was not going to die or be buried as she had. After I stuck my head out of John and Jennet's bedroom window to ascertain the street was empty—and it had been so for hours since a most stringent curfew was in effect—I let myself down my rigging. I rued the fact that someone might try to climb up the same way to get in, but perhaps the bundle of straw and warnings on the door would serve as safeguards. If not, I'd hidden pewter plates, extra clothes and the remaining wine behind heavy pieces of furniture.

Pulling my hat low over my face, carrying just one bottle of wine along to slake my thirst, I started for the river. My plan was to take a hired boat toward the bridge if I could find one; if not, I would run along Thames Street to reach the bridge. I could only hope that I was not spotted by bailiffs or the dreaded pair of plague examiners who patrolled each district. The penalty for leaving a plague house unbidden was heavy fines and prison. People who went abroad after knowing anyone who had been ill were to carry white staffs, but I even risked not doing that.

I was too soon out of breath, so I slowed to a fast walk. What Will would probably have called "rosy-fingered dawn" was barely visible. As I passed Blackfriars Gatehouse, I sniffed back a sob, remembering how we had danced and loved there. At Puddle Dock, I saw no boatmen waiting, nor even boats. The black river rippled past as if it too would flee the pestilence. For the first time in years, I longed for the gentle Avon with the small stone bridge spanning its banks, instead of the long, oft-crowded wooden one I must cross this morning.

I hurried on, praying that the old man at the inn had told me true. Other plague houses loomed ahead of me. From some of them came unworldly keening or shrieking that seemed to echo in the streets and in my skull. Those sounds followed me like disembodied voices. I felt I was fleeing hell, and there was only one way out.

I saw a three-story house being blatantly ransacked. From the upper windows, a man was throwing down bolsters, curtains and clothes to four louts below who gathered them up into huge bundles and dragged them to a nearby close. Thieves called anglers made an illegal living by snatching things through open windows at night with pinch-poles, but these looked like regular citizens gone mad.

Sir Walter Raleigh's grand Durham House loomed large as I passed it in the row of vast noble mansions, all with unlit windows. Surely, the so-called School of Night was not meeting during the plague. Had Dr. Dee or Kit told the others of the tricks played on both of them?

I gasped to see light pearling the cup of sky. Could I have judged amiss the time it would take me? I could only hope that some nobles wanted out of the city this late in the contagion and that I would have the strength to rush through the gates to freedom and safety.

South of St. Paul's—I could see the top of it from here, standing as silent sentinel over its suffering city—I heard voices singing. I pressed myself against a building as four men lurched down the street, bellowing a lusty, obscene song. Unfortunately, one of them spotted me and staggered over.

"Eh, then, lad! Eat, drink and be merry for tomorrow you die! Eh, wha's 'at yer toting? Got any food on you then?"

I prayed they were just drunk and not in the throes of the plague. From under my jerkin, I seized the wine bottle and thrust it at him, then, as he reached for it, ducked under his arm and fled.

As I neared the entrance to the bridge, the stitch in my side almost crippled me. I cut down Bridge Street; the wind from the river, which had been at my back, cooled my perspiring face. It felt bracing and smelled fresh somehow. I recalled the times I'd strolled the bridge's shops that hung out over the water with their living quarters perched above that. Surely, I could move faster this morning without the usual crowd pushing to buy fripperies and fashions. Who cared one whit for such when people were dying, when the entire city seemed doomed?

I gasped and broke into tears: the drawbridge at this end of the bridge was up, not down, making it inaccessible.

"Ho there!" I shouted, swiping at my tears and trying to pitch my voice low but still shout up over the tall wooden barrier to where someone must be able to work the lifting mechanism. "I need to cross!"

No answer. My heart pounded harder than it had on my run. The old man at the inn had lied or been ignorant of what he said, or else everyone who wanted out had gone. "Help!" I screamed. "Help me!"

The buildings atop the bridge stood three to seven stories high. It was a little city unto itself with a chapel, constable and guilds, besides the stores and houses. If there was only some safe way to go up and over this barrier, out along the backs of the buildings perhaps. But I'd heard people had tumbled to their deaths from there, battered and drowned by the raging waters pouring through the supports. I could recall the cascading rapids the day Will and I had been rowed out to see Edward Arden's head on a pole at the other end.

I had no choice but to wait here, hoping someone would open the bridge on this side in time for me to race to the other end. Perhaps if someone peered out or down, he would open for a comely woman rather than a boy.

As the child who had been taunted as "Gypsy" and "Egyptian," I had finally come to accept that I was an exotic beauty, and all that was enhanced by the mania for all things Italian these days. For that, but mostly through Will's love, I had come into my own.

So I took my hat off, loosed my hair and shook it free. If I judged it best to be a lad, I'd stuff it back up under my hat; if a woman's role would serve, that's what I'd be.

"I'm an actor too, Will," I whispered.

But I couldn't keep from crying again. Forlorn and bereft, I sat on a stone post that held the cable chains for the drawbridge, hoping, praying for it to be put down. Thinking I heard such a rumble, I vaulted up and stared at the top of it, but nothing moved.

Then I realized the sound came from behind: a coach drawn by four fine horses clattered across the cobbles toward me. I stepped aside as some sort of horn sounded, from the coach or bridge I was not sure.

The bridge entrance on which I stood shuddered as the chains grated and the drawbridge started down. I was so exhausted I wasn't sure I could race across the bridge and wondered if I could grab on to the back of the coach and ride as a footman. Two men drove it but no one stood at the back post. With dawn in my face, holding my hat in my hand, uncertain whether to put it back on or not, I gawked at the windows of the coach, covered with rolled, embossed leather flaps.

It was such a fine black coach-and-four that I wondered if I could be dreaming again, wishing for all the world that Will was in it and had come to rescue me.

Someone was looking out; a pale woman, I thought at first. No, it was a man with long blond hair. He swept the curtain open wide and peered at me from the depths. I smelled onions and recalled that, in my haste, I'd forgotten to wear mine.

"Dare I say I've found the lady with the mask and fan from a young boy's dreams? The Italian countess, I always pretended," a cultured voice said as the man with long blond tresses stuck his head farther out.

"Milord," came a stern voice from above as the young man and I gaped at each other, "you vowed not to so much as look out 'til we were clear of the city. Your lady mother will be much displeased—

"Oh, hang my lady mother and you too. You are a servant to drive the coach and that's all, Rollins, though I warrant you are to spy for my mother. But, Mistress," he addressed me now, "do you recall the Earl of Southampton from the clown Tarlton's memorial? I've seen you in the theatre many times in far better dress than your present attire, but I shall not inquire why such a glorious woman would be garbed like a rude lad in plague London."

Southampton! A delivering angel come to snatch me from the jaws of death if I played my cards right.

"Of course, I remember you, my lord, and have well noted your lordship too, on and off the stage. I swear to you, Lord Southampton, I am not ill but cannot abide this city one more moment and in this guise it was easier to flee."

He gestured for me to come closer. My mind's eye lit with the terrible scene of that trickster tumbler from Kenilworth years ago: I had merely bent down to look into his tent and he drew me in where I was assaulted until Will rescued me. But this young and charming earl, the wealthy patron of poets Will coveted, was hardly some cheap Italian tumbler. And then I saw there was another in the coach with him, an older dark-haired and bearded man.

"Alas, I am not at all a countess and only half Italian, my lord," I said as the drawbridge thudded into place to jolt me and rattle the trappings of his coach. "But I believe I can display the best of both worlds."

I could not let him leave me behind. Flirting was the last thing in the world I cared to do, but dire necessity made me bold. I would fall to my knees to beg if I must to escape plague London.

"What a coincidence that I speak half Italian, half English," Southampton said with a little laugh. "May I present to you my friend and Italian tutor, John Florio? And may I offer you a ride and respite from this cursed city at my country home, New Place at Titchfield? Have you not noted that we who are full-blooded English are fascinated by all things Italian?"

Despite mutterings from his driver, Southampton swept open the door to his coach and extended his hand. Flooded with relief, I took it to climb up and in.

Act Four

CHAPTER SIXTEEN

ᕆ

I slept with the Earl of Southampton and with John Florio too—that is, we all soon enough fell asleep as the coach lumbered away from plague London. However hard I tried to stay awake, the next three days blurred by.

I do recall the earl told me that, though the plague raged within the nearby city walls, his mother had prevailed upon him to stay with her in their nearby rural home. Southampton House lay not along the Strand as did most of the dwellings of other powerful nobles but in Holborn beyond Tyburn Hill and Lincoln Inn Fields.

Yet, despite studying Italian with John Florio, the young earl had become restive and bored. He'd longed to return to his hawks and hounds, hunting in the great deer park at New Place, his Hampshire estate southwest of London. But for Warwickshire, I was woefully ignorant of the lay of English land and was astounded to learn we had a three-day coach journey ahead of us. As I had nowhere else to go and hoped to convince Lord Southampton to become Will's patron, how could I protest being handed my salvation, and on a silver platter?

By day we bounced along roads so rutted they rattled our teeth. At night we stayed in sprawling country inns where the earl purchased some plain female garb for me, paid for my room and kept John Florio in his.

I had no notion that Hampshire was so wild, compared to my well-tended home shire. We plunged through deep forests where wolves still howled. More than once a big-tusked boar charged across the road. Upon occasion we emerged in clearings or hamlets where people stared or cheered us on. Some roads plunged through trees so thick they looked like tunnels. Erratic dirt tracks led from the main road into mazes of thickets. Giant oaks loomed overhead as we passed deep banks of spiny, yellow-flowered furze where the faint smell of wood smoke from remote, invisible chimneys or campfires wafted on the air.

Maud's death clung to me like that smoke or the reek of onions, though they had thrown them out of the coach the first day. Yet I felt I was in a foreign land, and London—even Will—seemed to slip farther away.

"I apologize," Southampton had told me the first day in the coach, "but I assumed you would know some Italian. I regret we two have been chattering on in it while you gazed out the window, but I thought you were merely melancholy and exhausted."

"Then at least," I told him with a small smile, "you were not saying something at my expense. You see, my Italian mother died when I was quite young, and my English father hardly spoke a word of it, though I've longed to learn."

"Then you shall!" my young benefactor declared with a glance at his more staid friend. I had come to learn that his lordship was as explosive as John Florio was pensive and as fashionable as his friend was modest, though the Italian tutor was handsome in an unruffled, austere way.

"I shall call you *Contessa* rather than Anne," he plunged on, his bright blue eyes alight with plans, "and shall share my tutor with you. John, we shall be her Pygmalion and bring to life our Galatea, our Italian *bellissima contessa,* though we have no need of Aphrodite to breathe life into her, *si*?"

"I'm game," John said, straightening from his slouched posture on the leather-tufted seat next to me, while the earl rode facing forward in the other seat. "My lord, you can fetch us venison from your huge hunt park on your own," John told him. "Hunting deer is not for me—and naught else either, so no goading in either language that I am after other game."

"Ha!" Southampton declared, and slapped John's knee. His teasing that I needed no Aphrodite to bring me to life brought to mind Will's poem *Venus and Adonis.* I'd meant to ask the earl if he could take on one more poet, a brilliant Pygmalion who brought his characters to life, a playwright he was already familiar with to whom he was distantly related through the Ardens. But I did not want him to think I had set him up for such, or that I was greedy for more boons when he had showered me with kindnesses already.

But late on the third day of our journey, when I finally worked myself up to broaching the subject, he cried out, "Here we are!" and, like the boy he still was in so many ways, yanked back the leather curtain. The most beautiful place I'd ever seen, including Lord Leicester's Kenilworth or the queen's Whitehall Palace, arose before my eyes, and my well-rehearsed mention of Will went right out that window.

After a sumptuous dinner that evening, at which I confess I continued to eat like a field hand—powdered beef and porpoise in mustard sauce, I recall—the earl gave me a tour of his ancestral home, a large, fortified mansion called New Place with vast grounds surrounding it near the town of Titchfield.

"I must admit that my grandfather built all this from church lands confiscated under King Henry VIII," he told me, looking not a whit rueful for that. "The gatehouse sits in the middle of what was the old church." He pointed and turned me with a light touch on the small of my back. He had loaned—given me, he insisted— the most beautiful clothing I'd ever worn, left here by one of his cousins who wouldn't miss it, he'd said. The tawny taffeta gown crinkled when he touched me or I walked, and I worried I'd soil my cork-soled, ivory-hued slippers on the grass or gravel.

"The great hall," he went on, "was once the monastic refectory, and the old cloisters beyond became the central courtyard. The two wings comprised the rest of the church. But let's go round to the back. I want to show you what we call the Wilderness."

With my hand on his proffered arm, as if we were lord and lady of this great pile, we strolled through knot gardens surrounding a splashing fountain and out into the stretch of tall, leafy bushes and tree-topped bowers that were let run riot in a natural state.

"I'm going hunting at dawn on the morrow, so I will leave you to John's tender mercies to begin your Italian lessons," he told me as our feet crunched along a gravel path. This was, I thought, the perfect place for a seduction, but I felt armed with several excuses, should it come to that. Somehow his youth, nearly a decade younger than my age, usually kept me from thinking of him that way, but perhaps men were men.

"I am grateful you rescued me from London, my lord."

"Ah, but in a way, you rescued me," he vowed, squeezing my arm against his ribs. "You see, I adore feminine companionship, only not that which others, who believe they rule my life, would foist upon me."

"I see."

"My beautiful, *carissima contessa*, I doubt if you do, for, thank God, you do not know my mother or the queen's chief man, Lord Burghley. Both of them are hell-bent on my wedding women of their choice, not mine."

"But is that not often the way of it, my lord? And do they not have your best interests in mind, even as does the queen?"

"Ha! The only two friends I trust are John Florio and Robert Devereaux, Lord Essex. The latter acts as an elder brother to me. Like him, I was presented to Her Majesty when I was but a youth, and she said fine things about me, but she ever has her own best interests in mind."

That reminded me of Will's opinion of our queen; perhaps Lord Southampton and Will would get on famously. I really should mention Will to him . . .

"And," he rushed on, as he indicated we should sit on a rustic bench beneath a weeping willow overlooking a small pond, "if my father had not died when I was but eight, I would never have become Lord Burghley's ward. At least he sent me to university and the Inns of Law, so I did not have to abide his rules all the time. But he tried to betroth me to his fifteen-year-old grand-daughter, Elizabeth Vere. I wanted none of her, I don't care if she is the Earl of Oxford's daughter. My mother is always after me to wed to preserve the earldom. 'S teeth, I am only eighteen years and not a stud stallion to be bred at someone's whim or profit! She's even threatened to hire one of my poets to plead with me in rhyme to take a wife."

I tucked that little nugget away too. Surely, Will could do that, though winning over this man's mother was certainly not the way to his heart.

His expression became even more sulky; he occasionally stamped a foot for emphasis. "She cannot fathom why I love the theatre above all else, when it is such a fine escape from her harping—the shrew!"

Will had been working on a play tentatively titled *The Taming of the Shrew*, so I also vowed to mention that later. My host seemed so peevish right now that I decided to pick a better time to ap-proach him about Will. But soon—soon.

The next morning I came to realize that, if the volatile Henry Wriothesley, Lord Southampton, was like the shifting tide, John Florio was deep water. While the earl was out dispatching deer, we sat together at a round table in the mansion's large library— Will would be wild to see this many books—while the tutor gave me some suggestions about speaking Italian: to elongate the vow-els, to let the natural lilt of the language flow forth, even to ges-ture to augment the emotional tenor of the words. Yes, I thought: I can vaguely recall all that from muted memories of my mother.

"By the way," he told me, his dark eyes intense, "though his lordship has not seen fit to mention it, I am not only a tutor, but an author in my own right, one of his many adopted causes."

"Poetry?"

"Nothing that imaginative. Besides, my wife's brother is the poet Samuel Daniel, and one of them in the family is quite enough. But I've written two published works entitled *First Fruits* and *Second Fruits*, a collection of speeches, proverbs, witty sentences and golden sayings, as well as an instructional volume, *A Perfect Induction to the Italian and English Tongues.*"

"How interesting!"

"I believe you mean that. I must say, I am impressed with how well you speak English, so I have no fear you cannot master Italian. Besides, it's running hot through your veins, I can tell."

He smiled—the first time I could recall he had done such. It lit his eyes and softened his stern countenance. I wondered if he was flirting. Though I felt nothing but fascinated and flattered by Southampton, this man evoked an intellectual allure I'd only experienced before in Will.

"You remind me somewhat of a friend of mine from home," I told him. "He lives and works in London now, when the plague does not rampage there, of course." Nervous at the mere mention of Will, I took an apple from the big bowl of them on the table and crunched into it.

"He's a linguist too?"

I chewed and swallowed. "In a way, but with our own language, the playwright William Shakespeare. Have you seen his work, perhaps *Love's Labour's Lost* or his historical trilogy on King Henry VI?"

"No, but the earl's carried on about him right and left."

"He has?"

I'd shirked my duty. I'd been so entranced by the gilded life here with silver plates and glass goblets and fine linens on my lavender-scented feather bed—and two intriguing men to study—that I'd only thought of Will when something reminded me of him. It was as if I'd escaped worrying about and longing for him for the first time since I could recall. I'd survived the plague. Could I somehow survive—escape—my passion for Will? And did I want to, however painful it became at times?

"*Contessa* Anna, you are woolgathering. I said, shall we start with basic phrases of greeting others? You look most—distracted and impassioned."

"Oh, no, I'm fine," I lied, though I felt myself blush as I had not in years. Was I attracted to this man? If so, it was the first time anyone but Will had turned my head that I could recall.

"It is a wonder you have not yet wed," John said, tapping a quill pen on an inkwell, "and a great puzzle to his lordship, because he worships, he told me, at the feet of your beauty—*'Adora ai piedi della Sua bellezza.'*"

I stood, forgetting to chew my apple—Eve's apple, if I wasn't wary—and went to stand at the window where the autumn air cooled my face. I swallowed hard, but the lump in my throat was not from that.

"His lordship has been a most gracious host," I said, hopeful of escaping such personal talk pointed at me. "Let's begin with the Italian then. I should like to learn enough today to greet our host properly when he returns with bounty from his hunt. Perhaps a witty sentence or golden saying from one of your books."

"And then," he said, pushing back his chair, "if I read you aright, perhaps we shall work on something like, 'I am deeply honored by your attentions, my lord, but I must confess I care for another and so must decline all but your kindness.'"

Frowning, I heaved my half-eaten apple out into the gardens and spun to face Florio with my arms folded across my breasts.

"You may not be hunting deer today, but you are hunting for private thoughts," I accused. "You presume to know a great deal about me, sir."

"Do not react so. I would be your friend, not your enemy. I just didn't want you to misunderstand your host's desires. He may worship at your feet, but it will not mean you can win his heart. His lordship likes to collect people—poets, artists, beautiful women— the same way he accrues portraits of himself, just to look at if not necessarily to touch."

"Are you truly his friend to be warning me against him then?"

"I am not warning you against him, for I know no one more generous with his wealth, more open, or more grateful for friends. I am just saying—as with words in foreign tongues that sometimes cause confusion—know yourself and Lord Southampton too and do not expect too much personal attention from him, any more than he would give a cherished, prized work of art."

He came to stand beside me at the window. As if in prayer at an altar, both of us clasped our hands before us on the deep stone windowsill. Our elbows almost touched. We gazed silently out over the grandeur of the distant, blue-green forest etched with scarlets, yellows and browns.

"He blows hot and cold, *Contessa* Anna," he said, picking up our conversation as if I hadn't challenged him.

"Do not all men?"

"Not me—always hot but seeming cold," he said with a deep laugh. I turned to face him; his eyes bored into mine.

"And brutally honest," I said. "'Tis a rare trait and one to be cherished in a friend. I believe you tutor your noble charge in clear-sightedness as well as Italian, then."

"It is you who must be clear-sighted, so let us get to work."

We got to work, but I can't say, however candid John Florio seemed, that I understood him or the totality of the warning he meant to give me about Southampton. Still, his forthrightness was a heady thing, and I liked him immensely for it. And that first private tutoring session pushed me into telling Southampton about Will after dinner. Not about our past, of course, but that Will was a friend from home, and I knew he longed to petition his lordship to become his patron for a long poem he was writing about Venus and Adonis as well as for his clever sonnets and his plays.

"And related to the Ardens, you say," Southampton repeated, looking excited. "We Wriothesleys are likewise entwined with them, the poor wretches. Ah, if only I knew how to find your friend Shakespeare in these terrible times, I would send for him to attend us here forthwith."

"I do know where he is to be the first three days of October—in but a few days," I blurted before I could think the better of it. If John Florio saw Will and me together, he'd read our hearts and probably ferret out the truth.

The earl seemed much more loggerheaded about such things. I believed I had finally discerned Florio's message to me: everything revolved around Southampton and was pursued only to please him. At first I believed I'd only been saved from a seduction attempt by the fact that, in truth, he seemed so effeminate. Besides his long, carefully curled blond tresses, he wore fanciful garb and a dangling earring and sometimes rouged his face and his pouty, rosebud mouth.

So perhaps there was another reason behind his vehement refusal to become betrothed to Lord Burghley's granddaughter or any other woman. Still he excelled at masculine endeavors and planned to pursue military glory in foreign wars with his dear friend, Lord Essex. So whether it seemed my host leaned toward favoring men or women or both, I guess the truth about Southampton was that he only loved himself.

One of the earl's footmen was sent to fetch Will from Stratford and to pay the Burbages for his loss from their company for a fortnight or so. I felt I walked on air. Will was coming to partake of this fantastical world of the rich and noble with me. Will was coming to be offered the patronage he'd longed for. Will was coming.

One day, then two passed. I walked about the grounds rehearsing Italian phrases but also quotes from Will's poems and plays, which ran repeatedly through my mind. "Let me not to the marriage of true minds / Admit impediments . . . Love's not Time's fool, though rosy lips and cheeks / Within his bending sickle's compass come . . . True. I talk of dreams; Which are the children of an idle brain, / Begot of nothing but vain fantasy . . ."

On the fifth day of my Italian lessons, I was reciting sets of standard questions for John as I paced in the library. I happened to glance out the window and saw Southampton, whom I thought had gone hunting again, strolling toward the Wilderness with his arm around the shoulders of a capless man. It looked like—yes, Will was here!

"Go on," John said when I stopped talking, then prompted me with the last question. "*Cosa desidera?*" What do you wish? "*Contessa, che cosa?*"

"*È qui. Il mio amico è qui,*" I cried, gripping the windowsill.

"Ah, and you want to run down to greet him," he said, coming over to stand behind me. "But since he's in such earnest conversation with his lordship, let's just go back to reciting with a clear head, *sì?*"

"*Giovanni, mio amico,* must you be such a hard taskmaster?"

"You are dismissed then—hopefully not to make an overeager fool of yourself."

If anyone else would have said that, I would have snubbed him. I could have kicked myself for my transparency, but I made it worse by blurting, "He's married with three children, but I knew and loved him first, and their marriage was forced!"

He pressed his lips together and shook his head. "Tread carefully then—that is, don't trip running down the stairs."

But I waited, pacing downstairs in the long gallery at the back of the house, until the two men came in nearly an hour later. "Anne," Will said, beaming as he gave me a peck on both cheeks, a quite proper greeting for a friend. "My good angel has wrought a miracle, and here I am not only in the earl's beautiful home but in his bountiful goodwill."

Southampton threw his arm around my shoulders and Will's too. "We are a marriage of three made in heaven, eh? *Mia contessa,* I've even prevailed upon your playwright-poet to write me a series of sonnets to get my shrewish mother off my back. I'll pretend to pine over them but still pick my own domestic prison, ha!"

Will was flushed with excitement and success. Despite the road dust that clung to him, he looked quite the conquering hero.

"I shall leave you two," the earl told us, "to discuss old times while I order a room prepared for you, Will, near mine and Florio's."

"John Florio," I told him as the earl left us, "is the linguist and Lord Southampton's Italian tutor."

"And yours, I hear." His voice took on a slight edge, but he smiled and nodded to the footman as he opened the door for us and we went outside.

"Wait until I tell you how he rescued me!" I said. "John and Jennet fled, Maud died and I was all alone, but—"

"He told me. I am ever grateful to him for that too."

I began to relax. After all, I'd helped him, saved him from penury, his family too, and set him up for future success.

"How did you find things in Stratford?" I asked as we walked past the fountain into the Wilderness.

"Susannah's quite a help to her mother, though a bit of a fussbudget," he said, as if I'd inquired about his children. "Judith is a handful too, but my son is so— Anne, I meant not to ramble on. And I thank you heartily again for sending them my portrait as if it were from me. Hamnet sketched it for me, stares at it often, he says."

Each time he mentioned his son, he became misty-eyed, but the moment we were hidden from the house, he seized me and I him. His embrace was so fierce he hurt me, but I only hugged and kissed him back harder.

"There," he said, setting me away at arm's length. "It won't do to have you go in all swollen-lipped with rosy beard-burn on your cheeks and chin. Would that—would that make either of your companions jealous?"

"If you are worried about the earl, think again. He's been a perfect host."

"Perfect? A high compliment. And Florio at your private lessons in the language of love?"

"Who says so?" I demanded, pulling back slightly from his strong hands. "The French think they speak the language of love."

"Don't try to change the subject, though I imagine your old swain the wine merchant would be willing to tutor you in that tongue too. Actually, Southampton made a jest of Florio teaching you with an 'agile' tongue."

"Southampton's jests are sometimes wide of the mark, and Florio calls all languages tongues."

"I can't wait to meet him. Quite cozy here, is it not, despite the scope and size of this place? Anne—forgive me, you've saved my hide again, and I am ever grateful, but I'd prefer to be a pauper rather than have you bargain too much away."

I yanked free of him. "Pretty words, but an insult to me nonetheless. I'll not have you go all green-eyed again as you did over Kit. Kit Marlowe is a different breed from these men."

"Ah. Then let me only say one more thing of that." We began to stroll back toward the house. "Lord Southampton praised my plays but asked me for just two lines from my long poem, which I told him was the story of the seduction of a handsome young man by a skilled temptress, an older woman. So, from *Venus and Adonis*,

I chose, 'Rose-cheeked Adonis with his amber tresses / Fair fire-hot Venus charming him to love her . . .'"

"I still mislike the tenor of your quote and your implications, Will Shakespeare. And to think I longed for you, thought only of you during the plague and these days here."

"To quote my new patron again, 'Ha!' But let's go in for dinner."

If Will was seething at the meal, I could not have cared less for so was I. It panicked me that John seemed to see beneath our pretence of politeness at the lavish meal. Afterward, the four of us took turns reading from *Venus and Adonis* and the death scenes from *Romeo and Juliet*. Southampton seemed thrilled that Will had named one of the feuding families the Montagues, for, as well as the Ardens, he had relations with that surname. I surmised that his lordship would be seeing many an allusion to his kith and kin in future works by William Shakespeare.

I excused myself early and left the three men talking literary pursuits. Though I had worthy observations and opinions, I was tiring of acting as if all was fine between me and friend Shake-speare. I swear, if London had not been a deadly place right now or if I had a home to retreat to in Temple Grafton, I would ride out of here—wolves in the woods or not—at first dawn. It also annoyed me that I could hear the earl's boisterous laughter clear up the grand staircase to the second floor.

Men! We women sometimes arranged the world for them, and they only looked askance and cursed us too, thinking they had contrived their own good fortune. But this country had a female monarch, one who moved men about like chess pieces as she had her numerous foreign suitors—no doubt the way she handled Southampton and his dear friend Lord Essex too. Whatever the earl, Will and the whole world might think of Elizabeth Regina, at least in how she handled men, I wanted to be just like her!

"He studies you," Will whispered the next afternoon as he and I retreated to a wainscoted withdrawing room to prepare to read a scene from his play in progress, *The Taming of the Shrew.* The earl thought it would be amusing to have me take the woman's part instead of a boy.

"The truth is," I hissed back, "Southampton has eyes only for himself."

"'S bones, I mean John Florio."

"Like you, he studies all things."

"Ah, then he is like me? Is that true in other ways too, such as an unslakable passion for you?"

"I weary of your empty, ill-informed accusations, both direct and deviously indirect."

"A good line. May I not use it for my heroine shrew, Katherina, who is 'as brown in hue as hazel nuts . . .' whose 'only fault, and that is faults enough, is that she is intolerable curst and shrewd and froward.'"

"I cannot abide you. I used to think I adored you, but you are working to change that every day! If I had ended up dead from the plague and in a mass grave like my dear Maud, you would probably have been relieved, for you would not have to fret anon that I am so much as conversing with another man."

"Ah," Southampton said, surprising us with his entry into the room, "I cannot catch the words but the tone suggests an exciting scene for this evening. May I not have a glimpse of it now? I've always found it hard to wait for gifts, which reminds me, Will, I have here a purse of coins for you to get *Venus and Adonis* published, including in it several crowns far different from the one on Her Majesty's head."

That wasn't very clever, I thought, but Will laughed at the jest, and I forced a smile as the fine leather purse exchanged hands. Will had told me he'd just written a flowery dedication to the earl for his prized poetic endeavor: *To the Right Honorable Henry Wriothesley, Earl of Southampton and Baron of Titchfield.*

"Well, then, a little taste of the scene you've chosen from the play," the earl prompted and perched on the edge of a chair like an expectant child.

"Will it not spoil your enjoyment of it later, my lord?" Will asked, no doubt hoping that we did not have to read this scene when we'd been bickering. Yet was that not exactly what Petruchio and Katherina were doing? Had Will again based yet another play on our own plight? This comedy sported another dusky-skinned heroine with hot Italian blood. Devil take him, the dog-hearted wretch had used me again!

I should have just stomped off in an impromptu exit and let Southampton wonder if that was in Will's precious play, but I took the roll of my lines he handed me.

"From Act II, my lord," Will said. "I've only written about half of the comedy but this will serve. On the road with the actors, there is little time or a quiet place to juggle learning new lines and writing them too."

"Say on, both of you. A play set in Italy, is it not? I should fetch my Florio but he's hardly a dramatic expert like I, and he'll see it soon enough this evening. Say on, say on."

Will pointed to a place on my roll, and I began with the shrew Katherina's words. She was the beautiful—at least he gave me that— termagant elder daughter of a man who refused to let his charming younger daughter wed until the shrew was off his hands. So the younger sister's suitors had recruited Petruchio, a strong, volatile man who insisted he could tame her and wed her at any cost, in fact, for a pretty purse much like the one Will still held in one hand.

Katherina: I chafe you, if I tarry: let me go!

Petruchio: No, not a whit. I find you passing gentle.
'Twas told me you were rough and coy and sullen,
And now I find report a very liar . . .

Katherina: Go, fool, and whom thou keep'st command!

Petruchio: And therefore, setting all this chat aside,
Thus in plain terms: your father hath consented
That you shall be my wife, your dowry 'greed on;
And, will you, nill you, I will marry you.
Now, Kate, I am a husband for your turn,
For, by this light, whereby I see thy beauty
(Thy beauty, that doth make me like thee well),
Thou must be married to no man but me,
For I am he am born to tame you, Kate—

I had always thought I would make a fine actor, that I could learn my lines and stay in my part, but this was too much. I hadn't seen these words before, so I was reading blind, and how dare he pick this scene for us to recite before others. "Married to no man but me?" The vile wretch!

"Something I ate . . ." I lied, dropping the roll on a chair and pressing my hands to my stomach. Though I tried to look as if I was not fleeing headlong, I ran from the room.

I locked my bedchamber door behind me and threw myself on the huge bed. Sobbing into the bolster until I was almost sick indeed, I rehearsed all I'd done for Will—none of which was deserving of his bitter treatment of me, especially after I'd gotten him his precious patronage from Southampton, the wretch. I curled up into a tight ball, lying on my side, and tried to hate him as I gasped for breath. I should be wed—wed elsewhere—with children, at least three of them. I should be wife to a man, however meek, boring and dull-headed, who adored and respected me, though if he were a bit jealous of me for my beauty and brains, I could bear that. But not this! Never this!

Yet I had to admit, I had known from the first that I was different; I was meant to forge a path of my own, to dance on a high, taut wire, as it were. And so it was with me and Will. I could try to change that, try to leave him and tell him to leave me alone, but then I might just as well have thrown myself from a high wire to the pavement of St. Paul's or into the rushing Thames. My tears finally spent themselves and, emotionally exhausted, I fell into fitful sleep.

That evening the earl sent a doctor from the nearby town of Southampton to me, but I told him I only needed sleep and would not unlock the door. In naught but my shift, I lay on my back and stared up at the lady with a unicorn elaborately embroidered on the underside of the huge canopy of my bed.

John knocked later to tell me through the door that Will had read Petruchio and Southampton himself had read Kate. I told him, in quite decent Italian, I thought, that I needed time alone, for I had not taken time to mourn the death of my friend and grief had quite crept up on me.

"Which friend is dead to you now?" he asked, still speaking *sotto voce*.

I rose, went to the door and pressed my mouth to the crack. "I trust you to keep such comments to yourself, for I mislike spies."

"His lordship thinks of Lord Essex as his elder brother. May you not think of me that way? I would have it otherwise, but I am wed even if you are not. I see the lay of the land and, despite being a linguist, *Contessa*, I know how to hold my tongue."

"*Grazie, il mio amico Giovanni*," I told him. He bid me *buona notte* in his lilting, smooth Italian. But I was no more back in bed than he rapped on my door again.

"I need my rest now," I called to him.

"No rest for the wicked," came Will's sharp voice.

My heartbeat kicked up. In her delirium, Maud had said that before she died.

"What is it, Will? I'm sorry I could not read that scene you'd set me up for to remind me of what I can never have."

"I chose it not for that. It was the best scene for him, considering the play is still in tatters. Now open this door, or I shall pound it down. I don't care who hears me or who rescinds his offer to support my work."

"Go, fool!" I spit his own words from the play at him.

He hit the door once so hard it shuddered on its frame. The lunatic would ruin the door and himself. I got up, yanked the bolt open and let him in.

He closed the door none too quietly and, with a frowning glance around my bedchamber and then at how scantily I was dressed with my hair all wild, he put his hands on my shoulders and pinned me against the wall. I was angry too—furious at him. But to be so close, to feel his strength and heat almost made me crumble at his feet. He pressed closer, thighs, hips and chest. His body was as hard as the carved wood behind me.

"I was wrong to suspect you were swept away by Southampton," he said. "It's that honey-tongued spouter of Italian you favor. I have proof now from my own eyes."

"As soon as the plague leaves London, you'd best report to Bedlam, for you have gone mad!" I told him, trying to shove him back. "He's kindly tutored me—"

"In many arts, I'll bet!"

I tried to slap his face, but my arm was snagged against his. I stepped on his foot instead. He swore but did not budge.

"I was tutored at your new patron's insistence," I ground out through gritted teeth, "but I was grateful for it, thrilled to get to finally learn my mother's language. If you must know, I find Giovanni Florio," I said, drawing his name out, "a very circumspect and kind person, unlike another of close proximity I could name."

"I saw him leaving you, then whispering sweet good nights at your door."

"You didn't see him leave me, because he only spoke through the door to tell me that Southampton had read the shrew's part. But do you know what? He's only the second living person, thank the Lord, who has grasped how much I have loved you, how much I have given up for you. And, no doubt, what an addlepated fool I am for such stupidity."

I cursed him and began to cry. This man did not deserve my tears, my time, my love. It was flattering perhaps, in some perverted way, that he was sometimes jealous of me, but he had no right—no right, but that I loved him and ever would, and he surely yet loved me above all safety and sanity.

I went on crying and talking. "Jennet's the only one I ever told that we were wed, and I think Maud guessed at the very end what we mean to each other—'my genius,' she called you the night she died . . . and John Florio only guessed it when I asked the earl to become your patron. He's only a wise friend, but the Lord knows I need friends, for in the plague I was so alone . . ."

"Anne, Anne, forgive me!" he cried and sank to his knees before me with his arms tight around my hips and one cheek pressed against my belly, making a fierce fluttering there. "I just cannot grasp how any man can keep his thoughts and hands off you, given but the slightest look or smile. I have let you down so, then I come back from Stratford raving about my children—my son . . . But for the other, she's hardly speaking to me, though she spends my money well enough . . . I swear to you, we did not lie together, but forgive me for all else . . ."

He went on and on as we clung together, until I slid down to hold him as we knelt, facing each other. We tumbled onto a patterned Turkey carpet and lay there, entwined limbs and lives, swept away, away. With his hands on me everywhere, trailing fire, we went mad indeed, kissing and caressing with a fierceness I had never fathomed. Then I cared not a fig for a foreign tongue, as there was nothing like a country-bred English one.

It was only after, when we lay perspiring and panting, that I realized we'd finally had the chance to share a real bed and had not done so—and that we'd never relocked the door.

As I got to my knees to shoot the bolt and turned back to Will, I heard the distinct double creak of floorboards in the hall, as if someone had hovered at the door.

CHAPTER SEVENTEEN

ℚ

"Will, it looks just wonderful," I said as we stood with Richard Field at a bookstall near St. Paul's, admiring the copies of *Venus and Adonis* for sale.

"Eleven left here out of fifty-four at this seller," Richard told us, straightening the pile of them and placing them in a more prominent position. "At least something's a success lately."

Richard's shop had printed the poem that Southampton's patronage had made possible. Will's first published work was doing especially well, we had heard, among university students. Since one of its topics was seduction, many young men had bought it as a guide for "the bold-faced suitor." Some copies had been reduced to tatters and already replaced. John and Jennet had told us that in Oxford, the poem had been read aloud in the inns by students who adored the classical sheen to a sensual story. Though he was more a playwright at heart, Will was becoming England's premier poet.

"It's strange to see something of mine in print," he admitted, stroking the copy he held. "I'm so used to seeing everything in my own written hand, or Anne's. At least my spasms haven't been half as bad lately, despite the fact I feel I'm writing day and night." He looked up from the book, his finely chiseled face so serious. "I thank both of you for your years of support and for playing key roles in the career I've had thus far."

Wanting to throw my arms around him, I settled for just nodding with tears in my eyes. Richard grinned and clapped him on the back. "I wager if we print your next long poem—and times improve—we shall all make a pretty penny," he told us.

Despite our forced gaiety, we all fell silent as if in mourning, not for the past but for the present. Too much spring rain had damaged England's crops, which drove up the price of food. The plague had killed ten thousand and, though it had abated, the playhouses, like most other London entertainments, were still closed.

The theatrical companies were barely hanging on. Despite rural tours, some had gone bankrupt; others stayed solvent by selling off their precious stores of costumes. Lord Pembroke's Men, of which Will, the Burbages and the clown Kemp were now a part, had pawned many of their backstage treasures—and, of necessity, to their rival, Philip Henslowe.

John and Jennet's wine trade was also dismal. Since no one had money for things that were not essentials, pack trains in and out of London were sporadic. Despite Will's success with his poem, the publishing industry was foundering. Rampant unemployment made the queen's government more unpopular than ever, which in turn kept the Privy Council on edge and eager to control disgruntled citizens. Even the Puritan-leaning city fathers feared the specter of domestic riots more than the rumors of a new Spanish invasion.

As is human nature, especially in terrible times, Englishmen were striking out at immigrants, as if they were to blame for everything. We'd heard ugly gossip about riots against the strangers of London, that is, against the foreigners, especially the French, the Dutch and the Jews. That very moment we three old friends stood admiring Will's first published work was the time that terror first took aim at us.

"Ho, Will! Oh, Anne, you're here too!" someone behind us cried. We turned and gasped to see Kit Marlowe, looking like a pale, gaunt ghost of himself. He'd thrown a hood over his head and had his hands on his sword hilt and belted dagger. Will's hand instantly went to his sword too, for we had not seen Kit since we'd made him look the fool in front of Dr. Dee.

"What's the matter?" Will asked as Kit took his hands off his weapons to pull us away from Richard. Will motioned to Richard to give us a minute, then the three of us huddled against the stony skirts of the cathedral.

"Whatever is it, man?" Will asked again. "And we'll leave Anne out of this, if you have some issue with me."

Kit shook his head, but I wasn't certain he had even heard Will's words. "They've turned on me," he said, "on all of us."

"Slow down," Will said. "You're not making sense."

Kit was breathing raggedly and sweating. He must have run here for some reason, then stumbled upon us. "Start over and explain," I said.

"'S teeth, they've broken into my rooms and taken Kyd," he

said in a rush and seized Will's wrist. "We've been living together, but they took him."

"Tom Kyd?" Will prompted.

"Hell's gates, who else? He was down on his luck for not selling any plays—'s bones, aren't we all, but I took him in. Someone—I swear, I know not who—nailed a libelous note to the door of the Dutch church, attacking them, the French and the Jews. 'Like the Jews,' it said, 'you eat us up as bread, so fly and never return . . .' I don't know what else."

"Lines from your play," Will said. "But I still don't follow you. You didn't—"

"No! I said, no! I admit Tom drinks like a fish and says things he shouldn't here and there, but the worst of this mess is that the libelous note was signed 'Tamburlaine'!"

"Who could miss that?" I asked. "But that doesn't mean you wrote it. As for an attack on the Jews, just because you wrote *The Jew of Malta*—"

"So the authorities came to question you?" Will interrupted.

"Because I've done things for them—the government—they've always given me a long rope, but now I fear they mean to hang me with it. I thought things were bad under Walsingham—may he rot in hell—but, I swear, Robert Cecil's worse."

I wished I'd told Will what I knew about Marlowe's spying for Walsingham, but perhaps he knew, for he just nodded at Kit's admission.

"But if they've taken Tom Kyd," Will said, when Kit looked furtively about, "this might affect all of us."

"That's what I've been saying. They might mean to sweep us all up, but I'm their chief target. They took Kyd because he lived with me, and they're hoping he will nail me—crucify me, rather. They ransacked my rooms and took papers, plays, my poems. They are looking for me, but they took him to question under duress."

"Torture?" Will demanded. "Under torture, who knows who he would name? He's been such a tosspot these last years, he'd say anything for a drink, so why torture him?"

"Because the powers-that-be are panicked! I didn't write that note, but they know I'm an iconoclast—hell's gates, all playwrights are at heart. I just heard there's a warrant out for my arrest. Cecil will blame us writers, however much Her Grace likes pretty plays at court. The Puritan city fathers hate us. We'll be the perfect scapegoats for all of this. When I was the darling of the masses, they dared not touch me—but now that someone else is beginning to take my place in this stinking land . . ."

For one moment, I thought he meant to strike Will, but he only swung his arm out as if to encompass all of England. He accidentally hit my shoulder.

"Sorry, Anne," he said, looking into my eyes at last. "Sorry if I . . . ever hurt you. Will, you brilliant bastard, watch your back as I must mine."

He ducked between us and darted off.

"He's overturned," Will whispered, "but this does bode ill for all of us."

"Does Tom Kyd know you dislike the queen?"

"If they torture him, what he truly knows hardly matters, for he'll say anything they want. I can't believe it's come to this—an excuse to get rid of writers if they so choose," he muttered as we walked slowly back toward Richard, who had moved on to a more distant bookstall. "Because, my sweet, if they probe my past, they can bring me down not only with my Arden connections but an extra marriage to boot."

"An extra marriage to boot," I echoed, kicking at a bladder ball some child had dropped. It skidded under a stall and bounced back out.

"Like us—resilient," Will said, not looking at me, speaking out of the side of his mouth.

"But do you think we should stay away from each other, at least for now?"

"I won't give them that—or anything. Without giving in to them, we must be clever and careful, both of us, that's all."

"Things will get better. I'm sure they will!"

But things got worse. We heard Tom Kyd had been put to the rack and had named Marlowe as guilty of all charges, including being a heretic and blasphemer as well as inciting the citizens of London to riot. Edmund Tilney, the queen's Master of Revels— and truth be told, the government censor—had treated Marlowe with kid gloves for years, no doubt at the behest of the now deceased Walsingham. Now Kit's plays, past and present, were brought in as proof that he wrote "with application to the times," meaning in a nutshell that some of his work criticized the current government.

Kit was found, arrested and stringently questioned, though not under duress. He was finally released but was instructed, Will heard, to report every day to the authorities—a sort of house arrest.

"Perhaps Kit still has a few friends in high places," I told Jennet as we washed and dried the bottles of wine John was digging up from their herb garden. I was grateful that their home had not been harmed after I had fled during the plague. "I just hope," I went on, "Will's friendship with the Earl of Southampton helps to keep him above the fray. The fact that the queen's own cousin, Henry Carey, Lord Hunsdon, has taken on the players in place of Lord Pembroke should provide protection too. They'll be known as the Lord Chamberlain's Men, since that's Hunsdon's title. Things just have to get better for London's players."

Despite closed theatres, Will continued to write plays. Though he sent most of his profits from *Venus and Adonis* to his family, he kept some back to publish a second classical poem, *The Rape of Lucrece*, which did not do as well.

It was not three weeks later that someone knocked on the door to my privy staircase after dark, late May it was. I'd been preparing for bed; my hair was loose, and I wore naught but my night rail and robe.

Barefoot, I padded to the bolted door. "Who's there?"

"I."

From that whispered word, I knew Will was in trouble. He'd vowed never to come to me here, lest we be spied upon.

I opened the door, and he darted in, then closed it and shot the bolt. With but a quick glance at me, he turned away and scanned the room, evidently to be sure I did not have little Kate with me or to ascertain that the drapes were closed. I had not yet replaced the one I had used for Maud's winding sheet. I watched in consternation as he blew out my single candle, pulled the top sheet off my bed and draped the half-covered window. Ordinarily I might have made some jest about his rush to get in my bed—with all of our fervent coupling over the years, we had yet never shared a real bed—but I pressed my clasped hands between my breasts and waited.

He came back to me, sat us side by side on the end of the bed and said, "Kit's been killed."

"What?" I could not believe it. I felt stunned, sick to my stomach. My thoughts flew to the fact that both Jennet and I had once wished him dead.

"I don't know all the details—supposedly in a tavern brawl in Deptford. I dined at Southampton's house tonight and word came to his lordship there."

"Where's Deptford?"

"Out by the docks not far from Greenwich Palace. But the thing is, he was stabbed to death in a tavern house run by a widow who has family connections to the queen's former spymaster, Francis Walsingham. Now the widow's working for his heir-in-terror Robert Cecil, for all I know."

"Will, that night I was half conscious in Kit's chamber," I went on, hating to bring that up again, "I heard him whispering to Mr. Mercer—the same man who questioned me and my men about the Ardens and you. Kit called Walsingham Wally, and it sounded as if he didn't want to play their games anymore. He no doubt didn't want to play them for Robert Cecil either."

I expected a tirade that I hadn't told him I'd overheard sooner, or a jealous snit, but his response showed me how truly distressed he was. "Ah," he said with a swift intake of breath. "It's a damned spider's web, all of it. 'S bones, how dare they close the London theatres and then stage this covert spy scenario of their own," he muttered and got up to pace. He'd made the room so dim he hit his shin against my only chair and swore, but continued, "Anne, there are things I want to say—things I *must* say in my plays."

"And yet you must tread carefully."

"Yes, but I *need* to say these things. I even have an idea for a play with a Jew in it, but one in which I shall try to show that they are people like everyone else. After all, Jews bleed, they feel, they love. And I've been helping to coauthor a play with several other playwrights, thinking they could not threaten all of us, but they have."

I stood and rushed to him. In the dim light, he looked like a specter, with only his seemingly disembodied face and hands visible. I threw my arms around him. "You've been arrested and questioned too?" I cried.

"No—not yet. Thomas Dekker and I were summoned before the queen's watchdog Edmund Tilney, who—believe it or not—is related to Lord Strange, yet we still got hauled in."

He held me to him with his chin resting on the top of my head. With my arms wrapped around his waist, I could feel his words when he spoke. Despite his despair, he radiated heat and strength.

"I didn't know you were collaborating," I said. He'd stayed away from me more lately, lest something happen to him and I be pulled in. "And Lord Strange has not forgiven you for staying with the Burbages and going to other patrons, so I think it's bad news that he's kin to Tilney. Tell me everything."

We sat on the bed again, holding hands. "The play written with others is *Sir Thomas More,* a historical, of course, set in the days of the queen's father's reign. It was barely finished but someone must have leaked it to Tilney. He insists several scenes showing how our forefathers had riots over foreigners be cut. The play disapproves of riots, but Tilney told us to rewrite or else. It's crazy—unconscionable! I even wrote a plea within it to the audience: 'Imagine that you see the wretched strangers, their babies at their backs, with their poor luggage, plodding to th' ports and coasts for transportation . . .' I thought that would put those in their place who want to ship strangers back to their own countries. Cannot a country care for others even if they are different? Has this modern world gone mad?"

"You cannot give Tilney excuses to ruin you. They've silenced Kit, and Tom Kyd has not recovered from torture."

"I know. I hear he's on his deathbed, and I think they set Kit up," he whispered, hunching over to put his head in his hands. "Not an accident, but an assassination. But, do you know what?" he asked, jerking erect again. "At least, Lord Strange has written a letter to Robert Cecil, demanding he steer clear of harassing players who are only writing imaginative plays, so hurrah for that."

But within a year we heard that Lord Strange had died a sudden, bizarre death, by poisoning, it was whispered. Rumors about his weird School of Night still circulated—that its members had been contacting the dead, that witchcraft was involved. If that was not all that made someone—perhaps someone in a lofty official position—want to rid London of him, perhaps he was dispatched for standing up for the players. We both rued his death, but, the sad truth be told in these perilous times, we were more worried about our own safety.

After all that, Will still wrote like a madman, scared but seething. When the playhouses opened again in June of 1594, the Lord

Chamberlain's Men presented *The Taming of the Shrew,* but it worried me that Will now thought of that shrew not as me, but as the queen. He wrote comedies for a while but began to produce history plays that edged on tragedy, such as *Richard II* and the two parts of *Henry IV.* He was aware that he was watched closely, but he seemed increasingly heedless of risk as he wrote and acted his heart and mind.

People flocked to see a William Shakespeare play, but then they had once made Christopher Marlowe their darling. I could only pray that Will's more bridled genius would keep him safer than Kit's wild ways had kept him.

I had seldom been more excited. During the Twelve Days of Christmas of 1595, after things had calmed down a bit, the Lord Chamberlain's Men were invited to play before the queen at Greenwich Palace. Since the company's costumer was puking his insides out and I knew the play and players well, at the last minute, I was asked to go in his place, dressed as myself too, though I'd volunteered to go as a lad.

The entire company went silent as the grave as we passed the tavern house near the palace where Kit Marlowe had been killed. Despite the cold winter wind on the palace barge that had been sent for us, James and Richard Burbage removed their hats, then the others snatched theirs off too.

To disembark from a barge at the palace water gate and then to walk right in was a heady experience for a Temple Grafton girl. Inside the vast palace, my head swiveled as if on a stick as we were escorted down a maze of corridors to a huge, decorated hall where a makeshift stage was set up. The play, *Love's Labour's Lost*, was very familiar to me, but since I was so excited, I prayed I would not miss a cue to help someone into a wig or doublet.

"At least this command performance got us the rest of our pawned costumes back," Kemp groused as he donned his patched harlequin jerkin for his role as the rural dolt Costard. "Our Willy might as well have named my part Custard, all the substance it has to it, eh, Mistress Anne?" he asked, breaking into a little jig and managing to covertly pinch my bum in his flurry of movement.

"Not true," I said, shaking my finger at him. "The point is that not only learned, wealthy men may fall for women and come to admit that our fair sex is the be all and end all of the world, but a country fool must admit it too."

"And to think such a pretty wench as you could have a brain— you could have fooled me!" he said and chortled at his own wit.

Kemp wandered off. Will liked the man for his talents well enough, and he was easier to control, he'd said, than Tarlton had ever been. Yet I knew Will longed to write deeper lines for his clown roles. I must remember to tell Will that Kemp wanted that too.

I kept an eye on everyone's appearance as best I could, darting behind the painted canvas backdrop to cover both sides of the stage, but I also managed to take as many peeks as possible around the corner of the curtain. It had been strung before the dais that served as the stage. And to think that this elevated platform was where the queen sometimes took her meals! Sounds and smells of the court's Christmas celebration wafted from the next room. Within this large chamber, the air was redolent of the box and bay boughs swagged above doorways and set in windowsills. Kissing bunches of white-berried mistletoe hung from the ceiling, though we'd been so busy we'd all ignored such. Holly leaves with red velvet ribbons edged the stage.

"My friend Jennet says," I chattered nervously to the lead actor, Richard Burbage, as I helped him into his purple surcoat for his entry as King Ferdinand, "that it was the custom in days of yore to count how many of the holly leaves were pointed—or male—and how many were rounded—the so-called female. Then whichever kind was in the majority supposedly decided whether the husband or wife ruled the roost in the coming year."

"That's a good one, Anne. But in this grand house a woman rules whatever the holly—or body—count, and make no mistake about that," he told me in a whisper.

And where was Will during all this banter? He sat on the back of the dais, hunched over paper he'd balanced across his knees, evidently scribbling something new or amending what he'd already done, then ripping it into small pieces. Maybe he'd been swept away by one of his strange moods during which he heard voices in his head. We had decided we would not hang together backstage, even though most of the players knew we were fast friends, or I would have asked him what he was doing.

The noise increased as the court moved from their dinner tables into the hall for the performance. The smells changed to the ladies' pomanders and powders.

As we retreated behind the backdrop, I saw Will was passing out small pieces of paper to the cast. A change of lines in this old play at this late date? It was probably something to suit the occasion, something about Christmas or the queen.

I was excited to glimpse her as I peeked around the canvas backdrop. I could see what seat was to be hers in the front row.

With a host of other courtiers I did not recognize, Sir Walter Raleigh awaited her arrival. Bending over my shoulder, James Burbage began to kindly name others for me.

He pointed out the queen's top man, Robert Cecil, Earl of Salisbury. I shuddered as I gazed at him, not because of his misshapen form, but because I knew he had become the new Walsingham, a more terrifying safeguard and spymaster of the queen. Burbage also pointed out Southampton's friend Lord Essex, who was a handsome young man—twenty-eight years of age, he told me. However compelling the man looked, he dared to look in a foul mood amidst the Yuletide revelry. There was Lord Southampton, making eyes and little covert gestures at a pretty woman in the queen's retinue, though he glanced over at Essex now and again. Well, that would make his mother happy if he fell for a suitable woman, I imagined, though I'd heard the queen did not like her ladies to wed while they served her. Until permission was given for courtship and marriage, they were to remain as virginal as their mistress.

"I've realized this play is just the opposite of *Taming of the Shrew*," I whispered to Will as he came to stand next to me for his entrance as Berowne. "There the man's the conqueror, so I believe I prefer this one."

"Perhaps Her Majesty will too, but we'll just see," he said, seeming out of humor. I wondered if he was always this sour when he played at court. It was almost if he had caught Lord Essex's foul mood from clear across the large chamber.

The white-bearded Lord Chamberlain himself, one of the queen's cousins through her Boleyn heritage, made a speech to announce the play. It was, he promised the court, one that would delight the ladies, especially her Most Gracious Majesty, and put the men in their places.

Will just grunted, squared his shoulders and made his entrance onstage. Surely, he would not do something rash to upset the queen. Peeking out, I could see she was intent on the actors, unlike the sulky Lord Essex who stared hotly at her, though she ignored him. Perhaps they'd quarreled. I'd heard that, though she favored him and Southampton, both men had been chastised for intemperate behavior since manners were always expected at court. I could not fathom that of the young earl so perhaps Essex was leading him astray. I cursed myself for continuing to watch the little drama with Essex and forced myself to pay attention to Will's play.

As the drama went on, I noted that the tutor named Holofernes now sounded much more pompous to show off his learning. He interjected Latin phrases into his English and rambled on and on. The audience laughed at his pretensions. John Florio, I thought. Had Will rewritten that character to mock John Florio? How dare he! It made me think I didn't know Will well anymore.

Worse, at the very end of the play, I was horrified to hear new lines. In the lighthearted group song at the end, the first verse was the same, mocking married men for not being able to court a new love in pretty springtime. But with Will leading, the words of the second verse now included, "The cuckoo then, on every tree, mocks women too; for thus sings he—Cuckoo, Cuckoo, Cuckoo! No word of cheer comes to the unwed woman's ear."

I peeked out onto the stage. Will had changed these words indeed, for two of the actors glanced again at the small pieces of paper in their hands.

Finally, the character of Armado spoke the last lines of the play, directly to the queen, it seemed to me: "The words of Mercury are harsh after the songs of Apollo. You that way—we this way."

Everyone bowed and danced the usual jig—Kemp jumping off the dais to cavort before the queen and even getting her up to dance a few measures with him to the great applause of our audience. I watched it all, now not with eagerness but unease. Was Will testing the waters to see how much he could get away with at the end of the play by challenging the queen herself? "No word of cheer for the unwed woman's ear," indeed! And the final implication was that, you, as queen, go one way and we the other.

I held my breath as the queen sent her entourage off for dancing, yet tarried with her servants, who brought us mugs of spicy hippocras and mincemeat pies shaped like mangers, in addition to the hefty honorarium. Though I was quite certain Her Majesty was making her way toward Will, when she nodded at me and spoke, I felt speechless.

"I am pleased to see a woman among the players, at least behind the stage, for behind every man—or men—there is a strong woman," she said, words I would ever cherish.

I felt dazzled by the glitter of her bejeweled gown; the sweet scent of her filigreed pomander swept over me. Up this close, she looked very old, ghostly, with her skin colored an unearthly white. Her curled, pearl-studded wig was too red, her lips, brows and cheeks obviously painted.

Yet she was magnificent. I managed a graceful curtsy before she moved on, but if I close my eyes I can still summon up the sight and impact of England's Gloriana.

"Master Shakespeare," I heard her say—and noted well that the buzz among the players muted—"I swear I need an explanation of the strange concluding words."

Rooted to the floor, I stopped breathing altogether.

"'No word of cheer to the unwed woman's ear,'" she went on in her clarion voice. "'You that way—we this way'?"

I did not know whether to laugh or cry as I saw Kemp reach into his doublet, pull out the scribbled scrap of paper Will must have given him and thrust it into the closest mince-pie manger.

With all eyes on him, Will bowed smoothly and said, "I admit it is an unusual ending, Your Majesty—that the couples do not wed immediately and that love does not conquer all because of the solemn oath the men have taken. So the women—at least for a year—go one way and the men the other. Of course, the women would wish to wed the men. As a result, 'no word of cheer comes to the unwed woman's ear.'"

"*Women's ears*, it should be," she clipped out, "not to put too great a weight on one little slip you have made. Pray, Master Shakespeare," she added, enunciating each word as if she were onstage, "do not make a greater error in one of your fine plays in the future."

She smiled and fluffed her feather fan in his face, but I prayed Will took her words to heart. I knew then that however much I had argued in the past that it was the men around Elizabeth of England who made her policy, but indeed Will had been right. Decisions came from the woman who ruled not only this palace and country, but its prominent people too, especially one increasingly popular poet and playwright.

. . .

It was in late August of the next year that a tragedy occurred to halt Will's subtle defiance of the queen's government policies. It was probably the only thing that could have stopped him, at least for a while, because he seethed with resentment and anger over things, from the downfall of his Arden kin to Kit's death—however much he had disliked Kit. Perhaps, I thought, Will knew he was indebted to him for the gift of brilliant blank verse blasting out from vibrant dramas.

The dreadful day began when I went to the bustling Maiden Head Inn to welcome my pack train from Stratford. Stephen Dench, after being greeted by his wife and three young sons, pushed past them and came to me.

"How are things in Stratford?" I asked, but I quickly sensed something was wrong. He wore a frown as severe as what I used to see from him when I'd turned down his wooing. We'd managed a good working relationship for years—I believe he thought I could not abide any man—but I feared what he had to say.

He drew from his money pouch a sealed piece of parchment he'd evidently folded in fourths to fit there. "A missive for you," he said, "given me by John Shakespeare."

That made no sense. Why would Will's father write to me? Never in all these fourteen years I'd lived in London had anyone in his family tried to contact me, and they'd always sent word to Will through my rival carriers, the Greenaways. Perhaps Will had mentioned to him I'd paid for his portrait. Or had he heard I was still in his son's life and wanted to warn me off?

"Thank you, Stephen. I appreciate all you do."

"It's not good news."

"Tell me, if you know."

He shook his head. "I'll let it be. Someone's died, that's it, and he thinks you should know."

I nodded and hurried away toward the Davenants'. Little Kate thrived and they had a newborn son, but were yet packing to move to Oxford, though no one had bought their business yet. But I could not bear the suspense any longer and broke the seal in the back alley. Trembling, I opened the parchment and read.

For Mistress Anne Whateley through her carriers to London since they be leaving afore the Greenaways and know where to find her—

Though he has not said so, I know ourn Will still sees you, cares for you. I have not forgot the kindness you showed ourn family e'en at great risk to yrself. I beg you tell him plain that his son, Hamnet, died of lung fever and is buri'd. If he comes home to comfort and to mourn, 'tis up to him. Yet if it be in yr. power, comfort him.

Yrs., John Shsp., Stratford, Day of Our Lord, Aug. 20, '96

Will's son, Hamnet, dead at age eleven! His only son, the son I knew he missed. He loved Hamnet and his own youngest brother Edmund best of all those he'd left behind. Hamnet, who Will said drew pictures of the portrait I sent them, Hamnet had died and was buried while his twin sister, Judith, Will's daughters and Anne Hathaway yet lived . . . Will's only son . . .

I did not even go in the house but, clutching the note, headed for Shoreditch where I'd find Will. The trip there was one I cannot recall; I walked as if in a trance, trying to choose the words, the gestures that might not break Will's heart. He'd been working hard on his play *The Merchant of Venice*. Another popular Italian setting, more strong, clever women characters, but a harsh play despite some merry jests, disguises, clowning and romance. I felt—and Will had admitted to me—it was hardly the comedy he'd promised his fellows and the queen's Master of Revels, Tilney, who had kept a watchful eye on him for years.

A watchful eye on Will for years . . . I had done that, and his father sensed it . . . He knew Will still saw me, cared for me.

I cared desperately for Will, and now this burden was mine. The son Will and I could never have together was dead, and I was the bearer of the dreadful news.

I had actually hoped to find him in a somber, thoughtful mood, but to my dismay, I found him backstage at the Theatre, jesting with Kemp, who was to play the clown Launcelot Gobbo, described in the *Merchant* as a "wit-snapper" and "merry devil."

"My clever friend," Kemp was saying to Will, who had his back to me, "you may have a skull full of hair-raising words, but you're losing your hair atop that skull. What's that line from *A Comedy of Errors* you tried to make us believe, you bare-pated churl?"

"Ah, let's see, my base-wit clown. I believe it was, 'What the Lord hath scanted men in hair, he hath given me in wit.'"

"Hey, then, 'tis the one behind you has all the wit I'd need to keep her company," Kemp said and swept me a bow fit for the queen.

"Anne?" Will said, turning and standing. "What goes? Have John and Jennet sold then? This varlet has been teasing me about my rising hairline, but he is a fool indeed if he can't sense my choler is rising at him too. Look, I've bought a gold earring to take everyone's eyes off my rising forehead."

He did indeed flaunt a small gold hoop in his left ear, for that pirate fashion was all the rage. It blurred to two hoops as tears filled my eyes.

Kemp rattled something else off in a sort of pig-Latin he sometimes used and darted away. I sat down on the bench where Will had been writing because my legs were shaking so. I was loath to ruin not only his soaring mood but his day, his year—his life.

"What's that?" he said, seizing the note from me. So it was decided, I thought, that I was too much the coward to tell him. Still, if there was just some way I could break it to him.

"It's from your father—" I blurted.

"But to you. Dear Lord in Heaven, I pray my mother hasn't died, and he trusts you to tell me."

So close but yet so far. I almost burst into tears. I wanted to cower behind a curtain and not have to say the words.

"Will," I told him, reaching over to put a hand on his arm as he sat down beside me to read the rest of the note, "Hamnet caught a lung fever and—"

"—and they want me home, and your carriers came before the Greenaways."

I shook my head as he skimmed the note. He sat back, dumbstruck, like a statue carved from stone.

"It—can't be," he whispered. "Died and I not there . . . hardly ever there."

I thought of things to say about how he needed to make his fortune here for the sake of his family, including his son, how his great gift to write would be stifled back in Stratford. But I said nothing. I had learned the day I'd tried to insist things could work out well for Kat that just being near—being there—was best. I clasped both hands over his, trembling on the note he had crumpled so hard the paper rattled. We sat like that awhile, and when I saw he could take no action, I knew I must do so.

"I'll go with you to get a horse and to pack your things to go home. Will, I am so deeply sorry."

He looked up at me. I was terrified to see his face blank—no emotions, nothing, as if he stared into space, into emptiness. Dry-eyed, distracted, he mumbled something. I realized later he must have quoted his own lines from the sad scene in the first part of *King Henry VI,* where the English hero Talbot holds his dying son in his arms, a scene that had always made even the stoutest louts among the groundlings cry:

> *Come, come, and lay him in his father's arms.*
> *My spirit can no longer bear these harms.*

What scared me most was that in the play the bereaved father then dies of a broken heart; it's as if he killed himself. But not Will—not Will, lost like Kat!

"Will," I said, "I'm going to hire us two horses and a guard to get you home. You need to go to your family, but I'll take you there."

Though he nodded, he still seemed to look straight through me. We were halfway home to Stratford the next day before his great, gasping sobs started. They shook him so hard I had to have him ride with me as he had once held me, devastated, on his horse so long ago.

CHAPTER EIGHTEEN

❦

"*Aye, I'll be able to* get it all thatched afore winter sets in," the man I'd hired assured me. "Just so's the carpenters and plasterers get out o' my way on time."

"They've promised me they will," I told him. "I've hired an overseer for the rebuilding, and he'll take care of all that."

We stood at the front gate, surveying my small Temple Grafton cottage I had now reclaimed and meant to make into my country home. How tiny it looked after living in London all these years, though I'd soon be in a small place there without the run of the Davenants' spacious home. They had sold their shop and house—unfortunately, to my old suitor, wine merchant Nicholas Clere, and his new French wife, so I knew I could not stay on.

I had hurried back to London to lease two ground-floor chambers from Will's friends the Burbages in the Blackfriars precinct; they had bought the old three-story refectory building there to live in and to turn into an indoor theatre. Besides my view of the mews with horses going in and out, I could see two mansion houses and the gatehouse I still coveted.

The once familiar Warwickshire accent of my visitor drew my thoughts back to Temple Grafton. "You give me a bit o' the money now to buy my reeds and get my scythe sharpened," the thatcher told me, "and all's well."

As I went in to get him some coins, I wondered if all would ever be truly well in my life again. I had not seen Will since we had parted at Clopton Bridge the day I'd brought him, laid low by grief and guilt over his son's death, back to Stratford, nigh on a month ago. Now I must head back to London yet again to bid farewell to my friends and to move my earthly goods to my new place. Yet Warwickshire drew me for the first time in years and not just because Will was near, if unseen.

Compared to London, the countryside seemed so serene and safe. I'd walked the woods and meadows and laid bouquets of late-blooming flowers on the graves of my parents, Father Berowne and Kat. I had sneaked into the unused church where Will and I had said our vows and stood there, lost in thought. Despite our separations and our sorrows, I did not regret I'd committed my life to loving him. Somehow, at the age of thirty-two, well into my middle years, I'd made peace with my past.

In short, I had restored my soul, but for feeling so deeply again my loss of Will, who yet remained within the bosom of his family as if he'd never again return to the stage—or to me. I tried to come to terms with that possibility but such eluded me.

Now, even after I'd paid the thatcher and he'd headed back toward Stratford, I leaned against my stone fence in the autumn breeze and let my mind's eye picture how the cottage would look when I saw it next spring. I was having it extended out the back and the east side to add a spacious solar with hearth and big bay window; a large pantry and kitchen with an open hearth and a fine bedchamber with a third fireplace, so a trio of chimney pots would sprout from the new roof. I would hire a maid to live here, someone to cook when I was in residence but tend the place when I was gone, especially the herbs and flowers.

I thought of Maud again, lost in her delirium, talking of her sweet-smelling herbs at the end. How I wish I could have brought her here. Perhaps Jennet would visit or let Kate come to me when she was older, and—hopefully—had even more siblings than little Johnny.

Indeed, I had lost my three best women friends, two to death and Jennet to her move to Oxford with my darling, eight-year-old Kate, who was like a daughter to me. I feared it would never be the same for us, though I had vowed to see them on my trips between Temple Grafton and London.

And between me and Will? I could not finish the thought.

I went inside to store some other things away for the rebuilding; I was leaving with the pack train on the morrow. Again, I walked through the place, surveying the small rooms where my mother had danced and sung, where my da had laid his plans to have his own pack train. And where, thank the good Lord, he had said I must learn to read and write. If only—

I jumped at a knock on the door. Could Will be here to tell me how things were with him, Will here . . .

I rushed to open the door, staring at the height his head would be, but a thin young girl stood there, her expression pinched, a blue cloak pulled tight around her shoulders. Looking into her eyes, I realized who she was, though I had seen her only once and that years ago when she was but a babe. I was certain it was Will's eldest girl, Susannah, thirteen years old now.

My insides leaped to think she'd come with dire news, for it had been exactly here I'd faced down those two neighbors of her mother's who told me Will was lost to me for good. Will—what if he was ill or had hurt himself in his despair?

"I know you are Mistress Whateley," she said, her freckled face hard and her voice harder.

"And I know you are Mistress Susannah Shakespeare," I said, obviously surprising her. "What may I do for you? Would you like to come in?"

"Don't mind if I do," she said, surprising me in turn. She stepped in, all curious, trying to take in the room and me without swiveling her head. She was at that graceless, gangly stage between childhood and womanhood I recalled all too well. I indicated she should sit, but she shook her head. I gripped my hands tightly in the folds of my skirt. Surely, Will had not sent her.

"They don't know I'm here," she said in a burst of words, "but I know about you, and I want you to stay away from my father."

"I haven't seen your father since I've been here, Susannah, but we have been friends for years, since we were younger than you. Has someone sent you?"

"I said they don't know I'm here. They don't know I overheard them arguing either. That's all they do now, 'stead of not talking, now that Hamnet's gone."

"I am very sorry for the loss of your brother."

"At least it's been good to have him back—Father, I mean."

"I can understand that. My father was often gone to London when I was growing up, and I missed him sorely, though he had to do it to support his family."

"Well, yes. My father has promised Grandfather he will help him get our coat-of-arms and promised Mother he will buy us a fine house in town too, but he says he has to leave to do that. I'd rather live—even live here in this little cot, if he'd but stay—so you just stay away! Grandfather sticks up for you, and that's bad too!"

"You are very brave to come here, and I thank you for your visit if not your harsh words. If you've come out all alone today, best I walk you back to town, at least a ways."

"And be seen together? Why would I want that?"

"Perhaps we could talk of other things besides what you've come to say. Did your father tell you how people love his plays in London, and how—"

"Mother wants the big house and nice things, but she doesn't want him in London!"

"Yes, I can underst—"

Another knock rattled the door and, this time, we both jumped. I prayed it was Will and not her mother come to fetch the girl. I went to the door and opened it, expecting the worst.

But a young, handsome stranger stood there, perhaps aged twenty-one or -two. As he snatched off his brimmed hat, I saw a russet horse was tied to my gate. The man was clean-shaven, with dark hair and eyes and a strong, square chin with a cleft in it. Though he was well enough attired, road dust powdered his broad shoulders. He seemed entirely surprised to see someone as dusky-skinned and exotic as I here in this shire of rosy skin and fair hair.

"I beg your pardon," he said with a slight smile that lit his face, "but this is the edge of Stratford, is it not?"

"This is Temple Grafton, sir," I told him, as Susannah came to peer around me.

"Then Stratford is . . . ?"

"There's a signpost just down the way," I told him, pointing. "Stratford is that direction, very close."

"I am sorry to intrude upon you and your daughter, but I am dreadfully inept at finding directions. If I do decide to set up a medical practice in Stratford, I shall have to ask my patients to come to me," he said with another smile as he nodded to Susannah.

All this while—after her gasp at his calling us mother and daughter—I was expecting Susannah to set him straight, but she just gaped at the man and blushed to the very roots of her hair. Her lips were slightly parted, her blue eyes wide, as if the man had entranced her. That reminded me how sheltered she was and what pluck it must have taken for her to come to face me down.

"I believe," I said in the awkward silence, "Stratford and this entire area would treasure another doctor, and the town physician is quite elderly. Dr.—"

"I'm Dr. John Hall, fresh from Queen's College, Cambridge, born in Bedfordshire."

"Well, Dr. Hall, if you are heading into Stratford, this young lady, Susannah Shakespeare, is returning also and would be glad to show you the way."

"Oh, I couldn't presume," he said, smiling at the still dumb-struck girl, "but I would appreciate the company into town."

"She's lived there all her life."

"Not your daughter then? I apologize . . ."

"Quite all right. She'll be able to tell you about the town, perhaps introduce you to her family, won't you, Susannah?"

To my utter amazement, she had not only changed her expression from sour to stunned but she now looked so sweet. As she stepped outside with us, I realized Susannah had probably rehearsed some sharp parting rebuke for me but now would look bad in the eyes of her new hero if she carried on so. Yet I yearned to tell her to enjoy—no, to treasure—her rampaging feelings in this moment, which now were centered not at all on me.

They left together, Susannah on Dr. Hall's horse like a princess as he walked, holding the reins. Ever the foolish romantic, I blinked back tears of hope for Susannah and of sadness for myself.

"It will be a damned outrage if we have to sublet this theatre after we've leased and remade it with great charge and trouble!" white-haired James Burbage exploded. He had just finished reading the notice to his son Richard, who beat both fists on the railing so hard I let go of it. The boy who had brought the message into the Burbages' new Blackfriars Theatre, where they'd been giving me a tour, scampered off as if he'd been shot from a firearm.

Richard shouted, his deep actor's voice bouncing off the walls, "Six hundred pounds this renovation has cost us, not counting the lease on the entire building! The artless, beef-witted joltheads!"

Will had told me both Burbages were hotspurs. Though their fiery personalities were matched by many of their fellows, Will was different. He only exploded when he was jealous, or perhaps—if his daughter had told true—when he argued with Anne Hathaway. The rest of the time, he seethed, even if he struck out at others, as he had at the queen by rewriting his old play.

The Burbages, who were also my new landlords, stomped about in the narrow aisle, so I moved out of their way. It was like watching a drama with heroic characters. If, indeed, city officials had somehow rejected their license for this indoor theatre, this display would perhaps be the only performance that would be allowed here, though we were in the first gallery rather than on the stage. The father and son theatre manager and lead actor of the Lord Chamberlain's Men were respected but feared too, and now I could see why.

With another curse, James wadded up and heaved the notice onto the stage. Then they tore down the stairs, shouting and cursing. I stayed where I was, for my tour—like this dream of theirs to own an indoor theatre—could well be over.

"And," Richard put in, his voice booming out as they appeared below me on the ground level, then strode up onto the stage, "it's partly because a few nosy, noble neighbors around here have signed a petition about noise and traffic before and after our performances! 'S blood, it's to their advantage to have us near, and there'd be no riots by apprentices to close us down since the penny knaves can't afford Blackfriars entry fees."

Indeed I saw there was no pit for mere pennies and standing room below: they had spent their hard-earned money to put in benches or chairs for all six hundred attenders. And they'd planned to allow well-heeled members of the audience who wished to be seen to sit on the edge of the stage for an extra fee.

"Those pious prudes, the Puritan city fathers!" Richard bellowed, gesturing wildly and stalking across the stage. He looked as if he'd tear his curly hair out. "They're using the neighbors' petition as an excuse. The city fathers are just enraged we found a way to outfox them with a theatre right in the heart of London. I see Cecil's hand in this, maybe Edmund Tilney's too, since we've stood up to him! 'S teeth, I wish Will was here. We need a calm head to fight a conspiracy—that's what it is, damn them all, the reeky maggot-pies, a conspiracy!"

My stomach knotted over the mention of Will and the fact that financial failure here at Blackfriars could mean financial catastrophe for the Burbages and their other playhouse. Giles Allen, the man who owned the land in Shoreditch on which the Theatre sat, had said he would not renew their lease when it lapsed, for the Burbages owned the building but not its site. So they could lose that venue and this one too.

And, I thought, squirming on my bench, what if they were forced to give up this Blackfriars building and the new landlord—like Nicholas Clere—made it an impossible place for me to live? I loved this area, and the Theatre was still only a bit farther away than it had been before I'd left Lilypot Lane.

Worse, Richard had told me Will was back in London, claiming he was ready to act, but that he had not been able to write. He had not been to see me. Clasping my hands on my knees, I hunched over them. I wanted to pray, but sound carried well in this vast room, and the men's words disturbed me.

I blinked back tears, which made the furious figures on the stage seem to shudder. The beautifully carved room was well lighted from two banks of high windows, but they'd added expensive candelabras that could be lowered when the wicks were trimmed. With all this space, stage machinery could fly in things— even people—from the lofty area above the stage.

It would be such a perfect place. They had been hoping it would inspire Will to write for it, the sort of more inward character plays he had longed to do for an intimate theatre with an educated audience.

I felt the cloak of dark despair cover me. The Burbages had boasted that this chamber had long been a backdrop for drama. Years ago, Parliament members had met to argue here, and it was the very venue where King Henry VIII's first wife, Catherine of Aragon, had pleaded before a tribunal not to be divorced. She'd lost, of course, and her wayward husband wedded his second bride, the current queen's mother, Anne Boleyn. Fated to fail, both women fell into the brutal hands of that destructive man. Henry VIII had six wives, I thought, and Will Shakespeare but two.

I started to cry in earnest, but stopped and stared below. For one moment, I thought my agonizing had made me imagine Will, for he'd made an entrance upon the stage as if he had suddenly been flown in by some *deus ex machina*.

"Will!" Richard cried and rushed to clap him on the shoulder while the older man hugged him. "I swear, our needing you here must have summoned you!"

I thought surely the Burbages would mention to Will that I was here, but they were so intent on their problems and each other. I considered stepping outside, but sat stock-still, remembering the first day I'd seen Will on the stage in Kit's *Doctor Faustus*. Why didn't he sense my very presence as I so often did his? Perhaps our days together were over now—our bond broken like our hearts had been.

As if pacing off a measurement, the three men walked back and forth across the width of the bare stage together. "We'll be in a pretty fix," James said, after they explained things to Will, "if we don't raise some capital—and somehow save the Theatre to keep Giles Allen from possibly tearing it down."

"If we're forced to sublet this place," Richard put in, "I say it's to Henry Evan's children's Chapel Royal troupe, not anyone else. I don't trust Philip Henslowe not to be behind this low blow and our looming loss of the Theatre too. Will, besides the continued pressure from the powers-that-be, the competition among the theatres has worsened since you've been away. We're glad to have you back as an actor, but it's your plays we need."

"But I still haven't been able to write," Will admitted, shaking his head more in amazement than denial. "I have several things going—but I feel so distant from them now—as if they are just gone—over." Like us, I thought. I couldn't bear sitting there anymore as an audience of one, so I stood to slip out. But the movement must have caught Will's eye: he turned and came to the edge of the stage, shielding his eyes with his hand from the window light, looking up at me. I stood frozen in midstride, staring down at him.

He snatched off his cap and said, "Anne Whateley, my angel from on high, I have much to thank you for."

"Will Shakespeare," I managed to get out, "like others who enjoy your plays, I am glad to see you back among your fellows."

To my surprise, Richard began a sort of pantomime behind Will's back, gesturing madly for me to talk to Will, to try to get him to write again, if that's what his aping a scribbler bent over a desk was meant to show.

James put in, "Anne has rented chambers from us out back by the mews. We were uncourteous to forget we were showing her about when the bad news came. We're off to tell our wives and to decide what to do, so would you walk her back, Will?"

I had to smile at that, for it reminded me of how lamely I had tried to give Susannah Shakespeare some time with Dr. Hall. I was about to reply that I could well find my short way home in these safe precincts, but Richard clasped his hands as if he were begging me. I wondered how much they really knew of Will and me. Surely, he had never told them, and I had not breathed a bit of it. Was it written all over our faces and lives? Did they think we were lovers but decided to act as if we were only friends from home?

"I would appreciate the company," I said, though I was hurt Will had not contacted me since we'd arrived in Stratford nearly two months ago. In the past, I'd snubbed and ranted at him as his Lady Tongue or Lady Disdain but best to get our twisted passions all thrashed out, I thought.

Will shook both men's hands then walked toward the back of the theatre to meet me where I would come down the stairs. I heard the Burbages' footsteps across the stage, then a back door slam as they went outside. Yet I stood, leaning over the balcony, just looking down at Will.

Turning his cap in his hands, he stopped and craned his neck to look sharply up.

"Will, it has been a while, has it not?" I asked, desperate to fill the air with words between us. "How are things at home now?"

"O, speak again, bright angel! — for thou art
As glorious to this night, being o'er my head,
As is a winged messenger of Heaven
Unto the white-upturned wondering eyes
Of mortals that fall back to gaze on her . . ."

Lines from the balcony scene between *Romeo and Juliet* were the last thing I'd expected. But I took his challenge and threw back Juliet's next line to him, only slightly amended.

"O Will, Will, wherefore art thou, Will?"

"I have been lost, my love, lost in despair of my loss, but I hope now I can go on."

"It's not something a father can ever get over."

"Not get over, no. Get through, perhaps. And with your help if you will lend it. Come down from on high then, my guiding and guardian angel, and let me make things clear."

I hurried down the staircase, wanting to throw myself into his arms but afraid to. At least I would give him my hand, but he gripped both my shoulders firmly and, holding me at arm's length, stared down into my face.

"Anne and I have come to an agreement," he told me, so serious and intent, "though not without argument and agony. I am going to buy the family a fine house in Stratford—probably the old Clopton town house—and buy them, especially for my father, though she thinks it's for her, a coat-of-arms. She is obsessed with lording it over those who whisper about why I stay away, and she refuses to set foot in London. So she's vowed that however I live and work here to accomplish my promises is my concern. I swear to you, she will have my house but never my heart, for that has been bestowed for nearly all my life elsewhere."

My insides cartwheeled. For a price Anne Hathaway was giving up emotional claims to her husband. "I see," was all I could manage and that in a shaky whisper.

"I hope you do. I was so guilt-ridden about Hamnet's loss. She was afraid I would blame her, while I thought the opposite. My girls were glad to have me stay a bit, and I came to know them not as children, but as blossoming young women whom I shall return to see when I can—them and my elderly parents in any Stratford house, small or spacious."

Did he know his daughters? I wondered. I should tell him of Susannah's visit, but I could not bear to break the bond between us.

"But the Burbages said you haven't been able to write," I countered. "You must write, for therein lies your future and your fortune."

"I had trouble writing there—without you. Anne, though I will no doubt go back again, the mother of my children and I have decided to live quite separate lives now, as if we haven't done so all these years. But I knew I could write again when I saw you, only I wanted to choose the time and place—to see if—if you would take me back one more time—one last time, as it were. Losing someone so dear to me, I realized how precious you are. I was told you had moved here and I was coming to call before Ellen Burbage said I'd find you here in the theatre with my friends."

He crushed me to him so hard I almost couldn't breathe. Strangely, then, I saw in my mind's eye his Susannah's pinched face and heard her voice telling me to stay away from him. But I could no more do that than stop breathing—and if he didn't loose me just a bit, that's what I'd do.

Despite the Burbages' pain and the possibility I'd have no place to live again, despite all the dear ones I'd lost and Will's griefs too, here was our home and happiness.

Like an invading army, we were going to steal the Theatre from Shoreditch: we planned to tear it down, move it across the river to Southwark and rechristen it as the Globe!

Three days after Christmas in 1598, in this dangerous endeavor, I joined Will, the Burbage brothers, Richard and Cuthbert, and their elderly mother, for their father had died last year. Other key players of the Lord Chamberlain's company—John Heminges, Will Kemp, Augustine Phillips and Thomas Pope—came too, for without a theatre, they would have to split up and work for others, and they'd become fast friends.

It was bitter cold and snowing heavily; the Thames, our escape route, was starting to ice up. But we were undaunted because we were desperate. The Burbages had been forced to give up use of the Blackfriars Theatre and had managed to lease it to the Children of the Chapel Royal company, though, as owners, they kept the building itself. That, at least, meant I didn't have to move again. As for the Theatre, the lease had run out and the landlord, Giles Allen, intended to dismantle the playhouse and keep the valuable timber, despite the fact that the lease stated that the Burbages could "take down any building they had erected." At least we stood on legal if not safe ground.

Unannounced during the holiday season, with a dozen workmen headed by our hired carpenter, Peter Street, we approached the Theatre just after the gray dawn birthed a thick white sky. Besides carting in wrecking tools in our hired wagons, the Lord Chamberlain's Men carried daggers and swords at the ready, lest we meet with opposition.

Though we'd hired two barges, I'd contacted many of the wherrymen Maud and I had sold scented cushions to years ago. They too would be lined up along the wharf to take piles of timber and our band of bold people across to Southwark. There, when the rough weather abated, we would erect the Globe playhouse close to that shifty Henslowe's Rose—and then another battle would begin.

"Ho, he's got armed guards there—two of them, at least, damn his hide," Richard whispered to us and motioned us back. "Kemp, go on up and distract them while Will and I sneak around behind so we can scare them off or tie them up without a fight."

My stomach knotted, but I knew better than to protest that Will, their precious playwright, could be harmed, for he hated being coddled. Lately, he'd been pouring out plays, amazingly light comedies like *Much Ado About Nothing* and *As You Like It*, though both of those reflected moments of great personal loss. He'd even agreed to do a humorous work requested by the queen, *The Merry Wives of Windsor*, because she favored the boisterous character of Falstaff from an early history play and wanted to "see him fall in love."

I'd held my breath to see what Will would come up with for Her Majesty, though he seemed only hell-bent on making money for himself and his fellows. He'd spent a tidy sum also to apply for a Shakespeare coat-of-arms to please his father and Anne

Hathaway and to buy what he called New Place for his family in Stratford. Though it needed repairs, it was a fine, large home that had once belonged to the town's most prominent family, the Cloptons. The bridge had been built by them and so named, and they also left a spacious country home outside of Stratford. It was as if Will were paying Anne off. At least, things between him and me had seldom been better, though we knew not to outright live together.

I alone knew he still had black moments of the soul from missing his son. He'd recently read me a scene he was adding to his history play, *King John*, a poignant speech that read, I recall, in part:

> *Grief fills the room up of my absent child,*
> *Lies in his bed, walks up and down with me,*
> *Puts on his pretty looks, repeats his words,*
> *Remembers me of all his gracious parts,*
> *Stuffs out his vacant garments with his form . . .*

However hard he worked to forget his woes, the ghost of Will's child was ever with him, the specter of one loved and lost.

Then too, he sometimes stumbled over his own feet in the street when he saw a boy who reminded him of Hamnet. In writing more sonnets, he seemed obsessed with the youth his son could have become. Will had vowed to me that he would dedicate all his sonnets to W.H.—Will's Hamnet—if he ever got them published. He'd also shared with me some earlier, angry sonnets he'd written, referring to me as the Dark Lady, from times he was jealous of me with other men. This included his patron the Earl of Southampton, who'd been out of the country for years, fighting foreign wars with his friend Lord Essex—both of whom slid in and out of favor at court for their hot-tempered ways. Right now, I could only pray we did not have a domestic war with hot tempers clashing here in the snow in Shoreditch.

Still, I couldn't help myself from trying to keep Will safe. "Richard," I whispered as Kemp strolled toward the two guards, "Will's hand's been cramping again, and if he hurts it—"

"Just so he doesn't hurt his head," he whispered back, "for I know you are his sounding board and his right hand indeed. Stay back with my mother so neither of you is harmed."

The feisty Ellen Burbage and I were to keep the men fed from the supply wagon and to paint numbers on the dismantled timbers so the Globe could more easily be rebuilt from them. When Richard and Will sneaked around and took the guards' weapons, I stayed back, but I did manage to trip one of the men, who scrambled away and began throwing stones.

Flushed with success with the oaf sprawled at my feet, I took a bow as the entire group of men—even to the carpenter's assistants—stopped and applauded me. Kemp swaggered over to sit on the lout and later ran him off, though we thought the guards might try to summon help. Without constables in this area, we had no fear of being stopped by the authorities, so it was only a question of Giles Allen coming in with hired hands to fight us.

Despite tearing down the building in which we had all invested our time, hopes and dreams, we were a happy, hardworking crew. Will winked at me as he passed, dipping out a mug of cider from a pot we had heated over a fire.

"The Globe's a much better name," he told me, as if we'd been discussing it just now again. "The works we enact there will encompass all of mankind and every place. England, Italy, Denmark—I have an idea for one set on a magical island in the New World . . . Brrr, I shall make it a hot, tropical setting."

His voice trailed off in the noise as timbers were wrenched apart and piled in the wagons that clattered down to the river. But by noon the first day, despite the thickening snow, Philip Henslowe showed up with a sputtering Giles Allen in tow.

"I'll sue you!" Allen, a short, fat man, shouted at Richard Burbage before Henslowe could speak. Allen shook his fist; he was red as a pippin from either his ire or the cold weather. "You're beating down the grass under all this snow, and that's yet my property. I'll sue for that!"

Everyone laughed at that threat, even Henslowe.

"I don't believe," Will said to Allen, "that even clown Kemp could have come up with a better line to lift our spirits. Sued over bent grass—that's a good one. I hope you won't sue me if I use it in a comedy someday."

"However," Henslowe shouted, wiping the smile from his face and pointing his finger to enter the fray, "all of you merry men—and women too—will regret it, if you try to put this—this ramshackle place near my Rose. We don't need two theatres there."

"Quite right," Will replied. "We need but one there, which is what will be left after we open our doors. One will conquer, I promise you—perhaps the one with all the new plays."

"Leave off and just plain leave, Henslowe!" Richard added, coming forward with a wrecking claw in his hands. "You took us for a pretty penny when we tried to get our pawned costumes back and kept some for your own actors, so now we'll just get some of that money back, eh? Keep working, men!"

And work they did—we all did. We had never been more exhausted or cold—or felt so renewed and hot with happiness. That time we joined hands and hearts to birth the Globe—but for when little Kate came into the world—was one of the best days of my life.

CHAPTER NINETEEN

❦

"Anne, come down here, will you?" Richard Burbage cried, windmilling his arm as I checked the top tier of gallery seats at the Globe to be sure their cushions were all accounted for. I looked over the railing at him. He stood at the edge of the stage, which thrust out into the pit where up to a thousand standing groundlings could pack in for a penny, while a total of two thousand cushioned seats were in the three elevated galleries.

"What's amiss?" I called down. Since I stood in a shaft of sun from the thatch-edged roof opening, I had to squint to see him well. Despite the sunshine, it was winter, so the breeze off the river was brisk. His voice carried well; the cries of seagulls soaring overhead did not mute his words.

"Ned Kinnon can't be found, and we'll need a book holder in an hour. You know the play well enough, and we're in over our heads, putting it together this fast."

I instantly began to sweat, and not just at the idea of managing the backstage for this impromptu performance of one of Will's previous plays, *King Richard II*. Like all his work, I knew it well and had even written part of it from his dictation when his hand spasms were bad. But this whole idea of a special presentation for the earls of Essex and Southampton when the city might explode around them in rebellion scared me stiff.

"Will you do it?" Richard asked. "We'll make a mess of it without a prompter. As King Richard of this group of actors, I command it of you."

I smiled at his lame jest, nodded and hurried down the stairs. The forty-shillings' payment the earls had offered was not to be sniffed at, however much of a success the Globe and Will's plays had been these last two years. Will was a full partner in the company of the Lord Chamberlain's Men, who had built and operated this renamed and reborn theatre. The Burbage family held half the shares; others, including Will—actually with some of my money invested too—each owned one-tenth of the endeavor.

Profits were up but costs were too, and we never knew when the plague of the Black Death or the plague of Puritans could close London's theatres. Now I feared the rumored Essex rebellion might come down on our heads and harm the company's good standing with the queen.

Will and I had had a terrible row over that three days ago when his longtime patron Southampton had requested a privy performance of this play for Essex and his friends.

"You know they want it played because of the abdication scene!" I had protested. "Essex and his rabble—"

"Southampton's hardly rabble!" he'd insisted. "Of all people, you know that. You've seen the interior of his coach, his country home. You've worn his cousin's costly clothes, enjoyed his hospitality and company, even privily."

I had frowned at his mocking tone, crossed my arms over my breasts and glared at him, daring him to go off into one of his jealous rages again, for my spleen was up too. And he knew full well there had been nothing sexual between Southampton and me. He was just in a foul mood, maybe worried his patron would get in trouble, bucking the queen. After what had happened to his uncle Arden years ago, I could understand that, but he'd been impossible lately, as if he were going through some middle-aged rebellion or crisis.

I'd leaned against the wall as if steadying myself to take him on. The solid old house where we had faced each other stood on the corner of the new Globe property. The Lord Chamberlain's Men used it for additional prop storage and the overflow of their tiring room costumes and wigs. Will used it to write and sleep in sometimes, but he also stayed with me at Blackfriars off and on besides keeping a rented room with the Mountjoy family, wig makers, in Silver Street. Will's favorite brother, Edmund, now twenty-one, had come to town to try his hand at acting, and Will had put him up on Silver Street. Will had told Edmund he must make his reputation on his own, not at the Globe where Will and Richard ran everything, so the boy had obtained a job at the Curtain north of town. Edmund had created all sorts of new concerns for us, but I shall address those later.

Suffice it to say that it seemed to me that Will was living and visiting and even writing all over London, driven, I'd say, by some demon I could not name. Ambition, perhaps. Guilt. God-given talent, for certain. His temper was often short. It was almost as if he sensed his days were numbered. The passion in his loving had even become fierce, almost desperate, as if he tried to lose himself in me but could not.

Finally, at least in my chambers, we had shared a real bed, one he had shipped at some expense in a dray from Stratford. It was his favorite bed, he said, one he'd used for years when he went home, for Anne had slept in their second-best bed for years.

Although we might have had young, busy Edmund fooled, the Burbage family knew of Will's and my *affaire de coeur* now—though not that we considered ourselves wed—and accepted it. Richard had told me he understood because he'd met Anne Hathaway on one of their country tours and "her daughters had to beg her to let them attend the play, while Anne refused to come as if we were presenting heresy or promoting treason. Hell's gates, I've never seen a woman bite the hand that feeds her the way she does, then flaunt far and wide that she is the wife of London writer William Shakespeare."

"I said, Southampton's not rabble," Will had repeated, when I did not rise to the bait of his innuendo and argument. From my woolgathering, I came back to the present with a start.

"But some of his hangers-on are," I said, "and they're not to be trusted. If a riot of apprentices can start in a theatre, so can a riot of crazed conspirators against the queen."

He muttered something I could not hear, but I knew he was disparaging Her Majesty.

"Will," I went on, hands on my hips as he stalked around his big writing table like a caged bear, "I know your privy feelings, but you risk everything by defying the queen and Robert Cecil. I regret that Southampton and his dear friend Essex do so, but that is their unfortunate choice. With all the scribblings on walls and wild broadsheets circulating, all we need is for someone to quote something from one of your plays to get you in trouble. It's bad enough that someone put a line about a hunchback on Cecil's door, so—"

"I am not Kit Marlowe!" he shouted, flinging gestures as if he were onstage. "I have a circumspect reputation, and the queen and court love my plays."

"They loved Kit's, for heaven's sake, and where did that get him? God save us, you cannot stand up to Cecil and those who have her ear!"

"Kit was their spy and he tried to defy them. I'll not be false to my conscience!"

"Oh, I've seen your playwright's version of that. Clever, last-minute changes of dialogue to challenge Her Majesty even at court and at Christmas. Have you done something to this play now, other than agree to its performance? Have you made the plot worse than it already is with a lawful monarch being deposed, just what Essex and Southampton are probably hoping for?"

"Leave off, Anne! 'S bones, you sound like a wife indeed with your shrewish carping!"

He surprised me by throwing both his inkpot and sanding dish into a corner where they made a black, gritty splash upon the wall and floor. Furious at his tantrum and his heedless behavior, I stood my ground. Of course, I knew he'd also been deeply affected by his father's current illness and wished he could be back in Stratford with him. The worry over possibly losing his sire had plunged him back into despair over his son's death, and he'd begun to write dark tragedies in place of the lighter works. Indeed, he was a man of wildly swinging humors lately.

I thought that his dangerous disposition perfectly suited his latest malcontent, brooding hero. I'd even wondered if he'd chosen the title of the tragedy to honor his dead son, though the plot was borrowed from an earlier play with a hero named Hamlet, not Hamnet. It was a work with the ghost of a dead father haunting a son, a play of revenge with a murdered monarch—and a play where a distraught young woman drowned herself in a brook over her lost love. That latter scene had stunned me when I'd first read it, but Will seemed to regard it only analytically as good theatre.

"I cannot help but speak my head and heart," I told him now as we stared—or glared—each other down. "Your reckless words and this play that ends with a dead monarch in these tense times could spell catastrophe for all that you—both of us—have worked for. They say Essex is demented in his fury, and you know Southampton will do anything that demon says."

"I'm not sure who is a demon," he muttered, seizing his cloak from the back of his chair and swirling it dramatically around his hips as if to imitate a woman. "Sometimes, royal or not, damn it, they wear skirts."

Before I could reply, he was out the door, dragging the cloak and stalking head down toward the Globe. In despair, I watched as he went in the back tiring room door and slammed it hard. We hadn't spoken since.

But now, two days later, though I had a good nerve to refuse, I did as Richard asked and went behind the stage with him to review what I must know. I'd seen Ned Kinnon, the Globe's book holder, at work many times, but I listened closely as Richard walked me through the play, act by act.

I would stand behind the curtains of the inner stage or one of the stage doors to whisper cues and commands. Should someone miss or drop a line, I would prompt them. Since this play had not been performed since it was written four years ago, that could well happen. After all, I tried to buck myself up, this was but a play, not reality. So what if, years ago, the usurper Henry Bolingbroke, beloved of the masses, forced King Richard II to give up his crown and kingdom? Surely, Essex and Southampton would not really risk rebellion against their queen, however popular they were with the London crowds.

Yet everyone knew both men were increasingly desperate as they fell further out of royal favor for their rash actions. Essex was the stepson of the queen's beloved Robert Dudley, Lord Leicester, and she'd favored him greatly, though he'd abused her love. Once, 'twas said, in a Privy Council meeting, Essex had shouted at the queen and started to draw his sword, a capital offense in her presence, though she'd forgiven him. From that time on, her chief advisor, Robert Cecil, Earl of Salisbury, homely and misshapen though he was, had been her fierce and dogged champion.

Both Essex and Southampton had also fallen from the queen's good graces for getting two of her maids of honor pregnant and wedding without royal permission. Southampton had married Essex's first cousin, Elizabeth Vernon, so that had bonded them even closer as kinsmen.

Charged with gross mismanagement of the Irish War, Essex had been under house arrest last year. I prayed that had settled him down. He'd been ill too, and that oft made a man consider his mortality. Yet the handsome, once-coddled earls, victors and heroes in the Battle of Cádiz, were still wildly popular with the masses and, I fear, that went to their heads too.

But worse, I wagered, than their public affronts to the queen, Essex had stormed unannounced into her bedchamber at Nonsuch Palace before she had donned gown and wig or had her elaborate cosmetics applied. When she'd laid down some conditions for his return to court, he'd declared in a letter later made public that, "her conditions are as cankered and as crooked as her carcass!" I'd seen enough of the prideful woman in the aging queen to know such personal slurs would never be forgiven even if some public ones were.

Conspiracy and paranoia were all the rage and, it was whispered, the plotters met, supposedly in secret, both at Essex House in the Strand or in Southampton's in the suburbs. It had turned into a battle of wills and words between Cecil and Essex, with all London taking sides. Will's and my disagreement over it all had tainted our trust and rent our mutual respect asunder.

"Anne, are you listening?" Richard said and touched my arm.

"Oh, yes. But what are those two padded chairs doing there?" I asked as one of the backstage men placed them on the very edge of the stage. "You don't intend to have the king hand over his crown from a throne?"

"You know Southampton favors sitting on the stage to see and be seen," he muttered with a frown, not looking me in the eyes. "Well, Essex plans to do the same."

I should have walked off then, but I stayed. On that day I held more than the playbook through the entire performance—I held my breath.

. . .

The Tragedy of King Richard II was one of the first plays Will had written that used history as personal conflict between two individuals: "Character is fate," as he put it once. Now, as I watched the nervous, pompous Essex react to the drama—and Southampton seemingly in thrall to him, even mimicking his motions—my stomach clenched with foreboding.

Throughout the drama, Essex nodded at certain lines and gestured grandly to his several hundred guests in the audience—some well-attired and well-kempt, some ragged and rugged. At the description of the deposed ruler as "plume-plucked," Essex jumped from his seat and danced about, mimicking a chicken with its head cut off—a dreadful image when one recalled that the queen's mother and Mary Queen of Scots had been beheaded.

Essex looked so demented and dangerous that I almost missed my next cue to get all of the Duke of York's attenders onstage. And I nearly fell to my knees when I thought I might have glimpsed Mr. Mercer, Walsingham's old informant, amidst the groundlings. Everyone had heard that Robert Cecil had inherited Wally's network of spies, so I'm certain Mercer was part of that package.

"Will, this cannot go on," I whispered as he made an exit. Even he looked worried now that he'd seen Essex close up after his long imprisonment and—some said—debilitating illness.

"It's just a play," he said, but his voice shook.

I feared for him. And for our new Globe, so beautiful with some of its silver-grained oak painted to look like Italian marble.

Even now, a mournful melody floated down from the ornate musicians' gallery. The winter day was bright and crisp, but I could not stop perspiring. I almost wished I could sink through one of the traps in the stage floor and hide in what the company called "hell," the place from which ghosts and sometimes special effects like fog arose.

As drums rolled to accompany the exit of actors from the stage, I began to shake as if I had the ague while Will, playing the minor part of the Abbot of Westminster, spoke the final lines of the fourth act:

"I see your brows are full of discontent,
Your hearts of sorrow and your eyes of tears.
Come home with me to supper; and I will lay
A plot shall show us all a merry day."

As if that indeed referred to his plot, Essex leaped to his feet and swept a bow to his audience, who cheered and threw their caps into the air with loud huzzahs. Expecting all of us to be surrounded and arrested at any moment, I clasped the playbook to my breasts and leaned against the stage exit. As Will came off, I saw him wipe his brow. I believe that by the time I cued the coffin bearers onstage at the end of the play—they supposedly carried the dead monarch's body—he realized he might have gone too far.

When three days had passed with no rebellion and no reprisals, I—foolishly—felt very relieved. Evidently, I thought, the stalemate between the old queen and her young favorite would go on.

I had just received a note from Richard Field telling me that I could pick up the copy of Ovid's *Metamorphoses* for Will at his print shop near St. Paul's. Will had ordered it, for he had lost his beloved, dog-eared copy, but I'd never said I'd pick it up.

Did everyone residing in Blackfriars think I was Will's servant? I fumed. The Burbages now thought I was his mistress. I'd be willing to be his helpmeet, but I was becoming fed up with running errands for a man who was sulky and still upon occasion suspicious of me with other men and who threw temper tantrums and expensive ink with equal abandon. Indeed, I just might abandon him after all these years of hanging on, I thought, as I crumpled the note and tossed it against the headboard of our bed he'd had installed in my chambers.

In that very bed we'd recently had an argument about love.

"I analyze that particular emotion as being just a prettier way of saying people's needs," he'd told me. "You know, something missing in one's life, which he or she finds in another person."

"That sounds rather cold and cynical," I said, pulling away from his embrace and sitting up beside him. I punched my bolster to make it fit my form and leaned back against the big headboard with its beautifully carved scene of the Garden of Eden—before the fall from God's grace, I'd figured. I folded my arms across my bare breasts, then pulled up the coverlet to hide my nakedness. "It makes love sound rather like going to market to barter," I protested. "I'll trade you this for that."

"Tit for tat?" he teased and reached to squeeze my breast.

I hit his hand away. "Whatever happened to those heartfelt sonnets you used to pen for me—and spring on me whenever I was angry?"

He suddenly looked quite smug. "Are you angry now, Lady Tongue?"

"Will you call me your shrew again and try to tame me? Perhaps if you call me Lady Disdain, I will say you are right."

I scrambled from his reach, pulled on a robe and strode to the table where he'd been writing. Gripping the back of the chair he'd abandoned when we'd tumbled into bed, I happened to glance down and caught these words, labeled under the heading of Sonnet 130:

My mistress' eyes are nothing like the sun;
Coral is far more red than her lips' red;
If snow be white, why then her breasts are dun;
If hairs be wires, black wires grow on her head . . .

"Damn you, Will Shakespeare!" I cried, pointing at the poem but not touching it, as if it were poison. "This sonnet is about me, isn't it? Where's the rest of it?"

"In my head, but wait until you see the couplet, telling . . ."

"I am not your mistress or your housemaid—I am your wife. I don't care what anyone thinks or knows or hears!" I shouted. He rose hastily with his index finger to his lips to shush me. "You don't believe in love, if you ever did!" I shouted, darting away from him. "All your love poems are lies! You've changed, you don't value me anymore—that is, except as something you can buy in the marketplace. Go and be hanged, William Shakespeare—go find someone else to be your muse and warm your bed. Get away from me!"

I had ducked under his arm, run into the other room, slammed the door in his face and wedged a chair under the knob. He rattled the door, pounded on it, but in the end had to crawl out the bedroom window. I wouldn't let him in the locked door so he probably had to go to the Burbages for help.

Even as I stopped by the print shop to pick up the *Metamorphoses,* I told myself that I only did it so that I could go to the Globe and throw it in his face and tell him I was undergoing a change just like all the characters in Ovid's tales. I also planned to give him back the betrothal ring he'd given me years before, which I oft wore on a neck chain, hidden in my bodice. I'd find another man who didn't call me shrew, who didn't write poems about my dark eyes and dark skin and black hair like wires and . . .

Now, seething, heading at a good clip for the print shop at St. Paul's, I rehearsed my little speech, ignoring all else. Ah, I understood now why Prince Hamlet wanted revenge, and no one had killed my father and married my mother! My own inner chaos soon echoed that of the streets—or was that a loud hue and cry from somewhere up ahead?

A woman came running at me, holding a young child in one arm and pulling another by the hand.

"What is it?" I asked. "What's amiss?"

"Essex and his rabble," she gasped out. "He's on foot—armed—lots of men, trying to raise troops to take the palace—take the queen prisoner."

She ran into a house and slammed the door. That sound, over the shouts from the next street, echoed in my soul. What if this rebellion put Will in danger?

I ran north toward Temple Bar and passed through it. A mob was coming, but it was too late to retreat, for, behind me, others shoved through that entry to the city. I heard the big bar itself slam down. I could see the mob meant to smash it apart, though even monarchs traditionally stopped and asked permission to enter here.

"Warn the palace!" someone shouted from the other side of the bar. "Have them put wagons across the road by Charing Cross so they don't get through! Warn the palace!"

Pressing myself close to the buildings to get past the mob milling before Temple Bar, I saw Essex and Southampton. Both looked feverish, with eyes glowing as if from within. Neither wore armor, though they swung their swords over their heads and screamed encouragement to their men.

"A plot has been laid for my life!" Essex shouted. "Men of London, lovers of justice, to me, to me! Follow me for justice against all tyranny!"

I pulled up my hood to cover my face and hair just as when I first came to London and feared I'd be accosted for my exotic appearance. I'd become confident and proud of my looks—at least until I'd glimpsed that wretched sonnet Will was writing. But despite all that, my instincts said to warn him—to get to him and his fellow players to tell them the rebellion was on and they must be wary, perhaps even flee. I did not believe for one moment that these brutish men who still passed by would succeed in overthrowing the last Tudor, not the queen I'd seen and admired. But still, Cecil might be out for blood.

"To me, citizens of London!" Essex screamed as Southampton madly waved a banner with his coat-of-arms. I thought of that first day I'd seen the earl as a youth at the memorial service for the clown Tarlton so long ago. So young, so sweet and shy. I thought of how he'd rescued me from plague London. Could anything save him now? He was nearly twenty-eight years of age and Essex thirty-four, both fully responsible for this madness. Perhaps they loved themselves entirely too much, and pride had been their tragic, fatal flaw. But I must not let them take Will down with them in this true-life tragedy.

Finally, the rebellious mob turned back from Temple Bar, evidently deciding to go another way. They surged down Fleet Street toward St. Paul's. Wedged in where I was, even I could tell that recruits did not appear. People hung from their windows, gaping and cursing, even shaking their fists. Someone kept shouting, "God save the queen!" Men they tried to drag into their mob fought and fled. The horde of rebels seemed to shrink, not swell.

When they moved en masse, at first I was swept along in their fringe, but I managed to duck into an alley and dart through it to Water Street and thence to the river. Others were escaping, not toward the insurrection but away from it. The two rebel earls had badly miscalculated. I ran along the wharves to Bridewell where, out of breath and terrified, I caught a wherry for Southwark.

"Aye, then, guess 'is lordship's gonna take Whitehall for 'is own," the boatman said. "Time for a change, either wi' Essex or Scots King Jamie, a man back on the throne after the old king's girls, Bloody Mary and Virgin Bess, eh? Get a man ruling, things won't be ruined like lately."

If I had not been in the middle of the wintry Thames, I would have told this dolt that it was a man who was ruining my life, ruining the calm of this city and the queen's day to boot.

I turned away, even though I had to face the cutting western wind. Tears stung my eyes. A rebellion in the streets and in my heart. Oh, I'd warn Will and the players, but then I must get on with my life. How stupid—how sinful—I had been to think I could keep a man who was not wholly mine, maybe never mine at all.

The Globe came in view with its flag flapping, a drawing of Atlas shouldering the world. How I had loved that theatre and its people. How I had loved Will, almost as far back as I could remember. I could go to live in my fine new place only a few miles from Anne Hathaway's New Place. But, though I loved to visit there, especially in the summer, my heart and home were here. I must decide what to do with my life away from Will, who obviously had cooled toward me. Love "is an ever-fixed mark that looks on tempests and is never shaken. . . . If this be error, and upon me proved, I never writ, nor no man ever loved"—horse dung! Damn that devil with the bewitching words!

I paid the boatman and nearly tripped when I disembarked on the Paris Garden wharf. Holding up my skirts, watching for slick spots on the path, I hurried toward the Globe. I went in the back way, through the tiring room door, for I knew they were presenting *The Merchant of Venice*, but surely they must be nearly done.

I came in on the first scene of Act V, where the lovers Jessica and Lorenzo banter sarcastically—more of Will's true nature coming out, I fumed. I stopped backstage between the rows of hanging swords in scabbards as the pair of speeches struck me.

Lorenzo: In such a night
Did Jessica steal from the wealthy Jew,
And with an unthrift love did run from Venice
As far as Belmont.

Jessica: In such a night
Did young Lorenzo swear he loved her well,
Stealing her soul with many vows of faith,
And ne'er a true one.

It was too much. In truth, the malcontents in Will's plays, even his comedies, spoke for him. He loved me not, but had only needed me in his difficult days—need, his own definition of love. Now, with fame and fortune, it was all over. For him, love was only a theme in a play, a joke, a vow of faith to steal a woman's soul . . .

Will and his fellows had made their bed with Essex and Southampton by choice, and that was that. As far as I was concerned, Will Shakespeare would never make his bed with me again.

Blinded by tears, I staggered to the back door and let myself out. As I rounded the building, I saw a late-paying customer slip inside the Globe, though the ticket boy tried to tell him the play was nearly over. Mr. Mercer, come to see but the last few scenes of an old play? While Essex and Southampton staged a rebellion across the river?

Feeling as deserted and defeated as they must be, I wiped my tears away and hurried back to the wharf.

As I first conveyed to you in this, my life drama, it was but three days later that I found myself fetched by a boy to the building that housed the queen's wardrobe where I faced Robert Cecil in a war of wits and words. He made it clear that my answers would affect the fate of the Globe's players, especially Will. Then he posed the inquiry that made me decide to write this *memoir*, to use the

French word for a probing of personal memories. Quite simply, the queen's Secretary Cecil asked what I myself had been asking for years, especially now that things seemed so bad between Will and me.

We stared at each other in a stalemate but hardly, I thought, a truce. Air from an unseen source shifted a battle banner behind his head. With a shudder up my spine, I realized what I said in the next few moments could save Will or damn him to death. I'd been so angry with him lately, cursing his callous behavior, but now, in place of that, fear flooded in. Fear for him, for me and all we'd worked for.

"But tell me," Cecil said, leaning on his elbows and steepling his long-fingered hands before his mouth, "before we go on, exactly what is William Shakespeare to you? Here you are, an exotic woman, a tempting vixen, when I believe I've heard he has a wife and family back in Stratford-Upon-the-Avon. Tell me true, Mistress Anne Whateley, what is the man to you?"

If he'd asked me that on the day of the Essex rebellion, who knows what I might have said. But now the emotions—yes, the need, as Will had said—the long-buried love I had borne him from our childhoods on rushed back to nearly overwhelm me. "Love is not love which alters when it alteration finds . . ." I believed those words at all costs. I believed Will had once meant those words and could mean them again. Though I'd as good as thrown him out of my life, I yet slept in his best bed.

"Mistress?" Cecil prompted as if I had missed my cue. For one moment I nearly broke into wild laughter. It was as if he had inquired if I were Will's mistress, but he was simply prodding me to answer him.

"I am trying to find the words to explain, my lord. I rather reckon it is like your relationship to and love for the queen."

"How so?" he demanded, sitting up stiffly and frowning.

"Will Shakespeare, sir, is a genius at what he does, much as is the queen in her realm. But they need helpers, do they not, guardian angels of a sort? She is a woman in a man's world where some want to harm her, a woman whom you, as your father before you, have honored and served. And Will is a rural poet at heart trying to make his way in London where I lived before he came. So you and I are much alike in our admiration—and our love—for those we have chosen to care for."

"Yes, but Her Majesty is far above my star, whereas you and Shakespeare—"

"But," I dared to interrupt him, on a sure path now, "the queen's God-given destiny is to rule the English people. My friend Will's is to write for her people and for the queen herself, who has shown him much generous favor. Yet they both need protection and prompting to be their best, is that not so?"

I could tell he was shocked by my answer, perhaps suspicious and skeptical too. I had probably overdone the histrionics he'd wanted to avoid if he'd dragged the players in here. But I could not help it. I held my breath, praying he had not had Mr. Mercer or some other spy dig up the fact that Will and I were registered to be wed in a public record book in Worcester.

He cleared his throat. "So you are his friend and his—his muse, as it were?"

"Exactly and succinctly said, my lord, for I know I rambled on a bit."

"A friend to his family then?"

"I am not much in Stratford, but I believe if you inquired of his father, he would say so."

"Well, then to business," he said, looking relieved but not half as much as I felt. "You have claimed that the Lord Chamberlain's Men played *Richard II* for Essex, Southampton and their ilk because they needed the money. Even if I grant you that, I have it on good authority that the way Essex conducted himself during the play was shameful and provocative."

That was *Mr. Mercer in the audience*, I thought. My, but he was getting to be a supporter of Will's plays lately.

"He did, my lord, and I can tell you how appalled the players were, especially Will. I must admit I was there backstage and can tell you he looked sick to his stomach at the way the Earl of Essex carried on, and not just because he was cavorting about to draw attention from the players. Why, Essex even pretended he was a chicken with his head cut off, which entirely mocked the solemnity of the history being presented, not to mention—"

"I see," he intoned, holding up both hands. "We shall let it rest at that, Mistress Whateley. As for heads being cut off, that will be the sad fate of Lord Essex and perhaps Southampton too—"

"He's so young and impressionable, Lord Southampton, I mean, at least he seems that way from a distance. Thank heavens your father took him in when he lost his own father so early. Essex has deluded him, my lord, calling himself an older brother. I fear he has greatly misled the younger man in several serious matters, after your sire, no doubt, did a fine job counseling him when Southampton was his ward."

There, I thought. Essex was no doubt doomed, but perhaps what I'd blurted out just now could help to save Will's patron's life.

I would never forget that, whatever his shame and sins now, South-ampton had been generous not only to Will but to me.

"Mistress Whateley," Cecil said, half rising, then sitting again, "you are dismissed with my thanks and the queen's wardrobe pieces, which Thompson here will carry for you as far as the door. After all, your receiving such was all you were here for today. You saw someone in charge whose name you did not catch, took the garments and went home."

"Yes, I understand. And thank you from the Lord Chamber-lain's Men too, my lord." My legs were trembling as I rose from my stool; no, my entire body was shaking.

"And," Cecil added as his man stepped forward with a bundle in his arms, "I'd suggest you keep to your pack train business, and steer clear of actors and such. A volatile, overly emotional lot, however much the queen seems to favor them. By the way, she'd like them to come to Whitehall for a performance of something light to clear the air—definitely not *King Richard II*."

Was he making a jest? I almost smiled as I dipped him a curtsy. "Shall I tell them a comedy then?"

"Do so, as I hardly believe you will avoid them, no matter what I counsel. You see, I have learned much of strong, clever women working with Her Majesty—protecting her, as you say. That is all, Mistress Anne Whateley," he repeated abruptly and gestured me away, evidently before he—not I—could say more.

I went, head high, not running from the place as I longed to do, but making my exit with measured steps. Though all was si-lence, I felt as if the queen's Secretary Cecil had just applauded me as the heroine in a play, hopefully a history and not a tragedy.

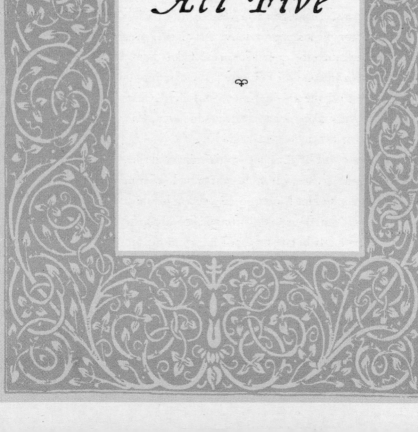

Act Five

CHAPTER TWENTY

꼬

The dangerous question about my relationship to Will that Cecil had put to me—and, I believe, I had escaped truly answering—was to endanger Will and me once more, not privily this time, but in a public trial. But allow me to unfold events leading up to that dread day.

After the ruined Essex rebellion, I had staged my own rebellion against Will, for I felt he had much changed from the man I knew. He was still seething not only over the loss of his Arden kin, but the government's handling of Essex and Southampton. Will's father had died too, in the fall of 1601, and that had sent him into black thoughts of his son's loss and his bleak relationship with his family. His plays—like the man himself—had turned bitter.

In a current work, *The Tragedy of Troilus and Cressida*, Will satirized life at court and the decay of nobility and heroism. It was, if I say so myself, a savage play. Some said he'd written the character of Achilles, sulking in his tent, to remind everyone of Essex's attitude toward the queen. I know not how he managed to get the whole thing past the Master of Revels. I was certain that, unlike Kit, Will was not in league with the powers-that-be. Perhaps, in the end, it was his genius that saved him.

As usual, we had argued, but this time I'd left town. For three months now, despite winter roads, I had gone back and forth between Oxford, visiting the Davenants and my darling Kate, now fourteen, in their cozy inn, and staying in my rebuilt cottage in Temple Grafton.

But as spring came to Warwickshire in late March 1603, I was going mad. The pleasure of furnishing my fine place, even walking the hills and meadows, did not quiet my heart this time. I longed to be in London, and, curse the man, I wanted to be with Will.

"I'll take that cheese there, if you please," I told the man in the row of Stratford Rother Market stalls that displayed pyramids of my favorite round, gold cheeses. My maid Sally had told me to buy from the first stall run by the tall John Lane, for his competition, the red-haired Rafe Smith, in the next one, was a blowhard and made lewd comments too.

I'd come in Sally's stead today, for I needed something to do besides keep the books for my pack train business and read Will's last letter to tatters as well as the new one I'd received from Richard Burbage. My big market basket was getting heavy with purchases, but I didn't seem to be able to stop buying things. As soon as I finished here, I told myself, I would go pick violets for Kat's grave.

And then, past the market cross and beyond a stall piled with early sallet greens and leeks, I saw Anne Hathaway. In bright blue taffeta and a feathered hat, she was dressed overly well for a foray to market. She trailed an entourage of four servants, two male, two female, with flat, square baskets she was heaping with goods, both produce and fripperies. Heavier than I recalled, she was turning gray at her temples. In an imperious tone, her high-pitched voice carried to me—to everyone, I guess, and perhaps that was the point.

John Lane gave a sharp snort and muttered, "Now we don't got the Cloptons or Ardens in these parts, thinks she can take their place—her highness! Comes every day, la-di-da, takes things, sends her daughter to settle up later."

"Her daughter Susannah or Judith?"

"The older one, dresses her fine too. You know the Shakespeares? The da's a 'portant, wealthy man, makes plays in London-town, can see why he don't come home much."

I saw a stir in the crowded market besides the pompous procession of Anne Hathaway. A portly man—I recognized the longtime town crier—mounted the steps from which proclamations were read. The bells of Holy Trinity began to toll. The steady, clanging cadence cut right through me.

"The queen is dead! Long live the king!" the man shouted over the din of the bells. His cheeks were shiny; he was crying. John Lane gasped and dropped the cheese, which rolled away under Rafe Smith's booth, but I did not budge. "Long live King James VI of Scotland, now our King James I of England! The queen is dead! Long live the king!"

I could not believe it. My legs began to shake.

"Hey, Lane," the redheaded Rafe shouted from the next booth, "he got that all wrong, 'cause we still got Queen Shakespeare and that pretty little Princess Susannah in these parts, eh? Like to bring them both down, I would."

I could not believe he dared to besmirch this solemn moment with his words and an obscene gesture as he spoke Susannah's name. John Lane only frowned and motioned for the other man to leave off. I did not wait for my cheese, but headed home.

Tears blinded my eyes, but I could still see the queen as she'd looked in my girlhood, garbed in gleaming satin upon her white stallion in that moment when her eyes met mine. I saw her at court, deigning to speak to me: "I am pleased to see a woman among the players, at least behind the stage, for behind every man—or men—there is a strong woman."

Of course, Her Majesty was aged, and rumors said she had been ill, but I could not fathom she was gone after forty-five years on England's throne. Will had written that the company had acted before her at Richmond Palace just last month; he'd said she'd looked delicate but was as demanding as ever. Gloriana had seemed to me invincible, a woman bestriding a man's world, one who had wanted but never wedded the only man she had ever loved—and she'd lost her Leicester years ago.

I stumbled but managed to keep from falling. I had lost the love of my life too. And with the death of the queen, I knew I had lost something of myself.

Her Majesty's griefs lately, like mine, had been many. How they said she had suffered when she'd signed the Earl of Essex's death warrant that sent him to the block. Southampton, at first condemned with Essex, had seen his sentence commuted to life in prison and had been languishing in the Tower.

Lugging my heavy basket, I left the outskirts of town and

headed toward Temple Grafton. I continued to cry, partly for the queen, partly because Will and I had parted awkwardly as friends, not lovers—and most certainly not as man and wife. And see what had happened to his plays since I was no longer his muse, not to mention that flippant, bitter sonnet about his mistress!

Since he was in London, he'd probably known of the queen's death two days ago. He would be relieved at his best or rejoicing at his worst. It would be just like him to write a poem celebrating Her Majesty's death instead of commemorating it.

When I heard a horse on the crosscut path behind me, I swiped tears from my face. The rider passed me, then reined in and turned in his saddle to look back.

"Mistress Whateley?"

Blinking back tears, I saw it was Dr. John Hall. He had a growing medical practice in Stratford and was well respected. I'd heard nothing but good things about the ambitious young physician. It was said he desired to become a writer too, one who dealt with diseases and their cures.

"Are you quite well?" he asked.

"I just learned in town about the queen," I said as he dismounted and kindly took my basket from me. "Have you not heard?"

"Ah, yes, we all mourn such a change." He seemed more philosophical than emotional—too much like Will, or perhaps all men. "'Tis an end of an era," he added, "though life must go on. A strong Protestant king is good, I think, though I find it hard to believe he is the son of that Catholic Mary, Queen of Scots."

"Life is full of surprises and turnabouts. I'm surprised you recognized me, for it's been nigh on eight years."

"I did not forget you. After all, you introduced me to Susannah."

I wiped my cheeks with the corner of my cloak. "Then you have become dear to each other?" Why had not Will told me? But then, as much as he was away from home, perhaps he did not know. Both of his Annes had lost him to his raving ambitions and desire for revenge. I could not fathom it was enough for Anne Hathaway to have that grand home and to put on gentrified airs. If I were she, I'd rather have Will—the old Will—and live in the middle of a cow pasture if I must.

"Susannah is kept much to home, and I am ever busy with my patients and stocking my new dispensary, but perhaps someday . . ." He sighed. "The course of true love never did run smooth, they say."

I wondered if he knew he was quoting Susannah's father from *A Midsummer Night's Dream*, but perhaps Will had been quoting a country saying. Considering my own life—and the queen's—it seemed a universal truth.

"Indeed," he rushed on, as if anxious to share his thoughts, "I do see her but only off and on. I am eight years her elder, and her mother says she's too young to be courted. Will you not ride the rest of the way home on my mount, if that is where you are heading?"

"I'll be fine, though I'd appreciate it if you'd take the basket and give it to my girl Sally at the house."

"I have seen how you've expanded it to quite a handsome place. All right then. Mistress Whateley, 'tis an honor to speak with you again."

I imagined I heard the rest of his unspoken sentence, *No matter what others—especially Susannah—say of you.* Yet I was on the girl's side. How could her mother keep her much to home if she and John Hall were in love? Surely he was an honorable man and had been open about courting her. He could certainly support a wife and family, and Susannah would still be near her mother. Anne Hathaway's imperious manner reminded me of the tantrums they say the queen used to throw when one of her maids of honor eloped. Why, when Will and I were eighteen, we were . . . were wed and then everything fell apart.

The moment John Hall rode away with my basket, I cut off the road and headed across the meadow, its grass still brown and much beaten down by melted snow and winter winds. But I saw hints of green, tufts of early flowers, especially around the hawthorn hedge. I leaned one shoulder against a sturdy horse chestnut tree where Will and I had sat once, eating apples, kissing and dreaming of our future. Of a sudden, my fierce desire to live life to the fullest swelled within me like spring sap.

The end of an era, John Hall had said. I broke into great sucking sobs. The queen was dead, but I was alive and I wanted Will. I wanted to be back in London, to go to the Globe, to live at Blackfriars near my friends. I wanted to be at Westminster when they interred the queen so that I could say farewell to her and, if he didn't want me back, fare-thee-well to Will!

The day of the queen's funeral procession to Westminster Abbey, April 28, 1603, there was stunning spring weather as if the England she had loved and long tended wished to bid her a sweet good-bye. The breeze was gentle, and shafts of sun slanted down into the cobbled streets surrounding the huge old building. Few but formal mourners would be allowed inside the abbey itself, so it seemed all of London lined the streets nearby.

I had found my place early; now the crowds were six or seven deep. Little children sat on shoulders. Even men cried; women sighed and moaned. People leaned from third-story windows to watch just as, I'd heard, they had the day she was crowned here.

Mostly people stood silent, but now and then someone would tell of a time Elizabeth the queen had ridden by or waved out the window of her coach at them. I too would ever treasure the times I'd seen her, but I sealed all that away with my dearest memories.

I hoped Will was nearby and in a respectful mood. I kept skimming the rows of faces for him. Her Majesty had shown him great favor, and he should be grateful for that.

I had been in London but two days after a stay with the Davenants on my way back from Temple Grafton, but I had not yet seen Will. I was afraid we would argue again over the queen, and I could not bear that right now. But mostly I'd stayed away—I was sure Richard Burbage must have told him I was back—because I didn't want it to look as if I ran to him the moment I returned.

Distant trumpets sounded as the procession came closer; the fanfare echoed off the abbey's gray stone walls. The crowd seemed to hold its breath as the first black banners of the heralds came into view. Between trumpet blasts, I heard the clip-clop of horses' hooves, then the footsteps of the nearly one thousand persons in the funeral parade.

The procession was both somber and magnificent. Black velvet swagged the four raven-hued horses and the huge hearse they drew. Over the catafalque, a black canopy bedecked with bunting and banners was carried on poles by six earls walking with slow strides.

People gasped and murmured when they saw atop the bier the

life-sized wax effigy of the queen with its painted face. Dressed in her crimson robes of state, she wore a crown on her red hair and held the orb and scepter in her hands. As the hearse bounced across the cobblestones, that image of her seemed to move as if it would shake off death itself and rise.

Next came Her Majesty's riderless palfrey, led by her Master of the Horse, then the main members of the nobility. The women wore mourning hoods and cloaks that made them look like nuns. After that followed row upon row of black-clad mourners, from courtiers to servants. The Children of the Chapel Royal went by, the company that performed musicals and plays in the Blackfriars Theatre, which Richard Burbage had leased to them. I saw Robert Cecil and Sir Walter Raleigh, marching at the rear with the Gentlemen Pensioners, who carried their ceremonial halberds pointing down. I felt dizzy with the passing of them all.

From my vantage point, I could barely catch a glimpse of the effigy and coffin as they were carried through the great abbey doors. The end of an era, Dr. Hall had said, and so it was. I was thirty-eight, but suddenly felt so much older.

As the mourners from the procession dispersed, either to go into the abbey or go home, even as the crowd thinned, I stood there yet. The next great procession in London would be held when King James and his entourage arrived from Scotland or perhaps the day of his coronation. The queen is dead; long live the king.

At last, as the shadows lengthened, breathing out cool air from the very abbey stones, I turned to go home. I thought I saw Will up ahead, speaking with a man, but I'd imagined the same whenever I'd seen someone of his stature or gait for months, both in

Warwickshire or here—pure wishful thinking. But this man, even capped and caped, did look like Will.

I quickened my steps, just as the other man hurried away and the one I sought turned around and, as if I'd called to him, saw me. Will indeed! My insides cartwheeled. Though my instinct was to rush to him, I halted and stared. His eyes widened, then he squinted—he'd been getting nearsighted the last few years—and smiled. "Anne!" he cried and strode so quickly toward me his black cape flapped like crow's wings.

I flew into his arms, nearly knocking him over. He lifted me off the ground and spun me around. "Burbage just told me that you were back," he said. "I was coming to call after all this, but was afraid I'd find you distraught over the queen." He put me down and kissed me hard, grappling me to him tightly. He slanted his mouth to get closer, to devour me, it seemed.

I met and matched him move for move and caress for caress, our public place in the street be damned. Frenzy flooded me; of a sudden it was hottest summer. I opened my lips beneath his and our tongues dueled and danced. I felt swept away from my spinning head to the very pit of my belly, when I thought—I had prayed—that such passion had now passed me by. But not with Will. Rampant lust and eternal longing filled me on this day of grieving.

"Anne, Anne," he gasped when we came up for air. "The truth is, I've been looking for you everywhere. I knew you'd be here for this."

"I wasn't sure you would be," I said so breathily it did not sound like my voice. I had clamped him to me, my arms around his ribs.

"I wanted to see her buried," he said simply.

We spoke no more, perhaps fearful of plunging into our old arguments. We held hands, staring into each other's eyes. Then we were young again, no matter how many years and troubles had gone by. We should not have been so intent on each other, though, for his brother Edmund appeared before we noticed him.

"I—I thought it was you," the young man stammered, his big brown eyes taking me in. I was certain who he was because he looked so much like Will, who had more or less adopted him. Only five years older than Hamnet would have been, Edmund had ever been Will's favorite brother. "Anne Whateley," the boy added, blushing, "Edmund Shakespeare at your service." He smiled and swept off his cap and made a small bow. Though he was but twenty-three, I saw his hairline was receding precisely as Will's had.

"Edmund and I watched the procession together," Will said, loosing only one of my hands, so that Edmund and I could make a proper greeting. "But as usual he was hungry and went to buy some meat pies—with my coins. So where are you hiding them?" he asked, pretending to be grim, as the younger man produced four pies from his satchel with a grand gesture as if he were a magician.

"I hear you are earning a name for yourself at the Curtain," I said. Had Will told Edmund about us when he'd told no one else? The young man seemed to be taking our presence so matter-of-factly.

"Edmund's good news," Will put in, taking a pie and handing it to me before he took one himself, "is that he is in love."

"I am, truly, for the first and last time ever," Edmund said, biting into a pie and getting gravy on his chin like the exuberant boy he seemed to be. He spoke with his mouth half full. "She is Frances Wembly, employed by the Mountjoys—wig makers—where Will has put me up. And when I earn enough to wed, we shall do so and both of you will be my guests. Are you still sure you want to go inside the abbey, Will? I'd rather not if—"

"I think Anne will go with me, and I know you have lines to learn and need to see your Frances."

"She doesn't like crowds or grieving, so she's working hard on one of the wigs for the Globe today, a huge one for a fairy queen, I hear."

"A revival of *Midsummer Night's Dream*?" I asked.

"You haven't heard that good news either," Will told me, squeezing my waist with his free arm. "The Lord Chamberlain's Men have now become the King's Men by order of our new monarch."

"Oh, Will! That's wonderful! The Monarch's Merry, Morose and Madcap Men, he should call you."

Will laughed and Edmund clapped him on the back as if I'd made the wildest jest. "We're to meet the royal entourage coming down from Scotland at Greenwich Palace with a group of plays prepared," Will went on. "So as for spending on costumes and wigs, the sky's suddenly the limit."

"If you don't want those pieces I was given from the queen's wardrobe, I'd like them back—keepsakes," I said. "And, yes, I'll go inside the abbey with you, if you vow not to say or do anything to disparage Her Majesty, at least today."

"No more," he promised. "I have tried to learn to let the dead rest in peace."

He and Edmund looked at each other, and Will hit his fist into the boy's shoulder before he left us. I could tell he was champing at the bit to be off to see his Frances. After we finished our pies and wiped our hands, Will and I walked slowly toward the abbey.

"You told Edmund about me—about us?" I asked.

"Not all, but yes, what a support and help you have been to me these years in London. I swear, the time you've been away, it was as if I lost my voice—my muse." He tucked my wrist in the crook of his arm and pulled it close to his ribs. I began to sniffle for the first time today; in Stratford I'd cried all I could for the queen's death.

"Anne," he went on, hanging his head a bit, not looking at me, but his fine, deep actor's voice was so intense. "I have been so vile to you lately—but that's because you have been my conscience too, and I could not bear that. I wanted to hate the queen, and you eloquently presented her good points. Like you, I knew Essex and Southampton were wrong, but I wanted them to win."

"It's all right, so—"

"It isn't! And the more we argued, the more I kept telling myself I had to keep away from you, that you were getting in the way of my work, and I had to protect my work at all costs. Then, I realized, you had always protected my work—and me."

I almost told him that I might have protected his very life when I stood up to Cecil with my own little drama, but I did not want to do anything but etch his words in my head and heart.

"And one more thing. I meant to write this to you, but I must tell you in person," he said, stopping and looking at me. "You once asked why I did not write you sonnets anymore, and I know you took great offense at the one you read the last night we bedded."

"Ah, yes, Sonnet 130 about your wretched, ugly mistress."

"I tried to tell you that night what the couplet was—the bottom lines, as it were. The point of it all was that the woman the poet loved was not idealized or imaginary, but very real—and he loved her yet with any slight flaws she might have."

"Tell me then, for I recall the rest all too well about dun breasts and black wires for hair."

"Poetic license—exaggeration, for you are the most beautiful woman—inside and out—I have ever known. But the couplet is:

"And yet, by Heaven, I think my love as rare
As any she belied with false compare."

"I see. And, though I have ever refused to dub myself your mistress, I shall never be false to you, poet—and you should know it."

"Oh, my Anne of rhyming and reasoning," he whispered as we began to walk again. We both hushed as we walked inside the huge double doors of the cool, dim abbey. And jumped back when, suddenly, the two guards at the door slanted their pikes before our faces.

"Others are still inside—your betters," one man clipped out, then looked closer at Will. "I seen you on the stage. At court and at the Globe." He looked at me, as if I should be someone he knew too. "All right then, only up to the entry to the chapel where they laid her. Best to come back next year and see the fine marble effigy, all painted and gilded too, that's what the new king has ordered for Good Queen Bess."

"We'll do that," Will said as they let us walk under their pikes they lifted as if we passed through a gate. We had heard they would inter the queen in an appropriate place, the Henry VIII Chapel in the north aisle, ironically with her lead coffin placed atop that of her unloved half-sister, "Bloody Mary." Feeling awed by the place and Will's words to me, I did not react at first when a familiar figure emerged from the chapel and strode toward us.

"Will," the cloaked but bareheaded man cried. In the torches still left burning, his long, auburn tresses shone almost as pale as his face. "And Anne!"

"My Lord Southampton!" Will cried and swept him a bow as I curtsied. "But—how long have you been freed from the Tower?"

He looked thin, tired and much older than I recalled, but he seized Will's hand with vigor. "It was one of the new king's first decrees, thank God for the queen's death to make him king! I had to come and see where they'd laid her, so I knew for certain it was ended. I—I will never cease suffering for my dear Lord Essex's beheading . . ." He had pumped Will's hand through all that and now he turned to me, tears in his eyes.

"Dearest Anne, yesterday Cecil himself brought me the news I was free and I partly have you to thank for my life too. He said you put in a good word for me the day he questioned you about Will and the players' part in the rebellion." He pulled me close and hugged me, then set me back. "You shall see how grateful I can be to both of you. For now, I must be off, so Godspeed to all and God save this king!"

At the entry to the vaulted Henry VIII Chapel, I stood as astounded as Will. We went no farther into the aisle where the queen's fine tomb would rise one day; he leaned against a massive pillar and held me at arm's length to stare into my face in the dancing torchlight.

"Cecil?" Will said, looking stunned. "He pulled you in over our part in the rebellion? Why did you not tell me at once?"

"I wasn't speaking *to* you then, my love, but was only speaking of you. In the end, he and I got on famously, and if you make some jealous or snide remark for that, I shall give you a black eye. Besides, he warned me to tell no one, though since he's told the earl himself now, I warrant that changes things. Will, in a way I lied to him and yet I managed to tell him the truth too."

"Ah, my love," he whispered and pulled me to him, "the consummate actor and author of her own words, the be-all and end-all of my plays and my days. My protector, my muse, my conscience—the wife of my heart. Let us pray on this day on which we buried the queen that we have also buried the tough times we've been through. Let's go out into the sun and treasure our days together."

In that moment, if the entire massive abbey had fallen down atop me, I would have died quite well content.

CHAPTER TWENTY-ONE

❧

I would like to end my story there, with naught but happiness on the horizon, but that would not be truthful, and I have sought to be so throughout these five acts of my life.

Indeed, times were good for us as Will became the new monarch's favorite playwright of the many he patronized. The King's Men were named grooms of the chamber and were allotted four and one half yards each of scarlet wool for royal livery of doublet, hose and cloak for the coronation parade. Despite his obtaining a coat-of-arms earlier, this was the height of Will's dreams. Though wool clearly showed they were gentry and not nobility, Will and his fellows had managed to help lift players from their reputations as impoverished, strolling entertainers to admired professional men.

Instead of profitable royal command performances but twice a year, the King's Men put on fourteen plays during each of the next few years as Will wrote like a madman, whether at the house next to the Globe, at his Silver Street chamber where Edmund lived, or, most often, with me in my chambers at Blackfriars. The Earl of Southampton had completely charmed Queen Anne, and many of Will's works saw revivals at Southampton House before the royal family and an adoring crowd of courtiers. Southampton did not forget his promise of gratitude to both of us, for I was always invited to these grand and elaborate events. Henry, Prince of Wales, loved Italian culture, and so he found me fascinating. Fortunately, Will only became jealous once in a while over that.

The best proof of Will's favor with the new king and especially with his theatre-loving Queen Anne came when a dire plot threatened king and country. This time, no one, not even Cecil, suspected Will of complicity, despite the fact that one of the key plotters was Robert Catesby, a Warwickshire man. Another conspirator had even leased old Clopton House outside Stratford to lay his plans. Under the leadership of a man named Guy Fawkes, the rebels planned to blow up king and Parliament by igniting barrels of gunpowder in the cellars beneath Westminster.

When the plot was discovered and the villains tried, tortured and executed, unfortunately, Robert Cecil ordered new legislation against all Catholic recusants, especially around Stratford. Susannah and Will's brother Richard ended up in their hometown courts with hefty fines for refusing to take Protestant communion. Will stomped about a great deal when we heard and more than once muttered a line he'd written in protest, "Every subject's duty is the king's, but every subject's soul is his own."

I heard from my maid Sally's gossip that Stratford folk were pleased to see the upstart Shakespeares put in their place. When

Will heard the word *upstart*, it distressed him even more for two reasons. First, that Anne was ruining the family's reputation in the land that had bred him and where he was working hard to become a leading landowner and citizen, for he blamed himself as absent head of the household. And second, because he too had been branded an upstart by his detractors years ago and had worked so hard to get past that slur. All this worried him, but the religious persecution at home riled him even more.

"I've learned a lesson from all of this," he told me as the two of us sat over a late supper in my rooms at Blackfriars. "'The fool doth think that he is wise, but the wise man knows himself to be a fool,'" he quoted from *As You Like It*. "In short, times change, the country's ruler has changed, but unfair persecution goes on. Your queen was perhaps not so very different from my king after all. So I'm going to write King Jamie a play to set his teeth on edge."

"Will, not again! If *I've* learned a lesson from all this, it is do not bite the hand that feeds you!"

He laughed and reached across the small, cluttered table to still my hand furiously forking him out more venison. "Just listen. I'm going to write him a Scottish play, so he'll let all else in it pass, born-and-bred Scot that he is. Imagine, a Christian king, planning to sponsor a huge Bible translation, and he's afraid of witches. Yes, I'm going to write our Jamie a play that starts out with three witches and a curse . . . and plotting for the throne and murder and . . ."

And so it went, with new characters and plots and scenes—and dangers—swirling around us as he created play after play, each one with darker visions, but ones I understood: *Julius Caesar; Othello*, his study in jealousy run rampant; *Macbeth* and *King Lear*.

Family events came fast and furious too. Jennet and John gave my godchild Kate a total of six siblings. Perhaps their healthy family was the result of Oxford's small-town air, or perhaps it was that Jennet had finally given up a bottle of fine wine each day.

Susannah wed John Hall, partly because I'd put it in Will's head that the next time he went home, he should see to it. John told Susannah he wanted to invite me to their wedding—I visited Temple Grafton off and on, just as Will did to tend his growing Stratford properties—but poor John was shocked to be told why I would not be asked. Yet he and Will formed a fine, mutual friendship, and Will said John always asked how I was getting on. More than once, the good doctor stopped by my front gate to inquire about my health when he rode between Stratford and Temple Grafton, so I reckoned he must take his wife's and mother-in-law's opinion of me with a grain of salt.

Will's mother died the year after the wedding, but worse was our loss of dear Edmund at age twenty-seven from a swift onset of the bloody flux. As if he'd lost his Hamnet all over again, at first, Will was inconsolable.

"I loved him too, you know," I told him as the two of us walked away from St. Saviour's Church on the south bank of the frozen Thames, where Will had paid to have him laid to rest and for the tolling of the passing bell.

Edmund's landlords, the Mountjoys, with the grieving Frances held between them, had just departed under a stone gray sky spitting snow. The bitter wind cut like a knife, but we hardly noticed. Edmund's loss had happened so fast, and now Will had to send the sad news home.

"I know you loved him," Will told me. "He and Frances loved

you too." We held tightly to each other in the buffeting wind. No boats were on the frozen river, and we did not want to walk its width, so we started home across the bridge. "And it was so good of you to ask Frances to stay with you, but it's best she be near her work—bury herself in it, rather. I've paid the Mountjoys for Edmund's room for the next year, so she can live there."

Halfway across the bridge, looking between the buildings, we stared at Londoners cavorting on the Thames, slipping and sliding on the ice amidst screams of joy. Seldom were the winters cold enough for the great river to ice over, but this one had been bitter and brutal.

We did not speak of the fact that Edmund and Frances had had a child together, a son, who did not live long, and who was buried next to him. They had not married in a church but had handfasted, or so Edmund claimed. In a strange way, I felt in burying him we had buried what Will and I might have been and might have had: a life in London as man and wife with a child or two while Will made his way on the stage.

"With all that's happened, I didn't realize it's the last day of the year," I said. My words came out muffled because my lips were so cold.

"And good riddance to the old year. That is, but for our marriage of true minds and hearts getting stronger each day. 'And ruined love, when it is built anew, / Grows fairer than at first, more strong, far greater.'"

"I favor that sonnet over a few others I've seen. But Will, not only Frances will bury herself in her work over Edmund's loss, but you will too."

"I will bury myself in my work, and also in you, my love, and I shall use that as a *double entendre* in some bawdy clown scene sometime."

"Or in a battle royal of courtship between some full-of-himself man and some shrewish, smart-mouthed vixen."

"One with hair black as wires."

"And the man will want to tame her but will find that he cannot."

"Anne, my beloved Anne, let's hie ourselves back to Blackfriars where it's warm and bright, however dark and cold the night."

And so we did.

"The Lord giveth and the Lord taketh away"—my da used to say that. And so it was.

Richard Burbage finally got the Blackfriars Theatre back from the boy players of the Chapel Royal, and Will and I took a one-seventh share in it. The intimacy of the place brought benefits but challenges too. Will wrote for it with a will, if I may pun upon that. But in that happy time, the Prince of Wales died and Will's brother Gilbert too, the latter at age forty-five, so all of us became public and private mourners again.

Still the king and queen decided to go on with the wedding of their daughter, the Princess Elizabeth, to Frederick of Hapsburg, and the King's Men put on fifteen plays for the celebrations of that royal event. The plays included *Cardenio*, based on a translation of Cervantes' *Don Quixote*, a collaboration Will wrote with his protégé John Fletcher. Will was also bringing along Francis Beaumont, training both men to be the King's Men's principal writers for the future. The demands on the company and Will's stamina had made him decide it was time to pass that torch.

"The subject for *Cardenio* just shows how things have changed in our lifetime," Will told me. We would both turn fifty next year, and he'd taken to philosophizing. Since he'd lost the spring in his step, he'd also quit acting, but for a few small parts.

"True," I agreed. More than ever these days, I knew what he would say before he spoke. "It would have been the kiss of death to write a play based on a Spanish story back in the days we were all terrified of the Armada."

He seemed to have come to terms with his once fierce feelings toward the former queen: with a bit of help from Fletcher, he wrote a history play called *All Is True* about the early reign of King Henry VIII, which ended with the baby Elizabeth's baptism and fine accolades for her glorious future.

I liked the play immensely but for one thing. In the character of Cardinal Wolsey, whose power declines in the play, I feared Will saw himself. Lines like "Farewell! A long farewell, to all my greatness!" and "I have touched the highest point of all my greatness, / And from that full meridian of my glory / I haste now to my setting" greatly worried me.

"I believe," I told him the day the play was first performed at the Globe, "*All Is True* will be my favorite of your history plays. But everyone's just calling it *King Henry VIII*, you know."

He heaved a sigh. Though it was his practice to be backstage during premier performances, this had already been played at Blackfriars, so we were sitting in the lowest of the three Globe galleries, dead center in the front row. "They may call it what they will," he said, "but I want to make the point that what has happened already will, in one way or the other, happen again in the history of mankind. The past is prologue. All is true."

"Like King Solomon's 'There is nothing new under the sun.'"

"Exactly." He squeezed my knee, as we watched the theatre continue to fill.

It was a lovely late June day in 1613, a bit windy with sea air off the Thames and gulls wheeling overhead. I was not nervous to sit with him in public, something we hardly worried about anymore. More than once some stranger had called me Mistress Shakespeare, and indeed, I had always believed I was.

I did not know this play as well as his earlier ones, for Will often had John Fletcher take his dictation now. I missed being an integral part of his initial creation, but we were as close as we had ever been.

The scenes of Act II rolled by, and, like the penny knaves on the ground and their betters around us, I was snared by the speeches, the wonderful words, words, words. Henry VIII's first wife, Queen Catherine, "like a jewel hung twenty years about his neck," was about to be replaced by his second wife, the enticing Anne Boleyn.

At the thought of two wives, I shifted slightly in my seat. No wonder Will's daughter Susannah hated me, for she believed her mother to be Will's first and only wife. My last time home, I'd crossed Susannah's path, this time as she shopped in the marketplace with her mother, and I'd been badly burned for coming to her aid.

"Hey now," the red-haired, handsome Rafe Smith had cried, coming out from behind his cheese stall, "if it's not their majesties, the Shakespeare high-and-mighties, come down to throw us poor dolts a few bones or a few coins." I stood at the next stall, owned by John Lane; like everyone else in the area, I turned and stared as Smith stripped off his jerkin and threw it mockingly at Susannah's feet. "I'd take off more'n that for you," he told the blushing girl, "aye, lay myself down for you and with you again and again."

"Susannah, do not even address the likes of that lout!" Anne Hathaway ordered her daughter and turned away, whether from Rafe Smith or from me, I was not sure.

"She's addressed me afore, hain't you, Mistress Hall?" Smith goaded Susannah. "Paid for my very best goods off and on for years, husband or not—"

The crowd was growing. Susannah was pippin-red and stammering in embarrassment and anger. Thinking her daughter was behind her, Anne had flounced away. This entire sordid scene seemed as if it led from the first act I'd seen here nearly ten years before, so what indeed had been going on? Will had not come back to Stratford this time, but best he get here soon and sort this out instead of just tending to his business affairs. Surely, Susannah, wed to the upstanding Dr. Hall, had not had an affair with this ill-bred man.

Before I could rein in my Italian choler, I strode between Susannah and the man. "I shall summon the constable if you do not leave off your insults and slurs, Master Smith."

He hooted a laugh, but worse, Susannah hissed from behind me, "Cease! I don't want the constable, Anne Whateley, and I don't want you to stand up for me or even near me!"

Susannah's mother, dragging her servants, was back; they formed a fence about the younger woman and moved her away from Smith and me. I faced him alone but with half the Stratford market watching.

"See?" he goaded with a rude laugh. "They think their chamber pots don't smell, that they can just dump a man like me in the sewer with the night refuse. But they'll see—they'll see."

"They and the rest of the town will see that buying cheese from your stall is a danger to one's taste in more ways than one, that's sure," I'd said and, head high, walked from the place and the staring people.

I'd told Will about it when I'd come back to London. He'd said that if Susannah's husband had not done so already, he'd settle the man once and for all when he went back next time.

Frowning at the memory, I jumped so hard at the blast of trumpets and the roll of drums from the musicians' gallery above that Will laughed. Small cannons popped near the roof to signal a noble troop of strangers arriving at Cardinal Wolsey's banquet. It was a play with fine sound effects and endless pomp. The musicians wailed away on their hautboys as Richard Burbage as the king danced with Anne Boleyn. Smoke from the cannons drifted down to the stage as if steam came out Henry's ears when he beheld the beauteous Boleyn.

"Those cannons make a stench," I whispered to Will.

He squinted up at the roof. "Still smoking."

We were well into the next scene when someone in the musicians' gallery cried, "Fire! Fii-re! Fiiiii-re!"

People around us vaulted to their feet. Some screamed and, trying to get out, bumped into one another as if in a comic scene. Will and I looked around, behind, below, then up. I could see flames not only licking at the roof thatch, but the entire ring of sky looked smoky.

Panic swelled as the hundreds of patrons in the two galleries above us clattered down the stairs, only to find them blocked by those on our level. The groundlings fled; actors shouted to one another. Will and I knew what we must do. Even if the building was consumed, the expensive costumes and precious playbooks must be saved or, royal patronage or not, the future of the King's Men was doomed.

Pressed in and pushed, we fought our way down to the first floor and bucked the exodus of the last of the shoving groundlings. The two wooden pillars that guarded the stage were burning partway down, and the curtain and railing of the musicians' gallery were aroar with orange flames. Pieces of charred or flaming thatch rained down as we ran for the stage. The players had the tiring room door wide open. That created a sucking draft that fanned the flames, but they were carrying armloads of costumes out the back of the theatre.

"I'll help them!" I shouted to Will.

"Go!"

In the increasing, choking smoke, I lugged out armloads of heavy court costumes. At least the actors were attired in some of the best today, if they weren't ruined by flying cinders. Backstage boys carried out thrones, tables, a cloud, a ship. The roar of the flames soaring skyward made speaking nearly impossible. Everyone dripped sweat; faces were so darkened with roiling smoke we looked like blackamoors.

The Globe, our beautiful Globe, was dying. Gasping for fresh air, I fell to my knees near the house where Will used to write. I saw John Fletcher in tears. Yes, everyone else seemed accounted for—but for Will, I thought, scanning the crowd. Surely, he had not gone into this house or down to the river, for a bucketful of water would be futile.

"Richard!" I screamed to Burbage and leaped up to pull at his arm as he stalked back and forth tearing his hair. "Where's Will? Did you see Will?"

"I saw him with you!"

"He told me to help. I haven't seen him since."

"We saved the playbooks and rolls from the tiring room . . ." he got out before we both stared at each other, wide-eyed. Will kept copies of everything he'd written under the stage, accessed only through the trapdoor. He'd intended to have it all published as his sonnets had finally been, but he'd been so busy . . .

"I'm going in!" I screamed.

"No! It's an inferno!"

He seized my wrist; I yanked and scratched at him to get free. I was out of his grasp and tearing toward the tiring room door before I had time to fear. I sucked in one last breath and plunged inside.

The entire interior seemed one huge bonfire. Heated air belched at me. Flaming timbers thudded into the pit and even onto the stage, and smoke blinded and suffocated me. I wished my skirts weren't so full, for they suddenly seemed like ropes around my legs, and I feared they would catch fire.

But the trapdoor to what the players called hell was only a short run away. Hell—to be trapped in hell and to die there.

I stumbled about at first, fearful I'd missed it. It had an iron ring recessed in the floor. I learned if I crawled on the boards, the smoke was a bit lighter. What if Will went down there and—

Where was that ring, that door?

"Anne! Anne!"

Burbage's voice, not Will's. My lungs were bursting to breathe, and I dared not answer him, or I'd suck in more smoke.

I bumped into a huge wooden chair—the king's throne, one that had been moved but not carried out to save it . . . save it . . .

Yes, it rested on the trapdoor, and if Will had gone down there, the weight could keep the door closed.

I began to cough and gag, but I heard and felt pounding on the door below me. I shoved the chair away and reached for the iron ring. It burned my hand. I screamed, sucking in more hot air and choking on the stench of burning wood and straw, the curtains, the sweet-scented cushions . . . Hacking, I wrapped my skirt hem around the ring, and then Richard appeared on his knees beside me to help lift it.

The door slammed up as Will shoved at it from the inside. He had been trapped in hell. How the players would joke of that—if we made it out. Richard reached to help Will up, but he thrust out the big leather box of what he'd almost died to save.

My eyes streaming tears, I lifted the box, and Richard pulled Will up. As we ran in the direction we thought was the tiring room door, the entire flaming musicians' gallery crashed behind us. Staggering like blind King Lear, we found the open door by the shouts of those outside. My hair was singed and my skirts on fire, but the players put it out by wrapping me in King Henry's heavy velvet cape. Will and I half crawled, half fell into each other's arms, not caring who saw us together or sobbing.

And then, like the others—and a growing crowd that came across the river—we simply stared at the destruction. The playhouse we'd saved and hauled across the river nearly fifteen years ago on that cold, cold day became a gigantic torch in the evening sky.

Crying, coughing, the players, the playwrights, the others—even most of the audience that had stayed—stood silently, many arm in arm, and watched the remains of the Globe crash to a seething skeleton.

Then we stood too, in honor of it all. With the rescued box of his work at his feet, Will held me tight to him, shaking like he had the ague. Finally, our legs gave out, and we sat down on the ground as the burned bones of the Globe tumbled to its brick foundation. As night came and some neighbors moved among us with food and drink, we watched the crimson flames mute to a golden glow.

Finally, sometime later, Richard Burbage cried in a loud voice, "We will rebuild. We will rebuild! The Globe is gone, but not our dreams nor our determination."

"A fine speech," Will whispered to me, his voice hoarse with smoke and tears. "So many fine speeches here . . ."

We were glad when it started to rain because it washed us. The final embers of what had made Will's fame and could have marked his funeral pyre hissed out.

CHAPTER TWENTY-TWO

꼬

But that same year in which fire took the Globe, Will gave me the most glorious gift. The Blackfriars Gatehouse had come up for sale, and he bought it for me, though he put it in a friend's name so that no one would know it was mine—ours—and so that, should he die, it would not go to his wife.

"I can't believe it's ours. I can't believe it!" I cried. We danced in it as we had once before, a pavane and a gay galliard, though we were soon out of breath in the latter.

"Ah, I fear my wild dancing days are over!" he told me as we leaned in the very corner where we'd once risked making love. "But not my dancing days between the sheets once we get that big bed in here."

Holding hands, we rushed from room to room, ecstatic, looking out every window, planning where our furniture would go. Ah, if only we had owned this place for all the years we'd been in London, I thought, then scolded myself for that. After all, the first time we saw this place together, Will had three pounds to his name and look at him now: in fame, fortune and influence, he'd outdone every other force in the English theatre.

"And we'll be close to the Blackfriars Theatre here," I rattled on, "to the Burbages, to Richard Field too. I can't wait to get Kate here to show her this place . . ." Then it struck me that our dear godchild was twenty-five years old and betrothed. Where had the years gone? Where had it all gone?

No matter, I told myself, thrusting those thoughts away. Anne Whateley now had a home every bit as grand as Anne Hathaway's New Place in Stratford, and much more to my liking. It would be our London house, for we were both back and forth to Warwickshire more than ever. It would be our safe haven, our—

We startled at a knock on the door. Things had been so up and down this year that we both froze, for, despite our joy, we feared the worst. Will's last living brother had recently died, so, of his seven siblings, only his sister Joan remained. All these years I'd been an only child, but which was worse—to be alone or to have so many to lose?

Will opened the door. The head of my pack train, Stephen Dench, stood there, grizzled and slightly stooped, a grandfather of nine already. If there was any reminder of years flying past, the people around us were that, for somehow Will and I never changed to each other.

"Heard at your place you'd be here," Stephen said. "Burbage told me."

"Some problem with orders?" I asked as I stepped forward and held out my hand for the paper in his hand.

He shook his head. "For Master Shakespeare, from home. His daughter, the doctor's wife, sent it with me 'cause our pack train left right away, thinking if I found you, I'd find him."

"I see," I said and handed the sealed piece of parchment to Will, as Stephen tipped his cap and thudded down the stairs.

Will stared at the epistle as if it were a poisonous snake. Since it was from Susannah, what if Anne Hathaway were—were ill?

He broke the seal and frowned when he read the letter. "Susannah's suing that man who gave her such trouble in public, Rafe Smith," he said as I stood there breathless, clasping my hands.

"For defamation—the things he implied?" I prompted.

"Now he claims she committed adultery with him and gave him the running of the reynes, and she's begging me to ask you to testify on her behalf in court."

"Adultery with the likes of him! And that she gave that bawdy beef-wit gonorrhea? He'll ruin her and John Hall!"

"And the Shakespeares, at least in Stratford. It's outrageous, an attempt to bring her—and her mother—down."

"That it is. But me to testify? Back in Stratford? Last time I stood up for Kat in court there I—we—lost so much, each other for too many years, and we don't have too many years anymore."

"It's not to be in Stratford, and that's another thing that frets me. It's to be at Worcester Cathedral in the bishop's Consistory Court."

"What's that?"

"The nearest high-ranking religious court. It deals with issues of morality and is presided over by the chancellor of the diocese. In short, it's serious. Curse that woman for flaunting herself."

"I can't believe it of Susannah, so—"

"I mean Anne! She's rubbed everyone's nose in my money and success, so is it any wonder they resent us! I don't believe these charges against Susannah, for she loves and respects John. Well, you will have to refuse this request, because on the stand, you must answer anything and everything they ask—"

"All is true."

"What? If they are out to besmirch Susannah's reputation, they will surely rejoice in ruining yours and mine. I can't let you do this, so she will just have to find someone else to testify."

"You may tell your daughter that you asked, and I accepted," I told him, propping my hands on my hips.

"No, my love," he ordered, shaking his head. "No. I'll absolutely not allow it, and that is final."

While I was waiting in an anteroom to be called to testify before the chancellor and court, I was strangely calm, perhaps numb.

Granted, I'd never seen massive Worcester Cathedral before and was awed by it, this place where, just over three decades ago, Will and I, though still in Stratford, had been granted a marriage bond. Then too this chapter house where the trial was being heard was impressive with its wainscoted walls, tiled floors and high-vaulted courtroom that Kate and I had peeked into before anyone had arrived.

The protocol for the proceedings was complicated. I'd been told I must address the presiding judge, the robed and bewigged chancellor, either as "worshipful sir" or "sir" and must refer to the court itself as "this venerable court." By peeking out the anteroom door,

I'd seen quite a crowd go in—including our dear Kate and her parents to boost my morale—and then the procession of the chancellor and his apparitor, who carried the court's mace and seal, followed by secretaries and aides.

As I waited for the cheese seller John Lane to testify before me, I admit I became a bit on edge. But God's truth, I would have been more afraid to face Cecil in the depths of the queen's wardrobe again—or at least I tried to tell myself so. After all, I had been through so much, from poverty to plague, from losses to great gains, from riots and rebellions to a catastrophic fire, so surely I could handle this.

I hoped to walk a line between helping Susannah and protecting myself and Will. In short, once again, to avoid admitting—or insisting—that I not only considered myself Will's other wife, but his first and only wife. I had wed him in a church in the eyes of God, legally registered, and that was that.

"Mistress Whateley," a man said as he poked his head in the door of the small room where I waited, "this venerable court is ready to hear your testimony now."

I had dressed plainly and somberly, all in gray; my bounteous hair, now threaded with silver, was piled up and greatly hidden under a brimmed hat with one black feather. He led me in, across the parquet floor and into the vast diocese courtroom filled with rows of benches. My heels seemed to click incredibly loudly as everyone pivoted his or her head to behold me.

Will sat in front along the right side as I walked in. He was with Anne, of course, and John Hall. The Halls had a six-year-old daughter, the apple of Will's eye, who was not present. The child was another reason I was certain Susannah would not stray from her marital vows, though I'd seen more than one London wife with a family who erred in that way.

Susannah had the Shakespeare family lawyer, Robert Whatcott, with her. They looked dwarfed by the size of the court and the height of the chancellor's dais looming over their small table.

To my left at another table sat Rafe Smith and his lawyer. I was thoroughly annoyed to see that the defendant looked the part of a clean-shaven and well-kempt man, one with his hands folded before him, when I'd been expecting cock-of-the-walk slurs and sneers. He even managed to look sad and shy. What an outrage, I wanted to shout.

Besides guests of the two interested parties, there were a few folk I did not recognize, and I knew not why they were here. Surely the court would not let mere curious onlookers into a hearing like this.

The man who had escorted me in left me standing in the elevated, railed dock to the left side of the chancellor and moved to stand behind my little prison. At this close range, as I looked up at the chancellor, I noted he was a handsome and imposing man with gray hair showing under his white periwig and broad shoulders swelling his black and red robe. He had clear blue eyes, but they were narrowed and focused on me.

"Anne Whateley, do you swear before God and man to tell the truth, the entire truth?" he asked. His voice boomed out like Burbage's on the stage. I told myself I must not shirk, that I must play my part with calm and courage.

"I do, sir."

I locked my knees and resisted the urge to grasp the high railing for support but stood erect, keeping my hands lightly clasped before me. I did not look at the Shakespeares, though I longed to draw strength from Will. When we were still in London, we'd rehearsed what I might be asked, that I must tell the truth and add nothing on my own. Still, as I'd said to Will, it was my outwitting and standing up to the judge at the hearing on Kat's death that had saved the day.

But this man was hardly a bumbling bailiff, nor was this Stratford's little Guild Hall, however grand that had seemed to me more than thirty years ago. Then my desire was to have my dearest friend buried in hallowed ground; now my task was to have my dearest enemy saved from shame, a huge fine or worse. I'd been appalled to hear that an ecclesiastical court such as this, charged not only with judging but punishing immorality, could order huge fines and public floggings.

One woman, I'd been told, had been found guilty by this very chancellor of similar charges and ordered to be stripped to the waist, tied to a cart and whipped three times around her town church and twice around her marketplace. The picture in my mind of Susannah being so abused in the Rother Market while Rafe Smith and all Stratford watched sickened me.

"Mistress Whateley, I must recount for you that Susannah Hall, née Shakespeare, is in this consistory court to sue Raphael Smith for accusing her of adultery," the chancellor told me, as if I had not a clue as to why I was here. "Are you familiar with that?"

I could have cried at the way he'd worded that question, but my insides cartwheeled. Susannah might be suing Rafe Smith, but she was being charged with precisely what Will and I might be accused of if something went wrong here. And then, ruination, shame and—worst of all—separation.

That terrified me. Will had been ill of an unnamed debilitating disease off and on of late, and Dr. Hall had told him he could not promise him many good years left. One would think the fact that his brothers had died at younger ages would force Will to stay calm, but it had quite the opposite effect. He refused to rest and went back and forth between Stratford and London to pursue his interests in both places—and in both places managed to see me.

Now two memories assailed me in that instant before I answered the chancellor. Years ago when we were but children on Henley Street, a neighbor of Will's, a William Wedgewood—why that name came back to me I knew not—was charged with bigamy and drummed out of town. And I recalled why I always avoided passing Bridewell Prison in London, however near it lay to Blackfriars: before its grim facade were held public whippings of women for various crimes, including adultery, and I could not stand the sight and sounds of such cruelty, no matter what they had done.

I began to shake; my stomach cramped. And yet I answered steadily and strongly, "Yes, sir, I am familiar with the charges."

"Then I must admonish you that, though you are here to testify for Susannah Hall, the plaintiff, what you say may be also of use in the adjudication concerning the not-guilty plea of the defendant Raphael Smith. For in deciding the case of the plaintiff, I will also decide the validity of the original charges against Mistress Hall and mete out justice to both sides. Therefore, will you now recount for the court what you observed the day that Raphael Smith publicly implied that Susannah Hall was guilty of adultery with him?"

"I will," I said and explained how Rafe Smith had mocked and accused Susannah before her mother, me and many others.

"Then," the chancellor said, "since he in turn accused her of such behavior publicly, he was publicly admitting to the same behavior, which few would do if it were not true or were he not in the throes of a humiliating rejection by a lover. Did he indeed seem humiliated that day?"

"Not humiliated, sir, but wanting to humiliate Susannah at any cost."

"Angry, like a spurned lover then?"

"No, but a resentful man who for years had been envious of the rising social circumstance and the conduct of Susannah and her mother, that is, the fact they have not been familiar but aloof to him, as I said, for years."

"Indeed, for years? You have known the defendant for years?"

"In fact, I observed his spite and malice twice, once in the time I have just recounted and once nearly ten years before."

"You can recollect an incident ten years before? Why so? What made it so stand out in your mind?"

"I believe we all know where we were and what we were doing when something dreadful or awesome occurred, such as where we were when we heard the Spanish Armada had been defeated or Sir Francis Drake had sailed around the world—or when we heard the queen was dead."

He nodded. "Say on, Mistress Whateley."

"I remember exactly when the defendant insulted Susannah and her mother ten years ago, though not to their faces that day. He spoke words I overheard—"

"Hearsay, worshipful sir!" Rafe Smith's lawyer interrupted.

"Objection denied," the chancellor cut him off. "I have asked her to tell what she heard, and so she shall. Say on, mistress."

At his last word, I heard Anne Hathaway cough. Without turning my head, my gaze darted to her. She was glaring at me, which I supposed could pass to an observer as her simply listening intently, but I knew better. Had this woman coughed or pretended to do so when the chancellor addressed me as mistress? Did the woman not want me to help her daughter? Did she not have one kind thought for me, at least for that? Or would she let her daughter suffer if she could get her long-tended revenge on Will and me?

"The defendant's words of disparagement toward Susannah and her mother"—here I slanted a stern look at Anne—"were spoken to John Lane from whom I was buying cheese in the next market stall. That scene is stamped in my mind because it was then that Stratford's town crier announced the queen was dead and King James was king."

"Then can you recount for us what Raphael Smith said or did at that time, in March of 1603?"

"He referred in a bitter tone to the Shakespeare mother and daughter as thinking they were local royalty and said he'd like to bring them both down."

"Them, but not the father?"

"I supposed he referred to the two women because they are the ones he saw, the ones who came to market daily."

"Because the father was oft away from Stratford, making his living in London?"

My pulse, already racing, pounded harder. "I warrant that is true."

"Yes, well, granted the defendant's father is a well-known person, playwright and poet of amorous subjects. I recall private copies of his *Venus and Adonis* being passed about when I was at school in Oxford. And now, they have been published for all to read—but back to business."

How I wanted to look at Will. Damn, but this man was biased against him, so probably against Susannah too. I had wanted to trust his judgment would give justice, but now I was not sure. Was he implying that because Will wrote amorous poems, his daughter would be of an overly amorous nature too?

"In your own observation, Mistress Whateley, what was the public demeanor of the Shakespeare mother and daughter, as you put it?"

Years of resentment at Anne Hathaway surged through me. Will was mine! He had always been mine, and it was Anne Hathaway's pregnancy with Susannah that took him from me. If I ever thought to be an actor, it must be now.

"The other cheese seller, the John Lane I mentioned, told me that they put on airs, at least the mother did."

"In what way?"

"Have you not asked John Lane, sir?"

I knew I'd said the wrong thing when I saw the chancellor grit his teeth so hard his jaw bulged. He cleared his throat and asked, "Do you know Anne Shakespeare well enough to judge if she were putting on airs, as you say?"

"I do not know her well, sir."

"So your testimony here today is not out of friendship with her or with her daughter, the plaintiff?"

"Susannah indeed asked me to testify but only because she

knew I'd seen the entire confrontation between her and the defendant, not because we are friends. Rather the opposite."

"Ah. How would you describe your relationship to the Shakespeares?"

"I have been in their house but once and that years ago. I did introduce Susannah to Dr. John Hall, whom she later married, and I believe she loved him from the first."

"Yet you claim you do not know her well and you hardly know that from continued observation of them."

"I know love when I see it, sir."

Amazingly I saw him almost smile at that, but freeze the expression before it widened. "So you are not friends with the plaintiff, Susannah Shakespeare, but are here to testify to help her?"

"I admit to the court I would like to help her, for it is unjust for any man, however jealous or resentful, to spread lies about a woman who only loves and has always loved one man."

"I see," he said. "I see you speak passionately and firmly. The court excuses you and calls Mistress Anne Shakespeare to the dock. That is all, Mistress Whateley."

I was shocked. I had been so certain he was going to ask me more about my relationship to the Shakespeares, and that would be a slippery slope. Relieved, I stepped down and brushed skirts with the other Anne as she passed me. I could almost have fallen flat on the floor when she whispered in passing, "For Susannah—my thanks."

Was she thanking me for defending her daughter today or for introducing Susannah to John Hall, I wondered. Maybe Will would know, but we'd kept a wide berth around each other today.

I went outside and walked through the old graveyard at the side of the cathedral, waiting while the rest of the trial went on, wishing I could hear, wondering if the chancellor had asked Anne Hathaway what she thought of me, or her own husband for that matter.

As people began to spill out the front of the chapter house and I waited for Kate or the Davenants to come tell me what happened, I saw the chancellor's aide come out the back door and motion to me. Perhaps he saw me pacing and realized I would want to know what the verdict had been.

Gathering my skirts close, I hurried to him. "His worshipful self," he said with a cryptic, wry smile, "has a gift he would give to the playwright, if you would be so kind as to deliver it to him when you can." Puzzled, I stared at him, for I saw he had no gift in his hands. Back in London it was not unusual for someone to send Will a letter of praise or a small gift if they liked his plays, but here—and from the chancellor?

"Will you see to it, Mistress Whateley, and tell no one else?"

"Oh, a spoken message? Yes, but how did the trial come out?"

"The young woman was acquitted and the defendant fined, berated and excommunicated."

I felt a rush of relief. I would have burst into tears of joy had not this stranger stood before me. "Well, do you vow it?" he prompted.

"I vow it, if the chancellor is certain I am the one to tell."

"A spoken but partly written message," he said, producing from up his sleeve a small, folded piece of paper he thrust into my hand. "Please tell the poet that the chancellor has adored his *Venus and Adonis* and later his sonnets and has always wondered who the Dark Lady of his inspiration was, and whether she was real."

"You know how poets are," I stammered as he stared at me. "All imagination and speculation."

"The chancellor hazards a guess that you would understand. You see, his vocation is this, but his pastime is solving crimes, puzzles and whatnot. And he mentioned this trial to his elderly father, who has kept the record books in the cathedral for years, and the old man recalled a very strange thing. Some years ago, someone in Stratford named Shakespeare—not the most common of surnames—had registered for a marriage license to one woman, and then the very next day was registered to wed another, and a great deal of money and pressure was put up to get the second registration to another Anne, no less. Is that not strange?"

My heartbeat thudded harder than it had inside. "Yes—strange."

"That paper you hold is a copy of the way the first entry was worded. He thought you could pass it on to the poet should he want inspiration for more poems or plays—amorous, even erotic ones—though you must tell no one of the source for that idea but Shakespeare."

"Probably just a slip of the pen—a coincidence," I managed, though I was breaking out in a sweat while I was yet tingling all over.

"So the chancellor believes. Oh," he said as he turned away then back again to speak partly over his shoulder, "he also said he might send a packet of his own poems for Master Shakespeare to read, if he would give him his opinion."

He let the door close behind him. Did the trial today really go in Susannah's favor, or had the worshipful sir slanted things her way to amuse himself and find a way to get Will to read his own work? Sometimes big things in this world hang on such personal pursuits.

As I saw Kate and her parents and started toward them in all haste, I opened the small piece of paper from the chancellor to Will. The short note was headed, "To Whom It May Concern" and contained only these words:

27 November 1582, Marriage bond issued for the wedding of William Shaxpere and Anne Whateley of Temple Grafton, Warwickshire. GRANTED.

Well, I thought as my tears blurred the words and one plopped on the paper, the old registrar might not spell well, but he had an amazing memory. I looked up just as Kate got to me and hugged me hard.

"You were wonderful!" she cried, and soon Jennet and John had their arms around both of us.

"Will said he'll see you later," Jennet told me. "I'm afraid despite this victory, he still has his hands full, for Susannah and her mother are going at it like cats and dogs outside the church."

"Everything changes and yet nothing does," I whispered, more to myself than to them. "All is true."

"I know you told the truth," Jennet told me, and I did not correct her for hearing me amiss.

We walked toward the inn where we'd stayed last night and left our horses. In one hand I held the note for Will and in the other clutched the signet ring he'd given me when we'd exchanged our wedding vows. It had been one of the world's strangest marriages, but if I could have him no other way, I was content. I breathed in the summer air and pulled off my hat and shook my hair free.

My dear Kate linked her arm through mine. The beautiful young woman Will and I had helped bring into the world had her whole life ahead of her, and, despite my past griefs, I would wish her no less depth and breadth of love than had been mine.

CHAPTER TWENTY-THREE

φ

If anyone wondered why Will went back and forth to London in the last years of his life, one could say it was partly for business and partly for pleasure to see friends and his plays performed. But it was mostly to enjoy our waning days together in our sunny gatehouse.

Sadly, if Susannah's trial had not given him enough grief, his younger daughter, Judith, Hamnet's twin, gave her father fits when she became betrothed to a highly unsuitable Stratford man. Suffice it to say that her Thomas Quiney not only had hardly a penny to his name and chose Judith when her father settled some money on her, but also got another young woman, to whom he'd promised marriage first, pregnant.

Will hardly scolded the girl—how could he after the mess he'd made of his early life with women?—but he was very disappointed to see family history repeat itself. Poor Anne Hathaway blamed him for being away so much and ranted day and night, he said, over what her daughters had done to besmirch her reputation. All that fretted him, kept him awake at all hours and aged him.

"But didn't Anne ever rant over what I've done to her?" I asked him.

"That's one topic she knows not to broach after how you've helped us—and her—more than once, the one topic that would break the agreement between her and me."

Will sat in his favorite chair before the eastern window of the gatehouse. Mine was right next to it, though I perched on his knees now. We were going to the rebuilt Globe tonight to see *Romeo and Juliet*, though I was hardly in the mood for family feuds and the deaths of young lovers.

"It would break the agreement between her and me," he went on, repeating himself as he sometimes did these days. "Her big house and a fine living in exchange for letting me have my London life—my real life, and yet Stratford lures me and calls me home. Anne, if we could only go back to that first day I was walking out of town and you asked to come along . . ." He sighed. "And come along you did with me, all the way, thank God!" he added and hugged me hard.

"All the way and farther yet to go."

"If I close my eyes, I can see the meadows and flowers we passed that day, I can feel them from years later under my naked knees and elbows when we made love on them, crushing their fragrance . . . and yet they will grow and bloom again when we are gone."

"I used to dance across those flowered leas. 'I know a bank where the wild thyme blows,'" I recited some of his beautiful words from *A Midsummer Night's Dream*, "'where oxlips and the nodding violet grows, / Quite overcanopied with luscious wood-bine / With sweet muskroses and with eglantine . . .'"

He went on, "'The lunatic, the lover and the poet / Are of imagination all compact . . .'"

Two old but always new dreamers, we could have lived all day with our memories enchanted, but we kissed instead.

In the spring of 1616, I was in Temple Grafton, for Will had taken ill on a trip home, and I had come to be nearer to him. Dr. Hall, who was caring for him, stopped by my house whenever he could to keep me apprised of his condition: his phlegmatic humors were out of balance, and he was being treated with bloodletting and poultices of sack and sliced radishes. I knew Will's health was bad, but I expected him to rally as he ever had from whatever mental or physical ills assailed him. He was fifty-two and had made out his will.

As a knock sounded on my front door midmorning, I jerked from pacing before my low-burning hearth. Expecting Dr. Hall, I rushed to answer. Susannah stood there, just as she had years before with a cloak wrapped around her shoulders. I gasped when I saw her solemn face.

"No—he's not," she said in a rush. "He's rallied a bit, but he tells me and John he longs to see you. I volunteered to tell you, to bring you to the place on the Avon he insists John take him. I pray you trust me."

"Of course, I do. Just one moment." I ran into my bedchamber and seized my cloak, for the brisk wind chilled the sun today.

"Sally," I called out the back door to where she was spreading laundered sheets on the bushes, "I'm going for a walk."

We hurried along the road to town unspeaking for a little ways before Susannah blurted, "Despite the note I sent you, thanking you for standing up for me at the trial, despite how I had treated you, I want to say it to your face. Now that I have John, partly thanks to you, I can see what you mean to him—to my father, I mean. Now I can see past things my mother fed me with her mother's milk."

Tears blurred my vision of her, but I steadied my voice. "It is often a burden to see our parents through adult eyes, but we must love them yet."

She kept up the furious pace we had set, but turned her head to me. "Did you help him write his plays?"

That question surprised me, but I told her truthfully, "I wrote down some of them from his dictation when he had hand spasms. He tells me that my habits—a tart tongue, a stubborn nature and the like—inspired several of the heroines, and—"

"And somehow, you are the Dark Lady of his sonnets," she interrupted. "I've read them, though Mother doesn't know."

"Here," I told her, cutting off the path toward the river. "There's a crosscut this way to the Avon."

"But how do you know where he said to meet him?"

"Susannah, I know."

Dr. Hall was waiting for us, but I didn't see Will at first, only a horse with no one on it. Fear and foreboding leaned on me hard again. But John Hall smiled and waved to me and, to my surprise, before Susannah, who did not blink an eye, bent to kiss my cheek.

He took her hand and pulled her down the path away from us, tugging the horse after him.

Then I saw Will on the very spot where Kat, Dick and I used to meet him when we were young. I was appalled to see the change in him these last ten days. His pallor was not white but gray, his cheeks sunken, his eyes fever-bright. He sat on a blanket on the grass in the sun but out of the wind and patted the spot beside him.

I steadied myself not to show alarm, not to . . . to make a scene. I forced a smile and sat down, then turned to embrace him, to hold him to me. He felt shrunken in his frame. My heart fell.

"It looks much the same," he said when we finally shifted slightly apart, "our Avon, even swollen in the spring, so different from the mighty Thames. I wish that we could walk its entire length today, just setting out upstream together . . ."

"Yes, my love. I too!"

"But I shall not admit impediments to the marriage of true minds—not even death."

"Don't speak of that."

"Anne, my dearest, I must. It comes to all of us, and I feel it in me. But, oh, what a dance we danced together, what things we have seen and done, what people we have met. Let's cherish those memories into eternity, not what might have been."

Blinking back tears, I nodded and clung to him again.

"I could not have done it without you," he whispered, stroking my hair, "not a bit of it, my muse, my love, my wife."

"And I've written my life story telling much the same, Will. I was going to show you—read it to you, but, after you thought the Worcester chancellor's poems so poor, I hesitated—"

"I can tell without reading one word it is wonderful, clever, bright—and honest. I wish not that you had read it to me but that we could act out all the scenes, even the tragic ones, for that too is life, my Anne—my life . . ."

We sat silent for a moment, our feelings precious yet painful, far beyond speech. I believe we thought that if we stayed very still, barely breathing, time would stand still too. But the wind whistled and the river rattled on and time fled too.

As we yet held to each other, he whispered so close in my ear that his breath stirred the tendrils of silver hair at my temple, "My Anne, I cannot tell you how desperately I missed you when we were apart. Forgive me for my jealous rages, for you have ever been true to me, but I felt so helpless that I could not make you truly mine. I blamed myself, and then I took it out on you."

"Forgotten and forgiven. You know, if I could pick one day here at Stratford, I'd choose the one where you passed my cottage to deliver gloves to old Father Berowne, and my heart thrilled to see you."

"Though you gave me a devil of a time . . ."

"Until you recited that sonnet about languishing . . ."

"'But when she saw my woeful state, / Straight in her heart did mercy come . . .'"

"Yes, I remember, my beloved," I whispered, holding both his hands in mine, our foreheads pressed together.

"You threw onions at me, but since then, you have showered me with the blessings of your love . . ."

He began to cough, then slumped against me, out of breath, out of strength, I prayed, not out of life.

Though I wanted to keep Will all to myself, to just lie on the grass with him in the sun and warm him, to stay with him whatever befell, I knew he was fading. Hoping John could help, I stood and summoned the Halls back. The three of us put him up on the horse, and John mounted behind to hold him there.

Despite the appearance of collapse, Will slitted his eyes open and his gaze burned into mine. Strange, but then I felt that old swift surge of desire he had always stoked in me. An ill, dying man, and me of an age where all such passions should have passed, and I felt the power of our need for each other again. Love is a need, he'd said once, and I'd argued with him, but it was true. Like water, food and air, love was a need.

"We will keep you informed," John said.

"Yes," Susannah told me, squeezing my arm, "no matter what, I promise."

Will's eyes were feverish, clouded, but his lips lifted in a slight smile of fond farewell. I clasped his right hand in both of mine until Susannah led the horse away and his cold fingers slipped from mine. I could not bear, *I could not bear* to let him go or see him go. It was as if my life, my story, were ended too.

William Shakespeare lived but three more days. I suppose his effort to see me hastened his death, but I would have done the same to see him once more. He was buried two days after his passing, not in the churchyard, but in a crypt below the floor stones of Holy Trinity as befitting a Stratford man of means. And he left word that Anne Hathaway was not to be interred with his bones.

I did not attend the funeral, but walked the spring meadows that day and many thereafter, sometimes alone, sometimes with

Kate—even once in a while with Susannah—but always pretending Will was with me, for, in a way, he was.

The first time I went to visit his tomb, where the Halls were going to erect a fine stone bust of him with an inscription, I somehow lost my betrothal ring from off its broken chain. I searched for hours, more than once, with Sally and Kate, around Kat's grave, along my path to town. I checked for it every time I went to put flowers on Kat's grave or stood inside the dim, cool church to try to talk to Will.

But I soon realized the places to find him were down on the Avon or in our favorite under-the-sky places, even in our Blackfriars Gatehouse, where I stayed when I went to the theatres in London and where I heard him speak to me from the words of his plays. As for the ring, I pretended he'd taken it with him, that he'd wanted it back as a remembrance of me.

Indeed, more than anything, I can find Will in the pages of what I have written too. I believe these five acts of my life I will entrust to my dear goddaughter Kate are a loving, living memorial from his other wife, the wife not of his hearth but of his heart.

Signed,

Anne Rosaline Whateley,
Mistress Shakespeare

AUTHOR'S NOTE

The third biggest mystery about William Shakespeare (after endless arguments on who really wrote the plays and what he did during the "lost years" between the time he left grammar school and first began to act in London) concerns whom he married. It's accepted by most historians that he wed "Anne Hathway [*sic*] of Stratford in the dioces [*sic*] of Worcester maiden." (All of the entries are originally in Latin.) But the same official record, which is kept in the Worcestershire Record Office today, is documentary proof that, on the previous day, he was issued a marriage license, called a marriage bond, to wed "Anne Whateley of Temple Grafton."

Many have tried to shuffle off Anne Whateley as a mistake of the pen or the ear, but they conveniently ignore that the recorder in Worcester (both entries are in the same handwriting) also mistook the words *Temple Grafton* for *Stratford* and failed to cross out or correct the previous day's "error" of the Anne Whateley/Wm Shaxpere entry when William Shagspere/Anne Hathway was written in. The Shakespeare name is "misspelled" in both cases, so that can't weigh in on one side or the other; the Elizabethans cared little for standardized spelling. Shakespeare signed his own name various ways, including the two mentioned.

Besides unstandardized Elizabethan spellings, there are other challenges to Elizabethan-era research. Dates are always a problem since the Julian calendar was used until 1582, when the switch was made to the Gregorian, which dropped ten days from the previous records. But more confusing is that their new year began on Lady Day (March 25), despite the fact they also called January 1 New Year's Day. So, dual dating for events can occur.

I have tried not to take liberties with history, although I have Marlowe's plays performed at times slightly different from what some sources claim. *Tamburlaine the Great* was probably first performed in 1587 instead of early 1588, and by the Lord Admiral's Men at the Rose. *Doctor Faustus* was most likely performed in the early 1590s instead of 1588.

I am indebted for help in having the entire marriage bond for my study to John France, Senior Microfiler/Digitiser, County Hall, Worcestershire Record Office, Worcester, Worcestershire, United Kingdom. At the writing of this note, part of the bond is available for viewing on the website http://home.att.net/~mleary/positive.htm.

Over the centuries, certain scholars have stood up for the possibility that there was a second Anne in Will Shakespeare's life. *The Man Shakespeare* (1909) by Frank Harris gives an extensive array of reasons supporting Anne Whateley; a 1917 play, *The Good*

Men Do, by Hubert Osborne hangs its plot on his belief in the dual Annes. Other writers and historians, such as Ivor Brown and Anthony Burgess in his 1970 critical studies on Shakespeare, make a case for the second Anne. I agree, relying as much on what seemed to be missing from Will's relationship with Anne Hathaway as with the research on Will's life on which I base this story. Will could well have had another wife.

I have studied the Elizabethan period for many years; wrote my master's degree thesis about one of Shakespeare's plays, *All's Well That Ends Well*; and have written numerous novels set in that period, including a nine-book historical mystery series with Queen Elizabeth I herself as the amateur sleuth. I have been to London and Stratford-Upon-the-Avon many times, always concentrating on Elizabethan events and sites. When I taught British literature at the high school level, I helped organize an Elizabethan festival in which the students played many parts. In short, for some reason, I am drawn to the Tudor era and its fascinating people.

Of the many books on Shakespeare's life that I have read as background and inspiration before I wrote Anne Whateley's story, three were of special help to me: *Shakespeare: The Biography*, by Peter Ackroyd; *Shakespeare*, by Michael Wood (which was also an excellent Public Broadcasting miniseries); and *Will in the World*, by Stephen Greenblatt. Many people interpret the Bard of Avon's life differently with, as the playwright himself said, "infinite variety."

Of my many books on Elizabeth Tudor, I leaned most heavily on Alison Weir's *The Life of Elizabeth I*.

Such minor things in this novel as the portrait of the playwright as a young man and the W.S. signet ring with the lovers' knot do exist. Now in the possession of the John Ryland University Library in Manchester, England, the painting is usually called the Grafton Portrait because it was found in a home in Temple Grafton. I like to imagine that Susannah Hall, after her mother died, gave it back to Anne Whateley. The ring was discovered in 1810 in a field close to Holy Trinity churchyard; it is in the possession of the Shakespeare Birthplace Trust in Stratford.

Also, it is fact that a young Stratford woman named Katherine Hamlett drowned in the Avon in 1580, leaving her milk pail on the bank. Of such small details are big stories made.

Sadly, the Globe and Blackfriars theatres were pulled down in 1644 and 1655, respectively, so that tenement buildings could be erected. But, of course, the Globe was rebuilt in modern times and Shakespeare's plays live on there and in many other venues. And so, although this novel is fiction, the pieces that support the story are as factual as research and serious speculation can make them.

Despite my years of research in the Elizabethan era, I especially noted several fascinating and surprising truths while writing this novel. Marriage in "the old days" was often delayed until a person's midtwenties, and a surprising proportion never wed, including several of Shakespeare's brothers. Illegitimacy rates were quite low because what we would call "shotgun marriages" were common— again a statistic with which Will Shakespeare was personally involved. Also my reading reminded me how many Elizabethans died early, not only as infants but as young people. I have not exaggerated the death toll of the Shakespeares or the Davenants. People were middle-aged at thirty, and someone like the queen who lived to be seventy was quite remarkable.

Although we do not live in an age where youth and health are "brief candle[s]" and radish poultices are used to cure ills, perhaps we should yet be reminded to use well our "hour upon the stage."

Karen Harper

KAREN HARPER

⌘

Shakespeare's
Mistress

⌘

CONVERSATION WITH KAREN HARPER

Q. *In* Shakespeare's Mistress *you delve into an aspect of William Shakespeare's life that no other fiction writer has explored. What fascinated you about Will's relationship with Anne Whateley?*

A. Other writers have used Anne Whateley in two dramas I know of, but no one—as far as I can find—has written her story in a historical novel. However, the "other Anne" theory has had its scholarly champions over the years. Proof of Anne's deep involvement in Will Shakespeare's life hangs mostly on the fact that an Anne Whateley of Temple Grafton is recorded in a still-extant marriage bond as betrothed to Will in an entry on the previous day to the one for him and Anne Hathaway of Stratford. (My Web site at www.karenharperauthor.com has more on this, including a link to the marriage bonds, which are in Latin.) Anne Whateley was certainly betrothed to Will, but was she his wife or his mistress? They might well have married secretly or plighted what was then called a handfast marriage. In that era, of course, the word *mistress* meant *Mrs.* or *wife*, not only *lover* or *kept woman.*

I see Anne Whateley's footprints in other places in Shakespeare's life besides in their marriage bond. In his will, he left Anne Hathaway his "second-best bed," and there has been much discussion over the years about who got the first-best bed. Also, Shakespeare arranged for a friend to inherit and then lease out the Blackfriar's Gatehouse, where he lived in his heyday in London—in other words, neither it nor its profits went to Anne Hathaway. And who was the Dark Lady of his sonnets and the inspiration for many of his feisty, bright female characters? I love writing mysteries, and in this case, clues point to "Will's other wife" as having a great impact on his life.

So much is fascinating about their relationship: It is a universal truth that the lives of famous people are fascinating, especially their secret selves. Although parts of Will Shakespeare's life are well-known, there are the "lost years," which gave me the freedom to blend Anne's lesser-known biography with Will's. The fiction writer always deals with the "what-if's" of life, and Anne Whateley is a very possible, exciting "what-if." If people can argue about what Will did in his lost years, or whether or not he really wrote the plays, let them take a look at my novel and then argue about Anne Whateley's possible role.

Q. How much of Shakespeare's Mistress *is based on fact and how much is fiction?*

A. Nothing that is known of William Shakespeare's life or times has been fictionalized, although, as in all historical fiction, I imagined scenes and dialogue. Also, since little is known of Anne Whateley's background—although much can be surmised based on facts—I did have to fill in blanks in her life. If Shakespeare himself, with all the research scholars have done on him over the years, has some mystery years in his biography, then a lesser-known historical character like Anne could be expected to also. In a way, as in all historical fiction, *Shakespeare's Mistress* is what Alex Haley, the writer of *Roots*, dubbed "faction," a blending of fact and fiction.

Q. Shakespeare's Mistress *is a combination of painstaking research and imaginative speculation. What sources did you use? How does Anne's life compare to real accounts of life in Elizabethan England?*

A. Over the three decades I have studied and written about Elizabeth Tudor, her court and country, I have gathered quite a collection of books on Tudor culture and personalities. Some of my earliest research books include *Pictures from English History*, selected and edited by Coleman E. Bishop (Phillips & Hunt, New York, 1883), *Henry VIII* by Francis Hackett (Horace Liveright, Inc., New York, 1929) and *Life in Elizabethan Days: A Picture of a Typical English Community at the End of the Sixteenth Century* by William Stearns Davis (Harper & Row, 1930). I have a great selection of books spanning the years, including several very recent biographies of Shakespeare, dated 2003–2005. (The latter are listed in the Author's Note at the end of the novel.) Of course, I also consulted many references I don't own, and I used Internet research too. Anne's life compares to actual life in Elizabethan England as closely as scholars can determine and as I can make it. Fortunately, the English people of that day wrote journals and books, everything from herbals to their wills and lists of their household goods. The queen's possessions, health, writing and speeches are well documented, and so are the lives of courtiers and even some commoners.

Q. What are some of the challenges of doing Tudor research?

A. As a writer of historical novels in which the majority of the characters are real people, I strive to stay with what is recorded. On the other hand, one thing a researcher quickly learns about Tudor "facts" and "correct dates" is that they can vary. The Tudors switched calendars partway through the era, and their concept of when the new year began can shift. As for sources not agreeing, scholars are yet arguing over the key conundrum of Shakespeare's life: Could a man from the "boondocks" of rural Stratford who never went to university write these brilliant plays? I say yes, indeed, and my story of Will and Anne shows how and why. (After all, American inventive genius Thomas Edison came out of small, obscure Milan, Ohio, where, like Will, he had to leave school early.) I've wandered off track here, but that's one of the delights of Elizabethan research.

Q. You clearly admire smart, strong, risk-taking women. What qualities make Anne Whateley such an ideal heroine?

A. I greatly admire women who have ordinary beginnings but manage to face extraordinary circumstances with strength, courage and force of character. When a lesser woman would have caved in from troubles and tragedies, Anne rises above them. She insists on having a life of her own if and when she cannot totally share Will's. Although women of earlier historical periods were often chattel, bargaining chips or worse, some women managed to make their own way in a man's world—and Anne is one. I celebrate that kind of woman in all my novels. This book frequently points out how much Anne was inspired by the queen, a woman who overcame many trials (talk about a dysfunctional family!) to become the powerhouse of her age.

Q. British literature is one of your passions. What authors or books have inspired you?

A. I taught Shakespeare's plays for years and see his work as a real window into the people of that time. I love Medieval writing such as Chaucer's (I took graduate courses on both Shakespeare and Medieval English literature), and I also learned a lot from reading and teaching later British writers. My father was an amateur Charles Dickens scholar, so I'm very steeped in how Dickens wrote—the emotional characterization, the detailed descriptions.

I could name many historical novels that set me on the path of wanting to write novels myself, but I'll mention just one from the 1950s, which I read in the 1960s: *Katherine* by Anya Seton, set in the Plantagenet era in which I later set my novel, *The First Princess of Wales*.

I must add that I have also been inspired by the many historical sites in England that I have visited on research trips to England—those Tudor castles and timbered manor houses speak to me. Despite the ever-present crowds, I think it's kismet that twice I was left by myself upstairs at Shakespeare's birthplace in Stratford so I could listen to the voices in the walls. In every book I create, I try to treat setting as another key character.

QUESTIONS
FOR DISCUSSION

1. What early hints do you see that the boy Shakespeare will become the writing genius? What sorts of traits do you see in your own children or grandchildren that indicate particular talents or tendencies?

2. Over the years, some Shakespeare critics and scholars have argued that it would be impossible for a boy with Shakespeare's small-town grammar-school background to write the brilliant plays he did with all their diversity and depth. Do you think such a mind could come from a rural background?

3. Although Will and Anne Whateley are in love from their early days, they disagree on many things. Do you think this weakens or strengthens their relationship? Can two strong-minded people who disagree on key issues really get along over the years? In love relationships, do opposites really attract?

4. Why do you think Will is so jealous of Anne? Is this understandable in him? When does jealousy become unacceptable?

5. The Elizabethan world might seem to be an era of freedom, compared to the Medieval world that bred it, but what are some of the strictures on personal freedom that would never be acceptable today?

6. Why does Anne so admire and identify with the queen? What women in public roles do you admire and why?

7. Part of Anne's backbone comes from her feeling different. Why does she feel this way and what possible other effects could this have had on her character and personality? Have you seen instances in which tough times molded a person one way or the other?

8. Many authors, both in fiction and nonfiction, have opined on why Anne Hathaway and her husband seemed to have such a long-distance relationship. Besides the possibility that another woman had his heart, what other differences between them do you see that made them less than soul mates?

9. Both of Shakespeare's daughters have problems with men, which greatly saddens their father. Susannah is sued for adultery and Judith marries a scoundrel. Are the sins of the fathers truly visited upon the children?

10. The story covers about forty years. What changes occur in the lives of the two main characters and in the Elizabethan world during that time?

11. Fear of the plague permeated Elizabethan society. In our world, such horrors are gone—or are they?

Also available from Ebury Press:

The Queen's Governess

KAREN HARPER

Katherine Ashley, the daughter of a poor country squire, is lucky enough to secure an education and a place for herself in a noble household. But it comes at a price. Thomas Cromwell, King Henry's ambitious courtier, has plans for Kat. When she finally achieves her ambition of becoming a lady in waiting, it is because Cromwell needs a spy in the new Queen's court . . .

Kat witnesses Anne Boleyn's fall from grace and, as a favour to the doomed queen, agrees to become governess and confidante to the young Elizabeth Tudor. Together they suffer bitter exile, assassination attempts, and imprisonment, barely escaping with their reputations and their lives intact. But when Elizabeth is eventually crowned, Kat continues to serve her, faithfully guarding all of the queen's secrets, even the one that could bring down the monarchy . . .

'Harper's diligent research, realistic portrayal, and insider/outsider heroine will hook those who can't get enough of England's turbulent history . . . enjoyable historical romp'

PUBLISHERS WEEKLY

Please read on for an excerpt
from Karen Harper's novel

THE QUEEN'S GOVERNESS

Available now

MAY 19, 1536,
THE TOWER OF LONDON

I could not fathom they were going to kill the queen. Nor could I bear to witness Anne Boleyn's beheading, but I stepped off the barge on the choppy Thames and, with the other observers, entered the Tower through the water gate. I felt sick to my stomach and my very soul.

The spring sun and soft river breeze deserted us as we entered the Tower. All seemed dark and airless within the tall stone walls. We were shown our place at the back of the small elite crowd. Thank the Lord, I did not have to stand close to the wooden scaffold that had been built for this dread deed. I had vowed to myself I would keep my eyes shut, and, standing back here, no one would know. Yet I stared straight ahead, taking it all in.

For, despite my distance of some twenty feet from it, the straw-strewn scaffold with its wooden stairs going up seemed to loom above me. How would Anne, brazen and foolish but innocent

Anne, stripped now of her title, her power, her daughter and husband, manage to get herself through this horror? She had always professed to be a woman of strong faith, so perhaps that would sustain her.

I yearned to bolt from the premises. I nearly lost my hard-won control. Tears blurred my vision, but I blinked them back.

The crowd hushed as the former queen came out into the sun, led by the Tower constable Sir William Kingston, with four ladies following. At least she had company at the end. Anne's almoner was with her; they both held prayer books. Her eyes looked up and straight ahead, her lips moved in silent prayer. I thought I read the words on them: "Yea, though I walk through the valley of the shadow of death . . ."

Before she reached the scaffold, others mounted it as if to greet her: the Lord Mayor of London, who had arranged her fine coronation flotilla but three years ago this very month, and several sheriffs in their scarlet robes. Then, too, the black-hooded French swordsman and his assistant, who had come from France. Anne's head jerked when she saw her executioner.

The woman who had been Queen of England hesitated but a moment at the bottom of the steps, then mounted. She wore a robe of black damask, cut low and trimmed with fur and a crimson kirtle—the color of martyr's blood, I thought. She had gathered her luxuriant dark hair into a net but over it wore the style of headdress she had made fashionable, a half-moon shape trimmed with pearls.

I saw no paper in her hand, nor did she look down as her clear voice rang out words she had obviously memorized: "Good Christian people, I am come hither to die according to law. Therefore I will speak nothing against it. I am come hither to accuse no man, nor to speak anything of that whereof I am accused."

I knew such contrition was part of her agreement with the king's henchman Cromwell. It was also the price she had to pay for having me here today. I could hardly bear it. Yet, for her, I stood straight, staring at her. Betrayed and abandoned, if she could face this, I could, too.

"I come here," Anne went on with a glance and a nod directly at me, though others might think it was but to emphasize her words, "only to die, and thus to yield myself humbly unto the will of my lord the king."

Damn the king, I vowed, however treasonous that mere thought. No man, not even the great Henry Tudor, had a right to cast off and execute a woman he had pursued and lusted for, had bred a child on, the little Elizabeth I knew and loved so well. The terrible charges against Anne had been trumped up, yet I dare not say so. I wanted to scream out my anger, to leap upon the scaffold and save her—but I stood silent as a stone, struck with awe and dread. But then, since no one stood behind us, I dared to lift my hand to hold up the tiny treasure she had entrusted to me. Perhaps she could not see it; perhaps she would think I was waving farewell to her, but I did it anyway, then pulled my hand back down.

"I pray God to save the king," she went on with another nod, which I prayed meant she had seen my gesture, "and send him long to reign over you, for a gentler or more merciful prince was there never. To me he was ever a good and gentle sovereign lord."

Shuffling feet nearby, nervous shifting in the crowd. A smothered snort. I was not the only one who knew this was a public sham and shame. No doubt, she said all that to protect her daughter's future, the slim possibility that, if the king had no legitimate son and Catholic Mary was not fully reinstated, Elizabeth could be returned to the line of succession—for the poor three-year-old was declared a bastard now. I swore silently I would ever serve Elizabeth well and protect her as best I could from such tyrannical rule by men. At least Anne Boleyn was going to a better place.

Again, I longed to close my eyes, but I could not. When had the terrible things I had borne in my life been halted or helped one whit by cowering or fleeing?

Anne spoke briefly to her ladies, and they removed her cape. She gave a necklace, earrings, a ring, and her prayer book away to them, while I fingered the secret gift she had given me. She gave the axman a coin and, as was tradition, asked him to make his work quick and forgave him for what he was bound to do.

She knelt and rearranged her skirts. She even helped one of her trembling ladies to adjust a bandage tied over her eyes. Huddled off to the side, her women began to cry, but, beyond that, utter silence but the screech of a seagull flying free over the Thames. I realized I was holding my breath and let it out jerkily, as if I would fall to panting like a dog.

To bare her neck, Anne held her head erect as if she still wore St. Edward's crown as she had in the Abbey on her coronation day. Then came her hurried, repeated words: "O Lord God, have pity on my soul, O Lord God, have pity on my soul. . . ."

I wondered if, in her last frenzied moments, she was picturing her little Elizabeth. I sucked in a sharp sob of regret that the child would never really remember her mother. At least I had known mine before she died—slain as surely as this so someone else might have her husband. That cast me back to my mother's death, vile and violent, too. . . .

"O Lord God, have pity on my soul, O Lord God, have pity on my—"

The swordsman lifted a long silver sword from the straw and struck in one swift swing. The crowd gave a common gasp, and someone screamed. As Anne's slender body fell, spouting blood, the executioner held up her head with the lips still moving. Horror-struck, I imagined that, at the very end, she had meant to shout, "O Lord God, have pity on my daughter!"

Near Dartington, Devon
April 4, 1516

"God have mercy on her soul. She's gone," my father told the two of us. "Dear Lord God, have pity on her soul."

"Mother. Mother! Please, please wake up! Please come back!" I screamed again and again, throwing river water on her face, until my father shook me hard by the shoulders.

"Leave off!" he demanded, his forehead furrowed, his eyes glassy with unshed tears. We knelt in the thick grass by the rushing River Dart, where her body had been laid out, covered by her friend Maud Wicker's wet apron, for her own clothes had nearly burned away. When I still shrieked as loudly as the gulls on the river, he commanded, "Enough, Kat!" Unlike Mother, he had sel-dom used the pet name I'd had since I couldn't pronounce my own when I was still in leading strings. That sweet, little comfort almost steadied me until he added, "You'll learn to accept much more than this, so bear up, girl!"

But I couldn't. I just couldn't and heaved great breaths in my frenzy. If only we had been here sooner! But by the time I returned home from keeping watch over Lord Barlow's daughter at Dartington Hall, where Father kept his lordship's beehives, the local tinker had come to our house to fetch us. While seagulls wheeled and shrieked overhead as if in warning, Father and I hied ourselves across the cattle field, toward the river.

Now, my cheeks slick with tears, I finally sat in sullen silence. He patted Maud's shoulder, then squeezed her hand before he let it go and stood, looking away, head down, leaning stiff-armed against a tree. Why did he seem only resigned, not more shaken? His wife, Cecily Champernowne, aged twenty-eight years, had hit the back of her head and bled into her brown hair. Her entire body was bruised and blackened, even her face mine so resembled.

[Years later, time and again, I tried to tell myself that stoic mourning was just the way with men, but even cruel King Henry piteously grieved the death of his third wife, Queen Jane, and William Cecil sobbed when his second son—not even his heir—died.]

"I—I am overthrown by it all," Maud said, talking to me as much as to Father. "She must have caught her skirts in the hearth fire." Sitting on her heels, several feet away, she wrung her hands. Gray soot and brown river mud smeared her sopped petticoats. Tears from her long-lashed blue eyes speckled her rosy cheeks. "I was drawing nigh the house for a visit and heard her screams. She rushed out willy-nilly. I—I believe she struck her head on the hearth stones, trying to get the fire out. God as my judge, I tried to roll her on the ground to smother the flames. But in her pain and panic, she ran toward the river. The winds—they made it worse. But I— She jumped in the water. I think she died of drowning, not the flames, though I tried to pull her out in time, God rest her soul."

Father muttered something about God's will. I swore silently that, if I'd been there, I'd have put those flames out fast.

That day a part of me died too—my entire girlhood, truth be told. I was ten years old. I was angry with God's will and even more furious that Father kept comforting Maud Wicker more than he did me.

In four months' time, Mistress Wicker became my stepmother. She was but eighteen, one of six daughters of the man who wove my father's beehives from stout wicker that he soaked in the river to get it to bend. Maud had always brought the finished hives to Father in a cart and had laughed at his silly stories, which Mother only rolled her eyes at. The only good thing for me about their marriage was that the arguing my parents had done now became all honeyed words. Father never raised a hand to his second wife, though she had a temper hotter than my mother's.

And Maud had a shrewish side she only showed to me. As I grew older, festering under her orders—and pinches and slaps, when Father wasn't about the house—I sometimes took to wondering if my stepmother had been with my mother when her skirts caught the flames, instead of just coming toward the house, as she'd said. That day two new hives had been left out back, and fresh cart tracks marred the mud. But the cart had also left tracks as it was trundled across the field toward the river. When I asked her once why, since it was not the way she went home, she told me she was just dawdling about the area so her father would not give her another task. As I oft did such myself, I let it go. But I'd found a willow green ribbon when I swept the hearth the night Mother died, and Maud Wicker loved such fripperies for her yellow curls.

I kept that ribbon buried in my secret box of dried flowers, along with a sweet bag given me by Lady Barlow of Dartington Hall, else Maud would have taken it for her own. The sweet bag was a gift, Lady Barlow said, for my helping to care for her Sarah during tutoring sessions with her older brother, Percy. Poor Sarah went about in a wheeled chair at times, her tongue lolling from her mouth, her body shaking when she had her fits. I used to help hold her quill and form her words on paper. I held her book for her so she could read from it. But there was a keen brain inside her, too, and—like me—she loved learning.

Also in the box, which I kept hidden in the thick hedge out back, were two smooth stones from the River Dart, near where Mother died, and clover from a pixie circle on the moors before they were chased off by one of the ghostly hellhounds. Everyone roundabout knew not to go out on the moors at night. Sometimes I wasn't sure if the cries of gulls in the creeping fogs weren't the shrieks of lost souls out on the moors. The box also used to hold my mother's garnet necklace, but Maud had wheedled it from my father when she bore their second child, a daughter this time. Her little Simon and Amelia were the loves of my life then, so innocent and angelic, until they began to act like their mother, throwing tantrums for things they must have.

Yet I did not mislike my half siblings as I did Maud. Things she did were not their fault. Rather, I pitied them even as I did my own father, who, like a dumb, rutting ram, had made his bed and obviously liked well to lie in it. Maud—whom I called Mistress instead of Mother, no matter how she fussed at me—would no doubt have made me toil for her all day had not the Barlows paid Father for my services to Sarah. They never knew I would have happily helped their child for nothing, as I learned to read and write while tending her.

Most important of all in my hidden treasure box, now that my necklace had as good as been stolen from me, I kept these pages of my story. Once I learned to write well, from the time I was about twelve years of age, when Sarah was taking her naps in her chamber, I borrowed pen and paper from her writing table and began this record of my life, hoping I would someday amount to something. Over the years, from time to time, I went back and amended it from a far wiser point of view. And, oh yes, in my treasure box, I also kept a list of hints I brooded over, hoping to prove Maud had something to do with my mother's accident, but who would credit it since it would be my word against hers?

Without my tasks at Dartington Hall and my walks to and from that fine gray stone manor each day, I would never have had time to hide these pages or to seize a moment to myself—*carpe diem*, my first snippet of Latin. Without the kindly Barlows, I would not have learned about the other world beyond our thatched longhouse built of moorstone with the attached shippon which housed our six cattle. I never would have known about fine needle-work or Turkey carpets or tapestries, or delicacies like squab pie instead of fat bacon, or Latin, let alone English sentences. I never would have heard of the other English shires beyond remote Devon, a distant world where a king ruled his people from great palaces. Without my times at Dartington Hall, I would never have learned such or yearned much. But still, it was not enough, and I longed to escape to—to I knew not where.

722